True Colours

Karen Surtees
and
Nann Dunne

Yellow Rose Books

Nederland, Texas

ISBN 978-1-932300-52-9
(Formerly 1-930928-17-3)

Third Edition

Revised, Re-edited, Reformatted in 2006

First Printing 2006

9 8 7 6 5 4 3 2 1

Cover design by Donna Pawlowski

Published by:

Regal Crest Enterprises, LLC
4700 Highway 365, Suite A, PMB 210
Port Arthur, Texas 77642-8025

Find us on the World Wide Web at
http://www.regalcrest.biz

Printed in the United States of America

ACKNOWLEDGMENTS

We wish to thank Sue Cole for generously sharing with us her knowledge of horses and her unique sense of humor; our Texans, Phil Belanger and Jennifer Allum, for their unfailing support and encouragement; and Bob Clements for applying his assiduous and meticulous attention to detail to our story.

In addition, we'd like to thank Cathy LeNoir of RCE, artist Donna Pawlowski, and editors Lori L. Lake and Jane Vollbrecht for making this new edition possible.

For Phil, just because after all the heartache she's still my best buddie. For Ms Bobbie, for putting up with me and Phil. And finally for Kat who's light will always be missed, but is remembered everyday.

— Kas

For my parents and all the other people whose shining beacons have guided my path. For my dearest, lifelong friend, Sandy, whose passing darkened my world. For my daughter, Maggie, who understands me and loves me anyway. And especially for the woman who "got down on her knees" to lift me up from my sad and lonely mourning; who restored my zest for life; who awoke and nurtured my passion for writing; and who has become my cherished friend, Kas.

— Nann

Chapter
One

"MARY THERESA GILLESPIE, get up off your duff and get moving!" With these words to herself, the veterinarian, known as Mare to her friends, rose from her desk chair and turned to look at the wall mirror. Her reflection showed a young woman of average height with long, golden hair, noteworthy green eyes, and a wry grin. "Okay, okay, I'm moving," she told her image.

A week of one-hundred-degree weather had been hard on a number of animals in the area and Mare had been scrambling to keep up with the mounting casualties. Most of them were suffering from heatstroke. The condition could be life threatening, so there wasn't the luxury of saying, "I'll be over later." When the call came, you hustled to get there.

And ailments didn't stop just because it was bedtime. Much of last night had been spent sitting up with a sick cow. Coming home and eating breakfast had probably been a mistake. She should have grabbed something from the fridge and kept going. That would have been easier than slowing down and having to start up again.

After pouring the last of her coffee down her throat, Mare glanced at the appointment pad lying next to the phone on the maple desk. No new calls had come in, but she had a couple of recuperating patients who needed to be checked.

As if on cue, the phone rang. She picked it up and leaned into the headpiece, catching it between her head and hunched-up shoulder. She picked up a pen and moved the appointment pad closer. "Dr. Gillespie," she said with a briskness she didn't feel.

A woman's voice said, "This is Dr. Gillespie?"

"Yes, it is." Mare tapped her booted foot on the floor.

"Dr. Gillespie, we need you at the Meridian ranch, right away. One of our horses looks sick. Can you come?"

"What seems to be wrong?" Mare scratched "Meridian ranch" on the appointment pad.

"She's breathing hard, her head is drooping, and she's

of listless."

That sounded like another one with heatstroke. She wouldn't be surprised. It didn't cool down much last night. "See if you can get her to take extra water. I'll be right out." Next to the ranch name, she wrote, "horse — heatstroke?"

"I'll meet you at the barn, Doctor. Do you know how to get here?"

"Sure do." Mare hung up the phone. Dressed in her usual worn jeans, plaid shirt, and short-heeled work boots, she was ready to start her day, but the phone call had her puzzled.

Who could be at the Meridian ranch? It had been closed for ten years. Maybe someone bought it. Well, whoever it was, she had to go see a sick horse.

Mare grabbed her ten-gallon hat, slapped it onto her head, and picked up her black bag. She strode out to her dusty four-wheel-drive Dodge pickup parked next to her house. With practiced ease, she set her bag in the empty spot behind the driver's seat and climbed in.

The bag held a sampling of what Mare called her "quick-fix stuff" including gauze, tape, suturing needles, sutures, stethoscope, peroxide, ace bandages, painkillers, etc. The camper area of the pickup carried more of the same supplies and housed a wide array of additional medications stored in a refrigerated compartment, plus the bulk of the equipment needed to care for large animals.

For the past three years, Mare and her mother had pooled nearly all their resources to outfit Mare's practice. They'd purchased the second-hand truck in her next-to-last year of studies, and the equipment was added gradually as their earnings enabled them. Last year, when Mare graduated and started her own practice, everything was ready to go.

Doctor Mary T. Gillespie, D.V.M., was the only vet within fifty miles of Meridianville, Texas. Actually, there wasn't much of anything within fifty miles of Meridianville. In the nine years she had been here, nothing had improved. She sometimes wondered why she stayed. Maybe because her mother loved it here. And was buried here.

Today's heat was as oppressive as the rest of the week's had been. Mare laid her hat on the truck seat and turned the air conditioner's deflector toward her face. It was quiet in town this morning. Only a few people were up and about as she drove down Main Street. She waved hello to Rochelle, who was opening the door to the Pot-O-Gold Diner, and smiled at Jess Perkins when he whistled at her.

Jess had become the closest thing to a best friend that Mare ever had. His family, residing in Meridianville since it had been founded, ran the general store. Mare's frequent trips to pick up stationery supplies for her mother provided an opportunity for him and Mare to become fast friends. She found Jess to be a like-minded individual who tended to keep to himself and who refused to get involved in the petty disputes that others their age squabbled over. Nearly six feet tall with light brown hair, he was an especially talented athlete. Everyone had expected him to go to college on a baseball scholarship, but he surprised them by winning a coveted Information Technology scholarship to Stanford University.

Now he ran a successful web and graphics company from his home as well as helping out his folks at the store. Jess and Mare often got together for a beer and snack, talking about whatever was in the news or what was going on around town. Mare made a mental note to ask him if he knew anything about the folks out at the Meridian ranch.

She followed Main Street out of town past the last few paint-flecked houses. Immediately, wide vistas of fenced range opened up, dotted with stands of trees, and on the left side of the road, she passed ranch or farm houses with outbuildings and an occasional field of corn. The only movement outside of her truck came from a flock of birds, silhouetted against a solitary cloud.

As she continued the eight miles to the ranch house, the results of Tom Meridian's callous abandonment of the town ran through her head.

Ever since Tom Meridian, great-grandson of the town's founder, had departed, the town had been slowly dying. Meridian sold off his huge herd of cattle, closed down the meatpacking plant he owned, took his family, and left. Nobody seemed to know why he left, but everyone was bitter about it. The name Meridian wasn't heard without S.O.B in front of it.

Most of the people in Meridianville had worked at the meatpacking plant just like their parents before them. With the town's biggest industry shut down, the residents were hard-pressed to provide for themselves. Many went back into farming, lived off land rented from someone else, and tried desperately to survive, hoping that someday things would get better.

Even children learned to make do: wearing worn-out hand-me-downs, eating only twice a day, and finding simple ways to play. They crumpled up discarded newspapers, tied them with string begged from the butcher shop, and used them as balls. Handles sawed off worn-out mops and brooms became their bats. Other children fashioned little playmates from corncobs and husks garnered from the patches of land their parents worked. The surrounding ranches and large farms weren't as hard hit, but the town's depressed economy had some effect on all of them.

Mare's mother, Jane, had been a freelance writer. A major newspaper chain engaged her to come to Meridianville to write an ongoing series about the town's difficulties in adjusting to the loss of its main source of income. She and Mare arrived about six months after the closing of the plant and spent six more months gathering material for the articles. They both fell in love with the beauty of the area and the strength of the people and decided to stay. Jane bought a three-bedroom, two-story, frame home on the edge of town and set up her office in the downstairs bedroom.

During the summer and on weekends, Mare had traveled throughout the area with her mother, assisting with interviews of those people most severely affected. From meeting so many desperate people and hearing their stories of hardship firsthand, Mare developed a deep-seated loathing for the Meridians. That dislike filled her mind as she neared the ranch.

All the land, as far as she could see on the right-hand side of the road, had been part of the cattle baron's holdings. Mare turned into the lane that ran a quarter-mile up to the Meridian ranch house. As she neared her destination, she could see that the house and the other buildings were clean and fresh looking.

Gigantic, even for Texas, the white stucco house sprawled from an attached, four-car garage to another building connected to it by a covered walkway. At a right angle beyond that building sat the barn, with a good-sized corral to the far side of it, containing two horses. A blacktop parking area formed a huge oval that started in front of the garage and sent a finger over in front of the house before completing its oval shape at the barn.

Everything looked fresh and new. Someone had done a lot of fixing-up. Mare stopped in front of the barn and stepped out of the pickup, her booted feet meeting the springy surface of macadam. A woman dressed in a short-sleeved, tailored cotton shirt, jeans, and high-heeled boots came through the open door and hurried over.

"Dr. Gillespie? I'm Erin Scott." The woman was several inches taller than Mare. Her blonde, curly head tilted, and cool brown eyes skimmed across Mare's face and form as the two women shook hands. "Follow me. I'll take you to the horse."

Mare got her bag from the truck and followed the woman into the barn, noting her smooth, athletic walk and nice, even, rich-girl tan. She wondered whether Erin Scott was the new owner. Her lack of a friendly "hello, how are you" shouted that she wasn't a native Texan.

Mare welcomed the cooler interior of the barn, even knowing that it soon would seem just as hot as the outside. As she looked for the ailing horse, her peripheral vision caught nameplates hanging at three of the six stalls and a tack room just to the left of the barn entrance. Through the open tack room door she could see part of a worktable with cupboards above it and a deep sink standing next to it.

Erin stopped in front of a palomino mare whose nameplate said Faithful Flag. "This is Flag," she said. "She's usually alert and high-spirited."

A cursory look indicated that the horse was in obvious distress. Her head hung low, she seemed listless, and she breathed rapidly through flaring nostrils. All were classic symptoms of heatstroke. Mare set down her bag, opened it, and took out the stethoscope, which she hung around her neck. She slowly walked into the stall, reached up to the high shoulder, and patted it. "Good girl, just let me take a look at you." There was no sweat on the animal's body, but in this heat, there should have been.

With the stethoscope, she listened to an elevated heart rate of seventy beats per minute instead of the usual forty. For a final confirmation of her diagnosis, she took the rectal thermometer from its plastic case. After dipping it into a nearby water bucket, she shook it down and then inserted it.

"How long has she been this way?" Mare asked.

"I noticed how she looked when I came into the barn this morning, and I called you right away." Erin chewed at the inside of her lip.

"Has she been drinking a lot of water?"

"I gave her extra when you told me to, and she drank most of it. Is Flag in danger?"

When Mare withdrew the thermometer and saw a reading of 103, the diagnosis was confirmed. "She's suffering from heatstroke. Heatstroke can kill, but it looks as though you caught it quickly, so there shouldn't be any problem treating it." Erin visibly relaxed, and Mare sensed that her brusque attitude was probably due to worry over the magnificent horse.

"Not used to dealing with horses?" Mare used Flag's tail to wipe the thermometer. She put it in its plastic case and set it back into the bag.

"More like not used to dealing with them in these conditions." Mare strode out to the truck for medication from the built-in refrigerator, and Erin followed her. "Take me up north, give me several feet of snow, and I'm okay. Present me with heat and humidity like this, and I'm sort of out of my depth. And I can see that this is going to be a steep learning curve."

"At least you were quick to notice something was wrong." Mare continued her explanation as they returned to the barn. "I'm going to give Flag a tranquilizer to bring her heart rate down and another injection to bring down her temperature. You want to come around here and hold her still for me? Better snap a lead rope onto her first."

Erin walked around the other side of Flag, snapped the lead rope onto the halter enclosing the palomino's head, and hung onto it.

Mare attached a 21-gauge needle to a disposable syringe and pulled 3cc from the bottle of Acepromezine. She injected it directly into Flag's jugular vein and went through the same motions with 10cc of Dipyrone. She dropped the syringes into a plastic trash bottle she kept in her bag.

She went out to the truck and brought back four bags of Ringer's solution and IV equipment. On her way in, she snagged a pitchfork, brought it back to the horse's side, and leaned it against the wall of the stall. "That's good, hold her nice and steady. I'm going to put a catheter in the jugular vein."

When the catheter had been inserted, Mare connected a bag of Ringer's to the IV tubing, opened the drip regulator hooked to the tubing, and let some Ringer's run through to push out the air. She then attached the tubing to the catheter. She reached for the pitchfork and hung the Ringer's on it, lifted it enough to keep the bag high, then adjusted the drip regulator. "I'll have to give her three or four of these to combat the dehydration."

While she ran the fluid in, one bag after the other, Mare explained some of the aftercare that would be needed: temperature taking, more injections, hosing down, and adding electrolytes to the water.

Erin looked skeptical, but said, "I think I can handle that. Will you need to come out to check her again?"

"Yeah, I'll be out sometime tomorrow. In the meantime, I've had so many cases of heatstroke this past week that I've printed out the directions. I'll just fill in the figures, and you can follow right along. You need to keep an eye on the other horses, too. Keep them out of the hot sun. Spray them down once in a while. Bring some fans in here and move the horses inside before midday. Until this heat breaks, all the animals are at risk."

The IV lines were finally dry. Mare unhooked everything, walked out of the stall, and laid the apparatus on top of her bag. From her breast pocket, she extracted and unfolded a sheet of directions. With a pen pulled from a pocket in her jeans, she filled in figures based on Flag's condition. She grinned to herself when she realized that Erin was still holding Flag's lead rope. "You can come out now."

Mare clicked the pen closed and replaced it in her pocket. As she handed over the directions, she said, "Come here, and I'll show you where you need to make the muscle injections." The extra-wide stalls made it easy for two people to walk side by side next to the horse. Mare pointed out the muscle area and made sure Erin understood. Erin's earnest look reassured her somewhat, but she still asked, "You're sure someone will do this? It's absolutely necessary."

"Don't worry, Doc. I might not be too keen on the idea, but we'll do whatever we have to do."

"Do you have a thermometer? If not, I can leave you one." Mare picked up the IV apparatus and her bag and went to the tack room sink to rinse out the tubing. After following her in, Erin opened the cupboards on the wall above the worktable.

"I think we most likely have one. A lot of stuff was left in these cupboards."

Curious, Mare strolled over to look for herself. The cupboards were filled with a hundred items that could be used in the care of animals. She thought it curious that the Meridians hadn't taken the supplies with them. She reached over and pointed. "There's the thermometer you need. I'll leave you some disposable syringes, needles, the medications, and some bags of electrolytes. You have the water and hoses and fans. You're all set."

Erin laid the thermometer on the counter and closed the cupboard doors. "I sure hope so. When will Flag be better?"

"Once she starts sweating and stops the rapid breathing, she'll be pretty well over it. That might take several days, especially in this heat."

"Okay, that's great. Everyone here's been worried about her."

After laying the injection and electrolyte supplies on the worktable, Mare removed the proper medications from her bag and held them up. "Got somewhere cold I can put these? They usually don't need to be refrigerated, but in this heat I'd rather play it safe."

Erin took the bottles from Mare's hand and opened one of the lower cabinets on the far wall to reveal a refrigerated compartment. Pushing some sodas out of the way, she set the bottles inside.

Mare waited until Erin closed the fridge and swung back around. "Flag should be okay, but you'll need to keep an eye on her for a while."

Erin picked up the black bag and joined Mare as she walked out of the barn. "We'll do that, and thanks. We appreciate your coming out so quickly. Believe me, it would have been disastrous if anything had happened to that horse."

"It wasn't a problem." Mare removed the drip tubing from under her arm where she had stashed it, and when they stopped at the pickup, she placed it back in the camper. "So, how long have you been up here? Nobody in town even knew the place had been sold."

"Oh, we've been planning this for a while. Seemed such a waste not to use the land since it was just sitting here. And none of it has been sold. At least as far as I know."

Mare's curiosity was piqued. "This must be costing you a fortune to rent."

"No, we aren't renting."

Mare's voice turned sarcastic. "Please don't tell me that the Meridian Corporation is letting you stay here for free."

Erin looked puzzled. "Well, it's like this..."

Mare finally caught on and held up her hand. "Wait a minute. Are you trying to tell me that you're the Meridian Corporation?"

"Well, not me, personally, but yes, I work for Meridian."

Mare's eyes hardened as she stared at Erin. "I can't believe they had the gall to set foot in this town again, but at least they had the sense to send a flunky." Mare thought about how that sounded. It wasn't this woman's fault she'd been sent down here. She let her eyes soften. "Sorry. That wasn't meant as a personal attack. You have to understand that the Meridians are neither liked nor welcome in this town. They all but destroyed it when they pulled out."

"That's okay," Erin said. "No offense taken. I didn't know they were so disliked down here."

"Well, they are, and if you plan on ranching here, you might have trouble hiring any help. I'm sorry to say it, but even though work's hard to find around here, as soon as people know it's the Meridian Corporation, I doubt you'll find many willing to work for you."

Erin ran a hand through her curls. "I can see you're not afraid to speak your mind. Thankfully, I don't have to worry about that side of running this place. My partner, Paula Tanner, takes care of that."

"So you'll be seeing to the practical side of things."

"Yeah, Paula will do the hiring, and I have to tell you, Doc, she has a way of getting what she wants even from the most resistant people. She got me down here and convinced everyone to carry on with the plans for this place, so I can't see us failing to get the people we need."

Erin handed Mare's bag to her. "How much do we owe you?" Mare named a figure and Erin pulled a checkbook and pen from a pocket and wrote her a check. When she handed it over, Mare noticed it had been pre-stamped with T. J. Meridian's signature.

"Would you be interested in being the vet for our livestock? We're expecting to turn this back into a working ranch, and we were hoping to sign you on a retainer. Or would you prefer we get someone from out of town?"

Mare considered this for the moment. Looking after the ranch livestock would be profitable and would enable her to do a few more things for those who weren't able to pay for their animals to be taken care of properly. Still, wasn't agreeing to work for Meridian almost like selling out to them?

"Why don't you think about it and then let me know when you've made a decision?" Erin offered her hand to Mare. "Thanks again for coming out right away. As I said, it would have been hell on earth here if anything had happened to that horse."

Mare took Erin's hand and shook it. "Okay. I'll let you know my decision when I come back to do the follow-up on Flag." Mare noticed a delivery van pulling up beside her truck. "Looks like you have something to take care of. I'll see you tomorrow."

Erin looked over her shoulder. "Yep, you're right. Thanks." Turning, she walked toward the van.

Mare slung her bag into the truck, her mind still mulling over the opportunity that had been presented to her. She absently listened as the driver of the van shouted over to Erin. "You have a Miss T. J. Meridian here? I have a personal package that needs to be signed for."

"I can sign for it," Erin said as she reached the man. "She's not available right now."

Mare felt a chill roll down her spine. One of the Meridians was here? Well, well, well. Maybe she ought to drop in and say hello. Welcome them back after all this time.

She breezed past Erin, who was signing for the package, then rapidly climbed the three steps to the porch to approach the open doorway. Behind her Erin called out, "Dr. Gillespie? Uh— hey, wait a minute." Mare glanced back. Before she was even through the doorway, she saw Erin put a cell phone to her ear, and heard her say, "Paula, honey, we have trouble at the house."

And then she was striding across brand new carpeting.

Chapter
Two

TJ SAT BEHIND the office desk, staring at her computer monitor, not noticing the black panthers and other big cats that prowled their way across the screen. She knew she ought to be working. She should be on the damn machine in front of her, looking at the proposals for upcoming business developments. But the inclination just wasn't there and hadn't been for a long time.

She pushed a strand of her long, dark hair back behind her ear. She didn't want to be in here. She would much rather have been in her room. But Erin and Paula had insisted she get out of bed today, and she wasn't capable of resisting when they forcibly got her up. All her screaming and cursing, all her threats did nothing to dissuade them from their task and make them leave her alone. She thought she might have hit Paula, and in some way she felt sorry for inflicting that on her friend. But, as with everything else these days, the feeling meant little to her.

She had only agreed to come down here to the ranch because they had gone on about it so much while she was in the hospital. The only way she knew how to shut them up was to agree, and for seven blissful days, they left her alone.

She nearly succeeded in getting away from everybody then, but the night nurse had come in on her rounds and found her wrists cut and bleeding. A quick call to the doctor, and several stitches later, and she was tucked back in a clean bed — under observation this time. Erin and Paula were furious with her, and from that moment on, they ensured that someone was with her at all times.

She hadn't considered that her failed attempt to kill herself would result in more doctors and more tests. Still, she eventually escaped the clutches of the medics after they instilled in her enough skills to cope with her disability. The stipulations were that she continue with psychological counseling sessions and go to physical therapy sessions twice a week. She hoped returning to the ranch and giving Erin and Paula so much to do would make them forget about that. But they were hard taskmasters and always made sure one of them was free to drive her to her appointments.

She picked up a pencil and twirled it through her fingers. She had another counseling session with her psychologist, Peter Tauper, scheduled for this afternoon, and that was what had put her in this foul mood. Her last session hadn't gone so well. Peter wanted to talk about her father, and TJ adamantly refused. Her father had nothing to do with her current situation. In fact, it was about the only thing in her life she couldn't blame him for. She didn't see how talking about him could help her now. Peter said she had demons to get rid of and they might as well tackle them all, but TJ pulled her silent, I'm-not-even-here act on him.

He'd gone into the waiting room then and had a long talk with Erin. TJ knew she was being stubborn, but why couldn't anybody understand that the mere thought of her father was repulsive to her? He'd ruled her life while he was alive, and she wanted nothing to do with him now that he was dead.

Erin lectured her on the way back to the ranch, wanting to know why she refused to cooperate with her treatment. Why bother going if she persisted in being obstructive? TJ pointed out that she had no choice in the matter since she and Paula wouldn't allow her not to go. She hadn't wanted to see Peter in the first place and would rather all of them get on with their own lives and stop fussing with hers.

The last hour of the drive had been completed in silence. On their return, TJ asked to be taken out to see Flag, but Erin told her coolly that she and Paula would be tied up for the rest of the afternoon and it wouldn't be possible. That, of course, had sent her mood spiraling downward even farther. She would be glad when the alterations on the house were completed and she could get about without assistance.

Then last night they'd had a big argument. Erin and Paula wanted to get someone in full time to help TJ. What they meant was they wanted to get a nurse. TJ was vehemently opposed to the idea. It had taken her long enough to allow Paula and Erin to help her. There was no way she would allow a total stranger to see her in this condition.

The pencil she was playing with snapped. She looked at it, stunned, unaware she had been holding it that hard, then threw the pieces across the room. This afternoon she would make Erin take her out to see Flag, or she wasn't going to the counseling session.

The sound of voices in the hallway drew her attention. Erin

was trying to stop someone from doing something, but the voice she didn't recognize wasn't having any of it and quite vocally stated that she was going to give "Miss Meridian" a piece of her mind. The door to her office was flung open, and in charged the owner of the unknown voice. TJ watched as the intruder hurried toward her, pulling up short several feet from the desk.

A woman with long blonde hair stood there, her face flushed and her breath coming in uneven gasps. Erin rushed in through the door a second later, a pleading look on her face. TJ's mood darkened further. Erin could have physically stopped the smaller woman or even called the police, but apparently she had resorted to fruitless argument.

The visitor took two deep breaths, and her breathing calmed. "Are you T. J. Meridian?" she asked.

"I am."

The woman put her hands on her hips and stared hard, looking like she was struggling to quiet her anger.

"You and your family have some nerve coming back here. Don't you think you've done enough damage to this town?" She moved forward and placed her palms flat on the edge of the desk. "Ten years ago, your father destroyed this town, destroyed the livelihood of everyone in it. These people made your father and his company a fortune, then he upped and left. Hell, he wouldn't even sell the land to them so they could work it themselves, and now you've come back? Just what do you hope to achieve here?"

TJ listened as the woman vented her tirade against her and her family. How was she supposed to respond? Everything was true. If the woman had known that her father had pulled out from the ranch to prevent TJ, herself, from becoming obsessed with it, no doubt she would have had more choice words to say.

TJ knew that coming back here to put things right would be difficult. That was why she had planned to appoint a manager to oversee the project, but the injury changed all that. She had hoped to keep her presence here quiet. Obviously, that wouldn't work.

The young woman's words hurt. TJ wasn't her father. But nobody seemed to remember that. They always tarred her with the same brush. Even in death, he still ruled her life, and it looked like she would spend what was left of that life repaying his considerable debts.

She felt her anger build: anger at her situation, anger that Erin and Paula were being stubborn about her seeing Flag, anger at the world in general for not letting her lie down and die like she wanted to. "Have you finished?" she asked in a quiet voice.

"For now."

"Good. And you are?"

"Mare Gillespie. Dr. Mare Gillespie. I'm the local vet who just looked after your precious horse."

TJ flicked a glance toward Erin, who had the grace to blush, then looked like she wanted to hide. TJ bet Flag was ill and they kept it from her, probably thinking it would upset her.

"I see," TJ said. "And do you make a habit of bursting into people's houses? That doesn't seem like a good way to attract business, if you ask me. As for your opinions on my family, they're neither wanted nor appreciated. I suggest you leave quietly, before I have you thrown out."

Mare's lip curled. "I come here to treat a sick horse, and I discover the return of a sick family." TJ opened her mouth to respond, but just then Paula came running into the office. She stopped abruptly and ran a hand through short, dark brown hair as she looked toward TJ.

Instead of speaking, TJ's glance went from Paula to the vet, then back to Paula, and with a jerk of her head, she signaled dismissal. Thankfully, Paula recognized TJ's intention. Without question, she grasped the woman's arm and tightened her grip when she scowled.

Erin spoke up with an urgent tone in her voice, "Dr. Gillespie, Miss Meridian has asked you to leave, and I think it might be wise for you to do so."

Mare's gaze had been locked on TJ's during this whole exchange. "I'll be back tomorrow to check on your sick horse." Her voice flattened, giving a false sense of spent anger. Her gaze switched toward Paula. Slightly taller than Erin and solidly muscular, Paula showed a look of confident strength in her dark-brown eyes. Mare spoke firmly. "I would like to suggest that you take your hand off of me. I'm leaving."

Paula hesitated and looked at TJ. TJ's eyes were narrowed and her jaw set, but she nodded and Paula released her hold.

Erin jumped in. "I'll show you out, Doctor." She walked toward the door, then looked back. The vet hadn't moved. She stood where she was until TJ's gaze swept back to her. With one last challenging look, she turned and followed Erin out.

PAULA NERVOUSLY WATCHED TJ. She could see the anger building in her eyes and knew if TJ didn't say something soon it was going to be hell on earth around the ranch for the next few days. TJ was used to fending off insults aimed at her family, but illness for her horse was another matter. Maybe Erin should have told her Flag was ill. These days the animal was the only thing that kept TJ going. She took a deep breath as she anticipated that TJ was about to start a tirade.

"Why did we require a vet for one of the horses?" TJ's voice sounded normal.

Paula frowned. This was much worse than she had thought. If TJ wasn't shouting, she was furious. "Erin went to the barn early this morning and thought one of them looked a little distressed. She decided it would be wise to err on the side of caution and have the vet check it out." It was unlikely that TJ would let her get away with not naming the horse involved, but it was worth a try.

"Was it Flag?" TJ asked softly.

"Yeah, it was."

"What was wrong? Is she going to be okay?" Paula noticed that TJ had picked up a pencil and was twirling it through her fingers, another bad sign.

"I don't know. I haven't talked to Erin yet."

"Fine. We'll wait for her to come back then." The motion of the pencil quickened in her hand.

Paula took a deep breath and tried to still her nervousness. Oh yeah. Hell was about to materialize on a little-known ranch in Nowheresville, Texas.

ERIN WALKED TWO paces behind as the vet left the house and strode over to her vehicle, muttering under her breath. She liked this Dr. Gillespie and still wanted to have her looking after the animals for them, especially if the passion she had just shown transferred to her work. What she didn't like or understand was her attitude toward TJ.

Erin had first met TJ at Harvard and over the years developed a strong friendship with her. But in the beginning, it had taken her months to break through TJ's icy reserve. TJ was distant with everybody and rarely socialized. If provoked, she was openly hostile, even violent if pushed too far. It took a long time to be able to see past that, but when Erin was cornered one evening by one of the more aggressive homophobic groups from the campus, it was TJ who had come to her rescue.

Silence had descended on the jeering group. They stopped shoving her around when TJ's voice was heard. The three weaselly college guys just stood there and looked up at the tall figure, assessing her, apparently trying to figure out whether she was actually a threat. The first mistake the group's leader made was to smile, because when he did, so did TJ. It was chilling to see, and Erin couldn't understand why none of the group recognized their immediate danger.

Their second mistake was not realizing that the woman standing before them would be able to use the strength her tall, muscular body held. If there had been a weapon among them, it would have been a bloodbath. As it was, a few broken bones later, it was all over.

Erin had immediately changed her opinion of TJ Meridian and spent the next few months breaking down barriers and generally being a pest until she gained acceptance and friendship from her. In that time she learned a lot about her: her contempt for her father and his practices; her mother's constant badgering over what was right — and what wasn't — for her daughter; her lack of free time; and the way she constantly studied, trying to appease the demands of her family.

The only thing that seemed to make TJ happy was when her younger brother visited. The look on her face when Lance told her he'd been accepted into Harvard Medical School was priceless.

When the women's time together at Harvard came to an end, they kept in touch through the Internet, snail mail, and the occasional phone call. And Erin's admiration for TJ grew. After TJ's parents died, she took over Meridian Corporation and began to make changes. Market analysts said she was mad, that her changes were economic disasters. They were wrong. The shareholders loved her. The stock kept rising, and everyone was happy. Except TJ.

For some reason, everybody thought she was her father. The press said she was ruthless, more interested in profit than the repercussions her decisions had on those involved. The day TJ hired Erin and Paula as consultants on the ranch project, there were protesters outside the building. Not protesting about the corporation, but about the person running it. The woman Erin saw that day was a shadow of the one she had been. The pressures were already taking their toll.

Yes, TJ had restructured the company, and yes, people had lost their jobs, but it was nothing like what her father had done. Severance packages had been more than adequate, and where possible, people were moved to other positions within the corporation. In some cases, TJ had given financial incentives and help to other companies to encourage them to relocate to areas where she had pulled hers out. But unlike others who would have paraded their generosity for all to see, TJ refused to take credit for, or publicize, anything she was doing.

So hearing Dr. Gillespie vent her anger on TJ hurt, and she

knew it had hurt TJ, too.

"You know, you were kind of nasty," Erin said.

Mare swung around and stared angrily at Erin. "You have no idea what this town has suffered because of her. You have no idea what she's like."

She turned toward the pickup, but Erin reached out and grabbed her arm and swung her back. "You have no idea what she's like!" Erin said forcefully. "You haven't been through the hell we've been through with her the past year. You haven't been through the pain she has. What happened here happened ten years ago. At a guess, I'd say you were fifteen, sixteen years old? Well, she was eighteen. Do you think an eighteen-year-old girl had anything to do with making decisions about closing manufacturing plants and factories? TJ isn't her father, and it's about time people started realizing that."

Mare made a wide sweep with her arm. "Look around you. Where did all this come from? Where did those prize horses come from? That one I treated today is worth more than my house. The Meridian ranch is probably worth more than the whole town." She shook her head. "You're asking me to feel sorry for her because she's being blamed for the things her father did? Well, maybe she didn't make the decisions, but she sure as hell laid back and let the money drop into her lap, didn't she? Where would she be today without her father? Would she be a part of Meridian Corporation? Sure, tell me you believe in the Easter Bunny, too. While she was living like a princess, people in Meridianville were wondering where their next meal was coming from, worried not just for themselves, but for their children, too. I don't think I was nasty. I just told her the truth."

"You dislike her because she's rich?"

"No, I dislike her because her father produced that money by climbing over the lives of people from places like Meridianville. You want me to believe she cares about them? Tell her I'll believe in the goodness of her motives when I see her turn that money over to them."

Erin's anger had died away to plain frustration. "Have you ever heard the expression, 'Give a man a fish and he'll eat for a day; teach him how to fish and he'll eat forever'? Well, that's what TJ's trying to do. She wants to rebuild the economy here and bring people's lives back to them."

"Right." Mare suddenly felt too tired to argue any more. She climbed into the pickup truck and started the motor. "I'll be back to see Flag. Make sure you follow those directions." Stifling a yawn, she put the truck in gear and left.

Erin walked slowly back to the house, dejected. If she

couldn't convince even one person that TJ's motives were good, how were they going to convince a whole town?

TJ'S OFFICE WAS ominously quiet as Erin approached the room. She gently pushed open the door and stepped in. Paula stood over by the window, gazing out at the horses in the corral. TJ was still seated behind her desk, hands angrily twirling one of the many pencils that she kept in her desk caddy. Paula turned around, grimaced, and indicated she should close the door. Erin already knew from the silence that they were in for one of TJ's infamous outbursts of anger, and that could be painful indeed. "Has she left?" TJ asked in a precisely controlled voice.

"Yes." Erin didn't elaborate, knowing that it would only annoy TJ further. When TJ wanted to know anything more, she'd ask.

TJ flung the pencil to the desk, leaned forward, and stared pointedly at Erin. "Just when were you going to tell me that Flag was ill?"

TJ wasn't yelling, and that increased Erin's concern. "I only noticed this morning that she didn't look good. I got the vet out right away, and I would have told you once I found out the prognosis."

"And what is the prognosis?"

"Flag has heatstroke. We'll have to watch the other horses as well, at least until the temperatures drop. With the right care she'll completely recover." Erin felt Paula come up behind her and rest a hand on her shoulder, silently giving her support.

TJ turned her attention back to the computer screen. "Fine. Both of you can leave now."

"TJ, look, we weren't trying to..."

"Get out." TJ's voice grew colder, and Erin winced at the change in tone.

"But, TJ..."

The plaintive plea in Erin's voice broke what flimsy restraint TJ had over her anger. "Last time I looked, I was just a cripple, not a child, though for some reason you insist on treating me like one. Now, get out and leave me alone."

Erin opened her mouth to try again, but Paula tugged her away toward the door. "Not now," she said. She turned her gaze back to TJ, who was still staring at her computer screen. "TJ, I'll pick you up in two hours to take you to your counseling session."

"I'm not going," she said, without looking up. Paula gave Erin a wry look, then led her out of the room and closed the door.

Erin pulled her arm out of Paula's grip and looked at her. "Are you going to let her get away with that?"

"She's upset. It won't do us any good to antagonize her. Let's go check on Flag and let TJ cool down. In an hour or so, I'll go get her and take her for a visit to Flag, then I'll kidnap her and take her for her session."

"She isn't going to be happy about that. She'll tell you again that you're treating her like a child."

"Yep, she will. And when she stops giving us the silent treatment, we'll stop treating her like one."

Erin turned to walk down the hall, and Paula followed her. "Problem is," Erin said, "this time we gave her a reason. I should have told her about Flag."

"Yes, but I don't think that's what she's upset about. Did the doc say something that hurt her?" They entered the kitchen and Paula walked over to the coffeemaker and poured two mugs of coffee. She added creamer and sugar to Erin's, then sat down at the breakfast bar.

"Yeah, she was kind of nasty. She said the town hated the Meridians for what they did, and TJ had some nerve coming back here. I tried talking to her, tried to tell her that TJ wasn't her father, but she wasn't very receptive." Erin took the mug that Paula slid over to her.

"Maybe bringing TJ to the ranch wasn't such a good idea," Paula said. "Sounds like the atmosphere isn't going to be great, and that might not help toward her recovery."

"Maybe not, but we can't exactly go back to the city. You never know, maybe the attitude of folks around here will be the incentive she needs to pick herself up again."

"Yeah. Either that or it'll kill her," Paula said.

"We can't let that happen." Erin's face conveyed her determination even as a note of uncertainty sounded in her words.

"And we won't let it happen. But at this point, we can only play it by ear, see how things go. Which reminds me, what's the story with Flag?"

"The doc's coming back here tomorrow for some more treatment. In the meantime, there are some things we need to do." Erin reached into her pocket for the directions the vet had given her. "Here's a list of the care Flag's going to need for the next several days." She put it into Paula's outstretched hand.

Paula skimmed down the list. She looked up at Erin. "You're going to do all this?"

Erin's short laugh burst from her throat. "Nuh-uh, my dear. *We* are going to do all this. It will be a learning situation for both of us."

Paula whistled and her eyes took on a gleam. "When do we start?"

Erin shook her head in amazement. Paula was always eager to try something new, no matter how much work was involved. "Right now would be good. We need to get some fans set out in the barn with one of them fixed on Flag, and we need to give her a soaking with cool water every few hours. You can see there are a couple other things on the list for us to do soon, and some to do later."

Paula handed back the list, put the coffee mugs in the dishwasher, and grabbed a handful of cookies from the cookie jar. Chocolate chip cookies were her downfall, and Erin always made sure to pick up some when she went food shopping. "Okay, let's get to it." She handed a couple of cookies to Erin as they left the kitchen in search of fans.

THE DOOR CLOSED behind Paula and Erin, and TJ let out a ragged breath. She slumped back into her chair and looked sightlessly at the computer screen. Those two were as bad as her mother used to be, not letting her make her own decisions. Why did they keep treating her like a two-year-old child when she was the CEO of a major corporation?

She pushed herself farther from the desk, maneuvered her chair from behind it, and wheeled herself to the window. The office was on the first floor, just like her bedroom and all the other amenities she needed. The sunken living room had caused a problem, but it hadn't been too hard to rig a ramp to allow her access. The stair lift wasn't being installed until next week, and neither was the concrete ramp that would allow her to get off the front porch by herself.

At the moment, she was totally dependent on her two friends, which she hated because it only made her feel more like a child. All she wanted was to be left alone, but they hadn't allowed her that since the hospital. Even now, although she had promised them she wouldn't do anything stupid, they still didn't trust her fully. Flag's illness was a classic example of that.

What did they think she was going to do, kill herself? Well, they probably did, the more logical part of her mind reminded her.

They should have told her about Flag. But she would have worried herself sick until the vet arrived. Erin did the right thing in not telling her Now she was going to have to apologize for being such an idiot and for losing her temper.

TJ heard voices and looked out the window. Paula and Erin were chattering to each other as they walked to the barn, arms loaded with equipment. They certainly didn't look too upset from her outburst.

PAULA HOOKED THE last fan to the rafter, making sure it pointed toward Flag's stall. "Okay, that takes care of the fans. Each horse will have one. What's next on the list?" She put aside the stepladder, brushed her hands together, and cocked an eyebrow at Erin who was reading from the doctor's instructions.

"Some of these things — shots, temperature-taking — don't have to be done until about four o'clock. We're not to give her as much grain, and we need to add some salt to her feed to make her drink more. And put a bag of electrolytes in her water. The doc left the stuff for the shots and a couple bags of electrolytes. They're over there on the worktable. The medications are in the fridge."

Paula took care of these as Erin read them off, one by one. "Now," Erin said, "we need to give Flag a bath. Well, not actually a bath. We need to spray her down, especially her head and up inside her legs, to keep her cooled off."

She looked up at Paula who was waiting for the next direction. "Put a lead rope on Flag and take her out of the barn. I'll get the hose."

Paula clipped the lead rope on Flag and led her out. "She doesn't look all that great. Still seems listless."

Outside, Erin turned on the faucet, unrolled the hose from its carrier, and pulled it toward the palomino. "The doc said it might take a while. Best thing we can do is follow the instructions." Erin flipped the nozzle to the spray setting and lifted the hose toward Flag's head, showering her thoroughly. Paula, still holding the lead rope, jumped out of the way.

"Yo! Watch it, will you? Flag's supposed to get the bath, not me."

"Sorry," Erin said and snickered.

She sprayed along Flag's back, then leaned down and sprayed the undersides of the horse's hind legs. She made sure to get plenty of water on the large veins as the instructions said. Spraying the underside of Flag's body, she worked her way to the forelegs and sprayed the large veins there.

She could see Paula's jeans showing between Flag's forelegs and somehow the hose slipped and sprayed her, too.

"Yeow, Erin! You know how cold that well water is? Cut it out!"

Erin stood up and looked at Paula wide-eyed, the picture of innocence. "I'm so sorry. You don't think I did that on purpose, do you?" She walked up past Flag's shoulder until she was about four feet from Paula. "Now, this is on purpose." She flipped the nozzle adjustment to the stream setting and doused a now fuming Paula. "You know, you really do look like you need to be cooled down."

Paula hurried Flag back into the stall and unhooked the lead rope on the move. Even before Flag was in place, Paula was squishing after Erin. As she rounded Flag's hindquarters and shut the stall gate, Erin got her again with the stream of water. She put her finger on the nozzle to narrow and strengthen the stream and caught Paula full in the face.

Nearly doubled over with glee, Erin hadn't noticed the extra bucket of water sitting next to the stall gate. She also hadn't counted on the kink in the hose. As she pulled the hose forward, the kink closed, cutting off the supply of water to the nozzle. Erin turned back to see what had happened to the hose and when she turned forward, Paula let loose with the bucket of water, right toward Erin's unguarded face.

"Yaaahhh!" Erin dropped the hose, crossed her arms over her head, and ducked, too late. While she hid her head, Paula grabbed the hose, flipped out the kink, and soaked Erin with the stream of water until there wasn't a dry spot left on her body.

"I give up, I give up," Erin said, trying to run away.

"You'll give up when I say so." Paula chased her relentlessly, keeping herself between Erin and the doors. She finally took pity on her after a full minute of the water treatment and turned the faucet off.

The two of them, dripping wet, looked at each other and got a fit of giggling. Erin pointed at Paula and gasped. "You looked so funny, trying to hold onto Flag and get out of the way of the water at the same time."

Paula's giggle mingled with a snort. "You should have seen your face when the kink stopped the water and you turned back around to see a bucket of water coming at you. Thought you had the upper hand, huh?"

"I should have known better. You always seem to come out on top."

"And I like it that way," Paula said with a leer, and the two went off again into gales of laughter.

They took deep breaths and had almost regained their composure when Paula reached into her breast pocket and scooped out a couple of dissolved chocolate chip cookies. Her chagrined look re-ignited the hilarity.

The two finally got themselves under control. "I know one thing for sure." Paula waved a finger at Erin.

"What's that?" Erin's laughter still bubbled in sporadic bursts.

"Next time, you get to hold the horse, and I get to hold the hose."

TJ HAD CONTINUED sitting at the window. It was a pleasant distraction from having her head in a computer all day. She'd seen Erin and Paula bring Flag out for her bath. It had been apparent that Flag wasn't up to par. Her head, usually lifted so proudly, hung down, and her walk was sluggish.

TJ's eyes shifted to the distance as she remembered the first time she had seen Faithful Flag. Her father had squelched TJ's near-obsession with horses when he had closed the ranch. After his death, she determined to make up for lost time and promptly hunted for a jumper to start training for competitions. As soon as she saw the glorious part-thoroughbred, the two fell in love with each other. TJ hired the best teacher money could buy and had him train her and Flag together.

Picture after picture ran through her mind of times past when she and Faithful Flag moved as one: soaring gracefully over jumps, striding perfectly between them, and winning over all comers. Twin, solid-oak display cabinets with mirrored backs sat in adjoining corners of the office filled with trophies and ribbons won by the tall, blue-eyed rider as she put her beloved horse to the test. And always, Flag came through.

With these reminiscences, TJ's eyes started to mist but squeals from near the barn drew her attention back to the present. As Paula ran Flag back into the barn, Erin was chasing her with a streaming hose. Several shouts were heard and presently, the two women exited the barn, arm in arm, dripping with water and beaming.

At that moment, the wealthy, beautiful, supposedly arrogant TJ Meridian felt very much alone.

PAULA RAN LIGHTLY down the steps, all showered and changed after the water fight. It felt so good to get out of those boots once in a while. She headed to the kitchen, hoping Erin had fixed some sandwiches. Paula had waited while Erin jumped in the shower first, because TJ would be needing her lunch, and that was Erin's responsibility today.

"Good girl," Paula said aloud as she entered the kitchen and saw two places set, complete with sandwiches and iced tea. She sat down and lifted the top slice of whole wheat bread. Corned beef and Swiss cheese, one of her favorites. She slapped the slice back in position when she heard movement.

Erin entered from the hall that led to TJ's office. "TJ decided to have lunch at her desk." She joined Paula at the table, and they started eating. "Guess you have to change your plan about kidnapping her. There's not enough time for her to see Flag before you need to leave for the therapy session."

"That's okay. I'll just go in there and tell her she's going, or else. See what happens. She can visit Flag later."

The two women ate quickly, then Paula rose. "Maybe TJ's right about us treating her like a child. Let's see how far I get treating her like an adult."

"Lots of luck." Erin gave her a sympathetic look.

Paula knocked on the office door, opened it, and walked in. "Time for your session, TJ." She couldn't tell whether TJ had actually been conducting some business or was just hiding behind the computer screen. Her empty lunch tray had been pushed aside.

Inscrutable blue eyes looked up from under coal-black brows. "I told you I'm not going."

"You say you want us to treat you like an adult, but when we try to, you act like a stubborn kid." Paula walked over and half perched on the edge of the vast desk, her voice stern. "You know, you set the tone around here. If you want us to think you're a grownup, then you have to start acting like one. Because, so far, you haven't been."

TJ looked toward the window. Her fingers found an ever-present pencil, picked it up and started a quick tattoo on the desktop. Paula was on tenterhooks, not knowing what to expect, or whether she was even going to get an answer.

The even tattoo became ragged, slowed, and gradually stopped. "Go get the van."

Surprised at her easy victory, Paula jumped up and nearly ran to the door. "I'll pick you up at the porch." She hurried out, leaving the door open for TJ.

TJ sat for a while longer, still gazing out the window. Maybe if she went through the motions of cooperating, they'd leave her in peace. This morning sure hadn't been peaceful. As far as TJ was concerned, the vet had been an intruder—an annoying one. Why didn't she just take care of Flag and mind her own business?

For some reason, TJ couldn't get her out of her mind. Maybe it was her unaccustomed brashness. Most people quailed in front of the Meridian power, but it didn't even slow that little spitfire down. TJ came out of the short reverie and wheeled herself outside.

Paula worked the wheelchair down the steps and over to the open door on the passenger side of the van. TJ's long arm easily reached the bar that had been installed above the doorway, and she hoisted herself in and fastened the seat belt. Paula folded the wheelchair, opened the sliding door, and placed the chair on its edge on the floor in front of the back seat. After closing both doors, she jogged to the driver's side, got in, hooked her seat belt, and started up.

They drove for a while in silence until Paula said, "Hey, I'll take you to see Flag when we come back, if you'd like. Erin and I have to give her some shots just about then, and maybe you'd like to come watch us. We'll probably have to give her another bath, too."

"So it was Flag who got the bath today?" Paula's head jerked around for a quick glance at TJ, then came swiftly back to the road. But TJ was pretty sure that Paula saw the tiny quirk at one side of her lips.

"Why, TJ, I do believe you're teasing me." Paula automatically flicked the back of her hand at TJ's thigh, then suddenly looked embarrassed for her friendly gesture. TJ watched out of the corner of her eye as Paula blinked rapidly and swallowed hard to arrest unexpected tears. Paula got herself under control and cleared her throat. "I guess that means you saw us come out of the barn, dripping wet, huh?"

"Yes." TJ couldn't keep the longing out of her voice. Paula didn't say anything, but TJ knew her far too well to assume that Paula hadn't heard the yearning so evident in that one word. She bet Paula was glad they were pulling up in front of the counselor's office building. Paula jumped out, got TJ back in her wheelchair, and took her in for her appointment without another word. She and Paula were silent in the waiting area until Peter Tauper appeared and beckoned Paula into his office.

A few minutes later, Paula returned, wheeled TJ into the office, and left. Peter came out from behind his desk and sat in a stuffed chair across from TJ. Mahogany shelving filled with leather-bound books rested in the corner near his neat workspace. Several signed, abstract prints hung randomly about the buff walls, interspersed with framed diplomas, testifying to Peter's expertise. A couch and matching chair made a cozy nook against the far wall with green carpeting and soft overhead lighting completing the décor.

"Well, TJ, Paula tells me you had some excitement this

morning. With the veterinarian?"

"You could have asked me if anything had happened, you know. You don't need to have one of my own employees spying on me."

"Paula isn't spying on you. Actually, I just wanted to get her impressions of whether these sessions seem to be helping you any. She volunteered the information about this morning. You want to tell me about it?"

Peter put his elbow on his chair arm and leaned his chin on the back of his hand. A man of medium height and build, Peter wore his light brown hair short and a darker mustache and beard graced his fair-complexioned face. Wire-rimmed glasses covered eyes that were, disconcertingly, of two different colors, one blue, one brown. It gave one the eerie feeling that two people lurked behind his personable face.

TJ shrugged. "Not much to tell. She came to take care of a sick horse, and when she found out I was in the house, she came charging in and let loose a diatribe about my family ruining Meridianville. Old news."

"Did you get mad at her for running down your family?"

"No, what she said was right." The more TJ thought about it, the more she admired the vet's guts. She was wrong to burst in like that, but most people wouldn't even try.

"And did you feel responsible for it?"

"Me responsible for what my father did?" TJ shifted her shoulders in her chair. "Of course not."

"How do you feel about what your father did?"

TJ slammed her fist down on the arm of her wheelchair. "This is not about my father! Get that through your thick skull. I refuse to sit here and discuss him. We're supposed to be discussing my suicide attempt and what caused it, aren't we? That had nothing to do with my father. He's dead. D-E-A-D, dead. You got that?"

Peter spoke in a soft voice. "Don't you see, the reason you get so upset when I ask about your father is because you have some unresolved issues concerning him. We need to get those out in the open to see what bearing they have on your attempt to end your life. You need to talk about him."

"Well, if that's the only way you think you can find what pushed me to try suicide, then we're both in trouble. I will not, I repeat, I will not discuss my father with you or with anybody else. Period. Go get Paula. This session is over." TJ leaned her head down and closed her eyes. She didn't need to look up to know that Peter was bitterly frustrated, but he had obviously learned that once she made up her mind, she was done for the day, which she was.

"When you come next week," he said, "we won't talk about your father. We'll explore other avenues."

I won't be here next week, TJ wanted to scream, but knew she couldn't. The only thing standing between her and being committed to a mental hospital was the promise to attend these sessions. She wouldn't let anyone put her in a mental hospital. She'd die first. TJ's eyes flew open, but Peter had gone to call Paula. *I didn't mean that, I didn't mean that.*

Paula came in, wheeled TJ out to the van, and drove home. TJ didn't speak a word in spite of Paula's several attempts at conversation.

Chapter
Three

MARE PUSHED HER front door open and trudged through, letting the screen slam shut behind her. The heat inside was almost as oppressive as it had been outside. She mentally kicked herself for not leaving the air conditioner switched on. She threw her bag into the corner, took off her hat, and jammed it on the hook near the door, then headed to the kitchen.

She flipped the switch by the side of the refrigerator and listened as the air conditioner rattled to life. In a few minutes, the rooms were noticeably cooler. Holding a beer grabbed from the fridge, she slumped tiredly into a chair at the kitchen table.

God, what a day. When a day started out bad, it stayed that way, didn't it? She was exhausted. The call to the Meridian ranch in the morning had been a hellishly perfect start to a hellishly nasty day. She had been on call after call after call. The animals in the area were suffering badly, and if the heat didn't break soon, some of the ranches would be losing livestock.

Mare loved working outside, but today the soaring temperature had been a formidable challenge. She had to admit she had put herself in a bad mood by mulling over this morning's argument with TJ Meridian. Not that she particularly regretted barging into the woman's office and telling her what she thought, but her conversation with Erin afterwards weighed heavily on her mind.

Erin had been right. She didn't know TJ Meridian. She only knew of the father's reputation, and yes, she had judged the daughter on it. And yes, she didn't like that the Meridian family had made money from the town when they had left the town with none. And yes, in an ideal world, turning that money over to the town would solve its current problems. But this wasn't an ideal world. Throwing money at the problems would be a stopgap solution at best, and it wasn't likely to happen anyway. So now she was feeling a little bit guilty about her outburst to Erin and maybe just the tiniest bit guilty that she had invaded TJ

Meridian's home.

The shrill sound of a ringing phone startled Mare from her thoughts. She climbed to her feet and reached for the wall phone. Oh, Lord, she prayed that it wouldn't be work. She didn't think she had the energy to restock the truck tonight. Summoning enough enthusiasm to keep the weariness from her voice, she answered, "Dr. Gillespie."

"Hey, there."

Mare smiled as she recognized the deep voice. "Hi, Jess." She pulled the chair over from the table and sat down. "What're you up to?"

"Well, I was hoping I could persuade the local vet to come out to dinner with me."

Mare sat back and took a sip of beer. "That's a lovely idea, but I'm beat and honestly just don't have the energy. I'm going to have a bath and crawl into bed."

"Hmm, did you stop for lunch today?" Silence greeted his question. "I thought not. Rochelle said she hadn't seen you. Tell you what. While you hop in the bath, I'll hop over to the diner, get 'chelle to pack us up something, and I'll bring it over with a bottle of wine."

Mare thought for a second. She hadn't eaten much today, just the sandwich Mabel Stirkle had brought out to her while she was looking at their cattle. And she hadn't seen much of Jess recently. He'd been away on business, and she hadn't had the chance to sit and talk since he returned. It was about time they caught up with each other. "Sure, that's a great idea. See if they have any of that blueberry pie, will you?"

"No problem. Be there in about an hour, okay?"

"Yep. An hour is fine."

Mare didn't bother to get dressed up for Jess's visit. She jumped into a pair of old sweats and a T-shirt. He arrived promptly at eight with a couple of roast beef platters, a red wine, and blueberry pie. They ate in the kitchen, chatting about how the Astros were fighting for a playoff berth. Jess proudly announced that his company had just won a lucrative contract to design a web site and graphics for a major manufacturing firm. He was in a good mood because the job would pay handsomely and allow him to buy the new truck he wanted.

After they cleared the table and did the dishes, they retired to the living room and settled at either end of the couch.

"Where were you rushing off to this morning?" Jess asked as he lounged back onto the comfortable, plump cushions.

Mare looked over at him, wondering how much to tell him about the Meridians being back. She knew whatever she said within these walls would stay here. After all, Jess hadn't gone blurting out the fact that she was gay when she told him. She thought he'd understand that letting everybody know that TJ Meridian was at the ranch would only create trouble. While that family deserved all it got as far as Mare was concerned, they could still cause an awful lot of problems for the town, if they wanted to.

"I was going up to the Meridian ranch. They had a sick horse." She looked over, expecting to see shock on Jess's face and seeing none. "Did you know it had been reopened?"

"We knew someone was up there. We've made a few deliveries."

"Oh really? Didn't think your dad would approve of dealing with the Meridians."

"The store needs the money just like everyone else. Besides, no one mentioned the Meridians. Some woman named Scott opened an account and paid a whole stack of cash in advance. Dad couldn't afford to turn it down."

"Well, I met the owner today, and it's one of the Meridians — the daughter."

"No kidding? I thought they were all dead. Some car accident, or something. But hell, if they're back, the folks around town aren't going to like it."

"Yeah, I know. That's what I told her."

"You told her?"

"Actually, I marched into the house and yelled at her."

Jess's quick laugh burst out. "She got treated to Mare Gillespie's infamous temper? Bet she loved that."

Mare thought about TJ's reaction to her invasion. "She really didn't seem that upset. It was Erin Scott who lit into me as she was more or less throwing me out."

"What's she like?"

"Who? The daughter?" Jess nodded. "Long black hair, intense blue eyes, great bone structure. And now that I think about it, she was very pale, like she was just getting over an illness or something. She had a real quiet voice. She didn't raise it once to me, even though, technically, I was trespassing." Mare's words trailed off as her conscious mind took note of what her subconscious had observed earlier in the day: the slump to TJ's shoulders, the listlessness in her eyes. Something she couldn't quite put her finger on was wrong with that picture.

"Tall or short?" Jess said. "The Meridian woman — was she tall or short?"

"I couldn't tell. She didn't stand up while I was there. Just sat in her chair and presided over it all." Mare rose and walked toward the kitchen. "You want a beer?"

"Yeah, please." As soon as Mare returned with the beer, Jess continued his friendly inquisition. "So Miss Meridian is pretty good-looking?"

"Beautiful," Mare instantly replied. Jess chuckled, and Mare blushed when she realized what she'd said.

"You found her attractive then?"

"Physically? Yeah. But inside she's just another Meridian."

"It's not like you to make a knee-jerk diagnosis, Mare. She might not be what you think she is."

Mare looked over at Jess. His face held an expectant expression, and the conversation had turned uncomfortable. "So, how's your mom?" she said.

A huge grin split Jess's face, and she knew her question had given away her attempt to hurriedly change the topic of conversation. She knew him well—that he was tempted to pursue the subject—but he relented. "Mom's just about the same as when she talked to you day before yesterday." Mare made a face at him, and he stuck out his tongue at her. "But she's disappointed that I have to go away again so soon."

"Go away? But you just got home."

"Yeah, but this new contract means I have to spend a lot of time at the manufacturer's headquarters finding out just what each department wants on their web site. Management intends to use a lot of on-site pictures and has asked me to advise them what will work best. I figure I'll be there a month or more."

"So tonight's dinner was a going-away party?" Mare said, teasing, but she was disappointed, too. She'd miss having Jess to talk to.

"You could call it that, I guess. And now it's time for me to go home. I know you're tired, and I want to get an early start tomorrow." Jess stood and pulled her to her feet. They said their good-byes and hugged at the door, and Mare watched Jess drive away before she locked up. As she headed to bed, one sentence of Jess's surfaced in her mind and nagged at her until she fell asleep. *She might not be what you think she is.*

SOME PEOPLE AWAKENED at the same time every morning, rain or shine. But not Mare. The alarm clock had to drag her from slumber. That is, when she was still in bed asleep. Because animals often got sick at night, vets didn't always have that luxury. But this morning the insistent clang pulled her from the depths, and she sat up groggily. The last few days had been a hell of activity with so many heatstroke cases mixed in with the normal sicknesses and injuries. And hell was the right word. If the heat didn't break soon, she just might be the one who did. She thanked whatever gods may be for air conditioning.

But the barns weren't air conditioned, and neither were the fields or ranges. Mare was outside more than she was inside, and the heat drained her energy like a swift siphon.

While she almost sleepwalked through her shower, breakfast, and restocking medicines and supplies in her bag and pickup, her thoughts centered on her trip back to the Meridian ranch today. She wondered what her reception might be. She hadn't been especially tactful with either Erin or TJ Meridian, to put it mildly. Or Paula, for that matter.

She mused about the three women. Erin seemed nice. Paula seemed tough. And TJ? Mare wasn't sure how to categorize TJ or how she felt about her. Maybe mostly still angry with her as a Meridian, but also partly apologetic for bursting into her home and lambasting her the way she had.

Finally, bag and truck restocked, Mare embarked for the Meridian ranch. She drove slowly through town with her windows down. She hit the accelerator more forcefully when she reached the open spaces, hoping to grab a breath of cooler air. Even so early in the morning, shimmering heat waves from the asphalt road surface distorted the horizon. Surrendering, she wound up the windows and turned on the air conditioner.

Through the undulating distortion, Mare saw a boy on a bicycle some distance ahead of her. He looked to be about ten years old, and she thought she recognized his shock of red hair. He pedaled furiously, then heard her truck, and turned to glance behind him. As he did, the bicycle swerved and shot off the road. The front wheel struck a chunk of stone, and the sudden stop catapulted him into the dry ditch that ran alongside. Mare slammed on squealing brakes and turned off the motor. Bag in hand, she ran to the boy's side.

Besides relatively harmless brush burns, he had received a nasty cut on one leg where it had skidded across a piece of broken glass. He sat up and was trying hard not to cry, but tears rolled from his pale blue eyes, down across his freckled cheeks.

Mare squatted next to him, checked to make sure there was no glass embedded in the wound, and applied pressure to stop the spurt of blood from a damaged artery. "Aren't you Johnny Robertson?" Mare knew that speaking to the boy would help ease his pain. She recognized him as one of the sons of George Robertson who owned a nearby farm. The boy nodded and sniffled.

"You'll be okay, Johnny. Just let me clean this up and get a bandage on it, and we'll get you in to Dr. Hunt."

Mare heard hoofbeats and saw TJ Meridian slowly approaching on a sleek, black mare. TJ guided the horse up to the fence and stopped as her cool blue eyes took in the accident scene.

Reflexive contempt momentarily locked Mare's tongue, but for Johnny's sake she swallowed her pride and asked for assistance. "Miss Meridian, we could use some help here. I have a cell phone in the pickup. Could you call for the ambulance? Then we'll try Johnny's family."

Mare saw unexpected compassion in TJ's expression as she looked at the youngster. She reached to the belt encircling her long, blue tunic and unclipped a cell phone that Mare hadn't noticed. When her gaze turned to Mare, the compassion had disappeared to be replaced by the usual cool disinterest. "9-1-1?"

"Yes, we have 9-1-1 here."

TJ made the call. "They're coming." Her terseness eased as she spoke to the boy. "What's your phone number, Johnny?" TJ punched in the stated number. "Sorry, there's no answer at your house."

The timbre of TJ's low, soft voice unexpectedly resonated with something in Mare's emotions.

She quickly returned her attention to the wound. "If you would come down here and hold Johnny's leg, I could get a pressure bandage on it." When there was no answer, Mare looked up at TJ and caught the slight twitch that flitted across one side of her face.

"I...don't think so."

Mare strained to hear the soft voice and was dumbfounded when TJ turned the horse's head, clucked to it, and trotted off, pulling the phone again from her belt.

Mare couldn't believe it. She thought even a Meridian would want to help an injured child. But TJ's refusal confirmed that they were a pretty heartless bunch. She turned her attention back to Johnny who hadn't taken his eyes off TJ until she rode away. "That lady's beautiful," he said almost reverently.

"Yeah, she is." *At least on the outside.*

"Who is she?"

"She's a new neighbor. She owns the ranch across from your farm."

Mare heard a vehicle approaching. Looking in the direction of the sound, she saw a Land Rover come toward them, then pull over to the side of the road nearby. Erin Scott jumped out and hurried to Mare's side.

"TJ called, said you needed some help." Erin hunkered down

by the boy. "How do you feel?"

Johnny blushed at this attention from a stranger. "I'm okay. The doc's taking care of me."

"Erin, this is Johnny Robertson from one of the farms across from the ranch. Johnny, this is Miss Scott. She works for the lady who was on the horse."

"Glad to meet you, Johnny." Erin offered her hand, and he sat up straighter and shook it respectfully. "I expect we'll be staying at the ranch for a long while, so I hope to meet your family one of these days."

Another pickup slowed to pass them, then zoomed to the side of the road. A husky, redheaded man leaped from the cab. "Johnny! Are you okay?" He ran to the boy and grasped his shoulder.

"I'm okay, Dad. Doc Gillespie helped me."

"Thanks, Doc. What happened?"

Mare told George Robertson about his son's mishap. As she finished, the ambulance arrived, and the EMTs took over. Mare picked up her bag and walked back to her pickup with Erin following her. "You on your way out to the ranch?" Erin asked.

"Yes, I was. I'll be right along." Mare turned to meet Erin's eyes and saw that she felt rebuffed by Mare's attitude. "Thanks for offering to help," she said more warmly.

"Afraid I didn't do much. You had everything under control."

"I don't get it," Mare said. "TJ wouldn't help, but she sends you. What motivates her? Does she think she's too good to dirty her hands with us little people?"

"Never. As you get to know her, you'll find she's a very complex person. Many times even I don't know what motivates her. But I respect her. She has a noble heart."

"Humph! I doubt if I'll ever get to know her that well." Mare opened the pickup door and stepped in. "Shall we go take care of her horse?"

"I'll turn around and be right behind you." Erin took a tentative step forward. "Give her a chance, Doc. You might be surprised at what you find."

"Right." Mare used one of her favorite words, but her derisive tone negated any sense of agreement. She turned the key and started the pickup as Erin walked away.

AFTER ASKING ERIN to come and help the vet, TJ spoke to Paula. "I'm coming in. Meet me at the barn." She closed the phone before Paula answered and then concentrated on balancing herself on Ebonair's back. The straps that were connected to the front of the saddle came across her thighs and buckled to the back flaps. These gave her enough stability to ride with little difficulty if she went slowly, but on horseback TJ wanted to fly.

With Flag, TJ became such a unit with the palomino that Flag's legs became her legs and there was never any question of sliding off. But Ebonair wasn't Flag, and TJ had to stay constantly alert, even at a simple trot. She slowed the animal to a walk as she got nearer home, giving her a chance to cool down.

Finally, she reached the barn where Paula dutifully waited outside on the ramp with the wheelchair next to her. A lift, made of a T-shaped piece of metal connected to a chain, dangled overhead from a makeshift roof. An electrical wire threaded through the chain and ended at a two-button box connected to the underside of the T-bar.

TJ pulled Ebonair next to the ramp and Paula hooked the horse to a lead rope attached to the side of the ramp. Then she undid the straps on one side of the saddle while TJ worked on the other side. TJ reached up, grasped the T-shaped bar with both hands, and with sheer strength pulled herself up out of the saddle, swinging her upper body to help free her legs. After Paula guided TJ's body and legs into proper position over the wheelchair, TJ thumbed one of the buttons on the electrical box and the T-bar slowly descended and lowered her into the chair. Ebonair skittered at the noise, but TJ was well out of harm's way.

"Why didn't you let the lift pick you out of the saddle?"

"Just felt like doing it myself. Stretches the muscles everyone's always nagging me to exercise."

TJ hooked herself into the chair, reached into a pocket of cloth hanging from the chair arm and pulled out a towel. Briskly, she scrubbed the perspiration from her face while Paula unlocked the wheels and maneuvered the chair into the tack room. Paula opened the fridge and pulled out a couple of sodas. Handing one to TJ, she popped one for herself and sipped at it. TJ popped hers, tipped it back, and drank it down without stopping.

"You okay?" Paula said. "I still don't think it was a good idea for you to be out in this heat."

"It's still early morning, Paula. If it was really bad, I wouldn't have taken Ebonair out. I'm fine, just thirsty from sucking in all that dry air."

"What happened out there?" Paula tilted her head. "Erin goes flying out of here, then you come flying in."

"A boy from one of the farms fell off his bike. The vet was on the road and apparently saw it happen. She was taking care of him and needed some help." TJ dropped her head and a grimace tugged at her lips. She took a deep breath, then lifted her head and her ice-blue eyes swept up to meet Paula's nearly black ones. "But I couldn't do a damn thing except make a couple phone calls." The pained gaze moved away.

Paula grasped TJ's shoulder and squeezed it. "Hey, you did what you could, okay? Calling Erin was the smart thing to do." When there was no response from TJ, Paula walked behind the chair and started pushing her. "Come on, let's get you in the house."

"And to the bathroom."

That wasn't meant to be funny, but it amused Paula. At least TJ had something else to occupy her for a while. Might help take her mind off her latest bout with her disability. "And to the bathroom," she said.

THE BATHROOM THAT was part of her personal suite was the first room TJ had ordered remodeled. It contained every contrivance she needed to take care of her own needs without assistance.

The second remodeling work was the wooden ramps: one into the sunken living room for convenience, and one behind the barn to enable TJ to get on and off a horse. TJ was tall and solid, and neither Paula nor Erin, alone, was strong enough to help her in mounting and dismounting. The ramp and T-bar combination had been a lifesaver for her.

Once Paula was sure her help wasn't required, she went back to the barn to unsaddle Ebonair. She looked into Flag's stall as she went by with the saddle and thought how glad she was the doc was coming out today. TJ's pride and joy seemed a bit better, but she wanted to hear that from the doc.

Paula sprayed off Ebonair with a hose, then turned her into the corral with her own horse, a chestnut mare named Running For Fun—Runny, for short.

Ebonair was Erin's horse, and every time Paula saw her aboard the mare, she thought how perfect it was that Erin, a curly-headed blonde, had chosen such a sleek, black horse. The contrast between the two made a gorgeous picture.

Paula took the bridle into the tack room and hung it on the wall. As she walked out, she heard two vehicles come to a stop outside the barn, one after another. A short moment later, Erin and Mare walked side by side into the barn, chattering about the injured youngster.

They stopped when they saw Paula, who stepped forward and offered her hand. "Dr. Gillespie, I'm Paula Tanner. We...ah...weren't exactly formally introduced." A light blush warmed Paula's tanned cheeks as she recalled just how they did meet.

A slow, sardonic grin worked its way across Mare's lips. "Glad to meet you, Paula." She held the taller woman's hand for a moment, lifting it up with hers. "I have to admit I like your hand better here than clutched around my arm."

"Yeah. Sorry about that," Paula said, her tone brusque. "When TJ says jump, I jump. If you're the one in the way, you're the one I land on."

Erin spoke quickly. "Maybe we can get off to a better start, now that things have calmed down."

Neither Mare nor Paula committed themselves, each eyeing the other warily.

Finally, Erin broke the silence that had fallen. "Come on, Doc, take a look at Flag. She looks a little better, doesn't she?"

Mare went through the usual routine, taking Flag's temperature and checking her heart rate. "She does seem to be improving. Let me get some more Ringer's in her."

After Mare walked back to the truck, Erin glared at Paula. "What's wrong with you? You about bit her head off."

"I'm not too happy with anyone who upsets TJ, and she sure as hell did upset her. Mouthy little son of a bum."

"Whoa! Is this the pot calling the kettle black? You've done your share of mouthing off at TJ. You wouldn't have dared to say some of those things before her injury."

"That's true," Paula said, "but some of those things I've said purposely to get some kind of reaction from her. TJ scares me when she pulls that I-don't-give-a-damn act. I'm afraid it might become real."

"Well, her anger at the doc looked a lot healthier to me than that fury she gets into when she's frustrated."

Paula scratched the side of her neck as she considered Erin's words. "You know, I think you might be right. I know the doc's words hurt her. I could see it in the way her jaw was clamped together when I got there. But, later, when I took her to her therapy session, she actually teased me about the bath you and I gave each other. Maybe the doc woke up something in TJ. I sure hope so."

Mare came back in, waving a drip clamp. "The darn clamp broke, and I had a heck of a time finding another one. Guess I know one thing to put on my shopping list."

Paula snapped a lead on Flag and held onto her while Mare

again put a catheter in Flag's jugular vein, set up the IV of Ringer's solution, and ran it in. "You have three beautiful horses here."

"Thanks," Erin said. "Runny, the chestnut, is Paula's, Ebonair is mine, and Flag is TJ's." She reached over and patted Flag's flank. "TJ's crazy about this horse. She's like a member of her family."

Paula snorted. "Better than her family." Then she realized her indiscretion and clammed up.

"She's a jumper," Erin said. "That was a sight to see. Flag and TJ looked like they were one solid animal instead of two separate ones. TJ won a lot of medals with her, before..." Erin's reminiscence came to an abrupt halt, and she seemed flustered. Mare gave her a questioning look. "Before we came here," Erin finished lamely.

"Why don't you write the doc's check while she's finishing up?" Paula looked pointedly at Erin.

"I left the checkbook in TJ's office. We can get it when everything's finished here. Give the doc a chance to cool off, too."

Mare looked at Erin. "If TJ's so crazy about Flag, why isn't she out here?"

Erin looked at Paula, who gazed placidly back but didn't say a word. "I think it bothers her a lot that Flag isn't well. Maybe she just can't stand to see her in this condition."

"So she lets you two worry about it."

"Look, Doc." Paula's voice sounded more like a growl. "You don't know a thing about TJ, so just keep your mouth off of her, and we'll all get along a lot better."

When anyone attacked her with words, Mare's first inclination was to strike back. Her mind was quick, and she had a wit that could turn a nasty phrase with the best of them. But something made her pause. Maybe it was the softness she saw in Paula's and Erin's eyes when they mentioned TJ.

So Mare didn't say anything. She unhooked the IV apparatus, picked up her bag, and walked into the tack room.

MARE TOSSED THE empty Ringer's containers in the trashcan and washed out the IV equipment in the sink. More wide awake this time than when she had first been in here, she looked curiously around the whole room. Other than the table, sink, cupboards, and refrigerator she had seen on her earlier visit, she noticed three Western saddles on racks, bridles dangling from wall hooks, a couple of space heaters stuck back out of the way, and a floor fan standing out ready for use.

One of the saddles, partially blocked from view by another, appeared to have extra leather straps attached, possibly for decoration. Or maybe to attach extra saddlebags. It was so fancy, she guessed it was TJ's. A closed can of saddle soap with a rag lying next to it sat on the rack as though its user had been interrupted in the midst of attending to one of the saddles.

Mare finished her cleaning and set out some more supplies on the worktable for Flag's continuing care. She put new medication in the fridge and went out of the tack room. Erin stood there alone. "Paula just went up to the house to get the checkbook. I'll help you with your stuff."

"Thanks," Mare said, "but I can manage. I left the same supplies for you as last time. Just keep doing what you've been doing, and I'll come back in a couple of days to check her again. If she gets any worse, call me."

Paula entered the barn. "TJ says would you please come to her office. She'll pay you for your services, but she wants to talk to you about Flag."

The request surprised Mare. Usually an owner cared enough to come to the barn and watch her treat the animal. But TJ couldn't be bothered. Just about the time Mare was ready to accept that TJ wasn't her father, she pulled something arrogant like this. Mare took her bag and IV apparatus outside and dropped them off at her camper, then followed Paula and Erin into the house.

Paula stayed in the kitchen while Erin escorted Mare to the office. Erin knocked on the closed office door then, after a slight hesitation, opened it and walked in. Mare's gaze met one that reflected her own noncommittal attitude. TJ certainly did radiate power, and not just from her manner. Mare could see it in her eyes and feel it from the respect Erin and Paula showed her.

Erin motioned Mare to a seat in front of the oversize desk. "Would either of you care for some iced tea?" She looked from one to the other, but they both declined.

In a calmer mood now, compared to her first visit, Mare sat down and quickly took closer notice of the office while she waited for TJ to speak. The room was easily fifteen by thirty feet, with a random hardwood floor of a slightly darker shade than the honey-oak furniture. A large, square, deep-blue rug held the desk, its attached computer wing, and several comfortable chairs covered in milk-chocolate-colored leather. The right side of the desk was bare except for the usual caddy of pens, pencils, paper clips, and rubber bands. Other ordinary office items graced the left side: a telephone with built-in intercom, a console covered with labeled buttons and tiny bubble lights, an appointment book, and two pictures. One picture was of a young man, with the same black hair and unforgettable blue eyes as TJ's. The other was of Faithful Flag. Bookshelves were everywhere.

A giant television screen covered part of the wall directly opposite the honey-oak desk. In the two corners of the wall behind the desk, Mare saw oak cabinets displaying trophies, medals, and ribbons. On one shelf of the right-hand cabinet lay a hat, quirt, and white gloves. The eggshell walls held several paintings featuring horse scenes. Mare wondered whether TJ still competed.

Broad, arched, floor-to-ceiling windows graced two sides of the room, and there were two other doors. The wider door apparently led to the screened porch that could be seen through one window. At the far end of the room, a couch, two stuffed chairs, and a television sat atop a dark blue and cream oval rug. The ensemble, complete with reading lamps, made a cozy nook.

"Do you need us for anything else, TJ?" Erin asked.

"No, just one of you stay by the intercom. I'll call you when we're finished."

"Sure enough." Erin patted Mare on the shoulder as she turned away, a friendly touch that brought an answering smile.

The smile still lingered as Mare brought her attention back to TJ. This time, instead of a pencil, TJ picked up a pen to play with. Her checkbook lay unopened on the desk. She seemed uncomfortable, shifting several times in her chair. A jacket hung on the back of the chair, just as before.

Never one to sit quietly unless she was concentrating on her work, Mare spoke up. "Flag's coming along very nicely. I expect she'll start sweating by tomorrow or the next day. That's usually the course of heatstroke. One more visit, day after tomorrow, will probably be enough. Erin and Paula have done a good job."

"Erin and Paula always do a good job. They've been keeping me apprised of Flag's care and recovery." TJ hesitated, took a deep breath, and let it out slowly. "I thank you for that." The remarkable eyes dropped to her fiddling hands. "I've had Paula and Erin asking around about you. By all reports, you're a very competent vet." The eyes swept back up and locked on Mare's.

Great God, woman! Those eyes are a weapon, aren't they? Mare didn't say anything and the silence drew out. She was more than a little miffed that TJ had been asking about her. She could have given her references. Determined to sit there forever, if need be, she refused to say another word until TJ did.

As they sat staring at each other, Mare saw something flicker in the depths of TJ's eyes. Was it amusement? One dark brow barely twitched.

Finally TJ spoke. "I'm planning to make Meridian ranch a working cattle ranch again and eventually reopen the meatpacking plant. That should give a shot in the arm to the economy around here. I'm going to need the services of a good vet, and I'd like you to think about accepting a retainer to take care of the livestock, both horses and cattle."

Mare still didn't answer, preferring to let TJ stew for a while. TJ had to know Mare was the only vet within fifty miles, and Meridian would be in dire straits if Mare said no. Of course, Mare would be, too, since she was barely providing for herself.

TJ waited, but when Mare didn't answer, she opened the checkbook and riffled back to the stub for the previous payment. "Paula said your fee for today would be the same as last time?" She looked up again, and Mare nodded. TJ wrote the check and handed it over. Mare stood up and accepted the payment, folding it and stuffing it into the breast pocket of her gold and brown plaid shirt.

"Will you think about the retainer offer? If you decide in favor of it, we can discuss remuneration on your next visit."

Remuneration? Holy Hannah! The word alone should be worth a hefty price. Trying not to let her expression give away her thoughts, Mare kept a blank face. "I'll let you know."

TJ pushed a button on the console, and a dim buzz sounded from outside the office. She reached out her hand and Mare shook it.

The large hand engulfed Mare's smaller one, but there was no undue display of strength, just a firm grip that hinted at it. "Thanks again."

"Right."

Erin answered TJ's summons and walked Mare to her truck. "Thanks," Erin said.

"Taking care of Flag is part of my job." Mare patted her pocket. "My fee is thanks enough."

"I meant thanks for being nicer to TJ. Paula and I were kind of nervous about it, but you two actually looked civilized this time."

"You suggested I give her a chance, and I decided you were right. I'm going to give her plenty of rope and see which one of us gets hanged."

Erin shivered dramatically. "That's not a very pleasant figure of speech."

Mare chuckled. "Maybe not pleasant, but probably appropriate." She got in the truck. "See you day after tomorrow."

"I'm looking forward to it."

Mare left and Erin went back to TJ's office. Paula had just brought in some iced tea, and after they sat down, she handed it around. Erin took a sip and asked TJ, "Well, how did it go?"

"She's going to think about the retainer and let me know when she comes back out."

"TJ!" Erin feigned exasperation. "I meant how did you two get along? Paula and I were nervous wrecks."

TJ looked down at her hands, which were quiet for a change. A slight lift of one side of her lips made Paula surreptitiously nudge Erin.

"She has a mind of her own, that's for sure," TJ said as she looked up. Seeing the tiny seed of amusement that struggled to sprout in her eyes warmed Erin's heart.

"She sounds perfect then, TJ." Paula surprised Erin with her quick endorsement of Mare. "You wouldn't want anybody working for you who didn't have a mind of her own." Paula grinned wickedly. "Would you?"

The small lift of TJ's lips turned into a bona fide lopsided smile. She shook a finger at Paula. "You're going to get it one of these days."

"Yeah, promises, promises."

"Get out of here, you two, and let me get some work done." TJ waved her hands to shoo them out, but the smile stayed on her face. "Come get me when supper's ready."

They got up and left the office. "Yes!" Paula shoved her fist up into the air. "I knew that little doc was having a good influence on her. I don't know what it is, but I hope it keeps up."

"Yeah, Paulie, and you managed to get a smile out of her." Erin's eyes were bright and shining. She grabbed Paula's shoulder and shook it as they entered the kitchen.

"She's even going to join us for supper instead of sitting there by herself in that office eating off a damn tray. I tell you, Erin, I am one happy camper. I'll even help you make supper."

This earned her a quick kiss. "Offering to cook? You *must* be happy."

Chapter Four

MARE ENTERED HER kitchen and grabbed a soda from the fridge. Drinking it quickly, she examined the contents of the fridge for dinner possibilities and decided on cold, sliced ham and the potato salad still left from the weekend. But first, a shower. She rinsed the empty can and tossed it in the container used for recyclable discards, then headed for liquid refreshment for the outside of her body.

After her shower and dinner, Mare sat at the piano in the sitting room. Most people would call it a living room, but her mom had always called it a sitting room and that's what it would always be to Mare—the sitting room where her Muse would appear. She lifted her hands and caressed the familiar keys.

The Gulbransen upright, purchased second-hand for Mare's first music lessons, still possessed a mellow tone. As soon as Mare had learned to play a simple tune, the piano became an ardent companion. Through the years, she turned to it in joy or sorrow, serenity or disruption, triumph or defeat. When her fingers transmitted these emotions through the piano's keys, the cherished instrument reverberated with a resonance that nourished her spirit. Magically, this transformation enhanced any happiness Mare was experiencing and soothed any discord. Music served not only to express her emotions but also to balance them.

With little conscious thought, she ran her fingers up and down the keyboard for a few minutes of loosening up, then leaped into George Gershwin's *Rhapsody in Blue*.

The strong chords, intricate melodies, and fast fingering spoke for the disturbance within Mare, and she lost herself in the music. "Why am I disturbed?" she finally asked, aloud, when she finished the composition. For a long moment, she truly puzzled over what had caused a strong enough impression to lead her to the keyboard for solace. Then the title of the piece struck her brain and immediately conjured up a memorable pair of blue eyes.

As she replayed the rhapsody, she pictured TJ Meridian sitting in the ranch office and relived their words and actions from their first meeting. Finally, her fingers finished and came to a rest. *Yep, that's her all right – a rhapsody in blue.*

Why couldn't she get TJ out of her mind? A strong urge to find out more about TJ and the Meridian family filled her.

Mare got up, went into the kitchen, and checked her appointment book. Nothing on her schedule couldn't be put off one more day. She decided to take tomorrow off and go to the library in Sharlesburg on a fishing expedition. Fishing for information about TJ Meridian and her family. Maybe that would help her feel better about the retainer, too.

Yesterday's offer of a retainer had sounded repugnant to Mare, coming from the daughter of the reviled Thomas Meridian. When Erin had told her that saying about giving someone a fish or teaching him to fish, her resolve had wavered. Then today, TJ herself had recounted her intention of rebuilding the town by resurrecting the ranch and meatpacking plant.

If she did, that would pick the town right up. And if she expanded her cattle herd, she'd need a vet, so by helping her Mare would also be helping the town. She'd make sure that rebuilding the town was spelled out in the retainer papers before she agreed to anything.

But Mare was still undecided. She got a second soda and sat at the table to finish it. Another thought sprang into her mind, and she had to chuckle at the persistence of whatever had touched her subconscious. If she signed a retainer, she'd get to see the mysterious TJ more often.

Mare turned and spoke to her reflection in the wall mirror. "Get yourself to bed, Doctor, and give your soppy brain a rest."

She did go to bed, but her brain wasn't cooperating with the idea of rest. It wouldn't shut down. Mare couldn't get TJ out of her mind. Something just didn't ring true, and it nagged at her.

Okay, she'd look at this like she was trying to diagnose an illness. What did she know that didn't seem to fit? First, there was this powerful, independent woman with two employee friends who were as protective of her as mother hens with their chick. They took care of the horse she was so crazy about, and she hadn't been to the barn to check on Flag either time Mare had been there.

Second, TJ stopped at an accident, seemed concerned, made phone calls, but didn't get off the horse to help. Matter of fact, that was the only time Mare had seen her away from her desk. She'd never seen TJ on her feet.

Mare bolted straight up in bed and tucked her legs up under

her body. Her long, pale-yellow, cotton T-shirt draped in soft folds against the tops of her thighs. Images of two ramps and a saddle with extra straps leaped to her mind.

TJ Meridian can't walk!

Mare sucked in a breath as though someone had kicked her. She tapped her fisted hands against the sides of her head, none too gently, as another image came to mind—TJ's pale and dejected expression when Mare first burst into her office.

What on earth had happened to her? Maybe Mare could find out tomorrow at the library.

Remembrance of her heartless remarks landed on her conscience like a load of paving stones, each one pelting her with guilt. Why hadn't Erin told her?

But Mare guessed the answer to that—TJ was afraid people would feel sorry for her. Worse, somehow, she'd slipped into feeling sorry for herself. That seemed so out of character, she must be tearing herself up. Mare wished she could help her.

Nearly exhausted by this emotional upheaval, Mare lay back down, mulling over that last thought. TJ Meridian had everything money could buy. Just how the heck could a vet from the sticks help her? Only thing Mare knew how to take care of was animals.

Finally, mind and body gave up, and she drifted to sleep.

TWO DAYS LATER, in the afternoon, Mare got out of her pickup and stretched. She winced as her muscles resisted and her joints popped. After spending most of yesterday in Sharlesburg, she had paid for taking the time off. Old man Thomas had phoned her at the ungodly hour of 4:30 a.m., saying some of his cattle had been spooked and got caught in the barbed wire fence. Could she come out and patch them up? That took the better part of two hours. Although the cattle weren't seriously injured, they had still needed suturing.

She got home just after seven and didn't see the point in returning to bed. Her morning clinic was unusually busy, with several of the local children bringing in their pets. That finished up just before lunch, allowing her to grab a bite to eat, then she was on to her rounds of the local farms and ranches. Now it was late afternoon, and she had saved the Meridian ranch for her last call.

Mare still had mixed feelings about this place and its owner, but the research she had done at the main library in Sharlesburg had given her a new perspective on TJ Meridian. And, yes, she had to admit to herself that she had been too harsh in her assumptions.

This might be her last trip to the ranch. Flag was well on the way to recovery. It would probably be safe to let her back out into the corral, either this evening or tomorrow. But now that Mare had some facts, she was sorely tempted to take the retainer TJ had offered for care of the livestock. She reached behind the pickup seat, grabbed her bag, and headed into the barn.

It was quiet, which was unusual. By now, normally Paula, Erin, or both would have come out to greet her. She had a quick look through the barn and the tack room, just to be sure they weren't around. All three horses were in their stalls, out of the heat of the day, protected by the coolness the fans provided. Mare put down her bag and stepped inside Flag's stall, giving her a brief check over. Flag was sweating easily now, and her breathing had stabilized. Satisfied with what she saw, Mare decided to look for Erin and Paula.

Leaving her bag behind, she left the barn and walked toward the house. She noted that the Land Rover wasn't in evidence, but the van was parked by the side of the house. From her previous trips, she knew that Erin or Paula could likely be found in the kitchen when they weren't in the barn. She was debating with herself whether to use the side entrance or go around to the front when she heard a loud crash from the kitchen. She ran the last few feet and bounded up the steps, opening the kitchen door and going straight in.

At first, she couldn't see what had caused the commotion, then she heard TJ cursing from behind the island.

"Hello? Miss Meridian? You okay?" she asked, not wanting to startle the woman by just appearing in front of her.

"I'm fine," TJ replied.

"You sure? I thought I heard you fall." Mare stepped closer to the island.

"I said, I'm fine. Would you just leave me alone?"

Mare was leaning on the island now and could see TJ's legs sprawled on the floor next to her overturned chair.

She debated whether to call TJ's bluff or let her get away with it. TJ might have hurt herself. She hadn't fallen far, but she wouldn't be able to tell if she'd broken something. Taking a deep breath, not sure how she was going to be received, Mare walked around the island. "You look fine, as well. I take it that studying the kitchen floor from such close range is one of your normal pastimes?"

TJ closed her eyes and struggled to push herself into a seated position. She felt hands on her arms and froze. "I can do it by myself," she snapped.

"I'm sure you can, but I'm here, so why not let me help?" Mare said gently. From what she had read while in Sharlesburg, TJ Meridian had once been an excellent all-around athlete and superb horsewoman. Seeing her in this condition, after the video footage she'd watched of her and Flag, was shocking. Still, if she let the proud woman know that, there was no way she'd accept her help. TJ opened her eyes and batted at Mare's hand.

"I'm not asking. I'm telling you. Leave me alone." TJ's body was trembling with effort.

Mare let go and stood back, staying quiet, but watching closely. When TJ got herself into a seated position, she grabbed hold of her chair and pulled it toward her, setting it upright. She pulled the footrests up, braced the chair sideways against the cabinets, and locked the brakes. She sat still a moment, breathing heavily.

Mare stepped forward to help but narrowed eyes held her in place. "Stay back," TJ said, her words reinforced with a scowl.

Mare turned her head at the creak of a door. Paula and Erin walked in and stopped, staring from Mare to TJ. "Dr. Gillespie," Erin said as she and Paula set bags of groceries on the counter. Without another word to Mare, she moved to help Paula lift TJ into her chair.

"Are you okay?" Erin asked.

TJ, obviously fuming, didn't answer. She unlocked the brakes, turned her chair around, and wheeled out of the kitchen.

"What the hell happened?" Paula said.

Mare let out a shaky breath, still worried that TJ might have hurt herself. "I came out to check on Flag, but couldn't find either of you in the barn, so I thought I'd come over to the house. I heard a crash as I got near the door. I came in, and TJ was on the floor. Somebody ought to go check if she's all right. She didn't fall far, but this floor is hard. She might have hurt herself." Erin and Paula looked at each other, then Erin left the kitchen, following TJ.

Paula stared at Mare intently. "You already knew, didn't you?"

"Yeah, I did," Mare said softly.

"How did you find out?" Paula walked over to the fridge and brought out a pitcher of iced tea.

"A few things added up: her saddle with the extra straps, the way you and Erin keep an eye on her, the ramps — one in the barn and another in the living room. The day she saw me helping Johnny Robertson and refused to get off the horse. I put two and two together." Mare hesitated briefly, running Johnny's accident through her mind, remembering the wrong conclusions she had jumped to about TJ. "Then someone in town said they thought that all the Meridians were dead. I was in Sharlesburg yesterday and thought I'd check it out. So I went to the library there, pulled up some back issues of several newspapers on the computer, and read all that I could find about the Meridian family."

"I guess you know everything you need to know, then."

Paula handed Mare a glass of iced tea and indicated that she should sit. "What did you find out?"

Mare blew her hair off of her forehead. "Where to start? I found out TJ went to Harvard and graduated summa cum laude. From there she went on to work in one of her father's companies and eventually took it over, but she never worked directly for her father. In fact, *Business World* magazine reported that she personally financed the campaign for a national park to take over land that he'd wanted to develop into a leisure complex. Now that took guts and plenty of money." Mare took a sip of the chilled tea and looked up at Paula, who was smiling.

"Oh yeah, I remember that. Boy, was he pissed at her. Even more when he learned that she'd convinced the board to sponsor the park, and that he'd paid for most of the publicity. Still, he'd signed the company over to her. He couldn't even get his buddy boys to vote her out, their stock options had shot up so much."

Mare gaped at her. "You're kidding, right?"

"Nope. She can be unbelievably devious when she wants to be."

"Considering who her father is, that doesn't surprise me."

Paula's smile slipped from her face. "So, you found out that TJ doesn't follow the work practices of her father. Does that mean you're willing to give her the benefit of the doubt, now?"

Mare shrugged, not yet willing to admit to anybody but herself that maybe there was more to TJ Meridian than met the eye.

"Was that all you learned?"

"No." Mare drew the word out. "I found out she is...was...a superb athlete who excelled in track and field and equestrian events. That four years ago her parents were killed in a car accident and she took over her father's holdings. And if *Business World* can be believed for a second time, she pissed off a load more people. Then, eighteen months ago, she and her brother were mugged as they left a charity event. Her brother was killed, and she was seriously injured. That's about it."

"There isn't much beyond that."

"I know a lot more than I did. I still don't know everything. But you and Erin were right. She isn't her father."

"TJ was a complex person before her injury. Now she has

more twists and turns in her psyche than a mountain road. It will be days before we get her over you seeing her in the chair. It will be ten times worse because she'd fallen."

"Days? Ten times worse? It's hard to believe that someone like TJ would get that upset." Mare was skeptical but she pondered it rather than argue about it. TJ sure had sounded upset, though. She scooted out of here as fast as she could, hardly even looked at me...and too proud to let me help her.

"What do you mean 'someone like TJ?' " Paula said and Mare picked up on the edge in her voice.

"You know. Beautiful, rich, intelligent, top of the world. She could have almost anything money can buy."

"Maybe so, Doc. But money can't replace what TJ has lost, and it can't buy what she needs."

ERIN HURRIED THROUGH the house, looking for TJ. She wasn't in the living room, and a quick glance in her office proved fruitless. She walked farther up the hall until she reached TJ's bedroom and knocked on the door. "TJ?" She got no reply, but she could hear movement behind the door. "TJ, can I come in?" Still no reply, though the movement stopped. "TJ?" Erin rested her head against the cool oak door and made her decision. She dropped her hand to the knob and pushed the door open.

Erin entered, but TJ didn't turn around and face her. She was staring at a framed photograph of her brother. Erin gently squeezed her shoulder then knelt in front of her. TJ tried to turn her head away, but Erin moved her hand to her cheek and wouldn't let her. "You okay?" Erin asked. TJ clenched her jaw and just nodded. "I need to check your legs and hips to make sure you didn't hurt yourself." Pulling her head away from Erin's cupped hand, TJ wheeled her chair aside.

"I told you, I'm fine."

Erin knew this was hard for TJ. Her back injury meant that some bodily functions had to be taken care of with tubes and bags. TJ was highly self-conscious about it and refused all help in that area of her care. For Erin to insist on inspecting her lower extremities would mean exposing not only the equipment but also TJ's pride.

"Honey, you can't know that. I need to check. Come on. The quicker you let me see, the quicker it'll be over with." Erin got to her feet and stepped up behind TJ. She wrapped her arms around the proud shoulders, pulled her into a hug, and kissed her hair. "Please, don't make this hard. It's only me." She felt her friend let out a long sigh. TJ's shoulders slumped even more, and she nodded her head. Erin hugged her tighter for a few seconds, then stepped back to give TJ room to maneuver herself around to the frame that allowed her to pull herself in and out of the bed.

Erin was fully aware that TJ's independent spirit hadn't allowed her to sit back and allow people to do everything for her. That was one of the reasons why everyone was so shocked that she attempted to take her life. To the outside world, TJ had come to terms with her injury remarkably quickly. Not even her closest friends knew what was going on in her mind.

Erin watched as TJ raised one of the chair arms out of the way and grabbed hold of a grip attached just above the bed. With a grunt, she lifted herself out over onto the bed and lay down. She loosened her jeans, and Erin pulled them down, taking care not to dislodge the catheter bag or the tubing strapped to her leg.

TJ, still not looking at Erin, had her hands clasped behind her resting head. "So, what's the prognosis? Will I survive?"

Erin continued her exam. TJ had a purpling bruise on her right hip about the size of her fist. "Well, you have some excellent bruising, but I don't think you've done any serious damage. Still, it might be worth getting an X-ray done on it."

"Uh-uh, no way." TJ pushed herself up onto her elbows and finally looked at Erin.

"And I thought you liked Dr. Hamilton. Or was it his assistant you liked? She was kind of cute," Erin said in a teasing voice. She knew TJ hated the local hospital. Dr. Hamilton had been recommended to take over TJ's care, and even TJ had to admit he was an excellent doctor. But he had taken a shine to TJ the first time he'd laid eyes on her, and he pestered her every time she went in for her checkups and physical therapy. For some reason, the good doctor wouldn't take no for an answer, no matter how glacial TJ acted.

Still, if TJ had fractured something in her fall, she would have to be admitted, but it would take all of hell's horses to achieve that feat.

TJ scowled at Erin. "I said no way."

"Okay, I'll make a deal with you. Your next physical therapy session is two days away. Let me get it changed to tomorrow, and if Sacha says it's okay, then we won't go see Hamilton. But if she says you need an X-ray and it shows something, then you have to behave and do as the doctor decides. Otherwise, I'll go get Paula and maybe Doc Gillespie to give me a hand and we'll take you up now."

TJ's lips pressed together for an instant, but Erin didn't flinch. "Okay, if Sacha says it needs an X-ray, I'll have one."

"And follow doctor's orders if there's anything wrong." Erin stared hard, letting TJ know she wouldn't get away with anything less than full cooperation.

TJ looked up, and when Erin saw the hurt in her eyes, she almost gave in. Almost. With relief, she watched TJ nod and blink away tears that formed but didn't fall.

"Good. Let's get you dressed again. Are you going to come out and join us?" Erin already knew what the answer would be but hoped for a different one, nonetheless. She suspected TJ would want to avoid seeing the doc right now.

"I'm a little tired. I think I'll stay here and have a nap," TJ said. Erin helped TJ pull her jeans back into place, then gently pushed her hair off of her forehead and kissed it softly before leaving.

ERIN WALKED BACK into the kitchen and made straight for the fridge. She grabbed a cold beer before sitting across from Paula and Mare at the island.

"How is she?" Mare said.

"About how I expected her to be—somewhat withdrawn."

"Has she hurt herself?" Paula asked.

Erin shrugged. "She has a nice bruise on her right hip that should probably be X-rayed just to be on the safe side. But a tank couldn't drag her to that hospital today."

Mare was shocked. "Are you just going to ignore it?"

"No," Erin said, "but if I pushed, TJ would just dig in her heels and refuse. Even if we got her to the hospital, she'd refuse help there, and it would be a wasted trip. You have to know how to deal with her to get anything done."

"So, what are you going to do?"

"TJ has a physical therapy appointment in two more days," Erin said. "Her therapist, Sacha Courtney, is about the only person in the medical world that TJ will listen to. So I'll phone Sacha and move the appointment up to tomorrow, and if Sacha thinks it needs an X-ray, TJ will get it done."

"Yeah," Paula said, "but getting her to stay in the hospital, if there's a fracture, is going to be hell."

"Nope, I settled that. If the doctor thinks she needs to stay, she will."

"And just what did you bribe her with to achieve that?"

Erin glanced over at Mare before looking back at Paula. "I didn't exactly bribe her. Besides, TJ's an intelligent woman. Even when she gets belligerent, she knows what's best."

"Come on," Paula said. "There's more to it than that."

"Well, I did threaten to have you and the doc here help get her dressed and to the hospital if she refused."

"Good girl. Yeah, that would have done it. On the more serious side, though, how is she? You've got a sixth sense about TJ. What are her true feelings?"

Before Erin could answer, Mare said, "Why would Paula and I helping get her to the hospital be a threat?" Mare leaned forward and folded her arms on the island surface.

Erin and Paula avoided Mare's gaze for several seconds before Paula spoke up. "Let's just say that TJ understands that some people, especially in this area, would take great pleasure in knowing that one of the Meridians was less than capable."

The insinuation angered Mare. "You mean she thinks I'm going to go running back to town and announce to everyone that she's a cripple? Like it was something to ridicule her for?"

"Bluntly," Erin said, "that's exactly what she believes."

"But I wouldn't do that. I haven't even told anybody yet that TJ was here at the ranch. I may not be a close friend, but I don't get any pleasure out of her condition."

"Well, you've practically admitted that most of the people in this town would love to ridicule a Meridian. You assume that she's like her father and the rest of his kind, why shouldn't she make assumptions about you?"

Mare already had her next hot protest ready when the pure logic of this statement left her dumbfounded. She suddenly realized her mouth had gaped open, and she closed her teeth with a click. Sitting back in the chair and sighing, she looked at each woman. "That makes such perfect sense, you've stopped me in my tracks."

Paula glanced toward Erin who wore a smirk on her lips.

"But, please," Mare continued with pronounced earnestness, "be assured that I would never, ever do that. I couldn't, even if I hated someone. TJ doesn't have to worry about me. Convince her of that for me, would you?"

"We'll try," Erin said, "though who knows how convinced she'll be."

Mare stood up. "Look, TJ and I were supposed to have a talk today about retaining my services. I don't want to bother her after this commotion, but tell her I'll stop back tomorrow morning."

Paula rose, too. "Wait a minute, I'll get your check."

Mare waved a hand. "That's okay. I'll pick that up tomorrow, too." Erin accompanied her out to the barn to get her bag, then they walked to her truck. Mare tossed her bag in, then turned when Erin put a hand on her shoulder. "In the world of big business, sincerity's in short supply. I apologize for not recognizing yours."

Mare reached up and patted Erin's hand. "No problem. I didn't exactly cut any of you a break, either. We were strangers, and it's just taking us a little work to get to know each other."

Erin slipped her hand from Mare's shoulder. "Well, I, for one, am beginning to think it's worth the effort."

"Me, too." Mare got in the truck. "See you tomorrow, first thing." She started the motor and reached for the gearshift.

"Doc?"

"Yeah?"

"You might have some trouble getting to see TJ tomorrow. Just wanted you to know that you might be on a wild goose chase."

"You get her in that office and leave the rest to me," Mare said. "I'm an expert at catching wild geese."

With a wave, Mare took off.

CRASH! ERIN'S EYES flew open as her dreams disappeared, to be replaced by visions of TJ lying on the floor. "TJ!" Erin leaped from the bed and yanked her robe on. As she reached the doorway and hunted for the light switch, Paula caught her arm.

"No lights," she said in a low growl. "And put your shoes on." Another loud crash sounded, then another, and another. It dawned on Erin that it wasn't TJ who had made the first noise. Someone was breaking windows. Erin could barely see her shoes. She stuck her feet in them and followed Paula who apparently had wakened first and had yanked on T-shirt, jeans, and boots.

"What's going on?" Erin whispered as the two of them ran down the steps to the first floor to check on TJ.

"You deaf? Someone's breaking the damn windows." Paula's snarl was enough to cut off any other questions Erin might have asked. "I called 9-1-1."

They reached the bottom of the stairs and heard several more crashes. "Go see if TJ's okay." Paula ran toward the enclosed gun rack that stood in the living room. Erin heard her curse as she stumbled over the ramp, and she was torn between checking on TJ and staying with Paula to make sure she didn't do anything rash. Paula's nasty mood didn't bode well for the trespassers. But TJ might need her.

Erin raced to TJ's door and rapped and opened it at the same time. "TJ, are you all right?" TJ had managed to pull herself to the headboard and was sitting up against it.

"Yeah, I'm okay," TJ answered dejectedly. "Did you call the police?"

"Paula did."

A cup-sized rock had been flung through one of the deep-set windows in the wall across from one side of TJ's bed, and the bottom half of the light sheet that lay over her legs contained a few scattered shards of glass. None appeared to have penetrated the cloth. Erin picked up the sheet, dropped it onto the floor, and got TJ a new one. In the dim light, she saw a piece of paper had been fastened to the rock. "There's a note here," she said as she untied it.

"Take it in the bathroom and read it." The flatness in TJ's voice worried Erin, but she did as directed. When she came back out, being sure to turn out the light before opening the door, TJ asked, "What did it say?"

Erin hesitated, but she knew TJ would have to be answered. "Something to the effect of telling the 'effing' Meridians to go back where they came from."

Erin heard TJ expel a puff of breath. "Guess our little vet didn't waste any time telling them who was out here and siccing them on us."

"She wouldn't do that."

"Who the hell else knew, Erin? All the utilities, the post office, everything's in your name." TJ's reasonable tone worried Erin more than an explosion would. TJ was hurt and it showed. But she was right, no one else knew a Meridian was here. Erin thought it was a darn shame. TJ seemed to like the doc. So much for trust.

Just then a shotgun fired several times. There were shouts, then a motor revved up and moved away, its sound diminishing down the driveway. A few minutes later, a patrol car pulled in, siren dying as it came to a stop.

"Go see what's up, Erin, and see if the horses are okay. Come back and let me know."

TJ sounded so woebegone that Erin put a hand alongside her face and kissed her cheek. "I'll be right back. Be careful of the glass, there might be some in the bed."

Erin hurried outdoors and saw Paula speaking with an officer. "Erin, this is Chief Jackson. Chief, Erin Scott." Erin and the police chief shook hands. The chief was a six-foot-tall, heavy-set man in his fifties with graying hair.

"Paula, did you see if the horses are all right?"

"The lowlifes did knock down the corral, but they left the barn alone, so the horses are okay. We just can't put them out until the corral is fixed."

"We heard some gunshots."

"Yeah." Paula sounded disgruntled. "I shot a couple of barrels over their heads to scare them off, then put a load of buckshot into the side of their pickup."

Erin looked around. All the outside lights were broken, too. The chief had left his car lights on so he could see to write in his notebook. "That should help identify them, Miss Tanner. I'll just take a look around, if you'll accompany me."

"I'm going back in with TJ." Erin got a nod from Paula and she left.

"T. J.?" The chief looked up from his note taking. "T. J. Meridian? I thought he was dead."

"He is," Paula said. "This is his daughter, Taylor Jade Meridian. She's called TJ."

"So, the news was right. There really is a Meridian out here." Chief Jackson's jaw clenched. He stopped writing and put his notebook in his breast pocket. His face looked like he'd smelled a polecat.

"Yeah, there is," Paula said in a grating tone. "But last time I looked, our laws protect everyone."

"That they do, Miss Tanner, and I'll sure check this out. If we can find the vandals, they'll be made to pay for the damage they've done."

Somehow Paula wasn't reassured, but she figured getting on the wrong side of the local law wasn't a good idea, so she kept silent about it. "You know a glazier who might fix our windows?"

Chief Jackson hesitated for a minute, then gave a slight shrug. He pulled his notebook back out and wrote down a name and number. "You might try this fella. He's kinda new in these parts, never knew the Meridians. He's got his main shop in Sharlesburg, but lives out here and runs a small operation from his house."

"Thanks." Paula stuck the paper in her hip pocket. "Come on, I'll show you the rest of the damage."

Chapter
Five

MARE FINISHED HER cereal and coffee and stacked the dirty dishes and spoon in the dishwasher. No emergencies had come in during the night, so her plan for an early visit to the Meridian ranch was still a go.

She had taken some time the night before to write down the points she would insist be placed in the retainer agreement. After tearing the list from the yellow tablet, she stuck it in her shirt pocket, picked up her bag, and got on her way.

NEITHER PAULA NOR Erin had gone back to sleep. They each quickly showered, dressed, and started cleaning up. Erin cleaned TJ's room, double-checked her bed for glass, and got her resettled. Then she sat with her until TJ fell asleep.

After hours of sweeping and cleaning, Erin and Paula finally stopped. Paula stretched and yawned, cracking her back and her jaw, one right after the other. "Time for TJ to get up. I'll go wake her while you fix breakfast. Cereal's fine for me." Paula went off, and Erin set out bowls, spoons, mugs, cereal, milk, and sugar. As she finished, Paula returned.

"TJ asked to have a tray in her office." Erin cut a chagrined look at Paula, who shrugged. "I couldn't talk her into coming to the kitchen. She's really out of sorts. Only good thing about today so far is the weather isn't terribly hot and it's not raining. With all these windows out, it's bad enough we can't use the air conditioning, but rain would be a real pain."

Erin herself felt a bit down. "I know what's bothering TJ. That damn vet had to be the one who spread the word of TJ's presence. She's the one who caused the night's troubles. And to think I trusted her."

"Yeah, she must've run right home and told everybody in sight that the Meridians had returned and were looking for trouble. Then sat around like Little Miss Innocent, swearing she hadn't told anyone about TJ. I think we've been played for a couple of suckers." Paula jerked her thumb toward the window. "Look, here she comes now."

THE FIRST THING Mare noticed as she walked toward the barn was shards of glass from the outside lights lying around the edge of the parking area. Then she spied the broken corral gate, and she ran into the barn. She breathed a sigh of relief when she found all three horses in their stalls with no apparent problems. She hurried out of the barn and turned toward the house. "Oh my God!" Sprinting onto the side porch, she knocked on the kitchen door, which was promptly opened by Paula.

"What happened out here?" Mare turned a puzzled look on Paula as she stepped in, then swung her gaze around. All three windows in the kitchen were broken.

"Why don't you tell us?" Paula said coldly.

"Me? How would I know anything about this?" Mare looked in disbelief from Paula to Erin.

Erin's voice dripped with disappointment. "You were the only one who knew TJ was here. All the utilities and the post office records are in my name. Only *you* could have told anyone. Obviously, her presence angered a certain element in the town, and a bunch of them came out here last night and busted the place up."

"Is TJ all right?" Mare nearly shouted. Her heart thudded in her chest until Paula answered.

"Yeah, no thanks to you. She could have been badly hurt."

Mare walked right up to Paula, stuck her face into the taller woman's personal space, and shouted, "If you think, for one minute, that I would condone anything like this, let alone cause it, then you don't know me very well. In fact, you don't know me at all."

Paula's nostrils flared and her fist closed, but Erin grabbed her arm and looked at Mare. "I think you better leave."

"I am not leaving. I came out here to see TJ, and I'm going to see TJ." Just as she had on her first visit, before anyone could stop her, Mare swung away and marched out of the kitchen into the hallway. She charged up to and through TJ's office door, not bothering to knock.

TJ looked up, startled. Mare strode over to the huge desk and placed her hands, fingers splayed, palms down, on its surface, leaning in toward TJ. TJ jerked back away from the desk. She huddled into the chair and hunched her shoulders as though warding off a blow.

Mare glanced back as Erin and Paula came running in right behind her. Erin reached to stop her, but Paula grabbed Erin and pulled her to a stop. Mare looked quickly back to TJ, and her voice crackled with sparks. "You really think I had anything to do with this vandalism?"

TJ's eyes shot daggers that answered the question better than any words could.

The jolt of hurt that ran through Mare astounded her. She took a deep breath and poured out her anger. "I don't know who the hell you people think you are. You come here out of nowhere. You don't use the Meridian name, like it's a big secret. Then somebody finds out you're here, there's some trouble, and right away I'm the bad guy — the terrible person who let out a secret that I didn't even know was supposed to be a secret. Did anyone ask me not to mention your name? No. But I got news for you, I didn't say a word about it." Except to Jess, but she knew he wouldn't have said anything. Irate, Mare picked up one hand and slammed her fist on the desk. "My life does not revolve around the Meridian ranch."

She stopped talking and glared at TJ. The slamming fist seemed to have awakened TJ from whatever funk she had been in. She suddenly grasped the chair handles, leaned forward, and glared back.

"Then how did they find out, Doctor?" TJ sneered, biting off the title like it was a dirty word.

"How the hell do I know? I'm not your personal protector. I'm a vet. I came out here to treat a horse, and that's what I've done. I didn't expect to be tried and found guilty of causing an attack on the high-and-mighty Meridians without even a chance to speak in my own defense."

"High-and-mighty Meridians?" TJ said through clenched teeth.

Mare stepped back from the desk, cocked her head, and put her fists on her hips. "Yeah. Look at you. Do you think just being a Meridian makes you better than the rest of us?" She knew she was skating on thin ice, but the dangerous chill growing in those ice-blue eyes aroused a curious excitement in her breast and she charged on, recklessly. "What do you do with that oh-so-superior intelligence you possess, besides sit and stare at a computer screen all day while the hired help does your work for you? Does it take an attack against the precious Meridian name for you to stop feeling sorry for yourself and start rising to life's challenges?"

TJ's jaw worked to force the words out. "How dare you come into my house and start preaching to me! Everything points to you as the cause of the attack. Shifting attention to me doesn't change that."

Unable to ignore Mare's taunts, she raised her voice. "And what the hell would you know about it anyway? You're not the one sitting in this chair, are you? You can get up in the morning, do what you please, run your own life. I have to rely on my friends, on machines and, yes, on hired help, to come even close to matching the freedom you take for granted. I have the right to feel sorry for myself if I want to."

The poignant truth of TJ's words flattened Mare's anger to exasperation. "Sure, you do, if that's what you want your life's goal to be. So you're disabled. So what? Susanne Wallers was born blind, but she learned to do everything around a busy house that a sighted person can do. She got married and raised three children and her oldest boy just won an art scholarship. He's proficient in a field she'll never be able to appreciate, but she's as proud and happy as any other mother would be."

Mare stood up straighter, crossed her arms, and said softly, "And I'm wondering where your heart is."

TJ looked scornful. "What's that supposed to mean?"

Mare waved an arm toward a corner trophy case. "All those trophies had to be won by someone with heart and courage. I'm wondering where you parked yours while you're indulging your right to feel sorry for yourself."

TJ's head jerked as though she'd been slapped, and her lips twisted. Out of the corner of her eye, Mare saw Erin grimace and make a move to come forward, but Paula, still hanging onto her, whispered something Mare couldn't hear.

TJ clasped her arms to her body and looked away, but she didn't speak.

After a slight pause, Mare continued. "Stan Birsek was paralyzed in a farming accident when he was fourteen. Fourteen! He took an in-home writing course, and now he produces a national newsletter for farmers. I could go on and on. Plenty of people have had to overcome serious handicaps. And they have, because they never gave up. They set their goals higher than just sitting around saying 'poor me.' "

TJ's gaze met Mare's, and an electric current sparked through Mare's heart. There came those damn eyes again. No fair.

The two women stared at each other for a long moment, seemingly mesmerized. TJ broke the contact to search for a pencil and picked one out of the desk caddy. Several unidentifiable expressions fought their way across her face while she spun the pencil through her fingers. Finally, she regained some calm. She looked back up at Mare and spoke quietly. "I don't have to explain myself to you, but I don't sit here saying 'poor me.' I sit in front of the computer screen running a multinational company. And you still didn't answer my question about how the town found out I was here."

The question was so far afield from Mare's current focus that it confounded her. She weakly waved a hand and shrugged. "I...um... Suddenly she pressed both palms against her face and dropped into the nearest chair. "Oh, hell. You're right. It was me."

TJ frowned. "What are you saying?"

"Johnny Robertson. Remember at the accident? I called out your name." TJ started to shake her head, but Mare saw the recollection dawn on her face, and they both said the same thing at the same time. "Miss Meridian."

Embarrassed, Mare nodded. "Then I told him you lived on the ranch across from his farm." She hid her face in her hands momentarily, then looked back up. "I came charging in here popping off to you, and I was wrong the whole time."

TJ's rich, low-pitched voice disagreed. "Not the whole time."

When her meaning struck Mare, she impulsively reached across the desk and laid her hand on top of one of TJ's, quieting them. "I had no right to say those things to you. I apologize."

TJ dropped the pencil, turned her palm up, and clasped Mare's hand within both of hers. "Don't apologize. It's about time someone kicked me in the butt and got me jump-started."

Paula and Erin quietly left the room, wide smiles rimming their faces.

TJ looked down at their entwined hands, then back up, and Mare's captured hand twitched. TJ let go, and Mare hastily withdrew her arm, a faint blush rising on her cheeks.

"You could be good for me, Doc. Most people tiptoe around my feelings, scared to make me angry. With good reason, I might add. I do have a somewhat volatile temper." A lopsided grin and cocked eyebrow accompanied the remark. "Do you think you can keep an eye on me and give me an occasional boot when I need one?"

"I'd be happy to!" Mare blurted out. Her twinkling eyes met an answering gleam from TJ. "And my friends call me Mare."

"Great. And mine call me TJ." For the first time, TJ graced Mare with a full smile. She pulled a sheaf of papers from a drawer. "Now let's talk about that retainer."

ERIN LIFTED ONE end of the wooden rail and rested it against the fence post, then turned and looked at Paula. "Honey, wipe the grin off your face and help will you?"

"Hmm? Oh, sorry." Paula quickly lifted her end so that Erin could hammer in the nails. "I was miles away."

"No, actually, I think you were about a hundred feet away. But I have a lot of work to do around here today, and I'd like to get the corral patched up so we can get the horses out of the barn." Erin finished securing her end of the rail and quickly walked over to Paula and started on hers.

"So what do you think?" Paula asked as she watched Erin hammer away at the post.

"About what?"

"Come on, don't give me that. You know exactly what I mean."

"Okay, you can let go now," Erin said. Standing back from the mended fence, she reached forward and shook it, testing its sturdiness. "I don't know, but I think TJ likes her," she said. "Wonder how she feels about TJ?"

"Guess we'll just have to wait and see."

Erin chuckled. "At least we know she's not intimidated by her."

"That's for sure. Are we done here?"

"Yep, all fixed. Let's go and let the horses out." They turned and walked toward the barn.

Paula, the taller of the two, draped her arm around Erin's waist and pulled her close. "What do you think they're talking about up there?"

"Don't know, and don't care. It's just nice to have her talking to someone besides us."

"Yeah, that is good to see. What time's her therapy appointment?" Paula asked as they stepped into the cool shade of the barn.

"Sacha couldn't fit her in until six this evening, but she's arranged for TJ to get an X-ray as soon as we get there so we don't have to hang around."

"Great. Mr. Thorton said that fixing the windows was too big a job with the glass supplies he had at the house, but said he'd have a crew out here this morning from Sharlesburg. And I also called Meridian's Security Department in Atlanta and asked Adam Lynch to send out a crew to get an expanded security system installed. If feelings around here are that inflamed about TJ being here, I don't want anybody to be able to get near the house or barn without one of us knowing about it. I wish TJ would reconsider getting some help in here. I'd rest easier, knowing she wasn't in the house alone when we're not around."

Erin stopped at Flag's stall. "You think TJ's going to agree with expanding the system?"

"I doubt it, but I'm not going to give her the chance to say no. We've got a busy time coming up. You need to get out and inspect the fences, outbuildings, and water sources. I need to start interviewing and getting the staff hired for the ranch and the plant, which is going to take me off of the ranch. After last night, if TJ won't get a live-in housekeeper or somebody, then I'm having it installed for my own peace of mind."

"You won't care if I make sure I'm out of the country when you tell her, will you?" Erin said with a grimace.

Paula connected Flag's lead rope. "Oh no, my pretty one, you're going to be standing right next to me, catching the flak and telling her you agree with me. Besides, if I tell her it's to make sure that Flag and the horses are safe, she won't say a word."

"She's going to see right through that, but you might get away with it," Erin said. She got Runny and Ebonair and led them out of the barn to the corral. "Why don't you come into the city with TJ and me this evening? We could all get a bite to eat and maybe catch a movie."

"You buying?" Paula let Flag go and watched as the horse playfully bolted into the freedom of the corral, quickly followed by the other two. Feeling Erin's arms wrap around her waist, she turned toward her.

"Only if you make it worth my while," Erin murmured as she pulled Paula into a kiss.

THE TRIP TO the city turned out to be better than either Erin or Paula had imagined. TJ was given a clean bill of health by Sacha, and in way of celebration, the three friends invited the physical therapist to eat with them. Paula picked out the wildest restaurant she could find, and they never made it to the movie.

Both Erin and TJ imbibed more than they should have, knowing that Paula was driving home. They weren't about to tell TJ she wasn't supposed to overindulge. It was the first she'd relaxed fully in a long time. They finally made it home just after midnight, and Paula and Erin put the tipsy TJ to bed.

From then on, life at the ranch moved at a startling pace. Despite the damage that Paula did to the vandals' truck, the chief was unable to apprehend them, which didn't surprise any of the women.

There were no more direct attacks on the house, but fences

were broken along the road and slogans were daubed in red
paint on the gates. TJ seemed unaffected by the events. Not even
a thrown bottle, which shattered the van's windshield as they
drove out of town, upset her. To the surprise of both Paula and
Erin, TJ agreed wholeheartedly with the installation of the
expanded security system. Adam Lynch and his team visited
shortly after the initial attack. They surveyed the property to
design the system, and the ranch house put up its first visitors.
Security cameras were placed in strategic areas along the
driveway and around the house, barn, and corral. The monitors
were mounted in TJ's office, directly under her wall TV.

That same week, engineers installed the stair lift so that TJ
had free rein of the house, and builders constructed ramps for
the porches.

Over the next several weeks, Erin made a thorough survey
of the ranch lands and water sources from horseback,
occasionally taking a sleeping bag and food to camp out
overnight. She arranged for repairs, clean up, and new
construction where needed.

Despite Erin's claims that Paula could hire away angels from
heaven, Paula was having a tough time organizing workers for
the ranch and packing plant. But with a consulting firm's plans
in hand, she moved forward with having the plant's machinery
computerized and updated.

Once that was well on its way, Paula hired Bill Jacobs away
from a ranch in Porter Valley to be the foreman of Meridian and
take part in its herd restocking. He selected prime livestock
direct from ranches he knew and later, when the cattle auctions
started, he'd be buying there as well.

Mare became a frequent visitor to the ranch and slowly but
surely she built a friendship with TJ. As she pulled TJ out of the
depression she had fallen into, TJ slowly took control of her life
again.

She had found it limiting to be so far away from Meridian
Corporation headquarters in Atlanta, Georgia, the southern hub
of commerce. To compensate, she had two more computers and
ISDN lines installed into the house, one in her bedroom and the
other in her office. She directed her administrative assistant,
Teresa, to field all her calls from the head office, routing only
those that required TJ's personal attention.

The company directors and department heads soon realized
that their commander-in-chief had returned, and where she had
once hidden in her office, she now directed from it. Business
meetings were conducted via videoconferencing. Those who
didn't know better had no idea that TJ wasn't sitting in her office

in downtown Atlanta. The phone rang incessantly, at all times of the day and night, as various departments and offices demanded her attention. Receiving and sending data and mail across the globe kept her constantly busy.

TJ seemed happier as her plans for the ranch and packing plant took on momentum. The only thorn in her side was the attitude of the town she was trying to help.

Chapter
Six

MARE FINISHED CLIPPING the blades of grass that were too close to the tombstone for the mowers to reach. She wiped the hand shears against the carpet of mown grass she was kneeling on and returned them to the tote bag at her side. Reaching over, she brushed her fingers across the letters chiseled into the granite monument. Jane Arnold Gillespie.

Hi, Mom.

Mare often marveled at the cemetery's quiet beauty. Jane's grave site sat atop one of the softly undulating hills, resting just beneath a sheltering tree that spread its branches over several graves in peaceful guardianship. Mare had planted colorful petunias, remembering that her mother loved many different flowers, but petunias were her favorite. This past spring, she had planted them again.

Today marked the first anniversary of her mother's death. In defiance of her terminal cancer, Jane had clung to life long enough to see Mare graduate and open her practice. A month afterwards, as though those two events were the milestones marking the end of her earthly journey, Jane succumbed.

Mare, bereft not only of her mother, but also of the closest friend she had ever known, had buried herself in her work. Many late evenings she spent at her piano, seeking solace in her music. On the first Sunday of each month, Mare visited her mother's grave and recounted the month's activities, believing that, somewhere, her mother was listening and watching over her.

"Guess what, Mom? I've met one of the Meridians and she's not at all what I expected. No, that's not completely accurate, and I know you're particular about accuracy. She's a powerful woman, with powerful emotions that she keeps damped behind a cold exterior. Don't ask me how I know that, I can just feel it. It's almost like there's some invisible thread linking us together, and though I can't tell what she's thinking, I can feel her emotions. Does that sound crazy?

"Anyhow, Mom, she's having a real problem with low self-esteem. She had an accident that paralyzed her legs, and she's lost confidence in herself. Sort of like an eagle with a broken wing that thinks it's not an eagle anymore just because it can't fly. But penguins don't fly, or ostriches or turkeys — hardly, anyway — and they're still birds. Someone's got to make her see that."

Rising and picking up her tote bag, Mare kissed her fingers and touched them to the stone. "I have to go, Mom. I'll keep you posted." She walked slowly to her truck, drinking in the peace and tranquility, storing it away in her heart. She drove home, musing over a woman with unforgettable blue eyes.

MARE STOOD AND stripped off the sterile latex gloves that had all but turned her hands into prunes. *And they call Sunday a day of rest!* She sighed and wiped at the sweat that threatened to run down her face. With one last dejected glance toward the dead animal, she looked at the worried face of Abner Stirkle who leased the small ranch where she had been working for the last four hours. "Sorry, Abner, there wasn't anything I could do. The others should recover okay, though. I think I got to them in time. Are you sure you haven't changed their diet or introduced something they might be reacting to?"

"Nope, Mare. It's like I said. They were fine yesterday, but I came up to put out their feed this morning and those three were down. I've wracked my brain trying to think what it could be, but I really haven't got any idea."

"Maybe you ought to keep the cattle nearer to the homestead for a while. Don Holland had a few of his come down with similar symptoms the other day. It looks as though they've been poisoned in some way. I'm still waiting on the results from Don's livestock. I'll send blood specimens off on yours, too, but it'll be a few days until I get the results. Keep a close eye on the herd, and if any of the others start to show signs, give me a call. If I'm not at the house then call my cell phone. That card I gave you has all the numbers on it."

"Thanks, Mare. I sure appreciate you getting out here so quick, I can't afford to lose cattle like this." Abner lifted his hat and scrubbed at his hair with his hand. He seemed to be considering his next words. "Rumor has it you'll be working up at the Meridian ranch. That true?"

Mare knew that it would soon start to spread around and that questions were going to be asked. She just hadn't thought they would be so quick about it. At some point, she would have to answer them. Taking a deep breath, she decided to be up front. After all, they were all going to benefit from her association. The signing fee that TJ had insisted she take had enabled her to get hold of some of the more expensive medications she had wanted to use, but hadn't been able to afford, and she'd been able to update a lot of her equipment already. "Yeah, it's true. They're going to have a lot of livestock arriving soon, and they needed a vet."

"Lot of folks around these parts aren't going to be too happy about that. The Meridians aren't liked around here. You should know that. You've lived here long enough."

"Yeah, I do know that, but let me ask you a question. Can you afford the four-hundred-dollar medication I just gave your cattle?" Abner looked at her unhappily. "I didn't think so, but the monthly payment I get from the contract I've signed means you don't have to, until you can. People may not like it, but it gives me options I didn't have before. We've all been living on the very edge the last few years, me as much as any of you, and I've tried to keep costs down. But some things can't be treated without money. People are just going to have to get used to it if they expect me to be able to keep treating their livestock, like I have, for the amount they're able to afford. Sorry, but that's just how it is." Mare looked over at Abner, waiting for a reply, but he just scuffed the dirt with his booted feet. "I'll come back tomorrow to check on them."

"Sure, and thanks."

Mare collected her things, grateful that no one else required her services this evening. She climbed into her truck, dreaming of a nice, relaxing evening at the piano followed by a soothing bubble bath and topped off by snuggling up in her sitting room with a good book.

MUSIC FILLED THE house as Mare's fingers moved confidently across the piano keyboard. She halted their movement when she heard a banging at the front door and hurried to answer it. She pulled open the door and saw Lew Sturgis. "Sorry, Lew, I didn't hear the bell."

The silver-haired gentleman's eyes crinkled as a friendly smile lit his face. "No problem, Mare. I could hear the music and knew I'd have to bang on the door to get your attention." He followed Mare into the house and took a seat at the kitchen table. Mare opened the fridge and poured two glasses of lemonade as she wondered what had prompted the lawyer's visit on a Sunday evening.

Medium height, slim, and tanned, Lew had been a friend of

her mother's for a long time and had taken care of her legal work, including her will.

After he and Mare had chatted while finishing their lemonade, he came to the point of his visit. "Mare, before your mother died, she called me to the house and handed me a sealed envelope. She didn't tell me what was in it, she just asked me to put it in my office safe and give it to you on the first anniversary of her death. I know it's Sunday, but I stopped by the office this evening, and I had this lying on my desk to bring to you tomorrow. When I saw it, I thought, today is the actual first anniversary, and since I was coming right by here on my way home, I brought it over." He reached into the inside pocket of his suit jacket, pulled out a buff envelope, and handed it to her.

"To Mary Theresa Gillespie, My Daughter." Mare's eyes misted as she read aloud the words scripted onto the envelope in her mother's strong hand. She turned the envelope over to open it, and Lew stood up. "I'll show myself out, Mare. I think you may want to read it privately."

Mare brushed a tear away and sniffled. "Thanks, Lew. And thanks for bringing it over." She heard the front door shut as her fingers closed on the letter. What could her mom possibly have wanted to wait a year to tell her?

Before she started reading, Mare laid the letter flat on the table. She ran her fingers over some of the words, then pressed her hands against the paper and closed her eyes. *Oh, Mom. You formed these letters, you touched this same paper. If only I could touch you! Why did you have to die?* The past year's loneliness gripped her heart with an almost physical force. Her hands slipped from the letter, and she hugged her arms to her body, rocking back and forth. She was so alone. But directly on the heels of that notion came another: Except for TJ.

Except for TJ? she asked herself, then reflected on it. Well, yes. In a very short time, TJ had pushed away some of her loneliness. She had someone to think about besides herself and a bunch of farm animals. She was even playing happy music for a change.

In a brighter mood, Mare picked up the letter. The beginning talked about her adjustment to living without her mother and Jane's undying love for her daughter. But the next part dropped a bombshell.

> *Mare, my darling, please try not to be too angry with me for what I'm about to reveal. When you were a youngster, I told you that your father, my husband, had died in an accident before your birth. I made that story up, Mare, so you*

would believe you had a father just like your friends had. And to prevent your searching him out and raising embarrassing questions.

Your father and I loved each other very much, but we never married. We had an affair in our last year of college, and you were conceived. Your father was planning to go on with his studies. He had a very bright future ahead of him that could have been ruined by the burden of providing for a wife and child. So, I broke off with him shortly after graduation and moved away. He never knew that he had a daughter, and I was too proud to hold him to supporting us. I vowed to take care of you myself, without his help, and I managed to do that.

I never intended to reveal this to you until years from now, but when I found I was dying, I knew that to withhold it from you forever would be needlessly selfish. Perhaps it was selfish from the beginning, but I can't go back and change that.

I'm not going to tell you his name. If you insist on searching for him, the time and trouble it takes you to discover who he is will give you an opportunity to decide what you'll do when you find him. He may be a happy family man who would be appalled to find that he had a daughter he never knew, and perhaps he shouldn't be told. Or, he may be happy to meet you. That's something you'll have to decide for yourself.

Please forgive me if I've hurt you. You know I would never have hidden this from you without good reason. I love you more than words can ever say.

Good-bye, my dear daughter, please don't think too harshly of me.

Your loving Mother

Mare put her head down on the kitchen table, stretched her arms out past her head—still holding the letter in both hands—and groaned. She set the letter down and patted it. A father. She might have had a living father all this time and never knew him. She had to find him. She had to.

The sudden revelation overwhelmed her, and tears dripped from her eyes, gradually becoming a torrent. She cried for the mother she had loved and lost and for the father she had lost before she had a chance to love him. She cried for what had been and for what might have been. Finally, she cried herself to sleep, there at her kitchen table, in a turmoil over what her search for a missing father might uncover.

TWO DAYS LATER, as Erin neared her destination, she slowed Ebonair's gallop to a canter, then a walk, giving the animal a chance to cool down from the hard ride. She guided the horse into the barn, a look of concern apparent on her face. After jumping down from Ebonair's back, she grabbed her travel pack from the saddle and dropped it on a chair. In routine order, she undid the girth and pulled the heavy leather off of the mare's back, resting it on a nearby box. She removed the bit and bridle, put a halter on Ebonair, and led her into the stall to await her grooming.

Paula had obviously seen Erin from the kitchen when she rode in, because she could now hear footsteps approaching from behind as she closed the stall door.

"Hi, love," Paula said. "Everything okay?" Paula's arms slipped around Erin's waist and moist lips pressed against the side of her neck. She relaxed back into Paula's embrace.

Erin turned within Paula's arms and hugged her back. "I missed you," she said as she snuggled into Paula's chest. "And no, everything isn't okay. We have a pretty big problem. I need to talk to TJ."

"I missed you, too." Paula gave Erin an extra squeeze and kissed her hair. "I haven't even kicked her out of bed yet."

Erin was surprised. TJ was known for rising early in the morning. "She okay?"

"Oh yeah, she's fine. Mare came over last night, and they spent the evening talking horses in the living room. Which, of course, progressed to watching TJ's videos of Flag in the nationals. I think Mare finally got out of here just after two." Paula grinned. "I don't think she knew what hit her. She hasn't exactly seen TJ's best side, has she? I did try to warn her that she'd be out of her depth when it came to talking horseflesh with TJ. But you know what she's like. She steamed right in there without any thought of the consequences."

"What did TJ make of the visit?" Erin had now torn herself from Paula's loving hold to groom Ebonair.

"Don't think I've seen her this happy since Lance told her he'd made Harvard Med. Mare has caught TJ's eye, that's for sure."

"Mare seems to be enjoying herself, too." Erin's thoughts returned to her message. "You think you could get TJ up? She ought to hear what I've found, as quickly as possible."

"You got it, honey. By the time you're finished here, I'll have TJ up and breakfast waiting for you." Paula picked up Ebonair's saddle and bridle and put them in the tack room on her way out, bringing a tickle of warmth to Erin's heart for her thoughtfulness. They'd been together for eight years, and Paula was still a sweetheart.

Forty-five minutes later, Paula had breakfast laid out and coffee poured. Erin sat at the island, still in dusty jeans and shirt, looking tired. TJ rocked back and forth in her wheelchair, mulling over what Erin had just told her.

"How many streams did you say were affected?" TJ stopped rocking.

"Looks like all of the southwest sector. But I took samples from every water source." Erin took a swig from her mug and watched TJ turn her chair and wheel herself from the kitchen.

"Be back in a second." True to her word, a few minutes later TJ appeared with a rolled map across her knees. She handed the map to Paula who unrolled it on the table and flattened it out, using the condiments as holders. TJ handed Erin a red marker. "Can you mark the affected areas for me?"

"Yep." Erin studied the map and marked it in several places before clicking the red cylinder's top back on. Paula picked up the map and folded it so TJ could see the spots Erin had marked. One by one, TJ traced the affected streams back through to their sources.

"They all originate outside of our land. Do you think someone has deliberately poisoned the water?"

Erin considered TJ's question. "I doubt it. Even if we did have livestock on the land, they wouldn't be down in that area. Our best grazing is to the north by the lake and river. If it were deliberate, it would make more sense to poison that supply."

"And the river and lake are okay?"

"They were when I checked three days ago. From the amount of dead fish I saw in the streams in the southwest, it's been that way for longer than three days. I backtracked as far as I could up the streams, but I couldn't find an obvious source or cause for the contamination."

The room descended into silence. Then Paula spoke up. "So, what are we going to do?"

TJ rocked back and forth in her chair again. "Paula, I want you to drive into Sharlesburg, charter a helicopter, and hand-deliver Erin's samples to our biochemical division in Corpus Christi. They should be able to figure out what the contaminant is and how to get rid of it. I'll phone them and tell them it's on the way and to assemble a cleanup team ASAP. You can call ahead and give them an expected arrival time."

"Right," Paula said. "And while I'm there, I might as well check out possible machinery suppliers for the packing plant. Do some comparison shopping."

"Good idea." TJ stopped rocking and tapped a finger against the map. "Erin, see if you can find somebody around here who does aerial photography and get them to do some visuals of all the water sources on the property. Let's make sure that the southwest range is the only area affected. Then go into town and see if you can find out who else is having problems. Mare said she would try to stop by today. I'll get an update from her, too."

Erin went to grab a shower and get changed. Paula got hold of Erin's bag and left with the sample to be sent to Meridian Corporation's biochemical division. TJ retired to her office to stir the resources of her vast empire to work on a solution to their current problem.

Erin popped her head around the door before she left for town. "You want anything while I'm there?"

"No, thanks," TJ said, staring in concentration at the computer screen. Then her head raised. "Unless we're out of cookies. I think Mare and I finished them off last night."

"You and the doc seem to be getting pretty friendly." Erin perched on the side of the desk. "I take it you like her?"

"Yeah, I like her. She's feisty and won't take any crap, not even from me. She knows how to kick my butt and make me forget about my problems. I like that. I respect it. And she smiles a lot. She isn't someone who lets life get on top of her, no matter how bad it seems." TJ's face fell. "She's the exact opposite of me."

Erin was touched that TJ had obviously spent so much time thinking about Mare. In the past, TJ's affairs had been short, and not all that sweet. No one had been able to get past that wall around her heart. When her father was alive, her love life had been non-existent. And thinking about it, Erin honestly couldn't remember anybody ever having this sort of effect on her friend.

"Well, it isn't as if Paula and I aren't like night and day now, is it? If you two were just alike, it wouldn't be as interesting." Erin glanced toward the window as she heard the rumble of an engine coming to rest. "Speak of the devil." TJ looked, and her face brightened as she saw Mare step from her truck.

Erin stood up from the desk. "I'll send her on in, shall I?" TJ nodded, her eyes still glued to Mare's slim and perfectly defined body.

Mare stepped into the now familiar kitchen and saw Erin walking toward her. "Hi, how is everyone today?"

"We're fine. Paula and I will be out for a while, but TJ's in her office, if you want to go on in."

"Okay. I'll see you later, then." Mare walked past as Erin grabbed the Land Rover keys and made for the door.

"Hey, Mare?" Erin called out from the doorway. "You know

anybody who does aerial photography?"

"There isn't anybody in town, but if you drive out to Bancroft, you'll see signs for an airstrip. Some guy there does it. Don't know how good he is, though."

"Great. That'll save me some time. See you later."

"Bye."

The door to TJ's office was open. As Mare approached, she looked in but couldn't see TJ. "Hey, TJ, you here?" she yelled.

"Be right with you!" TJ shouted from farther up the hallway. "Go on in and make yourself at home."

Mare went into the office and sat in one of the more comfortable chairs. She leaned her head back and relaxed for the first time since a five a.m. wake-up call. Uhhh. Less than three hours' sleep, and no end in sight. She should be out checking the other ranches, making sure they didn't have any cattle down. But an hour of relaxation here would be as good as a couple of hours' sleep. She heard the wheelchair and struggled to open tired eyes, but still managed to sound cheery. "Hi ya."

"Hi." TJ wheeled herself into the office. "You okay? You look a little tired. I didn't keep you up too late last night, did I?" Her voice didn't hold the slightest bit of remorse for the previous evening's marathon video session.

"Of course, you kept me up too late last night, but that was my fault. I could have gone at any time. I was just having too much fun." Actually, she'd been having too much fun watching TJ rave on about horses, and seeing the excitement on her face was worth the loss of sleep. "But I also got called out to the MacMasters ranch. Some of their cattle couldn't wait until office hours to become ill."

"You want some iced tea? I could rustle you up something to eat, too, if you'd like," TJ said.

"Sure, that would be great."

"Come on, then." TJ turned her chair around and proceeded through the doorway. "So," she said over her shoulder, "what's wrong with the cattle?"

"Not too sure. I'm still waiting on test results from a load of cattle I saw the other day, but whatever it is, it seems to be spreading. This is the third ranch to be affected." Mare rested her hand on the handles of the wheelchair but didn't push. She'd already seen how TJ reacted to what she saw as coddling.

"Mare? Could the cattle be ill because of some sort of contaminant in the water?"

Mare felt her heart rate pick up. Please don't let this be something else the Meridians were caught up in. "That's possible," she said cautiously.

"Where are the affected ranches in relation to us?" TJ asked as they entered the kitchen.

"The MacMasters ranch is the next one over from yours. The other two are to the south. Why?"

"Erin's been checking the fencing and water supply for the last couple of days. She came back in today to report that most of our water supply in the southwest section of the ranch seems to have been poisoned. She says the streams have dead fish in them. I wondered whether the same thing could have affected the cattle." TJ pulled open the fridge and took out the pitcher of iced tea that was constantly kept full.

Mare let out a silent sigh of relief. "It sure could. The cattle weren't found particularly near to water but that doesn't mean they hadn't drunk it. I'll need to go out and get some samples."

"Erin already did that. Paula's on her way to Sharlesburg now. She's delivering a sample to my biochemical division, and we should have an answer by tomorrow. There's a map on my desk in the office. If you go get it, I can show you what we know is contaminated, and you can figure out whether the ranches affected are on the same water source as our streams."

Mare spent the next hour studying the map, seeing where the streams originated and following where they headed. As far as she could tell, there were two more ranches likely to be affected, and then the contamination would reach Meridianville. "Do you think the town's water supply could be hit with this?" Mare asked as she finished the last of the croissants TJ had placed before her.

"Depends where you pull your water from and whether it goes through a treatment works first."

"We have natural aquifers, and it isn't treated. There hasn't been any need."

"Then, yes," TJ said in a serious tone. "If the aquifers become contaminated, the town could have a serious problem on its hands. I'm having some aerial photographs of the area done to see if any of my other water sources are involved. We have a massive lake up in the northern sector. If that's affected, we could be in bigger trouble because it's supplied from the river."

"Oh God, let's hope not," Mare said. "I need to get back to town and let someone know about this. I hate to run out on you, especially after the effort you just put into feeding me."

"No problem," TJ said. "You go. By tomorrow, I should have the photos and the results from the labs."

"Okay, I'll drop in and see what you've got." Mare jumped from her seat and pulled her keys from her pocket. She bent down, impulsively kissed TJ on the cheek, and was out the door, relishing her parting glimpse of a rather stunned-looking TJ.

IN THE RANCH driveway, Erin slumped back in the Land Rover's seat and switched off the engine. A welcome mantle of calm silence enfolded her. She had been up since the sun rose above the horizon this morning. Now it was well past midday. The drive out to the airfield at Bancroft had proved fruitful, and Paul Williams and his partner Jenny Gomez were readying their helicopter to photograph the ranch's water resources. Erin had also asked them to fly up the affected streams as far as possible, to see whether they could locate the source of the contamination.

She pushed the door open and got out of the Rover, groaning at tired muscles and noting with disappointment that Paula hadn't yet returned from Sharlesburg. She trudged slowly up to the house, removed her Stetson, and plodded into the kitchen.

TJ sat near the island, cradling a glass of something cold. "Hi," Erin said as she hung the Stetson on a chair back. "Photos will be done this afternoon, and the photographer's going to drop off the prints tomorrow." She opened the fridge and grabbed a beer. When TJ didn't answer, Erin turned to take a closer look at her. TJ sat rocking back and forth in her chair as was her habit when thinking. She was flushed and had the weirdest look on her face. Erin walked over to her and placed her hand on TJ's forehead, checking for a temperature. "You okay? You look a little flushed."

"Oh yeah, I'm fine."

Erin removed her hand, still studying her. "Okay, if you say so. Mare gone?" Erin swore that TJ's face lit at the mention of Mare's name, her flush becoming a full-blown blush. *Well, well, well, our TJ is well and truly smitten.*

"Yeah," TJ said, as she seemed to come back from whatever dream world she'd been floating in. "She's been having a few problems with cattle becoming mysteriously ill. I think some of the other ranches in the area are affected, too, which makes it unlikely that it's anything against us specifically. She's gone to warn the town that their water supply may be hit, since they're about ten miles farther down the water course affected."

"Is she coming back?" She saw TJ's face fall slightly.

"Not until tomorrow. I said I'd give her whatever the labs come up with."

Oh yeah, Cupid's arrow was certainly well aimed when he got those two.

PAULA RETURNED TO the Meridian household later that evening after a round of factory visits. Before leaving Corpus Christi, she'd gotten an update from the biochemical division on the samples. Whether the contaminant could be cleaned up quickly would depend on what it was. The division had already notified TJ that the samples contained an industrial byproduct, and they would have a complete breakdown of its components in the morning. They had organized a cleanup team, which would arrive at the ranch tomorrow afternoon.

Nobody was in the kitchen when Paula entered. She heard music coming from the living room so she headed that way and spotted Erin sprawled on the couch listening to Shania Twain on the CD player. Erin looked completely relaxed with bare feet resting on one arm of the couch and both forearms folded across her face.

Paula crept over and tickled the bottoms of the exposed feet. "Yo!" Erin yanked her feet back and pulled both arms down. She half-lifted her head, but it quickly flopped back onto the couch as her yelp turned into a groan.

Paula grinned, pleased with the results of her tormenting. "What are you groaning about?"

"While you were out having yourself a good old time all day, I came back and unloaded a dozen bales of hay. Then I mucked the stalls, which were a bit overdue. How can just three horses produce so much...fertilizer? Yuck." Erin made a face. "Wonder when TJ's going to let us hire some extra help? That's one job that's going to the top of my 'To Be Delegated' list. This gives a whole new meaning to the word 'pooped.' "

Paula sauntered slowly alongside the couch, bending over several times to twitch her nose and sniff loudly at Erin's body. Finally, nearing Erin's head, she remarked in a mockingly supercilious tone, "I detect a suspicious absence of unpleasant odors for someone who claims to have engaged in such an aromatic pursuit."

"Well, cutie," Erin said dryly, "that's because I did exactly what you would have done when finished. I made a mad dash for the shower."

Paula tousled Erin's curls. "Yep, you're a little damp."

A saucy smile slowly curved Erin's lips.

Paula leaned over to place a kiss on Erin's forehead only to be pulled down on top of her. "So, feeling frisky, are we?" Paula said as her lips closed over the soft sweetness of Erin's mouth.

"Hmm, that would be a yes, " Erin said when their kiss ended. She wrapped her arms around Paula and pulled her nearer.

"Where's TJ?" Paula asked.

"In the barn, fixing something on her saddle. talking to Flag, knowing her."

"So..." Paula snuggled into the warm embrace ar her fingers slowly down Erin's chest. "We have the h ourselves?" She undid the top button of Erin's shirt.

"Yep, all to ourselves."

Chapter
Seven

THE NEXT DAY Erin was on kitchen duty when she saw Mare's truck pull up outside the house. Her thoughts immediately turned to the conversation she had had with Paula on the couch the night before. Yep, love was definitely in the air. Mare walked into the kitchen, and Erin turned from the counter and waved the knife she was using to slice tomatoes onto sandwiches. "Hi, Mare. You're just in time for lunch—almost. TJ's still in her office. I'll get you when it's ready."

"Hi, Erin. Thanks. Everything okay?"

Erin's cheeks dimpled. "Everything's fine." She'd been thinking about something for a while and figured she might as well say it. "Your coming here to visit with TJ sure has given her a boost. Which gives Paula and me a boost, too. Thanks a lot." It had done more than that for TJ. Mare had brought her back to life.

"No problem. I enjoy coming here," Mare said. She walked into the hall, rapped on the office door, and stepped in. "Hey, the cleanup's underway."

TJ waved her forward. "Yep. The full results were e-mailed to me this morning. Lucky we caught this quickly."

"The town council notified District 6's Clean Water branch of the EPA about the animal deaths, too. They're supposed to send a team to investigate."

"Hope they find the bastards who did this. Come here. The photographer brought over the aerial photos of the ranch, and I was just looking at them." The desktop was covered with 8-1/2 x 11" pictures, in color. "Those show the two streams where Erin found the dead fish, but, look, here's the lake I was telling you about."

Mare walked behind the desk, to the left of TJ, and leaned her elbows onto one of the few bare spaces on the oaken surface. She swung her right arm forward and rested her fingers on the bottom edge of the picture TJ was pointing to. "That's breathtaking!" Mare tilted her head and looked at TJ's profile as TJ concentrated on the photo. *And so are you.*

Mare didn't have the courage to say the words aloud. She recognized that her feelings for TJ were growing stronger day by day. The more she learned about this complex and intriguing person, the closer she wanted to be to her. Both as a friend and...

TJ reached up to slide the picture closer to Mare, and her hand touched Mare's arm. The contact sent a jolt through Mare, and she snatched her arm away before she could stop herself.

"I think—" TJ's words froze in the middle of the sentence. Her lips twisted and her shoulders slumped.

Mare was suddenly aware that snatching her arm away had somehow hurt TJ. Without a word, she slid her left hand under TJ's palm and put her right hand on top of the long fingers.

TJ stared at their hands, and her voice sounded raspy. "Is my touch so repulsive to you?" Mare's eyes brimmed with sudden tears. *Oh, TJ, if you only knew...*

Mare turned around, facing straight at the side of the wheelchair. She lifted the strong hand she was holding and placed it over her thudding heart. "Repulsive?" A tear trickled down her face, and she half laughed and half cried as she struggled to talk. The door she thought she had closed on her emotions sprang open and so unhinged Mare that she threw caution to the winds. "Don't you know I'm falling in love with you?" Leaning down, she pressed her lips to a surprised TJ's slightly parted mouth, then just as quickly she drew back in embarrassment. "Look, I'm sorry. Maybe I'm presuming something I shouldn't..."

Cool eyes stared at her, giving nothing away. TJ entwined her long fingers in the material of Mare's shirt and gently pulled her back into a longer kiss. And ice turned to fire.

Mare was a lightning rod and TJ's tongue was the bolt. Unprepared for the strength of her own reaction, or that of TJ's, Mare pulled her lips away to draw a ragged breath. She released TJ's hand, which moved to push the side handle of the wheelchair out of the way. Then TJ looked up at Mare and raised her arms in invitation. Mare slipped into the open arms and gently sat on her lap.

She raised her fingers to the gorgeous face, stroking along the perfect cheekbone, the strong jaw. She smiled a little self-consciously then took the plunge. "Can we try that again?" So they did. In the circle of each other's arms, their bodies alight with the warmth of touching for the first time, they shed their restraint and lost themselves in the sweet passion of the kiss. Mare tilted her head back as she surrendered to the pressure of

TJ's aggressively searching mouth. She wanted to stay in TJ's arms forever.

Erin knocked and opened the door, interrupting the exploring kiss. A delighted smile stretched across her face. "Do you, uh...still want lunch?"

TJ's whole attitude seemed to beam. "We'll eat in here if you—"

Mare put a hand over TJ's mouth and shook her head, passion still evident in her breathless voice. "No, I have to make some calls right after lunch. We better go to the kitchen," she said with a low laugh, "or I might never get out of here." Erin nodded and hurried back to the kitchen, obviously eager to pass the happy news on to Paula.

TJ kissed Mare's fingers, then Mare stood up and made an attempt to calm herself while TJ resettled the chair arm. Walking behind the chair on the way to the kitchen, Mare thought a neutral subject might be in order, so she asked a question that had been on her mind for a while. "How come you don't use an electric wheelchair?"

TJ's voice was laced with humor. "Pushing this one around gives me a lot of upper body exercise, and I want to keep strong. I have an electric one in the garage that I use in the city. Besides, this one is absolutely quiet."

"Oh, so you like quiet, huh?" Mare knew she herself was anything but quiet.

TJ's long arm reached behind her shoulder, and she laid her hand on Mare's as it rested on the chair back. "Not always."

"Glad to hear that." With a singing heart, Mare bent down and dropped a quick kiss on TJ's hand, then pushed her on into the kitchen for lunch, which started off as a quiet affair. Erin and Paula didn't say a word, although they kept glancing at TJ and Mare who were constantly looking at each other from the corners of their eyes. Fleeting smiles crossed between TJ and Mare whenever their eyes connected, but they eventually settled down and conversation picked up.

"So," Mare said, "what is it that's contaminating the water supplies?" The question gave her a great excuse to look at TJ's beautiful face a little longer.

TJ sat back and chewed absently on her bread roll before answering. "Bit of a mixture of stuff: industrial slurry from some production process, various types of oil. The people at the lab seem to think it can be cleaned up if we can find the source of the contamination, though it may take a few weeks. The cleanup team coming today will give me more information. They'll work up the watercourse and find what's causing it. Chances are it's someone in Sharlesburg dumping illegally."

"There's a meeting in the town hall tonight," Mare said. "The mayor's going to tell us what the EPA plans to do." She looked at the others to see if they had heard about it, but from the blank looks on their faces she knew they hadn't. "It might be a good idea if you came to it."

THE MEETING HAD been going on for an hour, and nothing had been sorted out yet. Mare was getting bored. All they were doing was going around in circles. The EPA had sent out its scientists, and samples had been taken. Big deal. TJ already had the results. Mare had hoped TJ would turn up for this, though her presence might have been resented.

Apart from the EPA monitoring the town's water supply, they wouldn't commit to doing much more. Resources were in short supply. The agency said if the contamination turned out to be a threat, then maybe a cleanup team would arrive within the next few days. But TJ's team was already at the ranch. If her team found the source of the pollution and removed it, she'd solve the town's problem even without the agency's cooperation. As the meeting dragged on and the ranchers recognized nothing was going to be done right away, they got louder and louder. Mare sighed as one of the more vocal antagonists spoke up yet again. This time, though, she sat up.

"Who's to say the Meridians aren't behind this? They dumped this town before. Doesn't mean they won't do it again now that we're getting back on our feet." There were a few yells of agreement and catcalls of derision at the statement. But Mare was infuriated. TJ had been at the Meridian ranch for several weeks, and yes, at first Mare had been suspicious of her motives, but she knew better now. She was about to get up and tell them exactly what she thought of the accusation when someone beat her to it.

"Nah, I don't hold with that," a strong voice said from the back of the hall. Mare turned her head to see who had spoken, and Chuck MacMasters strode forward. "Her ranch lies across from mine and next to Abner's, so she must be affected as well. The Meridians may have all but bankrupted the town before, but they never did anything to harm themselves. If Miss Meridian wants to make a go of that ranch, and all signs point to it, then I can't see her poisoning her own water sources. Can you?"

Mare wanted to get up and cheer but instead got up to speak. "Chuck's right. Water in the southwest section of the Meridian ranch has been affected."

"Yeah, and you would know that, seeing as how you work for her!" jeered an unknown source. Mare didn't know quite how to respond to that, and she didn't have to. Another voice entered the fray.

"No, she knows because I told her and asked for her opinion. Do you have a problem with that?"

Mare turned and saw TJ in the doorway. *Wow! She sure knows how to make an entrance.*

Isolated murmurs skipped around the hall as TJ wheeled herself through the crowd, closely followed by Paula and Erin. None of the people had known TJ was in a wheelchair, since Mare hadn't thought to tell anyone. Many seemed stunned at the sight.

TJ let her eyes scan the crowd, putting all the menace her father was known for into the gaze, quickly turning away anyone who was staring. "What? Now that I'm here in person and you see that I'm not the mighty Tom Meridian, but a cripple, do you think I'm not capable of doing exactly what you suggested?" TJ taunted them, her steely voice full of implied power. Mare had never quite heard that tone before, but she didn't want to argue with it and neither, it seemed, did anyone else.

TJ brought herself to a halt several feet from the front of the hall, barely ten feet away from where Mare was sitting. "However, we find ourselves in a similar situation, don't we? I've brought a cleanup team to Meridian, and it might be beneficial to help each other out."

"We don't need your kind of help!" There was that voice again. Mare wished she could see who it was. She'd shut him up on a semi-permanent basis.

"Fine," said TJ without inflection. "I'll take my cleanup team and go. You can wait for the EPA to figure out what it is. But I should inform you that I'm cleaning my section of land, and until all sections upstream of me are cleaned as well, I'll be diverting the contaminated streams off of Meridian ranch."

That brought shocked gasps from everyone including Mare.

TJ turned her gaze to Mare and gave her a wink.

Did she just wink at me? Mare saw the glint of amusement in the eyes that had for several seconds connected with hers. TJ was enjoying herself.

An angry voice shouted, "You can't do that!"

"Try me," TJ said. "Now do you want to talk about this, or shall I leave?"

There was a buzz of conversation through the hall until the mayor, Steve Armando, spoke up. "The thing is, Miss Meridian, the town and its people don't want to be beholden to the

Meridians ever again."

"Good." TJ smiled and that, Mare saw, was actually more frightening than if she'd been angry. "Because I'm not offering this for free. I'm a businessperson, and as all businesspeople know, there's always a deal to be done. I can have a cleanup team working within hours sorting this problem out, or you can wait until the EPA decides to move. Shall we talk?" TJ locked eyes with Armando, who nodded his consent, then her cool gaze swept around those gathered in the hall, seeing their begrudging agreement. "Okay, then let's get to work."

Mare relaxed back into her seat and watched the woman she was slowly coming to think of as more than a friend. TJ was remarkable. There she was, sitting in a room full of people who essentially hated her, and she'd just taken over the whole meeting.

"First," TJ said, "I need to know who else is likely to be affected by this pollution and what type of water source their domestic supply comes from."

"Why?" Abner asked.

"So my teams can fit a filtration unit to protect your family's home supply."

"Miss Meridian," Mayor Armando said.

"Please, call me TJ."

"Right. TJ. We're worried about the town's water supply. We don't know whether it will be contaminated."

"That's okay. My team can fit filtration units to the pump house so the town won't be affected. With the council's approval, of course."

Armando looked stunned. "What?"

TJ raised an eyebrow. "Do you think I'd sit back and watch people become ill because of this? I may be a Meridian, but I'm not my father."

MARE TOOK A quick glance at her watch as she stepped from the town hall into the cool, fresh air the night had brought with it. The meeting had started at six, and TJ had arrived just after seven. It was now close to eleven, and they were still going strong. TJ was a wonder to behold. Every time someone threw up a problem, she had an answer, no matter how stupid or petty the concern was. The whole town was rapidly coming to understand that Tom Meridian had been a reasonable businessman, who'd just happened to be a total bastard. His daughter, though, was a genius. She got things done, not because she used threats— though they had all seen she was good at that, too—but because she knew exactly what to do.

When TJ told them what she wanted in payment for her help, the mayor and the town's residents had been taken off guard. Mare had to admit to being surprised herself, though when she thought about it, she knew that money wasn't TJ's main concern. Getting the ranch and eventually the packing plant up and running was. So, for payment, TJ had told them that she wanted all those unemployed who had any farming, carpentry, or mechanical skill, to work for her at the ranch and the packing plant on a minimum one-year contract.

There had been another silence at that, but Paula had brought a copy of the contract with her and passed it around. They could see right away that it was a good deal. Those being employed would get a reasonable wage and extremely desirable benefits, including the building of a medical center in Meridianville. Mare thought it would probably take time for the worst detractors to accept that TJ was different from her father, but she had made a very good start.

Now Mare was on a mission for coffee and food as she walked over to the diner. TJ had obviously been going nonstop since Mare had spoken to her at lunchtime. Paula and Erin told Mare they'd both tried to persuade her to finish for the day, but to no avail. TJ was on a roll and had no intention of stopping while there were things still to be sorted out.

Paula had then been dispatched back to the ranch to check in and make plans to continue to coordinate the cleanup team. Most of the team had been visiting the affected ranches all evening, and tomorrow those likely to be affected would also have filtration units installed.

The door of the diner swung open easily as Mare stepped into its brightly-lit interior.

"Hey, honey." Pleasantly plump and bubbly, Rochelle had been a waitress at the Pot-o-Gold Diner for as long as Mare could remember. "They still going at it over there?"

"Hi, Rochelle." Mare slid onto a seat at the counter. "Yep, they're still at it. Can I get three coffees to go?"

"Sure can. Anything else?"

"You got anything to eat I can take back across?"

"Brad can make you up some sandwiches, and I have some pastries left. Will that do?"

"Thanks. Three ham and cheese on white with mustard will be fine." Mare propped her head on her hand and watched Rochelle call the sandwich order in to the kitchen, then busy herself taking care of the coffee and pastries.

ERIN SIGHED AS she looked around the hall. She was more than ready for bed. The day had been long and hard, but TJ looked as though she'd be going for a couple more hours. When she had the bit between her teeth, TJ rarely stopped until she'd finished. They could be here most of the night. A light nudge to her side prompted her from the doze she'd been falling into, and she sniffed the waft of coffee from a steaming cup being held in front of her. "Thanks, Mare, you're a life saver." She sat up and took the coffee and the offered sandwich.

"Does she ever stop?" Mare inclined her head toward TJ who sat at a table with several other ranchers, arranging for their cattle to be herded over to the sections of Meridian land where water sources were clean.

"Not until it's finished, she won't." Erin took a hearty bite out of the sandwich. "It's how she gets things done."

"She's so focused, she didn't even notice who put the food and coffee in front of her."

"I know. It used to worry me when I first got to know her. When she was studying, if you didn't stop her and practically force-feed her, she could go for days without eating. She was a full-time job all by herself."

"That I can believe," Mare said. "You okay? You look a little tired. I guess she's been working you hard."

"When TJ works hard, we work hard. It used to be she'd do all the legwork herself, but now, well, she lets us help out more."

"I was surprised she came tonight. I thought she might send you or Paula, but I didn't think she'd come herself."

"We were pretty surprised, too. But she knew she couldn't get anywhere with these guys unless she came down here herself and got in their faces. Besides," Erin said, "she knew you'd be here."

A smile sprang to Mare's face. "And am I ever glad I didn't miss this. It's about time this town got to find out who TJ Meridian is, and not who they think she is. But it's late. I need to get to bed and so do you, and even if she won't admit it, so does our friend over there. Do you want to tell her it's time to go home or do you want me to?"

"I think you have more chance of surviving than I do."

"We'll just have to find that out, won't we?" Her coffee finished, Mare got to her feet and wandered over to the table where the discussions were taking place. The men looked up as she approached, but TJ had her head buried in papers. She didn't know Mare was near until Mare placed her hand on TJ's shoulder and spoke. "Gentlemen, I know you still have a lot of questions for Miss Meridian, but I think it's about time you let her get home. She's been working on this since early this morning." The men immediately began making their apologies.

Mare could tell TJ was stunned. The shoulder under her hand stiffened, and TJ cast a near-glare at her. But Mare stood her ground and gave a stern stare back. The battle only lasted a second or two, then TJ's body relaxed. *Wow, it worked.* Mare mentally patted herself on the back and joined TJ in saying goodnight to the assembled ranchers. As she pushed TJ down the aisle, Erin stepped in beside her. She bumped Mare with her shoulder, gave her a mischievous glance, and mouthed, "Good job."

Chapter
Eight

MARE WAS SO busy attending to poisoned cattle and being involved with the contamination problem that her quest for her father had been postponed. The frustration of not being able to search for him was playing havoc with her nervous system.

Until she could discover something definite about him, Mare decided to keep quiet about her parentage—even with TJ. It surprised her how quickly telling TJ had come to mind. It was almost an automatic response. But TJ already had enough on her mind. Besides, Mare didn't know if he'd even want to acknowledge her, and she didn't want anyone to witness her humiliation if that happened. For the same reason, she decided against using a detective agency, except as a last resort.

Finally, Mare was able to free up at least part of a day by rearranging several of her calls and coaxing the elderly Dr. DiNicola, a vet acquaintance in Sharlesburg, into covering emergencies. The night before her time off, she tried to come up with an organized plan. She knew her birth certificate didn't show anything, so where could she start? At the college?

Standing at the bookcase, she looked through her mother's college yearbooks, which stood right next to her own. She removed the fourth year one and took it to the couch. She sat in the corner of the couch, under the floor lamp, pulled her legs up under her, and leafed through the pages. Contrary to the usual custom, no flowery sentiments were handwritten across the pictures. That brought a look of chagrin to Mare's face. Her mother always hated to see people write in books, but couldn't she have bent her rules? Everybody wrote in yearbooks. But not in Jane Arnold's. Mare's hope that a message would give away her father, or even a friend of her mother's, was useless.

The graduates were displayed according to their major field of study. Mare wondered what he could have majored in if he had an outstanding opportunity where a wife and child would be a hindrance. Maybe looking toward a medical career? Chemistry? Biology? Those seemed like good places to start. She found the appropriate pages and pored over each picture, hoping to see some familiarity to her own looks. Moving from major to major, she spent two hours in a fruitless pursuit. She had no idea what he looked like. Why was she wasting her time? In frustration, she slammed the book shut and tossed it onto the low table next to the couch.

Just then the phone rang. Mare snatched it up and snapped out her name, regretting it within the second. No one said anything and her frustration spoke again. "Look, if this is a joke, go play somewhere else."

"Mare?" The velvety richness of TJ's voice came through even though she spoke tentatively. Mare's face softened as her heart speeded up.

"TJ! I thought someone was trying to be funny. Sorry I didn't get by there today. Just didn't have the time. Are you okay?" Mare closed her eyes and pictured the beautiful face that found constant display in the gallery of her mind. She should have called TJ.

"I'm fine now. I won't keep you. I know it's late. I wanted to make sure you were all right and...I guess I...just wanted to hear your voice."

This touching revelation from such a proud woman filled Mare with a sense of awe. When she could find the words, she answered. "It's good to hear yours, too. Any further news on the water problems?"

"I'll fill you in when I see you. Do you think you'll make it by here tomorrow?"

Mare felt bad at having to hide the truth. "I might not, TJ. I have some business to take care of out of town, and I'm going to try to see to it tomorrow. If it's not too late when I get back, I'll give you a call, okay?"

"Two days without seeing you? I'll be getting Mare Withdrawal Syndrome." TJ's soft laugh melted Mare's insides. "Sounds like you have another busy day coming up, so I'll say goodnight."

"Goodnight, TJ. Sweet dreams." Mare hung up and sat savoring the call. Then her mind turned back to her search.

A thought occurred to her, and she retrieved the yearbook. She turned to the back pages, and sure enough, an address was given for each graduate, including her mother. Mare didn't know much about her mother's early life. Jane's parents had both died before Mare was born, and Jane never talked about her childhood home. She'd left there after graduation and never returned.

So an address was a start, something tangible to work with.

Mare got up and wrote the address on her appointment pad. She stretched, yawned, and went to bed, satisfied to have found another avenue of approach.

THE DAY HAD been a waste. After hours of searching through the neighborhood, Mare had found only one woman, a grandmotherly type, who remembered her mother as a young girl. The woman recalled that Jane had gone to college, but she wasn't able to shed any light on her boy friends. "Jane's mother was a friendly person, but she was very discreet about her own business. If you tried to trade gossip with her, it was mostly all one way."

Mare listened to the few tales the neighbor remembered, then graciously thanked her and left.

It was late when she returned home, dejected with the futility of her search. She flopped on the couch and reached for the phone, then figured it was much too late to call TJ. She looked yearningly at the instrument that could connect her with the woman whose mere voice made her heart sing. She would call TJ first thing in the morning.

What could she do for the next step in her search? Try as she might, Mare couldn't come up with a solution other than to hunt down and call each and every male in Jane's graduating class. The only bright side she could see was that their names more than likely wouldn't have changed. Jotting down a note to pick up a computer program that listed current names, addresses, and phone numbers on CDs, she decided she would set a regimen of making twenty calls a night.

Her father might be out there somewhere, and if he was, Mare was determined to find him.

THE MERIDIAN RANCH had changed virtually overnight. The day after the town meeting, cattle started to arrive from the ranches affected by the contaminated streams. Keeping the various herds separate had been a problem at first. But that became easier when a truckload of men drove up from town to give a hand with getting herds into the correct pastures.

Those same ten men also became the first to be hired by Paula, and by the end of the day, the ranch was once again fully operational. Of course, with the hiring of hands came a few more problems. The cookhouse needed a cook, which was soon settled as two of the new hands' wives offered to provide those duties. Paula immediately hired them on the same terms as the hands.

Many of the men and their families lived in town. A few of them opted to stay there, but once they had gotten a look at the accommodations, most decided to move onto the ranch. The bunkhouse initially would be home to the single ranch hands, and the families would have the houses. TJ planned to have new houses built for single ranch hands on the basis of two sharing each house. The bunkhouse then could be converted to a gym and leisure center, complete with a pool.

The day after the arrival of the cattle from the other ranches, Bill Jacobs, Meridian ranch's new foreman, arrived with his wife, and they settled into their new home. The first thing on Bill's agenda was to get the hired hands together and find out what experience they had. Most of them at one time or another had worked on ranches, though few had been permanent hands due to the economic situation in the area.

The next thing was to ensure that each of the men had a horse. Several men had their own, which they would bring with them. The others, though, were without a mount. On any other ranch this might have caused a major problem because horses weren't exactly inexpensive. But after a short discussion with Erin, Bill found himself with a bank account and budget to purchase quality horses for the ranch hands.

A barn near the bunkhouse provided sufficient stalls for the animals for the current work crew. Adjacent to the barn, a broad, fenced pasture held a run-in shed that could be used for feeding and shelter for a bigger herd of horses when necessary.

With the limited amount of work hands available, Paula hired several local teenagers to tend to the cleaning duties in both barns and to help with getting up the hay. The kids met at the local high school and were picked up in the van and driven to the ranch. After work had finished for the day, they were taken back. In addition to being paid, they were given opportunities to ride and to learn about the running of the ranch. The only condition of their employment was that when they returned to school in the fall, their grades must remain at a C or above. TJ didn't want any complaints that working at the ranch after school or on weekends was in any way detrimental to their studies.

Once the hiring was completed, Paula returned her attention to the refurbishing of the packing plant. TJ divided her time between running Meridian Corporation and overseeing the progress of the ranch and the cleanup.

Apart from helping Bill with buying the horses, Erin also kept an eye on the cleanup operation. Their main concern was to ensure that the streams no longer caused harm to the environment. The cleanup team backtracked the streams to within ten miles of Sharlesburg. There they had found an area of wetlands where containers of industrial waste had been dumped. Erin passed the information on to the EPA and left that agency to deal with the investigation of who was responsible for it.

TJ's cleanup teams worked with a team from the EPA to clean the wetlands and prevent further damage being done. Then they had moved back toward the ranches, cleaning the streambed. That process was going to take at least a week to complete, after which they would bring in pumps and oxidizing agents to re-oxygenate the streams. The final stage would be the reintroduction of fish stocks and placement of monitors to prevent contamination from occurring to that extent again.

All in all, it was a busy time for the three women. They rarely got a chance to sit down together for meals. TJ's outings on Flag were almost non-existent, due to being snowed under with work or there being no one available to assist her. Erin had offered to ask Bill to keep one of the hands near, but TJ had quashed that idea. They were still shorthanded, and keeping someone at the house just so she could go riding was a waste of resources. However, all work, no play, and no Mare began to take its toll on TJ's moods.

Paula and Erin noticed that Mare hadn't been around in some time and that her phone calls had been scarce. The times TJ had called her, she was rebuffed with flimsy excuses. Still, the whole area was busy recovering from the near disaster, and Mare was the only local vet. It was hard not to be judgmental, but she had to be as busy as everyone at the ranch, if not busier.

MARE ZEALOUSLY DEVOTED herself to achieving her target of twenty calls per night. Unfortunately, it cut heavily into her time for visiting with TJ. Her last visit to the ranch had been brief and somewhat upsetting. Neither Paula nor Erin had been at the house when Mare stopped by.

She was surprised when TJ answered her knock. "TJ! Are you here by yourself?" Mare's heart fluttered, but the joy of seeing TJ couldn't override the guilt she felt. She had almost totally neglected her for the past week.

"Yeah, I am. Come on in," TJ answered, sounding falsely cheerful.

TJ seemed drawn in on herself, and her whole attitude was tense. Mare bent down and kissed warm lips that quivered beneath hers. The sensation was arousing, but she realized TJ was upset and her guilt returned. They parted from the kiss, and Mare felt like groaning when TJ reached for a pen and started twisting it around and around.

"I'm sorry I haven't been able to get by any sooner."

"That's okay," TJ said. "Sit down, I'll get you something to drink."

"I can't stay." Mare's insides squirmed when she saw disappointment flicker across TJ's features. "I'm sorry. I have a call at the MacMasters farm, but I was so close, I just wanted to stop in and see you." Mare reached out and caressed the side of TJ's jaw. "I've missed you."

TJ sighed. "You've been really busy lately, huh?"

"Yeah, I have. Too many things going on that I have to take care of. Too many sick animals." Mare gave a short, dry laugh. "I feel like I'm on a roller coaster, and it won't stop to let me off. I've tried to phone you during the day, but the line's always been busy. And by the time I get home, all I want to do is flop in bed. Sometimes I even take the phone off the hook." Of course she had to in order to make the calls about her father.

TJ made a half-smile, half-grimace.

Mare glanced at her watch. "I have to run." She bent and brushed a kiss on TJ's lips, then turned quickly and opened the door. Catching the odd expression on TJ's face almost made her turn back, but remorse propelled her through the door. She shut it firmly behind her, ran to the truck, revved it up, and sped away.

Mare's tears started as soon as she left the house area. TJ was hurting. But she'd understand when Mare finally explained it to her. "If you ever get a chance to," a small voice whispered inside her head. "You might never find your father." No! She would find her father. She would!

As the days stretched into two weeks, Mare's frustration continued building. So far, her calls had been in vain. The few men who remembered Jane as a classmate had no recollection of her boyfriend.

Mare felt overwhelmed. An already heavy caseload of animals that needed her attention had been stretched to the limit with the addition of the ones that had been poisoned, and although the poisoning problem had slacked off, she had had to play catch up. With the buildup of nervous tension from not finding her father and another kind of tension from not seeing TJ as often as she wished to, she became extremely irritable. Mare recognized this and fought to control it, but that was just one more weight on her back.

Finally, she squeezed in time to spend a morning at TJ's.

When she entered the kitchen, Erin handed her a steaming mug. "Hi, stranger. Guess you've been as busy as we have."

"Yeah." Mare avoided elaborating. She saluted with her mug. "Boy, it can be the hottest day in the summer, and I still need a cup of coffee to start my day. Thanks. Is TJ in her office already?"

"No, she's not finished her morning wake-up routine yet. She has exercises she has to do three mornings a week. Paula's giving her a hand. She'll be in soon." She added an extra dish and place setting for Mare on the island.

Mare sat at the island and Erin joined her. "Erin, just what happened to cause TJ's paralysis? Would you mind telling me? I mean, I read about the mugging where her brother was killed, but it didn't mention exactly what happened to TJ."

Erin didn't hesitate to tell the story. "Soon after Lance graduated from medical school, he and TJ were returning to their car after a theater performance. A gang of thugs stopped them and demanded their money. TJ handed over her purse and encouraged Lance to give them his wallet, which he did. They were trying to avoid trouble." Erin pushed the bagels and cream cheese within Mare's reach.

"A couple of them had been eyeing up TJ and decided they wanted more than just money, so they grabbed her. She fought back. TJ wasn't someone you wanted to mess with in those days. The muggers should have left while they had the chance. Then Lance joined the fray. TJ and Lance were making some headway against them, when one of them pulled a gun. He shot Lance in the chest. He was killed instantly. TJ went berserk and had plowed through four of them — did a lot of damage, too — before the guy with the gun decided she had to go, too. He shot her in the back, and the ones who were still able to, beat her senseless. Then they took off, leaving her for dead." Erin's voice wavered, and she paused.

Mare stopped in mid-bite and laid the bagel down. "Please go on," she whispered.

"You wouldn't have recognized her in the hospital. She was a total mess. Her face was battered. Her nose was bloodied, her lip cut, her eyes blackened and swollen shut. She had bruises all over her body, and her hands were covered with cuts and scrapes. When she came to, she never even moaned. The first words out of her mouth were, 'How's Lance?' " Erin reached across to a shelf and pulled a tissue from a porcelain box, using it to wipe the tears that trickled down her face.

"She went berserk again when they told her he was dead. She screamed like a wounded animal and probably would have thrashed around had she been able to. But she was strapped down. The bullet had entered her spine and was pressing against the cord. They couldn't even operate on it. She's still carrying it around in her back. And I guess she'll be paralyzed for the rest of her life, unless there's some miraculous breakthrough."

Mare had sucked in her lips.

"You should have seen her before. She was majestic, like royalty. People would stop and stare at her." Erin's face had been distressed, but now it lit up and her eyes revived. "But, my God, Mare, look at her, she's still magnificent. Paula and I are half in love with her ourselves."

Then her face darkened again. "But TJ didn't see it that way. She blamed herself for Lance's death. She got terribly depressed and tried to kill herself. That's why she goes to a psychologist regularly. She wasn't allowed to leave the hospital until she agreed to see one."

"She sees a psychologist?"

"Yeah, not that he's doing much good. If he'd get off of the subject of her father, he might have a better chance at helping her out."

"Her father?"

"Yeah, she has some bad hang-ups about her father, and she won't talk about them to anybody, not even Paula and me, even though we've seen — "

"What's going on here, show and tell?" TJ wheeled furiously into the kitchen, her face contorted. Paula came in right behind her and looked at Erin with a stricken expression.

"I thought I'd made it quite clear that nobody was to speak of my father in this house." White heat shimmered from TJ's body as she flung her rebuke at Erin in a low, threatening voice. "It's not enough my father had to mess with my life while he was alive, now you're helping him do it while he's dead."

Mare could see TJ's words had stung. Erin's paleness matched Paula's ashen expression as she said, "I only told Mare what I thought she deserved to know. I didn't tell her anything about your father."

TJ's lips pulled back from her teeth in an ugly grimace. "I make the decisions who knows about my life and who doesn't, get that? No one tells anybody anything about my father, but me." TJ threw her shoulder forward, resisting Paula's attempt to clasp it. "Is that crystal clear?"

Erin nodded.

TJ wheeled around to leave the kitchen.

Mare had been watching this exchange with surprise that Erin and Paula seemed to be so afraid of TJ's anger. When TJ swiveled her wheelchair, Mare quickly rose and blocked her exit. Erin threw a half-shocked glance at Paula who also looked startled.

The wheelchair accidentally bumped into her shins. "Get out of my way." TJ still seethed, but she wouldn't look up.

Mare didn't budge. Her voice was firm and forceful. "Talk to me, TJ."

TJ sucked in a noisy breath. "I don't want to." Then she looked up, and the anger and pain pouring from her eyes made Mare flinch. TJ's voice was harsh. "You think you can just waltz in here whenever you please and pry into my family relationships?"

Mare's voice had lost some of its forcefulness. "We weren't talking about your father. Erin just barely mentioned him."

"You don't know a damn thing about my father except the gossip you've heard. Is that why you made a show of getting into my good graces? So you could hang around and get some juicy tidbits to feed the rumor mills? But once I made some headway into changing the town's thinking about me, I wasn't as much use to you anymore, was I? So now you come back looking for something stronger to pass around?"

Her eyes seemed to bore holes into Mare's. "Get out of my way!" Mare was shocked into immobility. Erin got up, took hold of Mare's arm and led her, without protest, away from the doorway. TJ propelled the chair into the hallway like a torpedo.

Mare threw herself down on a chair, put her elbows on the island, and placed her hands on either side of her pale face. She closed her eyes for a minute to regain her composure. Dropping her hands, she turned hurting eyes toward Erin and Paula who stood together at the edge of the island. "What is she talking about? Does she really think I came here just to get some dirt on the Meridians? I thought we settled this already."

Erin looked away then back to Mare. "I know you've been busy, but what would you think if someone hung around almost every day, waited until you cared about them, then just practically disappeared?"

"And," Paula said, "with only a few hurried phone calls making blatantly false excuses?"

With a pained expression on her face, Mare put her fist to her mouth. "There's a reason for that." She sniffled, fighting back tears. The idea that TJ must hate her tore at her heart.

"Oh yeah," Paula said, sneering, "give us the pitiful routine. Let's see what excuse you come up with this time."

"I thought my father died before I was born, but I just found out he might be alive. Every bit of free time I've had, I've been searching for him."

"What?"

Mare sniffled again and some tears overflowed. "It's true, honest." She reached into the hip pocket of her jeans and pulled out a wallet that was chained to a belt loop. She opened it and extracted a folded piece of buff paper. Handing it to Erin, she said, "Read it. It's from my mother. It's all there." While Erin and Paula read the letter, Mare made use of the tissues in the porcelain box.

She saw their expressions turn to belief as they finished reading. "I've been calling the men in my mother's graduating class. Every night I call twenty people. That's why I couldn't stay on the phone with TJ. And those excuses were so bad because I never was very good at lying." She wiped her face and eyes. "Now, TJ hates me." She bowed her head, and the tears came in earnest.

"You've hurt her pretty badly, Doc. She took all this as your turning your back on her. Abandonment, I guess. Maybe even betrayal." Paula handed the letter back toward Mare, but Erin intercepted it.

"TJ's a proud woman." Erin's face was filled with concern. "You do something that attacks that pride, and she writes you off. I'll go talk to her."

Paula looked wary. "You sure? Want me to go with you?"

Erin shook her head. "No sense in both of us stepping into the line of fire." She patted Paula on the arm and left the kitchen.

Mare dried her tears and listened to this exchange with interest in spite of her upset. "Why are you and Erin so afraid of TJ?"

Paula sat down in the chair next to Mare. "I guess it looks that way to you, but we're not so much afraid of her as afraid *for* her."

"You mean because of the suicide attempt?"

"So, Erin really has been talking too much, huh? Partly that, but mostly because TJ has an unbelievable temper. She keeps a pretty tight rein on it most of the time, but when she lets loose, run for cover! When she's that angry, sometimes she does things that physically hurt her or someone else. We try to keep that from happening by giving in to her when she's on edge."

"Or by moving people away from doorways."

"You got it."

ERIN LOOKED INTO the office and there was TJ, her head pillowed on her arms on the desk, her shoulders shaking. As soon as Erin stepped through the door, TJ rasped, "Get out." But Erin kept moving toward the desk.

TJ picked up a square, solid bronze paperweight and, without even raising her head to look, flung it straight at Erin. Erin knew TJ's aim was unerring, and she was already stepping to the left. The paperweight, thankfully, sailed past her and hit the wall with a thud.

She walked up next to TJ and put a hand on her shoulder. Head still down, TJ slapped her hand away. "I said get out!"

"TJ, honey, we shouldn't jump to conclusions about Mare. Again." Erin put out her hand and caressed TJ's head.

"You think I'll believe another of her excuses?" TJ's voice broke.

Erin leaned over and put her head next to TJ's and laid her body up against TJ's back. "Oh, honey, sometimes love hurts."

"How would you know? You have Paula."

A laugh rumbled through Erin. "Yeah, thank goodness. And you have Mare. Honest. I have proof."

Erin could sense a subtle change in TJ, and she lifted away from her, pulling her upright at the same time. "Read this. It's from Mare's mother." Erin reached in her breast pocket and handed TJ the letter. She watched as the cloud lifted from TJ's face. She grabbed a couple of tissues, wiped TJ's cheeks, and daubed at her eyes. "Mare's been on the phone for hours each night, trying to find her father. She's working her way through all the men in her mother's college yearbook."

"Why didn't she come to me about it?"

"Why don't you come back to the kitchen and ask her that?"

"She's still here?"

"You know Mare. Takes more than a few mean words to scare her away. But she is upset."

TJ lowered her hands to the wheels and backed away from the desk. "Do I look awful?"

"You look like you care."

TJ wheeled toward the door with Erin walking beside her. "Erin?"

"Yeah?"

"I'm sorry about the paperweight."

"At least it missed me."

"Yeah, I must need more practice."

MARE'S GAZE LIFTED as she heard the wheelchair come in, but she lowered it again as the wheels drew closer. Almost at once TJ's body appeared right alongside her, wheelchair turned backwards. Mare raised her eyes to the blue ones she loved, now rimmed with red, but still able to stir her heart.

TJ reached in her lap and handed Mare's letter back to her. Mare accepted it and took the time to put it back into her wallet with TJ watching her every move. Paula and Erin slipped unnoticed out of the room.

"Mare, I'm sorry. I — "

Mare reached forward and put her fingers against TJ's lips. "No apology necessary."

TJ clasped her hand, kissed the fingers, and removed them. "I want to say this. I need to. You're the last person I would ever want to hurt, but I keep doing it, because I find it hard to trust people. I'm sorry. I don't ever want to hurt you again." TJ leaned forward and kissed her gently.

Then she sat back. "But I do have a question for you. Why didn't you come to me to search for your father? I have resources all over the world, half of them sitting around waiting for me to put them to work. You shouldn't have to be doing this by yourself."

Mare felt a blush creep up her face. "What if you find him, and he doesn't want me? I would be humiliated." Her voice was almost too soft to hear. "I didn't want you to see that."

TJ leaned her elbow on the arm of the wheelchair, put her chin on her fist, and waited. Finally, curious as to why TJ hadn't said anything, Mare looked up. "You're trying to tell a woman in a wheelchair that you're afraid of being humiliated?" One eyebrow lifted higher and higher. "I could give lessons in how to be humiliated."

At first, Mare seemed surprised, then embarrassed. Then a laugh burst from her throat. "Okay, I get the message. When can you start the search?"

"As soon as you give me as much information as you can about your mother and your father. I'll e-mail it to the central office in Atlanta, and a team will get on it right away."

"I can give you that information right now. I've memorized every detail of my mother's history, as much as I know of it. And I reached up to the P's in my calls."

"Okay, come on in the office, and you can tell it to me while I put it in the computer. When you stop here tomorrow evening, I'll let you know what's going on."

"Let's go." Mare jumped up to start toward the door, then turned quickly, grabbed TJ's face between her hands, and kissed her hungrily. TJ threw her arms around Mare, pulled her so close the warmth of their bodies mingled, and kissed her back.

When they finally separated, Mare sighed. "I've waited too

long for that." Then she brushed her fingers across TJ's lips. "But it sure was worth the wait."

TJ just grinned like she would never stop, and they headed into the office.

Chapter
Nine

MARE GOT A phone call from TJ first thing in the morning. "Hi, Mare. When you come out this evening, could you bring the picture of your mother that's in the yearbook? The office wants me to scan it and send it."

"Sure. I have a couple of late calls so I'll be out around eight. Is that okay?"

TJ's voice dropped to a lower tone, and Mare closed her eyes, enjoying it. "Fine. I don't care how late you come, just come, okay?"

"Wild horses couldn't keep me away."

"Good girl. Bye."

"Bye, TJ."

When Mare got to Meridian ranch that evening, she spied TJ at her desk, poring over some figures on a printout and beckoning Mare to come in. TJ's head lifted for Mare's kiss, then she playfully pushed her away. "Hang on for a minute, okay? Just let me finish this bit."

"No problem." Mare laid her mother's yearbook on the desk, then noticed that the door to the left of the office was open. Curious about where it led, she walked over and stuck her head through the doorway. The hall it opened into started at the living room, came toward Mare, then continued on to a dead-end wall. There were two doors to Mare's left and one to her right. These she knew went to the dining room, kitchen, and porch. Three doors graced the opposite wall. Two were open and one closed. There was one more door at the dead-end. "Where do all these other doors go?" Mare pulled her head back in from the doorway and aimed questioning eyes at TJ who was so engrossed in the paperwork on her desk that she didn't seem to hear her.

Mare repeated the question, and TJ answered without raising her head from her work. "Those are mine. Exercise room, bedroom, bathroom."

Mare stuck her head back into the hallway and pointed toward the fourth door. "How about that one?"

TJ hadn't heard Mare clearly, but her eyes closed and she said rather impatiently. "Wait a minute." Her eyes opened and fell to the papers. "Please," she added.

"Oops, sorry." Mare walked over, dragged one of the chairs behind the desk, and sat down next to TJ. She rested an elbow on the oak surface, leaned her chin on her hand, and gazed at TJ's profile with a tantalizing grin.

After a minute under this adoring scrutiny, TJ's lips contorted, trying to suppress a reaction. Finally, she set her pencil down and turned toward Mare. "What?"

"Oh, nothing that can't wait. Please, finish your work. I wouldn't dream of interrupting you." Mare batted innocent eyes at TJ.

"Look, woman." TJ snarled the words, reached out a long arm, and grabbed the front of Mare's shirt. With a fierce look, she yanked Mare toward the edge of her seat until they were nose to nose. "You've already interrupted me, and now you'll pay the consequences."

Belatedly, Mare recalled Erin saying TJ had a lightning temper. She opened her lips to apologize, and TJ placed her other hand behind Mare's head, pulled it nearer, and closed her mouth on Mare's. Finally, TJ slowly released the kiss and let go of Mare's head and shirt. She drew back and licked her lips, obviously having savored every split second of Mare's change from alarm to surrender. "What was that question again?"

"Uh...give me a minute, now. I'll remember." Mare rolled her shining eyes at TJ, amused at her own stumbling. "Okay, okay, I remember! I asked you what the other door at the end of the hallway is for."

The rapid change in TJ's expression puzzled Mare. TJ's face hardened, and she spoke between clamped teeth. "That's my father's office." She retrieved the pencil and twirled it over and over between her hands.

"Don't you use his office?"

The pencil broke. "No. Bad memories." TJ got a faraway look in her eyes. She lifted her right arm and absently rubbed at the underside of it.

Mare's gaze dropped to the arm, and she saw three scars. The first, a thready one at TJ's wrist, shouted suicide attempt, which Erin had referred to. But Mare's eyes were captured by the other two. Each an inch long and slightly curved, they were spaced about three inches apart, farther up TJ's arm.

A feeling of horror spread through Mare as she grasped the

probable significance of TJ's words. She moved her hand to TJ's arm. Her touch seemed to pull TJ back to the present but generated tremors in her muscles. Distress closed Mare's throat but she forced the words out. "These scars...your father did this to you?"

TJ's silence was answer enough.

"But how? Why?" Mare looked up from the scars and searched TJ's frozen face.

"I hate him."

TJ spit the words out of her mouth with such fury that Mare cringed. What could she do to help TJ? Maybe at least hold her. "Can I sit on your lap?"

TJ stared almost vacantly at Mare for a moment, but she pushed away from the desk and lifted the nearer chair arm. Mare moved onto her lap, sliding both arms around her and moving her body close. They sat there together for a while in silence, then TJ's body shuddered. Slowly, TJ lifted her arms to embrace Mare. She started to cry. Mare cried with her, moving TJ's body slowly back and forth in a tiny rocking motion. After a while, TJ quieted, then said with trembling voice, "There's a box of tissues in the desk drawer."

Mare reached to the drawer, pulled it open, and felt for the tissues. Her hand closed on the box, and she brought it out and sat it on the desk. Pulling several tissues from it, she dried TJ's eyes and face, then her own. She tossed the damp tissues in the trash basket under the desk and wrapped her arms back around TJ, pulling the dark head against her and kissing her cheek. "Do you want to talk about it?"

"No!" The abruptness of the answer left no room for doubt. TJ's arms tightened around Mare.

Mare patted her head. "That's okay, sweetheart, you don't have to. Just relax. I'll hold you for a while. Just relax."

They sat together for so long that Mare was beginning to wonder if maybe her sitting on TJ's lap might tire her. Then TJ spoke into the base of Mare's throat. Her low, toneless voice poured like a river breaking through a dam. "The scars are from a belt buckle. He used to beat me all the time: sometimes because I antagonized him, sometimes because he didn't like how I acted, or what I said, or who my friends were. He could always find some reason." Mare pressed her lips to TJ's forehead and slowly caressed her hair with her hand.

"He was a big man, that's where I get my size from. And he was strong. Mostly he beat me with the strap end of the belt, but one time he got insanely angry and beat me with the buckle end. I have some scars on my back, too."

Oh, TJ, how could anyone be that cruel to you?

"My mother wouldn't stop him. She didn't want to lose what he could give her. She said he hated me because I was supposed to be a boy, an heir for his companies, and my father never forgave me, nor her, for my being a girl. I don't think he ever beat her, he just ignored her, all the while insisting that she turn me into some kind of showpiece that his friends would admire. But she said she didn't love him anyway. Never had. She had the advantage over me, there. I started out loving him." TJ's monotone broke, and long-damped emotions crept into her voice.

"I wanted him to love me back. But he told me my birth was a mistake, that I was no use to anybody. He would scream that at me while he beat me. He was the grownup, and I was only a child, so I thought he must be right. I was a mistake, a failure, not worth anybody's love. My father. My father was telling me this. And I believed it. All those years I hated myself for not being the son he wanted. I still hate myself, only now it's because I hate *him* so much! I wanted him dead and he is, but I'm still tied to that hatred. It eats at me."

The bitterness of these words dragged at Mare's heart. "Didn't Lance fill his need for a son?" she asked quietly.

At mention of her brother's name, TJ's tone softened. "He loved Lance. We all did, even Mother. But Lance wanted to be a doctor, not a businessman. Father was as furious as I've ever seen him, but he didn't beat Lance. He yelled and threatened and nagged him until Lance got so depressed he couldn't eat or sleep. He was in agony. So I went to Father and told him that whoever led the companies needed to be driven by a love of power or by greed, and neither one motivated Lance. He could never run Meridian, because his heart wasn't in it. I, on the other hand, not only loved power, I thrived on it. I offered to let Father groom me to head Meridian Corporation, if he would let Lance become a doctor.

"Well, Father finally admitted to himself that no matter how much he wanted Lance to take charge, it would never work. So the deal was made. Father accepted me as his heir. But he made me pay.

"I loved this ranch, and horses were almost an obsession with me. In my second year at Harvard, Father became fanatically determined that nothing should interfere with my studies. So, he shut down everything in Meridianville, without a care for the people he was hurting, and moved us to Connecticut."

TJ reached for another tissue and blew her nose. Mare gave

her an extra squeeze and continued to caress her.

"I got furious when I found out he was closing the ranch. The horses were my only solace, and from pure meanness, he ripped that away from me. We got into a terrible screaming match, and he went completely berserk. He grabbed the wrong end of the belt and beat and beat me with the buckle end. He stood in front of the door, so I couldn't get past him. I could feel my back was bleeding in several places, and I put my arm up to ward off some of his blows. So I got cut there, too." She rubbed her scarred skin again.

"Erin and Paula had come home with me for spring break. Paula was out, but Erin heard the screaming all the way upstairs, and she came running." TJ's face and voice turned ugly. "She came running in and saw him beating me. She yelled at him, but that had no effect, he just kept beating me. So she picked up a bronze statuette and hit him over the forearm with it. She broke his damn arm, and still he tried to hit me, but he couldn't." TJ smirked at this, then a touch of admiration entered her voice. "Paula showed up then. She didn't know what was happening, but she knew it was trouble. She shoved him away from blocking the door, and she and Erin grabbed me and hauled me out of there." TJ shook her head. "Those women have some kind of guts."

Mare could feel the tension in TJ's body start to slack off.

"They took me to the hospital emergency room and had my cuts sutured and the welts treated. They also had the sense to have the injuries photographed and a hospital report sent to the police station. My father never beat me again. In fact, because of their quick thinking and support, I was able to pressure him into giving me one of his companies, lock, stock, and barrel. And I built it into three times the company it was before...and finished at the head of my class...and got Lance into pre-med. You might say Erin and Paula were my saviors."

TJ lifted her head from Mare's shoulder and sat up straight. Her face wore a troubled, almost embarrassed look. "I can't believe I told you all that."

Mare put her hand on TJ's cheek. "I'm glad you told me. That makes three of us who love you to pieces." She leaned forward and entered into a kiss of unconditional love.

Afterwards, Mare sat back against TJ's arms and gazed into a somewhat happier face. "TJ, I want you to do a big favor for me."

"Another kiss? I guess I can force myself." TJ leaned forward.

Mare pushed her back with one hand. "Oh no. Not yet. First,

you have to promise me something."

TJ stayed leaning against the hand and could feel its warmth spreading over her chest. "Anything."

"Hmm. I'll keep that in mind. But I want you to promise me that you'll talk about all this with your counselor."

"Mare!" TJ threw herself back against the chair and turned her head away.

Mare wrapped her hands around TJ's arms and shook her. "Listen to me a minute. Please?" She waited until TJ turned back toward her. "I can listen to you, I can sympathize with you, and I can love you. But I am not professionally trained to help you, and that's what you need. Professional help. You've carried this hurt and bitterness and hatred around for a long time, and you need to deal with it."

Mare could see TJ was wavering, but still unconvinced. "You say you thrive on power. Well, you have the power to change your life, to get rid of the demons that are fighting to hold on to you. And the decision is completely yours—no one else's. Will you fight for love and happiness for the future? Or will you surrender to hatred and defeat from the past?"

Mare was fascinated by the way TJ could signal a smile without actually smiling. The corners of her lips would lift ever so slightly, just as they were doing now, and her eyes would grow warmer. "You do have a way with words, Mare."

"Is that a promise, then? You'll tell your counselor?"

"Okay, okay, I'll tell him." TJ didn't sound convincing.

"Say you promise."

With a sigh, TJ put her hands halfway up in surrender. "I promise. On one condition."

"What's that?"

"That you come with me?" TJ's voice was quiet, small.

That voice touched Mare to the depths of her soul. She hugged TJ. "Of course, I will." Then Mare grinned mischievously. "Now, before we get to work, let's see if you can still force yourself into another kiss."

It wasn't much of a struggle.

Chapter
Ten

TJ AND MARE were still waiting for a positive word about the search for Mare's father. TJ's team of six men had finished contacting the men from the yearbook, and when that was unsuccessful, two started back at the beginning, figuring some clue might have been missed. The other four investigated new avenues.

In the meantime, Mare had come over this evening to help TJ go over the mountains of paperwork involved with the contamination cleanup, including the legal paperwork required to help prosecute the company that had been dumping the waste. The EPA had found the company that was responsible and was bringing suit against them. TJ was handling a private civil suit for the ranches that had lost livestock.

Finally, TJ put away the pen she had been holding and slapped her long hands down on the table. "We've been working hard all evening. Time to stop and have some fun."

"Really?" Mare said. "Like what did you have in mind?"

TJ slid the side of the wheelchair up out of the way and opened her arms. "All evening, I've wanted to hold you and kiss you. If I don't get to do it soon, I'll burst."

"Oh yeah!" Mare stepped over to TJ, sat on her lap, and put her arms around TJ's neck.

TJ slipped her arm around Mare's shoulders and gazed at the delicate face. "You are so beautiful, Mare, you take my breath away." Laying her free hand against Mare's face, she kissed her forehead, eyes, cheeks, and nose. Then their lips met: soft pillows of warm, moist flesh, sliding, slipping, opening, and surrendering to two eager tongues. Mare's hand reached out to TJ's shoulder and started to lower the thin strap that held up her loose silk top, then she hesitated and moved the strap back to its original spot.

TJ pulled her lips away from Mare's, and disappointment flooded her expression.

Mare's heart thumped. "What? What did I do? Was I wrong to think of doing that? I know you never seem to want... She stopped, unsure of how to finish the sentence. Unsure of herself.

For a long time, Mare had wanted desperately to make love to TJ, but she had been shy, especially since TJ made no move to explore beyond kissing and hugging. She didn't know what to expect from TJ or what TJ might expect from her. Now the look on that lovely face confused her. Was TJ disappointed that she tried, or disappointed that she didn't?

TJ's cheek twitched and her eyes looked stormy. "No, you weren't wrong. I wanted you to do it. I want to take you in my arms and never let you go." The emotion vibrating in TJ's words struck an answering resonance in Mare. She meant to speak, but TJ continued. "But I want you to be sure of what you're getting into. I don't want us starting something you don't intend to someday complete."

"Don't intend to someday complete?" Mare said. TJ was just as confused as she was. "I love you, TJ. I want you. I need you. Sometimes you're so sure of yourself and other times – "

"I'm not exactly a whole woman, Mare," TJ interrupted hoarsely, tearing the admission from the depths of her being. "That could cause some problems with my...satisfying...your physical needs."

"Oh, but you are a whole woman to me, my love. I know you can fill my every need. I just wonder whether I can fill yours. I want to, so badly, but I'm not sure what would feel really good to you." She lifted her hand and caressed the strong face before her that hid such a vulnerable heart.

TJ's eyes filled. "I love you, Mare, more than I've ever loved anyone else. I can hardly believe you love me, too." She took hold of Mare's hand and returned it to the strap of the silk top. Mare's eyes softened as she brushed the straps from TJ's shoulders, barely breathing as the clinging material glided slowly downward, gradually revealing the sweet treasure it had concealed. TJ's desire flamed higher as she watched Mare drinking in the vision unfolding before her. Her mouth curved into a lopsided smile and her eyebrow shot up. "Suppose I give you a few lessons?" she suggested, her voice low and sultry.

"Oh, yes." Mare met TJ's gaze and wanted to drown in it forever. "You're so beautiful."

"So are you, my love." TJ pulled her again into an embrace, and she and Mare melded their mouths together.

Mare felt her shirt lift. Her body jerked as a strong, hot hand moved sinuously against her quivering skin, then clutched her bare stomach. Like a pebble dropped into a pond, TJ's touch sent circles of desire rippling into every crevice of Mare's being. Her breathing deepened and quickened, and her whole body became incredibly attuned to each touch, each caress.

Mare's hands glided over TJ's muscular stomach, sketching every ridge and valley, then proceeded to mimic, on TJ's body, every move TJ made on hers. The hands of the two women stroked slowly, sensuously upward, coming to, and cupping against, the softness of a breast. Searching fingers found their swollen targets, twisting them back and forth in agonizing slowness.

In perfect timing with this movement, a tantalizing tongue ran its curved tip against the tender roof of Mare's succulent mouth, alternately probing and retreating. In a battle of love, Mare's tongue challenged TJ's, making her push hard for every tiny taste of hotly defended territory.

Waves of sensation thrummed across Mare's skin from mouth to breast. Elsewhere, an indescribably sweet ache suddenly expanded into a hungry, throbbing demand. Mare, groaning into TJ's mouth, couldn't stand it anymore. Reluctantly she disengaged her fingers from their teasing task and twined both hands in TJ's hair. She pulled TJ's head away from hers and gasped for breath as their lips separated.

TJ's chest heaved, and questioning blue eyes, deepened by passion, opened upon yearning green ones. "Take me to your room," Mare said in a shaky voice.

TJ sucked in a hissing breath, and she seemed to glow with delight. She watched the play of emotions crossing Mare's expressive face, as she slowly drew her stroking fingers down the burning skin of Mare's ribs and stomach.

Finally, she moved her hand out onto the top edge of one wheel. Releasing her other arm from its hold on Mare's shoulders, she dropped it to the opposite wheel. Her low, passion-laden voice vaulted Mare's hunger a notch higher. "Hold on tight."

Mare drew both arms closer around TJ's neck. She leaned her head against TJ's and murmured a warm breath into her ear, "I'm never letting go."

TJ wheeled them down the hallway and into her room, eager to explore the intoxicating joys of their love's fulfillment.

ERIN'S HEAD RESTED in Paula's lap as they sat in the living room watching TV. Paula reached for another chip from the bowl balanced on Erin's stomach and crunched it between her teeth. "Hey, watch the crumbs, will you?" Erin smacked her on the thigh.

"Hmm. Sorry, I was just thinking about this show. You think those two characters really are lovers?"

"I think the producers very wisely left that up to the viewer. We can think of them any way we want."

"I guess. But I know if I traveled through the forest with you all day, our nights would be times to remember." Paula leered at Erin and grabbed a handful of a strategic body part.

"Whoa, woman!" Erin laughed and caught the bowl of chips that had bounced off her stomach and was about to dump on the floor. "Is that all you think of?"

"Only with you, honey." Paula slipped her arm beneath Erin's head and lifted it up into her kiss.

"Umm. Is it bedtime yet?" Erin set the bowl on the floor and put her arms around Paula.

They kissed again, then Paula said, "Not until you help TJ get ready for bed." She lifted Erin's shoulders all the way up so she could swing her legs around onto the floor.

Erin picked up the chips then stood up and patted Paula on the cheek. "Keep those warm thoughts, baby."

"Yeah? It's not just my thoughts that are warm."

Erin started toward the kitchen, and Paula's voice brought her to a halt. "Hey, Erin, did you see Mare leave?" Erin shook her head and bypassed the kitchen to look in TJ's office. It was empty.

Paula had gotten up, too, and she headed into the kitchen and looked out the window. Mare's truck was still sitting in the well-lit parking lot.

Erin set the bowl by the sink and walked over behind Paula. She smiled when her eyes fell on the truck. "What do you think?"

"If it means what we think it means, I'm happy for both of them, but especially TJ."

"Yeah, she was really broken up when she thought Mare had been playing with her. I'm so glad she has someone to love her. Have you ever noticed the wistful expression she gets sometimes when she looks at us?"

"Yeah, I have," Paula said. "Always made me feel bad that we couldn't help her find someone."

"So what would you suggest I do about helping her get ready for bed tonight?" Erin lifted Paula's short dark hair and nuzzled the back of her neck with her lips and tongue.

Paula shivered from the tickling lips and turned around. "I think you should wait until TJ buzzes you, if she ever does." Paula reached down and lifted a surprised Erin up in her arms. "I'm the one who needs your help tonight." Paula walked out of the kitchen, into the living room, and over to the bottom of the staircase, where she stopped and eyed the steps.

Erin giggled. "Put me down, honey. You'll hurt yourself."

Paula snorted. "You're probably right." She set Erin onto her feet. "Okay...race you to bed." The two dashed up the steps, shoving against each other. Still jostling, they ran down the hall to their room and dove onto the bed where they had a great time arguing about who won and who lost the race and what penalty the loser had to pay.

TJ never did buzz them.

MARE'S THOUGHTS WERE floating up through a filmy cloud, halfway between sleep and waking. The sudden realization that she was in a skin-to-skin encounter jolted her completely awake. She was lying on top of a naked body! Her eyes flew open, and her head jerked up, and she looked into the most beautiful face she had ever seen. TJ.

The peaceful features were relaxed, eyes closed. The calmness of sleep suited her. In slumber all her worries disappeared from her face, and the emotional pain that was her constant companion was soothed.

Mare lowered her head back down into the sweet valley where she had awakened, basking in the movement of TJ's slow, gentle breathing.

She sighed in contentment and, with a feather-light touch, caressed the strong arm that lay just to the side of her face, a long-fingered hand resting on her back. She had been worried last night when they reached TJ's room, unsure of how to proceed, or even if they should. It wasn't as though she hadn't been with a woman before, or that she wasn't overwhelmingly attracted to TJ. But from what she had been told about her injuries, she wasn't sure how much TJ was capable of feeling, or if she could feel at all.

She found out she wasn't the only one who had fears. TJ became almost shy when they entered the room. Mare soon learned that jumping into bed on the spur of the moment wasn't quite possible. TJ had been so self-conscious as she explained to Mare that intimate details had to be taken care of before they could proceed beneath the covers. Mare was touched by the gentle explanations TJ gave, and her heart melted further as she saw the proud woman reveal all the limitations of her injury.

What bothered Mare more than the tubes and bags was the thought that their lovemaking would be an entirely one-sided affair. TJ had tried to reassure her that she would be happy giving everything she had to Mare and that love and affection were enough in return. Mare hadn't been satisfied with that and had come up with some inventive ways to ensure that TJ enjoyed the experience as much as she did.

And, in the process of their mutual explorations, something unbelievably wondrous happened. They discovered that TJ's responses, once awakened by Mare's imaginative touch, left nothing to be desired. Both women found complete satisfaction. When it first happened, after they had lifted into the stratosphere of consummated passion, TJ cried. Their tears blended and Mare kissed every available surface of TJ's face as her awed lover struggled to speak.

"The doctors told me I might be able to have some sexual response. Other women had reported it, but I didn't believe them. I felt dead inside. As much as I wanted to make love to you, I had lost hope that I would ever even come close to feeling the way you just made me feel. My God, Mare, you've given me a new life."

They had cried together for a while, then eager hands and mouths renewed their quest to revisit the delights they had just become acquainted with. Again and again they soared above the mundane world until a glorious exhaustion finally quieted their loving frenzy, and they slept in each other's arms.

Remembering each delicious moment, Mare sighed once more, pressing her lips to the warm body beneath her, savoring the still-salty taste of her lover, before her lips languidly made their way up her torso. She looked up and stilled as her gaze connected with TJ's slowly curving lips.

Mare, filled with a need to kiss that seductive mouth, slithered her body up along TJ's without considering the fire it would rekindle in both of them. TJ's eyes gleamed, and her mouth opened, hungry for the kiss that Mare offered her. She wrapped her arms around Mare's awakened body and pulled her up, dragging skin against skin, until their heads were even. While their mouths tasted each other, TJ's hands started a journey of love down Mare's tantalized flesh. Mare slipped her mouth sideways and began her own voyage, sampling treasures found by questing fingers. Time had no meaning as, borne on the wings of tongue and touch, they ascended once more through the realm of passion.

MARE AND TJ finally made it into the kitchen to join Erin and Paula for breakfast. Erin set a steaming mug of coffee in front of Mare and a glass of iced tea in front of TJ. They all sat eating bagels and cream cheese for a moment without speaking. But everyone was smiling, and the new lovers absolutely glowed. Finally, Erin got up, came over to Mare, and kissed her on the cheek. "Welcome to our family, Mare. We're really glad to have you. Really glad." Her warm brown eyes twinkled. "Now maybe Paula and I will get an occasional rest from trying to keep TJ entertained."

"Keep your day job, Erin," TJ said. "You gals will never make it as entertainers." TJ gave her a shove. "Except maybe for each other. What the heck was that racket on the stairs last night?"

Both Paula and Erin blushed. "Uh...we had a race to the bedroom," Erin said.

"Oh yeah? Who won?"

"Neither one of us," Paula said, her eyes glinting. "We both had to pay up."

Mare and TJ laughed at the look on Erin's face when she tried to shush Paula, then accepting the futility of it, just rolled her eyes.

Chapter
Eleven

AFTER ERIN HELPED Paula with the dishes, they both disappeared for work and left TJ and Mare sitting at the island. "So," Mare said, "Abner tells me they're moving all the cattle back to their own ranches today. It's going to be calmer here without them, isn't it?"

"Yeah, but Bill and the boys will have plenty to do. Our cattle start arriving the day after tomorrow. And Paula has a few more hands for Bill to break in." Just ask her, TJ told herself. The worst she could do was say no.

"Are you okay? You seem a little quiet." Mare leaned closer.

"I'm fine." TJ lifted her head and decided to go for it. "You busy today?"

"I don't have to be. Why?"

"Want to go for a ride? We could go up to the lake. It's only about an hour or so on horseback."

"Sure, but shouldn't we have told Erin or Paula where we're going?"

"I'll take the cell phone with me, and we can leave a note. Besides, if they see Flag and Runny aren't in the barn, they'll know we're out riding."

"Let's get going, then. Do you need to take anything with you?"

"Nothing special, but we can take along something to eat and drink." TJ pushed herself over to the fridge and opened it to gather soda and snacks. "Grab the bag on the hook over there, will you?"

Mare expressed her frank admiration as TJ instructed her on how to assist with Flag and the lift that allowed TJ to mount her horse. Within thirty minutes, they were on their way.

"Hey, TJ, give me time to get used to Runny's gait, and then I'll keep up," Mare said. They made their way at a steady pace and eventually left the buildings of the homestead behind. Once in the open fields, Mare pulled abreast of TJ.

TJ glanced back as Mare came alongside, relishing her presence. Ever since she was a child and her father had given her her first horse, she had loved to ride. She had named it Artemis, after the Greek Goddess of the Hunt. Artemis had been her first love. TJ had spent every minute of the day with her that she had been able to, and they had been thoroughly devoted to each other.

Around then, TJ had begun to understand that her parents' attitude toward her wasn't like that of other families. She hadn't thought it abnormal for her father to hit her; after all it was her fault, wasn't it? Hadn't she been late? Hadn't she upset her mother? Weren't her school grades lower than they expected? She had done everything within her power to please them, and still it wasn't enough.

Her saving grace had always been Lance. He excelled at school and achieved A's across the board. His success sometimes managed to deflect their father's anger away from her, though not all the time. And, like Artemis, his love for his sister had been unconditional.

There was something liberating about being on top of such a powerful creature as Flag, even more so now that it gave her a sense of freedom denied to her by her wheelchair. "Come on, Mare, let's pick up the pace and let these two run off a bit of their energy."

"You go on ahead. I'm not so hot on a horse." Mare leaned down and patted Runny on the neck. "Let me get used to the big guy before I start running him ragged."

"And there was me," TJ said, "thinking you were a vet. Runny is a girl."

Mare laughed. "I know that. It was just a figure of speech. Now you go play on that horse of yours, and I'll be right behind you."

"Okay. I won't go too far, just enough to settle Flag down some. I haven't been able to take her out much recently." She turned Flag, and with a flick of the reins and a quick yell, urged her forward.

TJ was in heaven. There was no other way of describing what she was feeling. She was on her horse for the first time in days, riding like the wind, feeling its fingers lifting her hair. Not only that, but she was in the company of a woman who she now believed could love her like no other ever had. She let out a whoop of joy as she crested the rise she had urged Flag up.

The view from the rise was unhindered, and though it wasn't a mountain, she could see for miles. On the whole, the Meridian ranch was rolling prairie crisscrossed by streams and a river. Up to the north, near the lake, the land became hilly, and a whole section was wooded as it stretched to the mountains that were some miles distant.

She brought Flag to a stop and looked out over her domain. As a child she had never considered how precious this land was. Only when her father denied it to her had she truly understood what was being lost all over the world to development and urban sprawl. That was one of the reasons she had fought so hard to buy the land in Colorado her father had wanted. It was also the reason she had donated it to the national park system.

TJ inhaled the clean air and relaxed, enjoying the scenery in front of her. She twisted in her saddle as she heard Mare and Runny approach. "Beautiful, isn't it?" she asked, waving across the land.

Mare pulled up alongside her. "Yeah, it is. You enjoy your run?"

"Yep!" TJ said with contagious enthusiasm. "I haven't been able to get out much in the last week or so. Been too busy or there hasn't been anyone to spare to give me a hand. But it's great to be out here now, even if it is a little cloudy." Her grin widened. "Thanks for coming with me. Come on, it's about another forty-five minutes or so."

They started off again at a more leisurely pace now that TJ had rid herself of her excess energy. The ride was pleasant. TJ knew a lot about the land she owned and took great delight in showing Mare where she had played as a child. Her favorite places recalled fond memories of times before she had known her father's hate and punishment, times when she had believed she had a loving relationship with her parents.

It was nearly midday when they eventually reached the lake TJ wanted to show Mare, though they couldn't have told that from the sky. The fluffy white clouds they had started out under had built as they neared the lake. The air was warm and dry but the clouds had turned dark and ominous. Still, TJ was enjoying herself and Mare seemed to be, too.

The lake spread over about five hundred acres and curved away to the right of where they stopped. On the far side, trees grew down to the water's edge, but on this side, a pebble beach stretched before them.

"It's gorgeous. Did you spend much time here when you were a kid?" Mare handed a soda and candy bar over to TJ and took some for herself.

"As much as I could. If things got too tense at home, I'd sneak out on Artemis — that was my first horse — and come here." TJ pointed. "I had a hideout in the trees over there. Nobody ever found it."

"You want to go over, see if we can find it now?"

"Another time maybe. If we go up this way, we can circle back and head for home. How are you holding up? Ride not too much for you, is it?"

"I'll no doubt suffer for it tomorrow, but right now I'm fine. Mind if I get down and stretch for a while?" TJ shook her head, and Mare slowly dismounted from Runny. TJ hid her amusement when she saw Mare clutch hold of the bridle to steady herself until her feet became readjusted to the ground. Then Mare took the reins over Runny's head and began a slow walk along the lakeside. "Are there fish in here?"

"Probably. My father liked to bring his associates out here. An invitation to the ranch for the weekend was an indication that you were on your way up in the company." TJ leaned on her saddle horn. "Of course, he never brought Lance or me out here. I do remember him taking Lance to a ball game once or twice."

"How did Lance get on with your father?"

"You mean did Lance know what a bastard he was?"

Mare nodded.

"Not at first, no. I never talked to him about the beatings, and I didn't even try to make him see how cruel our father could be. For a long time, Lance believed he was a good man. Even if it was an illusion, I couldn't take that away from him."

Mare brushed her hair from her face and bent down, picking up a brightly colored, perfectly rounded pebble. "What changed that for him?"

"A number of things. Lance wasn't an in-your-face type of person, but when it came to what he wanted, he had a will of steel. If he wanted something, he put his mind to it and didn't waver until he got it. Father thought it was a particularly brilliant facet of his personality—until it was turned on him. Lance wanted medical school. Father wanted him to go into business. Lance took all the sciences in school. Father wanted him to take mathematics and business ethics. When Father recognized he wouldn't win with persuasion, he tried browbeating him into it. All it did was make Lance hate being at home or around him and eventually it got bad enough that Lance got depressed about it. He didn't understand why Father turned on him, but I put a stop to that as soon as I could."

"Did he ever find out about what your father did to you?" Mare picked up another pebble, this time a flat one. She sent it skimming and bouncing across the water.

TJ felt sad, remembering, but she wanted Mare to know everything about her. "I never told him, but yeah, I think he knew. He had to hear things. He was smart and he saw the bruises occasionally. When they were too noticeable to hide."

A forbidding rumble echoed overhead, and they looked up. While they had been talking, the sky had turned a threatening shade of dark gray. Mare readjusted Runny's reins and bridle before she remounted. "Guess we ought to head home before the skies decide to open on us."

TJ assessed the sky. "We better go back the way we came. It's the quicker route. Will you be okay if we go a little faster? We might be able to make it back to the house before the rain starts."

"No problem. I think I've gotten used to Runny here."

"Let's go, then. We can come back another time." TJ turned Flag, urged Mare to take the lead, and they headed home at a canter.

Fat, wet blobs of rain started falling soon after they made their decision to return. Mare clenched her legs around the barreled belly of her horse, concentrating on staying in her seat. She was comforted that TJ was close by, as the constant rumble of thunder was starting to unnerve both her and the horse.

The rain began to fall more heavily, rapidly soaking her cotton shirt and jeans. She wished she had brought her hat with her. At least that would have kept the rain from her face. The wind picked up and now had a decided chill to it. With the water and all, she'd be surprised if she got out of this without catching a cold. It suddenly occurred to her that catching a cold might not be in TJ's best interests either. She had no idea how illness might affect her.

While Mare was worrying over TJ, TJ was worrying over Mare. With each rumble of thunder, Mare tensed even more, and TJ questioned her wisdom in bringing an inexperienced rider out in such weather. A trickle of cool water was now a permanent feature running down her back, and she already knew that Erin and Paula were going to throw a fit over this badly timed excursion. If she got ill from it as well, it would only be worse.

The storm concerned her, too. Teeming rain made it difficult to see the ground, and she was loath to push the horses any faster when she couldn't see where they were going. The wind had picked up at a steady pace and lightning bolts flashed to the west. TJ urged Flag a little faster until she was alongside Mare. She made a signal with her hand, asking whether Mare was okay and got an affirmative answer. TJ thought hard, trying to remember if they could find shelter anywhere nearby until the storm passed, but nothing sprang to mind. They were still thirty minutes away from the ranch, and TJ decided they should carry on and hope that it didn't get any worse.

PAULA BOUNDED INTO the house with a soaked Erin hot on her trail. "Whew, where did that storm spring up from?" She ducked into the laundry room, grabbed two towels from the clean pile, and threw one across to Erin.

"I have no idea, but it looks as though it's set in for the afternoon. Did you notice that Mare's truck is still outside?" she asked as she towel-dried her hair, leaving the blonde locks in frizzy disarray.

"I did. Wonder what they're up to? You'd think they could at least have had the coffee on for us, considering the weather."

"Hmm. Well, they may be a little involved and didn't notice the rain. Why don't you go on up and run us a hot bath? I'll make us a couple of hot chocolates and join you in a few minutes."

Paula leaned over and placed a kiss firmly on Erin's slightly parted lips, while her hand blazed a trail of pure flame across a damp and sensitive breast. "You got it, babe."

Erin sighed and wet her lips as Paula turned and slowly made her way from the kitchen with a pronounced sway to her hips. The day was a washout, and she hoped there would be many more of them if it put Paula in this type of mood. She heard the door close upstairs and quickly moved to prepare the hot drink she had promised.

In her haste to get upstairs to the now hopefully naked form of her lover, she almost missed the folded piece of paper on the counter. She was tempted to ignore it, but she knew TJ wouldn't have left it lying around for no reason. It then occurred to her that TJ wouldn't have left it at all, if she were in the house. She unfolded it and read the short note.

> *Taking Mare out to show her some of the sights on the ranch.*
> *Should be back early afternoon. I've got the phone if you want me.*
> *See you later.*
> *Love,*
> *TJ*

"Hell!" Erin looked out of the window again and stared into the rain and lightning. The only way she could have taken her out was on horseback. Flag was okay in this sort of weather. Erin doubted TJ would have let Mare ride Ebonair — she was too big, but Runny was about Mare's size. She put the note down and forgot about the hot cocoa she was supposed to be making. She dashed out of the kitchen and up the stairs.

Erin flung the bedroom door open, barely registering the

fact that Paula was sprawled on the bed buck-naked. "Paula, what's Runny like in a storm?"

Paula looked pointedly down at herself, then at Erin. "I'm here in my birthday suit, and you want to talk about horses?"

"TJ took Mare out to see the sights of the ranch. I know Flag won't have a problem, and TJ is too good on a horse to worry about. But I don't know how good Mare is. Chances are she's on Runny, who's smaller than Ebonair."

Paula sat up. "Runny's okay as long as you keep a firm hand on her. Otherwise, she tends to be skittish. I can't believe TJ would go out without letting one of us know."

"She left us a note, and she's got the phone. Mare's with her so why would she let us know? I know we act like her mother sometimes, but she is an adult."

"You think they're okay? Maybe you ought to give her a call and make sure." Paula had gone to stand by the window, gazing out into the sky. "This storm is in for the rest of the day."

"Yeah, I know, but calling the cell phone might be dangerous. The last thing she needs is to be struck by lightning just because we wanted to check up on her. Besides, I'm sure she'll call if she needs us." Erin walked over and curled her arms around Paula's waist, cuddling her close to her body and absorbing her warmth. "They'll be fine. TJ knows what she's doing."

"Yeah," replied Paula, patting Erin's hand.

THE LIGHTNING WAS getting awfully close, and TJ wasn't too happy about being on top of Flag, or Mare being on Runny at this moment, but she didn't see what choice they had. Mare was keeping up well and Runny was behaving herself. Neither of the two horses was showing a great strain at the pace TJ demanded they keep. They weren't that far away now from the safety of the barn. She looked over to Mare's bedraggled form. Even soaked through and looking like a drowned rat, she was beautiful.

Thunder boomed. Mare knew immediately that something was wrong and tried to shift her seat to compensate for the horse's sudden awkward movements. Runny was having none of it as she pulled back on the reins to slow the horse down. Another flash of lightning and Runny again shied, this time over to the left, almost unseating Mare.

She looked frantically across to TJ, seeing that she had already noticed Runny's panicked movements and brought Flag alongside to help calm the horse down. Mare relaxed as she saw TJ lean across the narrow gap between them and give Runny a slap on the shoulder. The horse shook her head in the direction of the slap, seemed to take reassurance from Flag's presence, and calmed down.

Mare smiled through the rain at TJ and nodded when she saw her indicate that they should slow down. After all, it wasn't as if they could get any wetter. She pulled back firmly on the reins, and Runny obeyed the command, slowing her speed. They would have been perfectly all right if lightning hadn't struck an outcropping of rock nearby. An ear-shattering crack sounded. A clap of thunder shook the ground. Fragments of rock burst out like a spray of buckshot, and Runny immediately reared.

Mare held on for all she was worth but could feel herself slipping. She was thrown backward, clenching the reins. They were too wet to hold, and she was falling.

Flag charged past the rearing horse. TJ pulled the reins tight against the left side of Flag's neck and turned her back toward Mare and Runny.

She watched in horror as Mare fell. TJ's heart was in her throat as she rode up to the still form. "Mare? Mare!" She got no response. TJ looked around and saw that Runny had come to a halt not too far away, scared it seemed, to leave the presence of Flag. TJ guided Flag to walk in a circle around the prone figure. She leaned down and looked for any sign of injury. She couldn't see any blood or any broken bones sticking out.

"Mare, can you hear me?" she yelled again. Instinctively she went to get off of Flag but remembered the straps holding her to the saddle. She yelled out in frustration. For those few precious hours spent on her beloved horse, she had forgotten her limitations. Now Mare was in trouble and depending on her. She looked anxiously around, again trying to gauge the distance from the house. Even if she rode at the fastest speed she and Flag could manage, it would take another fifteen minutes to reach Erin and Paula, which would mean at least twenty before help would arrive.

She pulled the phone from its carrying case, and although she knew it was stupid to use it in such bad weather, she called the ranch, praying that Paula or Erin was home.

Chapter
Twelve

ERIN HAD HER eyes closed and was lying back, snuggled in
Paula's loving embrace, up to her chin in warm water and
bubbles. She couldn't think of anything more heavenly than
where she was now. Paula's arms were wrapped around her, one
hand caressing her inner thigh, the other cupping her breast,
teasing her with tantalizingly gentle touches. She groaned as
Paula's hand once again shied away from the need she was
stirring. "Tease," she whispered as Paula bent her head and
kissed her lightly, before sucking her earlobe and sending a
shiver down her spine. "God, you're so good at that," she said
with a sigh. The ringing of the phone went unnoticed.

God damn it! Where are you? TJ silently screamed as the
phone continued to ring without answer. She broke the
connection and rapidly punched in another number, hoping that
at least one of them had her cell phone switched on.

Paula jerked from the languid place she was in as a shrill
warble echoed from the bedroom. "Leave it," Erin murmured
lazily.

"Can't, might be important. Just because you can laze the
rest of the day away doesn't mean that I can, you know." Erin
tightened her grip in protest as Paula rose to climb out of the
tub. Paula kissed her soundly on the lips and was about to give
in when a thought crossed her mind. What if it was TJ? "Sugar?
Erin, move. It might be TJ." All sexual tension left the room as
both of them bolted from the tub.

TJ nearly cried with relief when the phone was answered.
"Paula! Paula, I need help. Mare's fallen, she's unconscious, and I
can't —"

"TJ, honey, calm down. Tell me where you are," said Paula's
disembodied voice.

TJ took a deep breath, struggling to calm herself. Frustration
at not being able to help Mare tore at her, coupled with attacks
of fear and guilt. "We're on the way back from the lake. We're

about a mile and a half away. Runny reared and Mare fell. I think she hit her head or something because I can't wake her up."

Paula repeated TJ's message aloud and stared urgently over at Erin who had scrambled into her clothes. Erin had already picked up the house phone and dialed. "Bill? It's Erin. Get a couple of the men together and meet me in front of the bunkhouse right away. TJ and Mare were out riding when the storm hit, and Mare's been thrown and is hurt." She paused for a second. "Great. See you in a minute." She put the phone down quickly, kissed Paula good-bye and was out the door.

"Honey, Erin and some of the men are on their way. Just stay by Mare, and if she wakes up, don't let her do anything stupid like move. They'll be with you in a few minutes, okay?"

TJ sat anxiously on Flag, already staring off into the distance, hoping to see the Land Rover even though they had only just set out. One hand nervously rubbed her wet jeans, the other clutched the phone she held to her ear. "She doesn't look like she's going to come around."

"She will, TJ. Don't you worry about that. She's too tough to let a horse get the better of her." Paula walked over to the house phone that Erin had recently used and picked it up, trying to figure out whether she ought to call 9-1-1 or the doctor. She settled on phoning Jon Hunt who ran the local doctors' service. "I'm going to get Doc Hunt to come out to the ranch. Let me know if you need him there, and I'll bring him as soon as he gets here. You hang in there. Erin isn't far away."

Erin skidded the Rover to a watery stop outside the bunkhouse and waited as Bill and two of the recently hired men ran from the building and piled in.

Bill said hastily, "This is Mark and Burt."

Erin nodded to them. "Thanks, Bill."

As soon as the doors were closed, Erin floored the accelerator and they were off. With the windshield wipers on high, she roared through the pools of water that had accumulated in the downpour. Going at a much faster speed than was safe, she fought to keep the Rover under control, fear pushing her onward. Several minutes later, a tall figure on horseback appeared in the distance. TJ had been right. They weren't that far from the ranch.

TJ heard the deep rumble of Erin's Rover before it came into sight. "Stay with me, Mare, I can hear Erin coming." TJ had positioned Flag so that she sheltered Mare from the worst of the slanting rain. When she hadn't been searching for rescuers on the horizon, she had concentrated on Mare, looking for signs of life. She could see her chest moving, so TJ knew she was breathing.

TJ had never been so glad to hear a painful groan as she was when one rumbled from Mare at that second. Mare's arms lifted toward her head, and TJ could tell she was coming around. "Mare, you need to stay still. You fell when Runny shied." Mare's eyes cracked open, and TJ sobbed with relief. "Stay still. Erin's nearly here. Are you okay?"

Mare tried to nod and immediately regretted it. "I feel like I've been thrown off a ten-story building." Both hands were now holding her head. "TJ?"

"What?" TJ's voice was full of fear.

"I'm lying in a puddle." Mare's voice held the petulant tone of a two-year-old child.

"What?" TJ couldn't quite believe her ears.

"I said I'm lying in a puddle. Couldn't you have at least trained Runny to throw me somewhere dry?" Mare tried to smile, but the pounding of her head wouldn't let her.

TJ couldn't believe Mare was joking about this. Didn't she have any idea how serious it could be? Hell, she only had to look at TJ to see what the consequences of a back injury were. "This is serious. You could be badly hurt." TJ looked up from Mare. The roar of the engine was closer, and she could see Erin's Rover. She'd be here in a minute.

"Nope, I'm just a little banged up. I hurt way too much for it to be anything more serious." Mare draped one of her arms across her eyes to stop the rain from hitting them.

Erin slammed on the brakes and slid to a halt barely ten feet from where TJ had stationed Flag. Bill and his two hands hurtled from the vehicle. Burt went to get Runny who stood where she had stopped, reins trailing on the ground. Bill and Mark headed straight for Mare and TJ. Erin jumped from the Rover and sloshed through the mud to where Bill crouched.

"Hey, there, little Missy, what ya doing lying in a puddle?" Bill's voice was deep and rough from the years spent bellowing at cowhands, but it also held a gentle lilt to it.

"Ask TJ," Mare said. "She's the one who trained her horses to throw people in the wettest place possible."

"Hi, Mare. You hurt anywhere?" Erin asked as she knelt down by Bill in the mud.

"You mean besides my pride?" Mare raised an eyebrow then remembered nobody could see it with her arm draped over her face. "No I don't think so. Took a pretty good bang to the head, but nothing else seems to be hurting me. Though I can't say I'll feel the same tomorrow."

Erin looked up into TJ's stony face. Mare might not have lost her sense of humor over this, but TJ's whole body was rigid with tension, and it was agitating even Flag. "Okay, let me just quickly check you out, then we'll get you two adventurers home." Erin quickly ran her fingers through Mare's hair. She found a nasty bump on the back of her head but it hadn't split and bled. Then she carefully felt down her neck, looking for any deformities or lumps that shouldn't be there. "Any neck pain at all?"

"Nope, just stiff from where the rain and wind have been attacking it."

"Okay." Erin continued with her inspection. "Any pain in your arms and shoulders?" Again Mare replied in the negative. "Wiggle your fingers for me?" Erin watched as Mare complied. "Okay, what about your legs? Any pain?"

"Nope."

"Can you wiggle your toes and bend your knees for me?" Erin watched closely and sighed in relief. "Well, it looks as though you survived. Come on, Bill, let's get her up." Bill and Erin took hold of Mare's arms and eased her into a sitting position. "Feel okay?" Mare gave a cautious nod. "Bill and Mark here are going to get you into the Rover. I just want to make sure TJ's okay." Erin waited until Mark took her place, then she stood back as he and Bill lifted Mare to her feet and slowly walked her over to the vehicle. "Bill, there's a blanket in the back," Erin called. She turned and faced TJ. "You okay?"

"Fine," TJ said tersely. Her voice was strained with barely controlled distress.

Erin walked over and ducked beneath Flag's neck, patting TJ's faithful horse. "You sure?" TJ nodded this time. "Okay then, once Bill and Mark have Mare settled we'll get you off Flag and back to the house. Burt can ride Runny in and lead Flag."

"I'll ride."

"TJ, be sensible. You're soaked through to the skin. If you ride, it'll take you at least another fifteen minutes or so to get back to the house. Besides, I'm sure Mare would rather have you with her."

TJ stared down at Erin whose hair was now plastered to her head by rain that showed no sign of letting up. And if TJ had been thinking rationally, she would have known that Erin had only her best interests at heart. But right now TJ wasn't thinking rationally. All she could see was that, just like with Lance, she had been unable to help someone she cared about. She took Mare out on a simple horse ride, almost got her killed, and couldn't do a damn thing. She was inferior just like her father had kept telling her. "I said I'll ride." TJ pulled on Flag's reins and moved the horse off in the direction of the house.

Erin stood drenched, silently watching TJ's rigid form ride slowly into the distance. She waved to Burt to follow TJ, then trudged back through the mud to the Rover. She got in, slammed the door, and turned the defroster on full blast to clear the steamed windows. Mare sat in the back wrapped in a blanket with Mark sitting by her side and Bill sitting in the front.

"Where's TJ?" Mare asked.

"She decided to ride Flag back."

"What!" Mare yelled. "Is she nuts?"

Bill looked over at Erin. "You sure it's okay to let her ride back?"

"No, it's not okay to let her ride back, but are *you* going to tell her she can't? At least Burt's right behind her." She turned on the engine and put the vehicle into gear for the journey home.

"Is she okay?" Mare leaned forward so she could see Erin's face.

"I think she's feeling a little inadequate right now," Erin said. "And my treating her like a two year old and telling her she couldn't ride Flag home only made it worse." Mare sat back and stared out the window, hoping to catch a glimpse of TJ as they drove past.

TJ was miserable. She was wet, cold, and upset. Not even the joy at being on Flag was going to shake her from this mood. It had been stupid and reckless to think that she and Mare could spend a normal day together. And her stupidity could have cost Mare her life. She should have asked Mare about her riding skills, instead of just assuming she was comfortable, and she shouldn't have taken her so far away from help. If she had been thinking, instead of mooning over a day out with Mare, she would have realized that gray skies only meant trouble.

TJ urged Flag to a greater speed, needing to work out her frustration, trying to run from the desolation that was building inside her. She had thought she had adjusted to her injuries, but days like today forced her to admit she would never be able to forget them.

Paula stood anxiously at the front door when Erin and Mare finally drove up in the Rover. Erin had dropped Bill and Mark back at the bunkhouse, knowing that Paula would be able to help if Mare was unsteady on her feet. Erin jumped out and ran around to open the door for Mare. Paula came down the steps with a gray-haired man at her side. Erin and Mare recognized him as Dr. Hunt from Meridianville. Paula and the doctor escorted Mare into the house while Erin parked the vehicle.

As soon as she had settled Mare on the couch in the living room in Dr. Hunt's care, Paula ran upstairs to find some of Erin's clothes that would fit her. "Well, Doc, what's the prognosis?" she asked as she came back down.

"We've always known that Mare had a tough head on her shoulders. She has a mild concussion and should rest for the next couple of days." The doctor turned off his pen light and put his stethoscope away. "I'd like you to keep her awake for the next few hours, but there should be no complications. I'll leave you a checklist of signs and symptoms to watch out for — any problems, give me a call. And you, young lady," he turned to Mare, "should know better than to give an old man a fright like that."

"Think I gave myself a bigger one, Doc."

"Lucky for you that you didn't break an arm or a finger. That sure would have played havoc with your piano playing. You just take it easy for the next couple of days. I'll leave some painkillers for the headache you'll no doubt develop in the next hour or so. Next time don't make it an accident that brings us together, okay?"

"You got it, Doc. Thanks for coming all the way out here."

"You're very welcome. I'll see you soon. Take care of yourself." He picked up his bag and Paula showed him out.

Mare closed her eyes. Her head hurt more than she had let on, but she knew that complaining about it too much would have resulted in a trip to the hospital in Sharlesburg. She was worried, not about herself but about TJ. Erin had implied that TJ wouldn't take this incident well, and thinking about it, Mare knew she was right. As she had come around, Mare had heard the barely restrained panic and frustration in TJ's voice.

"Hey." Erin's voice broke into her reverie. "Paula stole some of my clothes for you. Let's get you out of these wet things. You want to take a bath or shower to warm up?"

"Thanks for the offer, but I'd rather just get changed and wait for TJ."

"Okay. You can use TJ's bathroom to wash up and change. There's a buzzer in there if you need any help. I'll start a fire and bring one of the spare quilts in here, and you can snuggle on the couch."

Erin helped Mare down the hall to the bathroom and walked back into the living room just as Paula closed the front door. They looked at each other with concern. "Mare okay?" Paula asked.

"Yeah, just changing clothes," Erin said as she walked to the fireplace to build a fire.

"Where's TJ?" Paula moved over to her side and passed pieces of kindling and wood.

"Riding Flag home. She wouldn't get in the Rover even

though the hands would have brought the horses back. One of the men is following her in on Runny." Erin twisted paper wicks to light the fire.

"I take it she isn't handling this as well as Mare is?"

Erin shrugged, her expression sad. " She isn't handling it at all. She's putting one almighty guilt trip on herself. I could see it. She hardly said a word when we arrived. She sat up on that horse proud as you like, and anybody looking at her could have told you it was a show."

"So, I take it we aren't going to tell her that she should have told us where she was going?"

"No, we aren't. Her self-confidence has just taken one hell of a thump, and us pointing it out to her isn't going to help one iota. Besides, she's an adult, and okay, she's an adult with special needs, but we have to let her have a life of her own. We can't control everything for her."

"Yeah, I know." Paula leaned her head on Erin's shoulder. "But it's hard not to be protective when things like this happen."

Erin turned and kissed the side of Paula's head. "Come on, let's light this, get Mare settled, then go over to the barn and wait for TJ."

Paula stood up. "I heard the doctor say something interesting to Mare. Something about her piano playing." She looked at Erin. "Bet TJ will like to hear that."

"Yeah, but let's wait until she's in better shape."

TJ saw Erin and Paula waiting for her when she rode into the barn. She hadn't called ahead because she knew Burt was right behind her. Still, she should have known better. Paula and Erin weren't likely to leave her by herself after something like this. They knew her too well.

They didn't speak as she pulled Flag to a stop near the ramp, and in silence they unbuckled TJ's legs. TJ reached up for the T-bar and took her weight on her arms as Paula handed Flag off to Burt, who made a welcome offer to rub down the two horses. While TJ manipulated the lift controls, Erin steered her into her chair. She handed her a towel and draped a blanket around her shoulders, then wheeled her out of the barn to the house.

Mare was wrapped up tightly in the quilt that Erin had provided. After calling the elderly Dr. DiNicola, her vet friend in Sharlesburg, to cover for her for a few days, she had closed her eyes and lain back on the couch, listening to the crackle and hiss of the fire that Erin and Paula had lit before they left for the barn. The faint scent of hickory smoke battled with that of the hot chocolate on the table by her side. Her head was pounding, and she felt slightly nauseous. The tension building in her shoulders from TJ's continued absence wasn't helping either.

She heard footsteps on the ramp outside and pushed herself into a seated position so she could look over the top of the couch. The door creaked open and she saw the front wheels of TJ's chair. "Hey!" she said with cheerfulness that she didn't really feel. TJ didn't reply.

Erin wheeled TJ into the living room and down the short ramp so she was near Mare and the now roaring fire. "I'll leave you here while I go run you a bath," Erin said as she pushed the brakes on. TJ remained silent. Erin looked over TJ's shoulder, catching Mare's attention. "Help?" she mouthed, and Mare gave a nod. Erin left them to go draw TJ's bath.

There was silence for a few minutes, and Mare was concerned that TJ didn't seem to be able to look at her. She swung her legs off of the couch and reached over, taking TJ's hand into her own. She didn't speak, just held tightly to the deeply chilled hand, her thumb unconsciously stroking along the back of it.

TJ stared down at the entwined hands, then looked up into Mare's eyes and took a deep breath. "You okay?" she asked quietly

"I'm fine. A hard knock on the head, but Doc Hunt has given me a clean bill of health."

"Really?"

"Really. So what's the long face for, huh?"

"I should never have taken you out today."

"Nonsense. Why not?"

"Oh please!" TJ slammed the brakes off, pushed herself backward, and turned away. "You could have been killed."

Mare stood up and walked to her side. "I could be killed walking down the street." She ran her fingers through the damp hair on the bowed head. "What was different about today?"

"I was different today. You walk down a street, and at least someone could help you. What could I do today? Nothing, that's what. I shouldn't have taken you out, at least not before making sure you felt confident on the horse. I should only have taken you out into the corral where I couldn't put you in any danger."

"TJ, honey." Mare moved to where TJ could see her. "You didn't put me in any danger." TJ opened her mouth to speak, but Mare put her finger across it. "No. Now listen to me. Am I an adult?" TJ nodded her head. "Okay, that's good. Do you consider me an intelligent adult?"

"Of course."

"Well, that's nice to hear." Mare lifted her hand and caressed TJ's face. "So considering all this, don't you think I'm capable of making a decision all by myself?"

"I guess."

"Then, if anything, it wasn't you putting me in a dangerous position. I put myself in one. But honestly, TJ, all we did was go for a ride. So I fell off the dumb horse. You were prepared, you had the phone, and you left a note telling where we were. What more could you have done?"

"I could have got down off my horse and helped, that's what."

"Oh, sweetie." Mare leaned forward and kissed her brow. "No, you couldn't, and I knew that before I went out with you. You did everything you could. You got Erin and the men out to me. Nobody could have done better whether they could walk or not." She stood up and moved behind TJ's chair. "I love that cute look on your face, but you can stop pouting. You're cold and wet, and we need to get you into a bath."

This at least got a grin from TJ. "You going to come with me?" she asked as Mare pushed her up the ramp.

"Oh, I might be persuaded to get a little wet again."

Erin had done a great job in drawing the bath. The bathroom, specially modified for TJ, was hot and steamy. The scent of exotic oils rose from the tub, and bubbles filled it to the brim. Mare looked forward to a long, sensuous soak, reassuring TJ of their growing bond in her warm embrace. It would be a chance to ease Mare's bruised and battered body at the same time as healing TJ's bruised emotions.

Mare assisted TJ in the use of her hoist and then climbed in behind her, pulling her backward until she rested comfortably in her arms. But Mare couldn't resist the close proximity of TJ's bare skin. Her gentle caresses maddened her love and what started out as a seductive tease rapidly disintegrated into an all-out tickle fest and water fight.

Somehow TJ managed to turn herself around in the water so they were face-to-face, and at the first possible chance, she claimed Mare's lips for her own. For what seemed like hours, they reacquainted themselves with each other's body, touching, tasting, holding. They then left the steamy warmth of the bathroom for TJ's bed. Mare delighted in TJ's attentions. For someone who was disabled from the waist down, she was surprisingly agile.

Chapter
Thirteen

IT WAS STILL dark when Mare opened her eyes. A soft breeze gently ruffled the drapes through TJ's open window before entering the warmth of the bedroom. Yesterday had been a demanding day for both of them, but they had come through it together. It surprised Mare how insecure TJ had been. She thought they had come far enough in their relationship that TJ's disability wasn't an issue.

It also brought home a frightening reality that TJ wasn't as strong and tough as she appeared to the outside world. Her emotional state was incredibly fragile. Mare hoped the previous night had been a big step in allaying her fears and insecurities.

Although Mare loved TJ's caresses and cries of passion, she enjoyed these quiet times in the middle of the night more. TJ's head rested on her stomach, her left arm wrapped possessively around Mare's waist, her other arm splayed up by her head. The worries of yesterday had been driven away, and she was at peace. Mare would never tire of seeing her like this.

She lowered her hand and softly ran her fingers through the somewhat bedraggled hair, frowning slightly at the heat coming off of her companion. She tried to move without disturbing the slumbering TJ, but TJ only tightened her grip and fussed. Mare returned to her gentling caress and let her hand drop to TJ's forehead once she had settled again.

Yep, she had a fever. With all that wind and rain yesterday, she must have caught a chill. Her temperature wasn't that high, just enough to cause a sheen of perspiration across the brow and make her hot to the touch. It would give Mare a good excuse to pamper her in the morning. TJ seemed to sense her thoughts and snuggled in closer. Mare tightened her embrace and settled back down. She closed her eyes and basked in the sensation of affection and love emanating from her sleeping lover.

The next time Mare opened her eyes, bright sunshine was pouring in through the windows. She groaned as every muscle and bruise on her body made itself known, despite the bath and loving touch of TJ the night before. She lifted her head and searched around. TJ had migrated during the night and was now sprawled on her back by Mare's side. Mare ran her hand over TJ's head checking for signs of the fever she had noticed when she woke up during the night. TJ still felt warmer than usual.

Mare looked at her watch, surprised to find it was after ten. It was unusual for TJ to sleep so late. Had Mare worn her out last night, or was the fever to blame?

Now that she was free of TJ's nocturnal octopus-like grasp, she decided to get up. Her stomach was demanding to be fed. After yesterday's ordeal and last night's strenuous activities, they hadn't gotten the chance to eat. She left the bed, managing not to disturb TJ. After donning one of TJ's T-shirts, which fell almost to her knees, she went in search of food and coffee.

The house was quiet as Mare walked through its rooms. Erin and Paula must be out working. The kitchen was empty when she entered, but there was coffee in the coffee maker. She opened the fridge and took out the milk, diving back in to grab a grapefruit. While she was busy puttering around, she heard a phone ring three times before it was picked up. She faintly heard Paula's voice deal with the inquiry. Several seconds later she heard footsteps approaching the kitchen. Mare grabbed another mug and poured a second coffee.

Paula smiled when she saw Mare standing by the counter dressed in one of TJ's T-shirts. "Hey, there. How's the wounded soldier today?" She reached out and took the mug Mare offered.

"Sore. I feel like I've been run over by a truck," Mare said ruefully. "On the plus side, my head has stopped pounding."

"I'm glad to hear it. You sure look better than you did yesterday. TJ getting up?"

"No, she's still asleep." Mare took a sip from her mug.

"You wear her out last night, Doc?"

"Maybe, but I think yesterday took a lot out of her, and she's running a slight fever. I think maybe she caught a chill or something."

"That doesn't sound good. I'll give her doc a call and find out whether we need to take her in to see him."

"Well, I plan on keeping her right where she is for the rest of the day."

"Did I hear Doc Hunt say something to you about playing the piano?"

"Yeah, I've been playing since I was knee high to a grasshopper. Calms me down when nothing else will."

"I'd like to hear you sometime."

"Stop by my house anytime I'm home. I love an audience."

After another half an hour of chatting with Paula, Mare was ready to return to TJ. Paula told her to yell out if they needed anything since she was working from TJ's office just across the hall.

TJ was still deeply asleep. She was in the same position as when Mare had left except she was now hugging a pillow. Smiling at the childlike scene, Mare crept quietly onto the bed, trying not to disturb her slumber. She was leaning over to place a kiss on TJ's cheek when her eyes popped open. TJ turned her head and captured Mare's lips on her own. She released her hold on the pillow, wrapped her arms around Mare, and pulled her down on top of her.

"Morning," TJ whispered as they broke the kiss.

"Good morning, sweetheart." Mare lifted her hand to TJ's face. "How are you feeling?"

"Great, now that you're here. I woke up earlier. Where were you?"

"Kitchen. Food and coffee were required. You're running a temperature."

"I know. My throat hurts, and I have a headache." She pulled Mare down for another kiss. "But I'll be fine. Will you give me a hand to do my exercises?"

"And what exercises would you like to do?" Mare asked as she ran her finger down TJ's bare chest, delighting in the instant reaction her caress provoked.

TJ took a deep, shuddering breath as the sensation caused by Mare's inquisitive fingers raced through her. Her body woke with a vengeance, craving more than a simple caress.

Mare let her fingers wander lower, pulling the sheet from TJ's body as she went. She could see the goose bumps ripple along her lover's body and the downy hairs on her arms standing at attention. She sent a smoldering gaze into TJ's eyes as her hand found its destination.

TJ stopped breathing altogether, her whole body taut with sensual tension. She couldn't feel it exactly, but she knew where Mare's hand rested and knew that her body was reacting to it. After her accident, she had never believed she would ever feel this way again. Now that she knew she could, she couldn't get enough of it, especially with Mare, who had brought her body back from the dead and was invoking the response right this second.

"Don't tease," TJ said, her voice low and urgent with desire.

Mare leaned closer and ran her tongue along the valley between TJ's breasts. "Who said anything about teasing?"

TJ LAY WITH her arm around Mare's sweat-slicked skin, her hand stroking the waist it rested on. Her breathing had now returned to normal after her early morning "exercises." Those sure were better than the regular ones. Mare had curled her panting body into TJ's side, and sleep had found her as her breathing calmed.

TJ listened to the sounds of the house. She hadn't heard the phone ring, so Paula either had turned off the ringer or had calls diverted to her cell phone. The silence was heaven, and she was enjoying the relaxation far too much for it to last.

How long had she known Mare now? Six weeks? Eight? Never before had she moved so fast into a relationship, and never had she felt so comfortable in one. Mare fit perfectly. All of TJ's bad moods and tantrums just bounced right off of her. She was stubborn and refused to take anything sitting down. She was a challenge, and TJ knew already that she loved her from the bottom of her soul. Just being around Mare gave TJ hope and enthusiasm for life. But did Mare feel the same? She could up and walk out at anytime, and there would be no way for TJ to keep her from leaving. *No, stop thinking she would act like all the others.*

She took a deep, steadying breath and let it out slowly, releasing the tension that had been building with her thoughts. She turned her head, nuzzled the blonde locks, and inhaled the heady aroma of her lover.

ERIN STARED AT Paula who had clamped her hand over Erin's mouth. "Shhh, TJ and Mare are still in bed. And Mare said TJ had a bit of a fever." Paula pulled her hand away.

"It's nearly one o'clock in the afternoon," Erin said. "Even if they're still in bed, I doubt they're sleeping." Paula slapped her soundly on the shoulder and pulled her toward the kitchen.

"What was that for?" she asked, rubbing her shoulder.

"That, Miss Scott, was for the obvious look of jealousy on your face. Besides, I'm guessing they're asleep because it's quiet now and awhile ago there was enough noise to make a saint blush."

"Eavesdropping, were you?"

"Hard not to. I've never heard that tone of voice from TJ before. Whatever Mare was up to sure sounded good."

"Hmm." Erin gave a sly look. "Maybe I'll ask for a few pointers."

"Oh, hush up, and don't torment them about it either." Paula took a couple cans of soda and the makings of a sandwich out of the fridge. "How's the work going out there? They nearly finished?"

"Just re-oxygenating the streams now." Erin reached over and snagged a piece of celery from the salad Paula had put on the table. "Couple more days at the most, and they'll be finished."

"Is everything set for the cattle?"

"Yep. Bill and the boys will have the holding area ready for the herd tomorrow. Then all we need is for Mare to check them out before we let them loose. That is, if I can pry her away from TJ."

It was after three when Paula decided enough was enough and caved in to her desire to make sure the two lovers were all right. Mare had seemed fine that morning, but the doctor had told her to take it easy. And although TJ's doctor had said by phone that a slight fever wouldn't be too much of a problem, Paula still needed to see for herself.

Besides, TJ hadn't eaten at all today and both of them could probably do with fluids. So she made up a tray of iced tea and some fruit and knocked softly on the door to TJ's room. She got no reply, but cautiously opened the door and entered. TJ was awake, and Paula walked into the room, placing the tray within her reach. Mare was snuggled tight underneath TJ's right arm.

Paula reached over and placed her hand on TJ's glowing face. "You feeling okay?" she whispered.

"Yeah, just achy."

"You still have a fever, so you need to drink lots of fluids to bring your temperature down." Paula crouched so she was near TJ's head and wouldn't disturb Mare with her questions. "When did you last catheterize yourself?"

"Last night."

"You'll need to get up and see to yourself soon, love. You don't need a kidney infection on top of everything else."

"You sure know how to spoil the mood, don't you?"

"That's what you hired me for. But seriously, Dr. Hammond said you need to drink plenty of fluids, and you can't do that for any period of time unless you —"

"I know, I know. But jeez, Paula, it sort of gets in the way."

"What does?" Mare mumbled.

"Nothing. Go back to sleep," TJ said and gave her a slight squeeze.

Mare's head poked up from where it was nestled on TJ's breast. She blushed slightly as she saw Paula in the room. "Hi."

"I was just reminding TJ she has to look after a few personal issues." Paula was conscious that TJ didn't like to talk about this aspect of her disability, but it was unlikely that Mare knew what the consequences would be if TJ neglected them.

"Oh," Mare said uncertainly, seeing TJ shooting daggers at Paula.

"And I thought you might like a snack and something to drink."

"Oh yeah," Mare said. "But first things first. I need to get cleaned up. My bed warmer here did too good a job last night. Could you grab me the robe from the bathroom?"

"Sure, be right back." Paula stood and walked into the bathroom.

Mare gazed up at TJ's face. "I'd suggest we take a bath, but I don't think we'd get very clean, do you?"

"No, I doubt we would. Besides, I really need to do my exercises. Sacha gets pissed at me if I miss out on too many sessions. Since I only have to see her once a month now, I like to keep on her good side."

Paula reentered the room. "Here you go. I dug a load of TJ's shampoo and stuff out of the cabinet for you to use." Paula handed over the terry cloth robe.

"Thanks." Mare leaned up and kissed TJ on the cheek. "See you soon." She slipped the robe on and made a dash for the bathroom.

"All right, boss-lady, you want to get your exercises done?" TJ nodded and pushed herself flat in the bed. "Here's a towel to cover your modesty, though after this morning's racket I don't know how you can profess to having any."

"Well, that'll teach you to work in my office, won't it?" TJ laid the towel over her middle so that her breasts and pelvic area were both covered before Paula started her lower leg exercises.

Paula took hold of TJ's right foot and slowly rotated the ankle to limber it up and help stop the joints from freezing due to disuse. Her skillful hands massaged TJ's foot before moving up to her calf. "I found out something interesting yesterday."

"Hmm?" TJ had her hands behind her head and was staring at the ceiling.

"Yeah, apparently Mare plays the piano."

"Really?" TJ pushed herself upward so that she was resting on her elbows.

"Really."

"I guess she might like the music room then." She let herself fall back to the bed, as Paula bent her knee to stretch the hamstrings.

"I guess she might at that." Paula could already see TJ's mind ticking over the possibilities.

Chapter
Fourteen

WHAM! AN ARM came down across the side of Mare's face and bumped her nose, sending jolts of pain to her brain and waking her from a sound sleep. She threw her own arm over her head defensively, and it took a couple of seconds for her to recall where she was. Then she remembered and jumped out of a bed that was vibrating with movement.

Moonlight shone through the double window, painting silver patches on everything it touched and illuminating the body thrashing about on the bed. As Mare watched, aghast, TJ raised her arms and crossed her forearms toward the back of her head. Turning her face away, she cowered in a protective mode. "No, stop, stop!" TJ's pleading voice galvanized Mare, and she ran around the bed and knelt at TJ's head.

"TJ, sweetheart, what's wrong?"

Mare reached a tentative hand, but TJ shrank back from the touch. "No! Stop! Please, stop!"

The light from the window lay full on TJ's face, and Mare could see that she still slept. She reached her hand to a shoulder and gently shook it. Suddenly, TJ's face changed from fear to anger and her voice from pleading to venomous. "Stop it, you rotten bastard. Stop it or I'll kill you. I wish you were dead!" TJ gasped, and Mare ducked barely in time to avoid the fist that punched out at her.

She took a stronger grasp of TJ's shoulder and shook much harder, laying her hand along TJ's face. "Wake up. It's Mare. Wake up."

TJ's eyes, seething with hatred, snapped open. Mare flinched and pulled her hand back, then, hesitating, she returned it to TJ's cheek. TJ's expression passed from hatred to confusion to anguish as Mare felt blood trickle from her nose. "My God, I've hurt you," TJ whispered.

"No, no, I'm fine. Don't worry. Can you move over and let me get back in bed?" TJ shifted to make room. Mare climbed back

in and scooted high enough that she could hold TJ's head against
her chest. She kissed TJ's hair and forehead, and caressed her
cheek. TJ put her arm across Mare's hip and up the side of her
body.

"Do you have these nightmares very often?"

"Mare, your nose is bleeding. What did I do to you?"

Mare wiped at her nose. She saw there was hardly any
blood. "I'm perfectly all right. I just kind of got smacked by a
wayward arm. But I'm okay. Now tell me about these
nightmares. You were begging someone to stop. Then you were
yelling and hollering. At your father?"

"Yeah." TJ's dry word puffed warm air against Mare's skin.
"That was the only place I would beg...in my dreams. I wouldn't
give him the satisfaction in real life. For a long time, I didn't yell,
either. When I was about fourteen, I started yelling at him and
threatening him. He only beat me harder and longer, but at least
I had that one small moment of satisfaction."

As Mare listened to these revelations, her breathing became
ragged.

"Mare?"

"Yes?"

TJ took several deep breaths, then spoke in what Mare
thought of as her "small" voice. TJ obviously found it
uncomfortable to ask even minor favors. "I don't want to talk
about my father. Can't we just go back to sleep? I'll be all right,
now."

"We can do that. But tomorrow, you're going to call your
counselor and set up an appointment for us to see him. Right?"

"Right. I like that you said, 'us.' " TJ moved just enough to
touch full lips to deep pink flesh. "Goodnight," she murmured
against it. "I love you."

The soft contact sent a warmly pleasant flush through Mare,
and she tightened her arms and rested her chin against TJ's head.
"Goodnight, my love."

DAWN'S RAYS STOLE quietly in through the window,
spread silently across the floor, and crept upwards, bringing
light to the entire room.

TJ lay without moving, her head still resting where she had
pillowed it during the night's interrupted sleep, her lips a hair's-
breadth away from a tempting morsel. She forced herself to
ignore temptation and relished the simple act of waking with her
love beside her. She wished she had the guts to ask Mare to move
in with her, but wasn't sure she could handle Mare saying no.

"What's that serious look for?" Mare's still sleepy voice rumbled against TJ's ear.

"Aha, you're awake!"

Mare reached her arms above her head and stretched, putting the object of TJ's temptation in motion. TJ's will power evaporated and her mouth swooped down, accomplishing its aim.

"TJ!" Mare grabbed TJ's head and shook it. "Let go!" By the second shake, she could see she was helping TJ, not dissuading her, and she dropped her arms in surrender.

TJ put her hands to good use, and Mare's voice sounded breathless. "Don't you think we're being a trifle decadent, here?" Without releasing the hold her mouth had, TJ nodded up and down vigorously, and Mare got the giggles. Starting to giggle, too, TJ let go and the two women collapsed beside each other, laughing out loud until they couldn't laugh any more.

"Aahhh," TJ said, wiping her eyes then grabbing her sides. "I haven't laughed that hard in years."

"Neither have I, not since college. And certainly not for such a delicious reason." Mare reached for a tissue from the bedside table and wiped TJ's eyes, then her own.

"Let's get up," TJ said. "I have a surprise to show you after breakfast."

"You know I don't like to be teased."

"Oh yeah? That's not how you acted yesterday."

"Well, that was different." Mare got out of bed and walked toward the bathroom. "There's a time and place for that kind of teasing. I'll run us a bath." She turned around with a gleam in her eyes. "Now there's a perfect pairing of sentences if I ever heard one."

TJ, thoroughly enjoying watching Mare's progress to the bathroom, shook her head. "And you called *me* decadent."

TJ AND MARE got to the kitchen in time to have breakfast with Erin and Paula. They took some kidding about hibernating out of season, then TJ brought up a few stories from Erin and Paula's past, and breakfast was a lively time.

At one point during the meal, TJ had whispered something to Erin and she had nodded. Mare's curiosity was at fever pitch, and her patience was being sorely tried. As soon as the other two had departed, she asked TJ what the surprise was.

TJ rubbed her chin and furrowed her brow as if in deep thought. "I don't know if it's time to show you yet."

"TJ, you're going to be in big, big trouble if you don't tell me what it is." Mare tried to look fierce, but it wasn't working. After a day and a half of a wall-to-wall love-in, every time she looked at TJ, she saw her gorgeous unclothed body. Which was absolutely marvelous, but also absolutely disconcerting. She wondered whether TJ was having the same problem. The thought made a blush move up Mare's cheeks. TJ ran her tongue from one side of her lips to the other and back again, a glint of pleasure showing in the depths of her eyes. *Oh, you betcha,* thought Mare.

"Come on," TJ said, "I can't tell you the surprise. I'll have to show you. Follow me." She took off out of the kitchen with Mare behind her.

On the far side of the living room was a double set of French doors, heavily curtained. TJ opened them and pushed them forward, then wheeled into the exposed room. She stopped and turned the chair toward Mare so she could watch her expression.

Mare's whole face lit as she walked to the Steinway grand piano sitting near the center of a room thirty feet long and thirty feet wide. The top of the piano had already been propped up, and the keyboard cover receded into the piano as she lifted it. Reverently, she ran her fingers along the keys, and their melodious tones filled her with exhilarating pleasure. She turned her awed gaze to TJ. "May I?"

"Sure." TJ barely got the word past the lump that suddenly formed in her throat. Mare looked like a kid in a candy factory.

Mare sat at the piano and, as was her usual custom, ran through some light pieces and exercises to limber her fingers. Then she played in earnest. This was the finest piano she had ever played, and she lost herself in enjoyment of it.

TJ closed her eyes and let herself float with the music. They sat for hours, transported together to an area of the mind that resonated with beautiful sounds, one leading with nimble fingers, the other following with sensual delight. Finally, coming back to earth, Mare halted.

TJ wheeled over next to her and met Mare's happy gaze. "How come you never told me you played the piano? That was magnificent." She could see they were going to have fun getting to know each other, in more ways than one.

Mare's face was suffused with peaceful energy. "Thank you. How beautiful this piano sounds. How did you know I played?"

"Paula heard it from Doc Hunt. Remember he said something to you about a broken arm or finger hurting your piano playing?"

"Yeah, now I remember. And Paula picked right up on that, huh?"

"She and Erin play guitar. Guess that struck a chord with her."

"Bad, TJ. Really bad."

"Sorry, I couldn't resist."

"Do you play an instrument?"

"Uh, no, I don't."

"What's the 'uh' for?"

"TJ sings." Paula, back from her journey to town, had been standing in the doorway for the past minute. "And don't let her tell you she doesn't. She has a gorgeous voice."

Mare's eyes widened, and she inclined her head toward TJ. "So, Miss Meridian, what would you like to sing for us? Hum a few bars, and I'll pick it up."

"Come on, ladies, give me a break. I'm just getting over a sore throat."

Mare looked at Paula, who shrugged and said, "She's right, I guess we have to hear her another time."

"But she called us ladies. Are we going to let her get away with that?"

"Oh no," Paula said. "How about when she does sing, she has to sing at least eight songs?"

"Sounds good to me. Think her throat should be more than okay in about a week?"

"Yeah, that sounds good. Same day next week, in the evening."

TJ's gaze was swinging back and forth from Paula to Mare as this conversation progressed. "You two are worse than a hanging judge. At least he makes a show of being fair before he condemns the prisoner."

"Yeah," Paula said, "but we aren't going to hang you."

Mare waved her hand. "I'm not making that promise. I haven't heard her sing yet."

"On that note," TJ said, "I think we better break for lunch."

Mare and Paula groaned, right on cue.

AFTER A SPIRITED lunch, Mare insisted that TJ call the counselor for an appointment. TJ sighed, but she followed through on her promise and an appointment was made for four days away.

That evening, Paula and Erin propped TJ in the corner of the couch before going to their own quarters, and Mare was lying there with her head in TJ's lap, luxuriating in her nearness. TJ played with her love's golden hair, wrapping and unwrapping it around her fingers, as she gazed into Mare's face, appreciating her beauty.

"I'll have to be going home, soon and get back to work." Mare's disappointment sounded in her words. "I'm sure Dr. DiNicola will be happy about that."

"How hard would it be to run your practice from somewhere besides your home?"

"Why would I want to do that? Everything I need is there."

"I was...sort of...that is..."

TJ's stumbling caused the light to dawn. "Are you suggesting that I work from here?"

"Well...only if you wanted to." Suddenly TJ was flustered. She had meant to wait a while before asking that question, and now here it had just popped out.

Mare sat up and edged as close as she could get, putting her shoulder against TJ's and taking hold of her right hand. "If I didn't have any other responsibilities, I wouldn't hesitate to take you up on that offer." She raised the strong hand and kissed it. "But I don't see how I can right now. Maybe when everything gets going and the economy improves, I can afford to get an assistant. Until that happens, I have to stay home." She held TJ's hand against her face. "No one's any sorrier about that than I am."

"I could lend you the money to hire someone."

"Thanks, but you know I can't do that. I want to pay my own way. My pride won't let me do it." That was the perfect choice of words to explain her decision. The head of Meridian Corporation did know all about pride, and she accepted that as a valid reason.

TJ reached her other hand up to Mare's cheek. "I want to kiss you, but you're going to have to come to me. If I lean over, I'll fall for you, literally."

Mare laughed at the little joke. She moved so that her body pinned TJ against the corner and made it possible for them to kiss. The push of one body against the other was like kicking embers into flame, a flame that was fed by the meeting of their mouths and the movements of their hands. Time ceased to exist.

Chapter
Fifteen

MARE HAD HEARD both Paula and Erin speak of TJ's dislike of the counseling sessions, but she hadn't understood what a profound effect the mere notion of going to one had. The days leading up to the session were a lesson that Mare wouldn't soon forget. TJ was a kaleidoscope of mood swings. One moment she was on a high, the next she was a brooding recluse. Even Mare had a hard time shaking her out of the depressed attitude. Paula and Erin assured her this was the normal build-up to TJ's meetings with Peter Tauper. Mare had to wonder whether her counselor wasn't a major part of TJ's reluctance to talk about her problems.

Mare suggested that she drive TJ to the session by herself, but Erin said that it probably would be better if she drove. Mare would be free to concentrate on TJ, especially if Peter actually got TJ to open up about her father. Though Mare was under the increasing impression that Peter wasn't going to get much enlightenment out of the resistant TJ, she agreed.

Mare spent the night at the ranch prior to the appointment. TJ was in a quiet mood, and they retired early, where they were content to lay in each other's arms.

The next morning, TJ sat and stared out of the window for most of the drive, giving one-word answers to questions as Mare and Erin tried to draw her into the conversation.

When they arrived, Erin jumped out of the Land Rover and lifted TJ's chair from the back. Mare clambered out and looked at the imposing building before her. An old, red brick structure four floors high, it had a small well-kept lawn in the front. Steps led up to the main entrance, and to the side was a ramp. The ramp, although advertised for use by the disabled, was quite steep, and Mare knew that even with TJ's incredible upper body strength, she would have difficulty negotiating it by herself. Mare disliked the place already, and she didn't even have to be there. If Peter was as bad as he sounded, no wonder TJ hated coming here. As Erin pushed the wheelchair around the Rover, Mare took TJ's hand and squeezed it.

"You okay?" she asked.

"Yeah. Come on, let's just get this over with." Erin, taking the hint, pushed TJ up the ramp to the building.

Mare's first impressions of Peter's waiting room were good. His secretary was a discreet distance from where his patients sat, allowing them reasonable privacy to talk, and the room was brightly decorated with colorful paintings hung on the walls. Mare especially liked the one of the sailboat on the ocean at sunset. It had a soothing quality to it. The chairs looked comfortable and were gracefully spaced. These touches, together with the varying plant life and the light from the undraped windows, made the room quite pleasant.

Peter's secretary was a white-haired woman, mid-fifties in age by Mare's guess. She greeted both TJ and Erin by name. She asked the usual pleasantries and informed Peter that they were waiting. TJ immediately wheeled herself over to the window that looked out the back of the building toward the nearby park.

The park was a field of grass and walkways hidden within stands of trees. The residents of the city were making the most of the warm and sunny day, playing ball and lying around the recreational areas.

Erin stayed by the desk, chatting with the secretary, while Mare went to keep TJ company. She slid into the seat nearest her and rested a hand on TJ's arm. Mare knew that anything she said wasn't going to ease the tension and trepidation TJ was feeling. She hoped her continued presence could do that.

A door opened, and a man with short, brown hair, a beard, and wire-rimmed spectacles entered from the inner room. Wearing a tan suit, white shirt, and brown tie, he looked to be about Paula's height. He glanced over toward Mare and TJ but made no greeting, walking immediately to Erin. They had a quiet conversation, and Mare saw Erin gesture across toward them.

Mare's hackles rose. From the description TJ had given during one of their midnight chats, she knew this was Peter. The fact that he hadn't even bothered to say anything to TJ but had headed straight to Erin spoke volumes about his attitude toward his patient. Mare patted TJ's arm, then stood and walked toward Erin and Peter.

"I don't really think that's appropriate," Peter was saying.

Erin looked over his shoulder and beckoned Mare forward. "Peter, I'd like you to meet Mare Gillespie."

"Doctor," Mare said as she shook his hand, which totally enveloped hers.

"Miss Gillespie."

Erin said, "I was just explaining to Peter why he might make more headway today with TJ if you were with her."

"And I was just explaining to Miss Scott why I thought that wouldn't be a good idea."

"And why would that be?" Mare asked.

"Because, Miss Gillespie—"

"Please call me Mare."

"Because, Mare, patients often feel inhibited when close friends or members of the family are included in this type of session. I'm trying to get TJ to open up about feelings that obviously cause her some distress."

"I see," Mare said. She took a moment to ponder his words. "And it makes no difference to you that I already know the details you're trying to get TJ to tell you? Or the fact that I wouldn't be here unless TJ had asked me to be?" Peter opened his mouth to reply, but Mare wouldn't let him speak, and her voice rose. "In fact, why don't we ask your patient exactly what she wants? It occurs to me, Doctor, that you would get a lot further in your sessions if TJ felt at ease with you, but she obviously doesn't. I can't say I blame her, seeing as you haven't even acknowledged her presence yet." Mare paused in her outburst, staring Peter in the face. Erin hid her mouth behind her hand to prevent Peter from seeing her amusement.

"There's no need to be confrontational, Miss Gillespie—"

"Mare," she said once again.

"Yes, Mare. As I said there's no need to be confrontational—"

"I don't believe I'm being confrontational at all. I'm merely stating the facts. Because, let me tell you, Peter, if I were the one sitting in that chair and the first thing you did when you came into the room was walk over and talk to my caregiver and not to me, I'd be a little put out. In fact I might even think that you were checking up on me, or maybe I'd be paranoid enough to think you actually had her watching me. Tell me, just how would that help me trust you?"

"Do you have any idea why Miss Meridian is in therapy?"

Mare opened her mouth to speak, but a familiar voice answered for her.

"Of course she does, Peter." All eyes turned to TJ as she wheeled herself across to them. "Why do you think I asked her along? Now, can we get on with this session, or should I leave this hellhole and go home?"

Peter hesitated, as though weighing the pros and cons of arguing the matter with TJ. "Okay, then. Let's go into the office." He swept his arm before him, indicating that Mare and TJ should precede him.

"I'll just wait here," Erin said.

Mare studied the room as she entered, noting Peter's impressive display of diplomas from multiple schools of medicine and psychology. With all his qualifications, she thought it a shame his manner with a patient wasn't as impressive.

TJ wheeled herself over near the window, and Peter sat behind the desk. The positioning of the players intrigued Mare. TJ was subtly telling everybody that she didn't want to be here, that the room felt as though it was imprisoning her, hence the window positioning. And Peter seemed intimidated by TJ. His sitting behind the desk immediately put a barrier between him and her. For someone supposed to be breaking down TJ's emotional barriers, putting a physical one in the way didn't seem too wise.

"So, TJ," Peter said, "how have you been since we last spoke?"

"Fine," she said, still looking out the window. Mare walked over to her and put a hand on her shoulder.

"Are you going to stop dreaming out the window and come join us?" Mare asked, gently reminding TJ that she was supposed to take an active part in the session, not just give one-word answers. TJ took off the brakes and wheeled away from the window, closer to Peter's desk. Mare took a seat nearby.

"Sorry," TJ said, shooting a quick glance at Mare. "I'm fine, thank you, Peter."

Peter looked back and forth between the two women. "Do you have anything in particular you'd like to discuss today?"

TJ remained silent until she heard Mare start to move behind her. She told herself to go on spit it out, knowing Mare was going to hit her between the eyes if she didn't. "Well," she said as she spared another look at Mare to gain support, "you've wanted to know about my father, so I guess we can start there today." TJ let her hand creep in Mare's direction, needing more than her gaze to bolster her courage. She felt the strong, yet gentle, squeeze as Mare grasped hold.

"Why, goodness, TJ. Yes, let's talk about your father. What do you want to tell me?"

The next hour and a half flew by for Mare as she sat through the ordeal of TJ telling Peter what her father had done to her. Mare's perception of Peter changed over the session. It wasn't that he wasn't good at his job; he just had no idea how to handle TJ. He obviously thought of her as an emotionally vulnerable and fragile person. While in some ways that was true, TJ had a wellspring of strength that Peter ought to be tapping. TJ reacted badly to anybody treating her as fragile.

Now that he had something to work with, though, he wasn't letting TJ get away with skirting around the issues of her father. Although TJ didn't particularly like that he wouldn't let her hide, neither did she try to be obstructive. Throughout the session, Mare felt TJ's hold on her emotions waver. The tense grip on Mare's hand didn't loosen at all. Mare kept her eyes on TJ's face so that whenever TJ looked over, she saw love and support looking back.

For TJ, the session was the longest she'd ever been in. Even while in the hospital and physically unable to get away from the sessions, she had been able to tune them out of her mind. Now, though, with Mare by her side, she couldn't leave the office when things started to hurt, and Mare's constant grip on her hand kept her mind grounded in reality.

She spoke of life in the Meridian household and the constant battle to be true to herself in the midst of her father's abuse. She spoke about things that she hadn't wanted to remember. She told of the times she had ended up in her father's doctor's office, being patched up from the vicious beatings; of the concerned look in the doctor's eyes, while refusing to report her father; of the time she had been hit so hard that he'd broken her arm.

When the hospital inquired how it happened, her mother told them she fell off her horse. The strange looks and whispers of the nursing staff told a different story, but this was the all-powerful Tom Meridian they were talking about. He wouldn't beat his daughter, would he?

When the constant onslaught of memories weakened TJ's emotional resolve, Mare's steady presence helped her continue.

Mare saw that Peter's whole demeanor toward TJ changed. He sat forward in the chair, asked appropriate questions, and very patiently listened to all she had to say. When she reached a stopping point and looked seriously done in, he said, "TJ, you've accomplished some excellent work today. I had a hunch you were holding something back, but I had no idea of the magnitude. I'll be honest with you. I thought you were just a rich woman unable to cope with your disability. But I see I completely misjudged your situation. To suffer that abuse and to lose the one person in your life who showed you unconditional love had to have been excruciatingly painful. Thank you for sharing it with me."

Mare had tears in her eyes from all she'd heard, and she could tell that TJ was so choked up she was about to lose it. She looked at her watch and saw that TJ and Peter had been talking well over the standard fifty-five minutes.

Peter looked at his watch, too. "Our time's up for today. I look forward to talking about this with you further during our next session. We may have a long road ahead of us, but at least now we're headed in the right direction."

With an abrupt nod, TJ wheeled her chair around and headed for the door. Mare had to leap out of her seat to catch up with her. She glanced back once and saw that Peter still sat behind his big wooden desk, looking thunderstruck.

For the drive home, TJ insisted on riding in the back with Mare. With her legs stretched out along the back seat and her body reclining in Mare's embrace, she felt safe after pouring out her innermost secrets. Mare sat quietly, accepting TJ's need for silence, concentrating on TJ's need for comfort.

MARE HAD JUST dropped her bag in its nook in the kitchen when the phone rang. She grabbed it and spouted her usual greeting. "Doctor Gillespie." The caller's slight hesitation suggested at once who it was, and warmth spread through her in anticipation.

"Hi, Mare. Are you going to be home in the next half hour?" TJ's voice oozed into Mare's body like oil into a wick, ready to be set aflame.

"For you, anytime, anywhere."

"Sure, tell me that sometime when you have a sick cow to take care of." TJ paused. "I want to stop by. I have some information about your father."

Mare came quickly back to earth. "What? Have they found him? Who is he? Where is he?"

"Yes, we found him. I'll tell you all about it as soon as I get there."

"TJ! I don't have a lot of patience." The low laugh sent a shiver of yearning through Mare.

"I know, my love, but I don't want to give it to you in bits and pieces over the phone. I'll be right over as fast as I can."

"Okay, but hurry, please?"

"You know I will."

After she hung up, Mare got a ready-made salad and a soda from the fridge and had a quick supper, too fidgety to even taste what she ate. They found her father!

Afterwards, a need to find some respite from her jangling nerves led her to the piano. She ran through a few light pieces, then launched into more robust compositions. Engrossed in her music, she didn't hear the door opening or wheels coming through the kitchen.

Mare finished the piece she was playing and stopped. Applause from behind startled her, and she swiveled around rapidly on the piano seat. TJ and Erin were clapping vigorously. Mare felt herself blush. "Thanks." She walked over to TJ and kissed her welcoming lips. "Come on into the kitchen. What would you like to drink? Soda, lemonade, beer?"

"Beer would be great," TJ said.

"Make that two." Erin followed TJ and Mare into the kitchen.

"TJ," Mare said, "tell me what you've heard about my father before I have a nervous breakdown." While she talked, she took three beers from the fridge, opened them and handed them around. She pulled a chair out of the way so TJ could wheel close to the table. Then she sat and scooted up next to TJ as Erin took a seat across from them.

TJ pulled a manila envelope from the pocket on the side of the wheelchair and laid it in front of Mare. "Take a look."

With trembling hands, Mare emptied the contents of the envelope onto the table. She grabbed the picture lying on top and stared at it for several long moments. It was a professional portrait of a distinguished looking, sandy-haired man with emerald-green eyes exactly like Mare's. Even the shape of his face was the same as hers except the man's was longer.

"He looks like me. I mean, I look like him. I looked at every man in that graduating class, and I didn't see him." Mare ran her fingers over the picture as though she could feel the face whose paper replica she touched. "Why couldn't I find him?"

"Your mother didn't lie to you, but she didn't tell you the whole truth, either. Your father and mother didn't go to the same college. My people ran through the men at her college, then through those at every college within fifty miles of it, and finally found him."

As she moved the picture off to the side, Mare's eyes fell on the name at the top of the first paper beneath it. "Michael Thomas Gillis, MD. My father." Mare gazed up at TJ through the tears that trickled down her cheeks. "He's a doctor! And look at his name—same initials as mine and almost the same last name. I guess Mother really did love him."

While Mare made her way through the papers and pictures, Erin finished her beer, got up, and whispered something into TJ's ear. She picked up a box of tissues from a counter and brought them to Mare, taking several out and handing them to her before setting the box within easy reach. Erin bent down and kissed her on the cheek. "I'm going home for a while. I'll stop back about ten o'clock for TJ. I'm very happy for you, Mare. I hope things work out well for you and your father." She touched Mare's shoulder. "Don't get up. I'll show myself out."

"Thanks, Erin." Mare wiped her tears and went back to examining the papers.

The investigators had taken numerous photos of the doctor, his office, his home, even of him entering and leaving the hospital where he practiced. TJ looked on with affection as Mare's expressive face lit with excitement at every new picture she saw.

She picked up the sheaf of papers and made an attempt to read them but couldn't. She turned toward the gaze watching her so tenderly. "I'm too nervous. Would you read it to me, please?" She placed the papers in the extended hand, sat back, and listened to TJ's warm voice fill her in on her father's life history.

TJ read through Dr. Gillis's medical school attendance, internship, and specialization. As she narrated the report on the doctor's specialization, three words jumped out at her. They had startled her at her first reading of the report, and she still stumbled over them. "Dr. Gillis specializes in neurosurgery and has won many awards. He is a recognized authority in the field of...spi—spinal cord injury."

Mare leaned forward to look into TJ's face. "Did you say spinal cord injury?"

"Yes. Kind of eerie, isn't it?" Her wide-eyed look swept to meet Mare's inquiring gaze. "SCI. Your father is a recognized authority in the field of spinal cord injury."

"My gosh, I'm getting goose bumps."

"Yeah, I did, too."

They sat staring at each other for a moment, then Mare patted TJ's arm. "Keep reading, okay? I want to hear everything there is to hear. We can follow up on that later."

TJ finished the career investigation notes and proceeded to the personal history. Mare's father had made his career his life. He had never married. He lived in a spacious, well-appointed house in an elite area bordering Dorburton Lakes, just outside Springerly, the city of his practice.

"Springerly's only a couple hours' drive from here." Mare's face and voice turned wistful. "All these years, my father's been just a couple of hours away."

Mare's expression tore at TJ's heart. "But you've found him now. You know what they say, 'Better late than never.' " Then she ran a finger along a line of text. "Dorburton Lakes. He must be wealthy."

Mare thought about that for all of three seconds. "Lucky me."

"And listen to this." TJ handed her a flyer as she continued to read aloud. "A student of classical music, Dr. Gillis gives semi-annual piano recitals on behalf of SCI patients who need financial assistance."

Mare beamed as she looked up from the flyer. "And his next recital is only a couple of days away. I have to go. Just think, he's a doctor, he plays the piano, and we look just alike. I can hardly believe it."

Suddenly needing advice, she said, "Now what do I do? Do you think he would want to know he has a daughter?"

TJ's sweet smile wrapped itself around Mare's heart. "I guarantee that once he knows you, he'll love you. But I don't think you should drop in on him unannounced. It's safer not to presume anything." Picking up the loose papers, TJ jogged them together, laid them on top of the envelope they came in, and placed the pictures on top of them. "I think going to the recital might help you be more comfortable with the idea of meeting him. But I think he needs that chance, too. How about if I talk with him, show him a report just like this one that explains the highlights of your background and the situation, and let him decide if he wants to meet you?"

Mare's face was a study in serious concern. "Could you do that before the recital? Then maybe we could meet soon afterwards."

"Do you really think I should approach him right now? This will be an emotional moment. It has to be. That might disturb his recital."

"Oh no. Music flows from emotion. The stronger the musician's feelings, the stronger the performance."

"All right, you're the expert. I'll try to set up a meeting as soon as possible. My team has already gathered information on you."

"You've had people checking up on me?" Mare's face darkened. She wasn't entirely comfortable with that idea.

TJ looked away, abashed. "It was before you even set foot on the ranch. Before I knew you. I mean, you were just a name to me. We knew the people in Meridianville wouldn't be happy to see me here, but I also needed to know if you were a reputable vet." She glanced sideways at Mare. "Look, I told you I'm not an especially trusting person, okay?"

Mare's expression slowly lightened, and she poked TJ's side. "Just don't ever do it again."

TJ threw a hand down to protect her ribs. "But the report didn't tell me half what I've learned through personal contact." Then she leered. "Especially how emotion strengthens a musician's performance."

Mollified, Mare wrinkled her nose. "Very funny."

TJ looked at her watch. "Hey, it's 9:50, Erin will be here in about ten minutes. Do you want to play?"

"Umm. I thought you'd never ask." In one continuous motion, Mare swung around, pulled the wheelchair arm out of the way, reached under TJ's shirt, and zeroed in on her intended objective.

TJ gasped, startled by her body's unhesitating response. "I meant the piano."

Transferring to a seat on TJ's lap, Mare growled in pleasure at her lover's reaction. "Quiet, woman, we only have nine more minutes." A moist mouth smothered TJ's laugh.

Chapter
Sixteen

THE NURSE CAME through the waiting room door, holding it open with one hand. "TJ Meridian?"

TJ laid down the magazine she had been leafing through and steered the electric wheelchair through the doorway. The nurse went ahead of her and held open an office door. "Dr. Gillis will be with you soon. Please make yourself comfortable."

Did every office in the world have buff walls? TJ wondered. But the yellow birch furniture, gold rug, and green upholstery gave the pleasant room a light warmth. Sunny prints of several master works dotted the walls, balancing the black-and-white austerity of the framed diplomas and awards.

Within minutes, the doctor entered the room. He walked over to TJ and shook her hand. "Miss Meridian, how are you? What a pleasure to meet the head of Meridian Corporation." TJ had faxed her credentials ahead, requesting that they be verified. She hoped to do away with any suspicions that her news wasn't genuine.

"I'm just fine, Doctor." TJ laid a manila envelope on the desk as Dr. Gillis moved behind it and sat down.

"Your message intrigued me. I do remember Jane Arnold, very well. I'm sorry to hear that she died last year. You said you had a letter from her that you wished to give me?"

"Actually, I have a copy of a letter from her. It's not addressed to you, but when you read it, you'll understand why I've brought it to you." TJ handed him the copy and watched as he read it.

At first he looked puzzled. Then his face went slack, and his jaw dropped. When he finished, he set the letter on the desk, his eyes still down and his breathing rapid. After a minute, he looked up at TJ, and his eyes showed the struggle he was having to comprehend what he had just read. "I recognize Jane's handwriting," he said in a bewildered tone. "I still have her letters to me." Then his voice firmed. "We had a daughter? Jane and I had a daughter?"

"Yes," TJ said.

Dr. Gillis sat there thinking. Suddenly, he asked, "Is it — are you — ?"

"No, not me," TJ said in a soft voice. She reached into the envelope, drew out its contents, and laid them in front of him. Mare's picture was on top.

"My God, there's no doubt she's my daughter. She looks just like me." He dropped his trembling fingers to the portrait and ran them over its surface, just as his daughter had done to his. "But she's beautiful."

TJ managed to get one word out. "Perfectly."

"Where is she? Can I see her? Can we meet? What's her name? Where does she live?"

TJ had a terrible time keeping a straight face. He even talked like Mare. "We'll make arrangements for you to meet. I've given you the answers to most of your other questions in the papers you have there, under the picture."

He pulled out the papers and read the name aloud. "Mary Theresa Gillespie." His voice broke as he made the same discovery Mare had made. "Same initials — almost the same last name." He put his head down against his hand. "Jane, Jane, Jane." His gaze lifted to meet TJ's sympathetic one. "She always was independent. An extraordinary woman. And I know she meant well, but she cheated both of us out of a lifetime together." Then he brightened. "But she left me a daughter. What's she like? Do you know her well?"

TJ finally let her smile break across her face. "Yes, I know her very well. She's an extraordinary woman, too, and a special favorite of mine. You'll love her. We all do."

His eyes lit up as he read further. "She's a veterinarian. A doctor, too. And she plays the piano. Our similarities are amazing."

They sat in silence for a while. Finally, Dr. Gillis said, "When can I meet her?"

"Perhaps you'll need some time to think about everything you've just learned. Maybe you want to investigate further." TJ knew this kind of news could be earthshaking to Dr. Gillis. He deserved some time to adjust. But it turned out he was just as impulsive as Mare could be.

"No. As your faxed information suggested, I had your credentials checked, and I don't see any reason to doubt what you've shown me. I want to meet my daughter as soon as possible."

"You have a concert tomorrow, right?"

"Yes."

"How about if she comes to the concert and checks you out, so to speak. Maybe, if she's willing, you could meet together after the concert."

"That sounds perfect. How many will be in your party?"

"Four of us. I have two friends who accompany me to public functions."

"I have a townhouse directly across from the hall. After the concert, a reception is being held there for a few of my friends. Please bring your whole party, and we'll have a chance to meet with less pressure on both of us. Having her friends around will, I hope, make her feel more comfortable."

"That's very thoughtful. I know Mare will appreciate it."

"Mare? Is that what she's called? I'll have to remember that."

"I'll say good-bye, Doctor. We'll see you tomorrow evening at the recital."

Dr. Gillis came around the end of the desk and took TJ's hand in both of his. Instead of shaking it, he raised it to his lips and kissed it. "Thank you, Miss Meridian. You've brought me the happiest news I've ever had."

The nurse appeared, summoned by a silent bell. "Nurse Hansen, please show Miss Meridian out. Good-bye."

"Good-bye, Doctor."

The door closed and Michael Gillis sat again at his desk. Thoughts of Jane wandered through his mind. The only woman he had ever loved. No one had been able to chase Jane's memory from his heart. Now he found out, too late, that she left him because she loved him. The tears he had managed to stifle during the meeting now ran down his cheeks, unchecked.

TJ DECIDED TO lay on the grand treatment for the occasion of attending Doctor Gillis's recital. A Meridian limousine took them from the ranch to the nearest airport. She provided one of the company helicopters to fly all four women to Springerly and directed the pilot to wait to take them home. A folding wheelchair, carried at all times by the helicopter, ferried TJ between vehicles. From the airfield near Springerly, a second Meridian limousine took them to the concert hall where TJ had reserved a box. The light shining from Mare's face when she squeezed TJ's hand in gratitude made every gesture worthwhile.

Paula had arranged for two Meridian employees to be waiting at the concert hall with an electric wheelchair. As the limousine approached their destination, the driver called ahead to alert them to TJ's imminent arrival.

The women being assisted from the limousine drew close attention from bystanders waiting behind police barricades to watch the cream of society gather. Each attractive in her own right, together the four women made an impressive array. Necks craned to see as first Paula, wearing a forest green gown, then Erin, in shimmering burgundy, emerged, followed by Mare, resplendent in antique gold. The chair was wheeled to the door of the limo, and all eyes watched as the two attendants assisted the last occupant from the limo into the chair. TJ was dressed in a cocktail length sheath, with the bottom two thirds of the material black and the top third a blue that matched her eyes. Thin, black, spaghetti straps held the top, while the neckline plunged to a diamond shaped opening, tied together above her breasts with a thin, black string that matched the straps.

Once settled in the chair, TJ raised her gaze to Mare. She knew Mare was so excited at the prospect of seeing and meeting her father that she could barely stand still, so she steered the chair right up to her. "Ready?"

"As ready as I'll ever be." Paula and Erin moved in behind them, and they entered the hall and were escorted to the box. All the extra chairs had been removed to make access easier for TJ so she wheeled right up to the rail. The others sat and looked out over the assembly.

Mare marveled at the perfect view from the box, which slightly overhung one end of the stage. "How were you able to get this box on such short notice? These have to be the best seats in the hall."

"I had Erin check out the person who had it, and she found out he's a local horse breeder. I offered to share our box at the Kentucky Derby with him and his guests, in return for letting me rent this one from him. He jumped at the chance, and here we are."

"I'll never get used to how easily you seem to make things happen. Or how you think of every tiny detail." Just as she finished speaking, an usher arrived and handed her a corsage of white orchids. Mare looked from the flowers to TJ.

"Uh-uh, that's not my doing. Read the card."

Mare pulled out the card from the envelope that rested on the florist box. "To my dearest daughter from your fa—" Mare stopped as her breath caught. She bit down on her lip and tried to blink back tears, but it was a losing battle.

Erin reached in her bag and handed her some tissues. She heard a suspicious sniff from Paula and gave her several.

TJ touched Mare's arm and tried to chuckle. "Hey, cut that out, you'll ruin your makeup." Seeing TJ's brimming eyes, Erin passed tissues to her, too. Then she took one and daubed her own eyes.

Erin reached for the florist box. "Here, Mare, let me pin this on for you." The greenery that nestled against the orchids was the perfect touch, forming a beautiful border against the antique gold gown and deepening the color in Mare's eyes.

Mare sniffled. "Boy, we sure look like a happy group." She jumped as the lights dimmed, then came back up. A nervous wreck, she grabbed the hand lying on her arm and squeezed it with her fingers.

TJ watched every movement of Mare's face as the lights dimmed again. The stage lights came up, and Dr. Gillis walked out for his bow. Dressed in a long-tailed tuxedo, he looked handsome and youthful. He walked to the piano and just before he sat down, he looked up at their box, nodded his head, and smiled. Had the size of their hands been reversed, TJ would have been suffering some broken bones. She hoped Mare's father was the decent man he seemed to be. If not, he'd answer to TJ. Mare would never go through what she'd gone through.

The music filled their minds and hearts as it filled the hall. Mare couldn't take her eyes from her father. She had an irrational feeling that if she looked away he would disappear.

Because Mare held her hand, TJ found herself in an awkward position. She tried to stay still to avoid interrupting Mare's concentration, but finally, just at intermission, a cramping shoulder forced her to move. Mare suddenly noticed she was crushing TJ's hand.

She raised the strong hand to her lips for a quick kiss and whispered, "I'm so sorry. I didn't mean to hurt you."

"I'll probably never write again with that hand, but it was worth it." TJ's look, filled with love, made Mare's heart flip-flop.

"Oh, TJ, he's wonderful, isn't he?"

"Yes, he is. Are you ready to meet him?"

"Oh yes. I can't wait. And I can't thank you enough for finding him for me." How was she the lucky one? What did TJ see in her that she fell in love with? Someday, Mare would have to ask her that.

"I'm just thrilled for you that my people were able to find him. If he had changed his name and moved away, like your mother did, it would have been a lot tougher."

"Poor Mother. She had too much pride for her own good." Mare looked sad for a moment, but then she shook it off. She gave a tug to the hand she still held. "Sort of like you, sometimes."

"Me?" TJ said. "Never. And you can stop that snorting,

Paula. You're supposed to act like a lady tonight."

Now Erin snorted and all four women laughed.

The lights dimmed again and the hall hushed as Mare's father reentered the stage to complete his performance — and to bring him closer to meeting his daughter.

NUMEROUS QUIET CONVERSATIONS spread a blanket of warmth through the reception. TJ tried to divert Mare's nervous impatience with small talk. "This has a good feel to it. The people seem happy and friendly." Again, Mare had latched onto a hand, but this time she stroked it rather than squeezed.

"Yes, yes. I wonder what's taking him so long?"

"I'm sure he had some backstage visitors. He'll be here soon. Have you thought about what you're going to do when he comes through the door?"

Erin and Paula were choosing drinks and hors d'oeuvres from a series of trays brought around by white-jacketed servers. They handed drinks to TJ and Mare.

"I'm not sure what to do," Mare said. "Any suggestions?" She took a reflex sip, totally unaware of what was in the glass.

"Maybe wait here and let him come to us. You wouldn't want to upset his usual routine. You think?"

Mare sighed. "You're right. I just want to run to him and throw my arms around him. But I know that isn't quite the thing to do."

TJ took a hefty drink from the glass she held in her free hand, and her eyes swiftly flashed up to Paula's. Paula had already tasted hers, and she grinned at TJ's surprised face. "Double Manhattan."

"Whew!" TJ said. "It's a wonder the cherry isn't dried up. Don't hand me anymore, even if I beg you, okay?"

"Darn, guess I'll have to drink your share." A sharp look from Erin brought a frown of mock disappointment. "You weren't supposed to hear that."

Erin was just about to answer, when a round of applause signaled the entrance of their host, and everyone turned toward the doorway.

Dr. Gillis was the epitome of charm and graciousness as he made his way through his admirers, gathering their congratulations and accolades. Although his eyes hadn't made an obvious search for them, TJ saw that he circled around their group, leaving them for last.

Finally, he arrived. Although he walked to TJ and took her free hand, his eyes immediately went to Mare. "Miss Meridian, welcome."

TJ smiled brilliantly, tilted her head to see Mare's face, and said, "Dr. Gillis, may I present Erin Scott, Paula Tanner, and...Dr. Mare Gillespie?"

Dr. Gillis smiled at Erin and Paula as he shook their hands and welcomed them. Then he grasped Mare's hand in both of his, and the two stood there looking into each other's eyes. Mare tried to talk, but tears choked her throat. Her father's eyes filled, too, and he gently drew Mare into his arms. The two stood embracing and crying quietly.

At last they parted, and Erin handed them tissues from her never-ending supply. "Hello, Mare." Michael Gillis spoke his first words to his daughter.

Mare's eyes brimmed again. "May I call you Dad?"

No one would have believed that Michael's face could light up any more than it already had, but somehow it managed to. "I'd be absolutely thrilled to have you call me Dad." He turned to include the other women in his look. "Why don't we sit on the couch and chairs over in that corner and chat?"

"Why don't you and Mare go ahead, Doctor?" TJ said. "You must have a lot to talk about, and we can mingle for a while."

Mare and Dr. Gillis excused themselves and went to the corner couch. They were laughing and talking even before they reached it.

Erin nudged Paula and tilted her head toward TJ. They watched TJ's rapt expression as her eyes followed Mare and her father. After a few moments, she turned and looked up at her two observers. "What?" An eyebrow crooked up.

"We were just enjoying one of the most beautiful faces in the world," Erin said.

TJ's eyes swept to Mare and back up to Erin. "She is beautiful, isn't she?"

"She is, TJ, but Erin meant you." Paula tapped TJ's creamy shoulder.

TJ's eyes widened in surprise, then a blush rose from her neck up over her cheeks. "Cut it out, you two. Are you looking for a raise or something?" she said, taunting them in friendly retaliation for embarrassing her. "Paula, go get us a couple more Manhattans, will you?"

"Just one more," Erin said.

Paula put on her best aggrieved look. "Why? We're not driving."

"TJ is."

The co-conspirators looked at each other in confusion. In a moment, they realized that Erin was teasing about TJ driving the wheelchair. "Erin," said TJ, "this is one time when I'll be glad to let you push me around...in the wheelchair, that is. Go for the Manhattans, Paula."

Erin rolled her eyes, but waved at Paula's hesitation. "Go ahead. I'll be designated driver for her."

The evening had turned out even better than TJ dared hope. Her heart swelled with happiness for Mare and for her own part in bringing her lover such delirious joy. One for the Memories scrapbook.

ALL THE WAY home, first in the limousine, then the helicopter, and lastly in the limo that met them at the airport and transported them to the ranch, Mare talked. Her meeting with her father had been a huge moment in her life, and she was totally wound up over it. TJ, Erin, and Paula happily let her retell, several times over, every word, every nuance of the conversation she had with Dr. Gillis. Her nervous energy was finally winding down as they reached the ranch and piled out of the car.

The driver retrieved TJ's lightweight wheelchair from the porch, brought it to the car, and helped her into it. She said, "I can take it from here, Jeff. Thanks for your help."

"My pleasure, Miss Meridian. Just call whenever you need me again." Jeff touched his forehead in an abbreviated salute, climbed back into the car, and drove away.

They made their way into the house. Paula hugged TJ and kissed her cheek. "I don't know about you gals, but I'm dying to get out of this gown and hit the shower. It's been a wonderful, but tiring night. Thanks, TJ. Happy for you, Mare." Paula gave Mare's shoulders a quick squeeze.

"Yeah, TJ," Erin said. "Thanks. Everything was lovely. Glad things worked out well for you and your father, Mare." Erin gave each of them a hug and a kiss, and she and Paula went upstairs to prepare for bed.

When Mare had come to the ranch earlier in the day to dress for her momentous meeting, she had brought an overnight bag with clean clothes. Now she followed TJ into her bedroom and lifted the bag onto the bed. She unzipped the bag and pulled out a pale green garment.

"What's that?" TJ tilted her head sideways and propped it on her hand.

"I thought I'd slip this on after my shower." Mare shook out the short nightgown. "At least for a while."

TJ reached to the console next to her bed and turned a

rheostat that dimmed the lights. "Why don't you put it on now, then help me undress? Forget the shower." TJ's voice had dropped into the seductive lower register that turned Mare's willpower to marshmallow fluff.

Mare undressed somewhat self-consciously, feeling TJ's eyes on her every movement. She thrust her arms and head into the satiny green chemise and wriggled her body to settle it past her hips. Finally, she mustered the courage to look up and was astounded by the sweet look of adoration spread across TJ's stunning face. In five swift steps, she reached the chair and gently melted her lips against the mouth that opened to greet her arrival.

Pulling slowly from the kiss, Mare moved the chair arm out of the way and swung onto TJ's lap. Two long arms embraced her. "I've had a wonderful reunion with my father, and it's all because of you. I'll never be able to thank you enough."

"I was thrilled to do it. You know that."

"I know, and that made it even better."

Mare's face turned stern and her words became more forceful. "But there is one thing that, no matter how excited I was at meeting my dad, I'll never forgive you for."

TJ looked dumfounded. "What?"

"This." Mare's forefinger bounced on the black string bow that held the front of TJ's gown together. "Every time I looked your way, this pesky black bow rose and fell signaling, 'Untie me. Untie me.' Like it was holding a couple of prisoners, begging for release. Drove me crazy!"

A delicious smile transformed TJ's concerned features. "Well, are you going to listen to it, or not?"

Mare tugged on the bow playfully for a few moments, pretending to untie it, but only rolling it between her fingers. "I suppose I should shower first." Now she had turned the tables and was driving TJ crazy with anticipation.

"You haven't done any heavy work. Will you forget the damn shower! Besides," TJ said, her tone dipping again, "I want to smell you and taste you and—" A gasp cut off her words as Mare pulled the bow's string and lifted one of the freed prisoners to meet her descending mouth.

THE NEXT MORNING, the four women spent breakfast time rehashing the musical event of the previous evening.

"Mare," Erin said, "the recital was a great experience. Your father plays beautifully." She collected the empty cereal bowls and stacked them in the dishwasher.

"You should hear Mare. She's pretty good, too." Paula cleared the cereal boxes, milk, and sugar as Erin finished putting the cups and utensils in the racks.

"I did hear her, when I dropped TJ off the other day. You're outstanding, Mare. Like father, like daughter."

The praise heightened the color on Mare's fair cheeks. "It takes years to play as well as my father does." She repeated the two words whose novelty awed her. "My father." The others smiled at how her face beamed.

"When did you say you'll see him again?" TJ asked. Mare had told the women every detail of their conversation, but TJ wanted to watch her say it again.

"He invited me for a late dinner this coming Friday, and I'm to stay over and we'll spend Saturday together. We want to see if we can set up some sort of regular visiting schedule." Her eyes, which had brightened as she spoke, now dimmed a shade. She put her hand on TJ's arm. "That's going to cut into our time together."

TJ looked down at Mare's hand, reached her own hand over, and patted it. Then her eyes swept up and grabbed Mare's heart. "Nothing's ever easy, is it?"

"Maybe," Erin said, "we could have you and your father over here a few times for dinner. That way you all get to visit with each other, and maybe you could stay awhile after he leaves." For confirmation, Erin looked at TJ who nodded with enthusiasm.

"That sounds like a good plan," Mare said. "By the way, Paula, don't we have a singing date tomorrow night?"

"Sure do." Paula turned to Erin who had missed the by-play the previous week about TJ's singing. "Mare's coming over, and TJ's going to sing. Eight songs."

When Erin saw TJ roll her eyes, she figured the decision had been made for her, but TJ didn't deny that she would sing. "Wonderful! You haven't sung for quite a while. I miss hearing you."

"Show up in the music room at six o'clock. That's performance time." Mare squeezed TJ's arm and got up. "Well, folks, I have to get to work. I'll see you tonight. Thanks for breakfast."

Mare leaned down and kissed TJ's waiting lips. "Umm. Thank you, too." TJ winked at her and Mare left.

"You okay, TJ?" Erin had noticed that TJ was quieter than usual.

"It has dawned on me that Mare's finding her father may have created a monster."

"What's that supposed to mean?" Erin said, and Paula stopped wiping the counter to turn and listen.

"You just heard one problem. Mare has only so much free time, so that means we won't see each other as often."

"But there's something else?"

"Yeah." TJ's anxiety showed as her gaze went from Erin to Paula and back. "What if her father is opposed to our loving each other?"

A look of consternation passed between Paula and Erin, then their eyes came back to TJ's vulnerable expression as she said, "Do you think she would choose me over her newfound father?"

Erin pulled a chair out and sat down. "Look, TJ. Granted, Paula and I have been very fortunate that both our families accepted us as lovers. And I know a lot of families have made life miserable for their gay children. But let's not borrow trouble, okay? Her father's a doctor, a famous specialist who's been all over the world. He's probably a lot more tolerant than you're giving him credit for."

Paula walked over to stand in front of TJ and planted her hands on her hips. "Plus, I don't think you're giving Mare enough credit for her own strength of character. I've seen her face when she looks at you and you're not watching. She's in love with you, body, soul, heart, thought, emotions, whatever. You name it, she's offering it to you. So instead of worrying yourself sick over something that might never happen, suck in your gut and show some gratitude. The woman is yours."

Paula and Erin watched a bevy of emotions cross the strong-jawed face until one overpowered the others — respect. She reached her hand out to shake Paula's, then pulled her close and kissed her firmly on the lips. "Thank you." One side of her mouth tilted up when she saw a flush cross Paula's startled features.

TJ turned to Erin who was trying to smother her grin. She wound her fingers in tight blonde curls, pulled her down, and kissed her lips, too. "And thank you." Swinging the wheelchair around, TJ left the kitchen.

Ignoring her self-consciousness at the kiss, Erin got up and put her arm around Paula's waist. "I am so proud of you, Paulie. You said exactly the right thing."

"Well, I'm more than just a pretty face, you know." Paula basked in the praise. "Hey, Erin."

"Yeah?"

"Have you ever wondered what it would be like to kiss TJ's gorgeous lips?"

"Maybe. Is this a trick question?"

"No, just curious. I've wondered myself sometimes."

"And what's your verdict?"

Paula slipped one arm over Erin's and the other around her waist, bringing her close. "It was very nice, but her lips don't belong to me. I think I'll stick with the ones that do." She dipped her head and met Erin's eager mouth with her own.

"Hmm. Me, too." The women parted and scrambled out the door, tickling each other.

Chapter
Seventeen

MARE'S ONGOING VISITS with her father had brought the two to the closeness that both yearned for. They had so many similar tastes that they quickly were surrounded with a natural comfort zone. Mare's narration of her life history continued with each visit as her father added bits and pieces of his own, intertwining segments of his and Jane's time together.

Unfortunately, TJ had proved prophetic in her assessment of Mare's limited free time. Because of the two-hour driving time each way, Mare's visits to the townhouse at Springerly or the main house at Dorburton Lakes generally extended through the weekend. Dr. DiNicola covered her practice, making this possible.

Ironically, Mare's extra duties related to the Meridian ranch's start-up made free time even scarcer. Mare rushed so much to keep on top of those duties and her practice's usual responsibilities that lunch together was usually hurried. In addition, a late call to a sick animal's side had forced a last-minute postponement of TJ's evening of singing, stealing away that chance for another night together.

Any physical closeness beyond hugging and kissing reached a point of non-existence while Mare concentrated on becoming acquainted with her father. She and TJ had talked it over and decided not to reveal their relationship until he got to know both of them better.

Paula and Erin tiptoed around TJ's moodiness, understanding the cause of it, but unable to do anything but sympathize. Contrary to past behavior, though, TJ's moods didn't deteriorate into nastiness, a welcome change they noted and attributed to Mare's influence

They all breathed a combined sigh of relief when, at last, Dr. Gillis's schedule enabled him to accept the standing invitation for dinner at the ranch. If nothing else, TJ would have Mare near for the evening, which might help to soften the edge of her frustration.

On the phone that afternoon, Mare promised to stay overnight if she could think of a suitable excuse to her father as to why he should follow her to the ranch in his own car. Waiting in the living room for their arrival, TJ shone like the sun when Erin informed her they had just pulled in with two separate vehicles.

Paula went out to meet their guests and escorted them in the front door. Dr. Gillis nodded to Erin, said, "Hello, Miss Scott," and walked briskly to TJ, accepting the hand that she offered as Mare gave Erin a hug. "Miss Meridian, I'm so glad I was at last able to accept your generous invitation. I would have been here sooner if my schedule had permitted it."

"I understand that, Doctor, and I'm delighted you're able to be here tonight. But, please, call me TJ, and this is Erin, and Paula."

Dr. Gillis nodded again to the two women, his eyes crinkling. "I'd be happy to, if you'll call me Michael."

TJ inclined her head. "Michael it is."

Erin slipped her arm through Michael's. "Mare has agreed to provide an appetizer of music for us, Michael. Please come with me. I'll escort you to the music room." They went toward the hallway with Paula following as Mare stepped up to TJ.

"We'll be with you in just a minute," Mare called to their departing backs.

After a glance toward the group to make sure they exited the living room, Mare turned and pressed her lips to TJ's, a darting tongue teasing its adversary into retaliation. Breaking away before she succumbed to total loss of control, Mare whispered, "Until tonight." The yearning felt by the two formed an almost tangible bond. TJ's eyes darkened, and her lids lowered as pictures of their past passion played across the screen of her mind.

"Hey." Mare chuckled, pulled a tissue from her jeans, and patted the moisture from TJ's upper lip and around her hairline. "You can't go in there looking like this. Your face will be a dead giveaway."

TJ's lips curved into the lopsided smile that Mare found so endearing. "Just how am I supposed to turn myself off?"

Piano notes sounded and Mare figured her father was trying out the Steinway. "I've got to get in there. I'll send Erin out to you. That will give you some time to regroup." Mare couldn't resist, she had to kiss TJ one more time, then she spent a moment quieting her own emotions before moving to the music room. True to her promise, she sent Erin back to TJ.

"Whoa, honey." Erin's eyes danced with merriment when she

got a close look at TJ's face. "No wonder Mare said you need help. Maybe a bucket of cold water?"

Both Erin and Paula were enjoying the development of the relationship between TJ and Mare. It even added some extra spice to their own passion by recalling their first encounters. The two had met in their second year of college but for months had shied away from confessing their mutual attraction until TJ had informed each of them of the other's interest. By their third year, they knew that theirs was a lifetime commitment, and their love had deepened and expanded ever since.

"Funny, funny," TJ said dryly. "Wait until I send Paula to Europe for several months and see how you feel."

Erin's jaw dropped and her face paled. "You wouldn't do that to us, would you?"

"No, but the look on your face is so comical, it's helping me cool down."

Erin cuffed TJ's shoulder. "One of these days, TJ, you're really going to get it."

"It sure as hell better be tonight," TJ said fervently, and the two of them chuckled. Feeling a lot calmer, TJ wheeled to the music room with Erin walking beside her.

When they entered, they saw Mare and Michael sitting at the piano, running through exercises. Paula sat over to the side with an empty chair next to her. Erin settled in the chair, and TJ wheeled alongside her. Paula leaned forward to include TJ in her vision. "Mare and Michael have a surprise for us."

When Paula spoke, both pianists stopped and turned. "Are you ready?" Mare said with feigned innocence. TJ swallowed hard, but managed to nod.

Mare and Michael bowed their heads to each other, turned to the keyboard and played a duet that swept the three listeners into their circle, twirled their psyches gloriously around in a high-stepping routine, then set them sweetly back to earth, finishing with a charming trill.

The duo rose and moved around past the piano seat to stand together and bow to the applause they heard. When they lifted from the bow, Mare saw that TJ hadn't joined in the applause. She sat with her head lowered, one hand across her eyes.

Mare rushed to her side, with Michael coming over right next to his daughter. Mare rested her hand for a moment on the raven locks. "TJ, what's wrong? Are you ill?"

TJ dropped her hand and raised her powerful gaze.

Her voice was filled with wonderment, and she blinked back tears. "You made me walk again. For just a few precious moments, I walked again." A brilliant smile appeared even as

Mare wiped away the tear that had overflowed onto TJ's cheek. "And not just walked, I danced!"

TJ threw her arms wide, and Erin jumped up and hugged her before Mare had a chance to collapse into her embrace. The action brought Mare back to her senses, and she turned and hugged Michael, who had been watching the obviously emotional exchange between Mare and TJ.

"I think our surprise was a huge success," he said, obviously pleased.

Erin stepped away from TJ, smiling at the thanks that had been whispered in her ear.

"Dad composed that piece." Mare's eyes shone with pride, and Paula and Erin both remarked on the beauty of the music and how it had moved them.

Martha, one of the women from the ranch's cookhouse, appeared in the doorway. TJ had engaged the two cooks to prepare and serve the dinner. "Dinner's ready, ma'am."

"We'll be right there, Martha." TJ wheeled around and led the group into the dining room.

Dinner was a thoroughly entertaining affair. Michael proved to be a nimble raconteur with a broad repertoire of fascinating anecdotes. With Mare's natural affinity for chatting, and TJ's expertise as an accomplished hostess assuring that each person contributed to the conversation, the time flew by. After the dessert, Paula and Erin excused themselves, allowing the others some private time to linger together over coffee.

The conversation continued without effort. TJ's charming hostess side was new to Mare, and she found it very appealing. Her father seemed to be totally captivated, too.

"TJ, Dad has made me a marvelously generous offer." The sudden closing of a curtain in TJ's eyes startled Mare.

"Oh? What's that?" TJ said, suddenly horrified that Mare might be leaving.

Puzzled by TJ's reaction, Mare halted. Michael picked up where she left off. "Mare's my only living relative."

Oh God, Mare was going to go live with him! The color blanched from TJ's face, worrying Mare that she might be ill. Michael, too, looked concerned. He hesitated, then continued.

"After some long, hard discussions, I've persuaded her to let me settle some of my estate on her now, rather than wait until I die. I'd rather be here to see her enjoy it."

"Are you all right, TJ?" Mare said.

TJ took a couple of deep breaths and began to recover her color. "I'm fine. Just a slight jolt there for a minute. I think that's a wonderful idea, Michael."

"I told Dad your law firm could handle the transfer from his lawyer. Is that okay?"

TJ's heart sang as she realized her worst fears would not be confirmed. "Yes, they'll do that. Just a minute, Michael, and I'll give you the names of my lawyers." She backed her chair three feet to the wall and turned it sideways. Reaching up to a metal panel holding a button and tiny bubble lights, she pushed the button and returned to the table. When Erin appeared, TJ sent her for a card, which she brought, handed to Michael, and then left.

"This will do fine, TJ. Now," Michael said as he got up from the chair, "it's time for me to leave this lovely company." He took TJ's hand, bowing low over it. "I've had a wonderful time and a delicious dinner. Thank you for inviting me."

"We were delighted to have you. And the invitation is still standing. Anytime you can fit us in, we'd love to have you."

"Thanks, I'll try my best to take you up on that. May I use your bathroom before I leave?"

"Certainly. Mare, there's one in the music room."

Michael allowed Mare to escort him to the music room. As she waited, she ran her fingers along the piano's keys, musing over what a good time she'd had tonight.

Michael moved to the sink to wash his hands. A soft light flickering through the chest-high window drew his curiosity. He stepped close and peered out. The window opened onto a dimly lit courtyard that contained trees, bushes, and benches. A flickering yellow citronella candle sat on a pathway next to one of the benches. Two people on the bench were kissing. The darker head lifted from the kiss, into a beam of light coming from someplace along the wall. He could see it was Paula. The other person sat up straighter, put an arm around Paula's neck and kissed her again. The blonde curls left no doubt as to who it was. Erin and Paula were kissing? Their hands moved, and Michael jerked his head back. What was he, some kind of voyeur? What did it matter to him what they were doing? They were adults, weren't they?

Still, Michael had been raised with the conventional idea that men are attracted to women and vice versa. He knew that wasn't always the case, but he'd never come face to face with the reality before, and he was a bit uncomfortable with it. He wondered whether Mare knew. My God, he wondered whether Mare... No, he didn't even want to think about that possibility. He could hear Mare's light touch on the piano. Deciding not to make an issue of something that was, after all, none of his business, he walked back into the music room, and Mare showed him to his car. They spoke a few minutes, kissed good-bye, and Michael got in his car and left.

Mare went back into the house looking for TJ who was no longer in the dining room. "TJ? Where are you?" She hurried into the hall and saw the light showing through the transom above TJ's bathroom door. She tried the door, then knocked on it. "TJ?"

"Just a minute," TJ answered in a singsong voice.

"I'll be right back." Mare dashed to the other bathroom, made use of it, then ran back to TJ's bathroom just as the wheelchair was coming through the doorway. Mare opened the bedroom door. TJ wheeled in, then swung around, lifted the arm, and went "ooph" as Mare landed against her stomach. Long arms pulled the supple body as tight as they could against TJ's chest, and two mouths joined for a banquet of treats.

They eventually parted and Mare reached for TJ's blouse straps. "Wait," TJ said, "let's get on the bed. I can move better there."

"Just a minute," Mare said in a perfect imitation of TJ's earlier singsong, bringing a grin to her lover's face. Mare slid the straps down, and TJ lifted her arms through. The top was cotton and tight enough that it wouldn't fall, so Mare sat a little away from TJ, put her hands, palms flat, thumbs down, on the top of TJ's chest, and slid them down, pushing the blouse lower in tiny tantalizing increments. This was a purposely slow process, made even slower by the massaging that went on with each lowering of the blouse. As her fingers slid against skin, Mare's thumbs played a counterpoint through the blouse material. When she almost reached the critical masses, now yearning for a bare touch, Mare stopped. "Now we'll get on the bed."

TJ clamped her hands on Mare's wrists. "My God, Mare, you can't leave me like this. Stop tormenting me."

"But you're so much fun to torment, sweetheart." Mare leaned in until her mouth was next to TJ's ear. "Just wait until you see what we do in the bed," she said in a sultry tone and blew her warm breath into the ear's sensitive opening.

TJ let loose of her wrists and said, in agony, "Okay, okay, let's move to the bed. Floor. Anywhere. Just do something. Anything. Help!"

SOFT LIGHT HAD just entered the room when TJ awoke. Mare's body covered hers, the top of the golden head even with TJ's eyes, which fit the curves and valleys of their breasts perfectly together. TJ blinked and smiled, remembering their escapades of the night before. Just when she thought they'd tried about everything, Mare came up with something new. Well, she was a musician and musicians were creative, right? She sure was that, and boy, did she ever know how to play TJ.

"Umm." Mare turned to press warm lips against TJ's neck and started nibbling. She stopped, and TJ felt a puff of breath against the dampness as a laugh bubbled out of Mare. "Believe it or not, I think I'm worn out."

"No wonder. You've been working like a madwoman, then you spend half the night using your wiles to turn me into a begging mound of jello. You *should* be worn out."

"A mound of jello? Now there's a picture. You're all muscle and you know it." Mare moved her chest back and forth against TJ's and giggled. "Well, almost all muscle."

"If exercise builds muscle, then you've got them on a strong path to change." Both women laughed.

Mare's voice sobered. "TJ, when Dad gives me that money, I have some plans for it."

"Like what?"

Mare moved off of TJ and onto the bed beside her so she could look into her face. "I've decided I'm going to hire an assistant. I can't stand being away from you for so long."

"That's wonderful news! How soon do you think you could get someone?"

"Hard to tell. How soon do you think I'll get the money?"

"Maybe a couple weeks, maybe a month. Depends on how fast these lawyers move. But you could go ahead and advertise, start interviewing. Things are going to be picking up around here, Mare. The area will be expanding. Your assistant will earn his own keep in a hurry."

TJ's business mind was gearing up. Mare recognized this and wanted to bring her back. "Does the offer for me to move out here still stand?"

TJ threw her arms onto the bed above her head, causing an interesting change in the appearance of her chest. "Pinch me, I'm dreaming."

So Mare pinched.

"Mare!" TJ's arms came back down in a hurry. "You didn't have to pinch there, for Pete's sake. They're still tender from last night."

"Oh, poor babies. Let me kiss them and make them better." Mare leaned forward and TJ pushed her back, laughing.

"No you don't. You have to get up and go to work, and so do I."

"Darn." Mare groaned and winked, twice. "But I'll be back, you guys."

Chapter
Eighteen

MICHAEL SAT IN his home office staring blankly at the computer screen. He had called up the financial worth file that enumerated all his assets and liabilities, with the intention of choosing how much of his estate to settle on his daughter. He had a problem keeping his mind on the figures in front of him. A picture of two women kissing insisted on intruding.

There were three women in that house and two obviously were gay. Didn't that hint that maybe TJ was gay, too? Then what about Mare? Erin and Paula appeared to be lovers, so did that mean Mare and TJ were? There did seem to be some kind of connection between them, but he had assumed that was because of their friendship. Besides, TJ was paralyzed.

Come on, he was the SCI expert. He knew that some people with SCI could still have sexual relationships. Maybe TJ was one of them. But he didn't want it to be with Mare!

A niggling aggravation behind this thought bothered Michael, and he was straightforward enough to examine it objectively. Was he more worried that Mare might be gay? Or that TJ might be? He turned this question over in his mind, searching for the impetus behind it. TJ was stunningly beautiful, charming, intelligent, and poised. And she definitely had an aura of — what? Power? Magnetism? There in the music room, when she had swept those remarkable eyes up, she just about bowled him over. He had taken for granted that her passion was directed at him, and he had to admit, it woke up something inside him. But maybe it had been directed at Mare.

Michael had engaged in sporadic relationships through the years, none very long nor worth pursuing. For the last few years, he had buried himself in his work, and his obsession with it had enabled him to learn all the latest procedures in his field and also to make several breakthroughs. Because of his hermit-like life, his reaction to TJ surprised him. But she was an extremely attractive and obviously passionate woman. And to be honest, he would be more upset if TJ was gay than if Mare was, at least for the moment. He found that somewhat embarrassing.

What if he wouldn't give Mare the money unless she — did what? He was sitting here thinking she was the lover of TJ Meridian, an extremely wealthy woman. Did he believe he could turn her into something false by waving a paltry couple of million at her?

But what would his friends think about Mare? That was a pretty stupid question. What was he planning to do — hang a sign on her? How Mare spent her private time was of no concern to his friends or to anyone else. Including him.

But he was her father. So what? Who put him in charge of her life? He was her father, not her owner.

What if he was totally wrong and making a mountain out of a molehill? This question cheered Michael and brought him out of his self-inquisition. Mare was coming over tomorrow night. He could find out some answers then.

Having made this decision, Michael went on to choose which assets to transfer to Mare and sent the information to his attorney.

MARE AND MICHAEL finished dinner and moved to his den for their coffee. They relaxed on a comfortable couch with a coffee table immediately in front of them. A grand piano sat at the far end of the room in an area set off by a broad archway. Another archway, to the right of the piano, connected the area to the living room in an L-shaped configuration.

At Dorburton Lakes, Michael employed a married couple, the Eschers, as housekeeper/cook and butler/chauffeur, and they took excellent care of him and his guests. Once they had served the coffee, they retired to the kitchen.

"I had a wonderful time at TJ's the other night." Michael waited until Mare finished with the cream and sugar, then he added some to his coffee and stirred it. "She's an exceptional person."

He watched as Mare's eyes brightened. "Yes, she is. She directs enterprises spread all over the world."

"I'm not much of a businessman. I have a financial consultant who manages my affairs, but even I've heard of Meridian Corporation. The few times TJ mentioned it at dinner I was impressed with her grasp of what each subsidiary does and how she's meshed them all together into a smooth-running operation." Michael hesitated for a moment. Watching Mare closely, but unobtrusively, he continued. "Tell you the truth, I was more impressed with her as a woman. She's stunningly attractive."

"Yes, she is."

"In fact, I've met a lot of glamorous women, but she's one of the most beautiful I've ever seen."

"I think so, too," Mare said, wondering where this paean of praise to TJ was leading. She didn't have long to find out.

"I was thinking about calling her and asking her for a date. Would you have any objection to that?"

Mare was speechless. After a moment, she found her voice. "No offense, Dad, but there's a difference in your ages."

"That's true, but it might be of less importance to TJ than it is to you. I'd like to ask her that myself. As a matter of fact, I was thinking of calling her tomorrow evening."

"Dad, I..." Mare searched for the right words to say without hurting his feelings. "TJ doesn't date."

"Well, there's always the chance that someone will change her ways. It can't hurt to ask."

Mare was in agony. Should she just tell him right out that she and TJ were lovers? Would he hate her? She didn't want to lose him already.

She never even considered the option of leaving TJ.

Mare finished the last sip of her coffee, set the cup in its saucer, and picked up her father's hand. She took a deep breath and looked him straight in the eye.

"Dad, there's something I have to tell you. Something important. I know you had no way of knowing this, and I would have told you at some point, when we got to know each other better." Mare hesitated, swallowing, her throat suddenly dry. This was a thousand times harder than she had thought it would be.

Her stomach tensed, turning over as she felt a wave of fear run through her. This situation had never arisen between her and her mother. Jane respected the privacy of others and expected the same from them. Besides, Mare had always thought her mother knew without asking pointed questions.

Mare gathered her courage. "You know how much you and I are alike, right? In the short time that we've known each other, we've been amazed at how many things we both enjoy, how similar our tastes are, right?"

Michael looked like he suspected what was coming and was braced for it. Mare saw his lips set and her courage slipped, but she seized hold and set it upright again. "Well, it so happens that you and I are so much alike that"—Mare gave a quick little nervous smile—"we've both been attracted to the same woman.

I'm gay, Dad, and I'm involved with TJ. We're in love with each other." Mare's eyes were pools of anxiety, pleading for understanding.

Michael's hand moved and Mare, her heart sinking, released it. But Michael surprised her. He turned his hand over so he could hold hers in both of his. "I have to confess that I'm not totally shocked by this revelation. After dinner at TJ's, when I was in the bathroom, I noticed a flickering light outside. I looked out the window, and I saw Erin and Paula kissing each other. So I wondered about your situation, and TJ's."

He gave Mare's hand a squeeze. "I hoped I was wrong. At first I was angry at the possibility that you and TJ were in love. Partly because I didn't want you to be gay, and partly because I was attracted to TJ. Do you understand what I'm saying?"

Mare nodded and swallowed, hoping to contain the tears that threatened to flood her eyes.

"Is it stupid to ask if you could ever change?"

Mare forced out a hoarse voice. "Dad, that would be like asking you to change your green eyes to brown." She tried a tentative smile.

Michael thought about that for a few moments, looking down at their entwined hands. Finally, he looked up. "This isn't easy for me, and there might be times when we accidentally hurt each other, but I'll honestly try to accept what I can't change. About the best face I can put on this whole situation is"— Michael offered his own tentative smile—"if I can't date TJ, at least you're keeping her in the family."

Mare started to cry in relief, and he took her into his arms, patting her back and soothing her with small shushing sounds.

Finally, Mare calmed down, and with the help of tissues, dried her tears. "I knew Mom would pick a winner."

"I am a winner, Mare, since you came into my life." Michael gave her an extra hug before releasing her. "I just want you to promise me one thing."

"What's that?"

"Not to tell TJ that I was developing a crush on her, okay?" Michael blushed like a shy schoolboy.

Mare reached up and patted his cheek. "Never, Dad. But crushes are okay, just as long as that's all they are. I think anyone who really knows TJ has a mild crush on her. How could you help it? She's wonderful. Of course, I am prejudiced."

"No, she is wonderful, and I probably always will have a mild crush on her. Beyond that, though, I'd like to see if I could do anything to help her. Do you think she'd let me look at her case history, X-rays, MRIs, and so forth? I'd like to keep up on her condition, in case we come across anything that could improve it. That's my field, you know."

"I know, and I thank you for wanting to help. I'll ask TJ. She's kind of close sometimes about her privacy, but in this case I think I can talk my way around her. Like you said, we'll be keeping it in the family."

"Perfect. Now how about if we cap off this evening with my duet that we played earlier?" Michael's voice caught for just a moment, remembering TJ's emotional reaction to his original composition. "The one she danced to?"

"Perfect," Mare echoed, and they rose and walked arm in arm to the piano.

Chapter
Nineteen

PAULA STUCK HER head into the hallway and hollered, "Hey, TJ, here comes Mare!" then ducked back into the kitchen and put another glass, plate, and setting on the island.

Erin turned from the fridge where she was getting the iced tea. "You could have used the intercom."

"Yeah, yeah, yeah. I know you were raised in polite society." Paula gave her a light pinch as she passed by.

Erin swatted at Paula's hand. "And so were you, though no one would ever suspect it."

The storm door burst open as Mare came through. "Hi, folks. Believe it or not, I have some extra time today, time for a real visit for a change." She hugged each of them, and her smile broadened as TJ came wheeling into the kitchen, right up to Mare's legs.

Mare leaned forward to kiss her, but TJ pulled back. "Something wrong?"

TJ flung up the arm of her chair and patted her thighs. "Yeah! I haven't seen you for days, and you're going to sit down and let me give you a real kiss." Long arms reached out, and Mare slipped into them and onto the volunteered lap at the same time. She encircled TJ with her arms and melted into a kiss of fire.

When their lips finally parted, Mare laid her head down in the V between TJ's neck and shoulder. She kissed her throat, then snuggled her body into a more comfortable position. "I want to stay here forever. Can I do that, please?"

Erin spoke up. "Might be a little messy. Lunch is soup and sandwiches, and TJ has to eat. She already skipped breakfast." As she spoke, she ladled soup into bowls and set one at each place.

"Oh darn." Mare slowly slid her tongue up the side of TJ's neck, across her cheek, and into her mouth, sealing its entrance with her lips.

"Umm." TJ's arms tightened around Mare, and they held the

kiss until Paula dropped some ice cubes down Mare's back.

"Yiii!" she yelled and leaped out of the chair, jumping up and down and pulling at her shirttail until the cubes fell out onto the floor. Mare threw a mock glare at Paula who was gleefully watching the impromptu dance.

"Sorry. I know if you get too hot, you can cool down with some ice cubes, and you looked like you were sizzling." Not appearing at all contrite, Paula picked up the cubes from the floor and threatened TJ who shook a fist at her. Paula reconsidered, tossed the cubes in the sink, and washed her hands. "Come on, let's eat. I'm starving." She helped Erin set the sandwiches out, and they all sat down to lunch.

The food disappeared quickly, and they sat around talking for a while. "By the way"—TJ's eyes swept between Erin and Paula—"did Mare tell you that you two outted her to her father?"

"What?"

"That's right." Mare gazed at them very seriously.

"How did we do that?" Erin asked.

"You remember the night he had dinner with us?"

"Yeah."

"You remember being in the courtyard?" Both nodded.

"You remember what you were doing?" The two looked at each other, then back to Mare. Erin had a slight blush on her cheeks, but Paula looked cocky.

"Damn right I do! It's a courtyard. We were courting."

Mare sucked in her lips to keep a straight face. TJ covered her mouth with a hand.

Mare cleared her throat. "Well, Dad used the bathroom next to the music room, and guess what he saw out the window?"

"Aw, hell," Paula said. "We didn't know he was there. We're sorry."

"What did he say about it?" Erin asked.

"Well, he put two and two together and figured if you two fooled around with each other, maybe I fooled around with TJ, too."

"And what did you say to that?"

"I said, 'Damn right I do!' " Mare's expression cleared and a huge smile split her face. TJ laughed out loud as Erin and Paula saw a joke was being played on them.

"Funny, funny, funny," Erin said, being a good sport about it. Paula took a moment longer to lighten up, and Erin pulled on her arm. "Come on, Paulie, that was payback for the ice cubes."

"Right," she said gruffly. "But what did Michael say? Was he upset? I can't tell you how much trouble some of our friends have had when their families first learned they were gay."

"He wasn't especially happy about it, but he'll work on accepting it. And I can live with that. That's enough talk about me. How are things coming along out here?"

Erin sat forward and rested her arms on the island. "Looking pretty good with the cattle. After we culled the sick ones you had pointed out, we turned the others onto the range and they're doing fine. Bill says the men are shaping into good, solid hands, and at the rate we're getting cattle shipped in, we should be up to full capacity in a couple more months."

Paula chimed in. "The plant's being brought on line, and the foremen and a skeleton crew are in place. We should have our first shipment of cattle to process by next week. TJ told them we'll get scattered shipments so the plant can be brought up to capacity slowly, giving us time to hire and train more and more workers. In the meantime, of the ones already hired, some are being trained to handle the beef, and others taught how to take care of the production areas."

Mare clapped her hands in appreciation. "And I have to tell you there's a lifting of spirits in town. People are walking with their heads up, a look of hope on their faces. They're starting to believe that the town is truly turning around." She looked at TJ. "And I'm starting to hear Meridian said once in a while without S.O.B. next to it."

"That *is* an improvement," TJ said.

Mare asked, "TJ, did you get in touch with your doctor to send your records to Dad?"

TJ shifted in her seat and rubbed a hand over her mouth. "Not yet."

Mare looked at her quizzically. She and TJ had discussed this on the phone, and she thought TJ was amenable to it, but her body language said otherwise. "Is there a problem? I mean, this is my father, sweetheart. He's an expert in the field, and he wants to keep your records on file in case there's a breakthrough, some treatment that might help you."

"Maybe it's because he's your father. I feel kind of exposed."

"Sorry, I don't follow that thinking. It's your insides he's going to see, not your outsides."

TJ had to grin. "I didn't mean that kind of exposed."

"You're going to make me tell Dad that you don't want him to look at your records?" Mare batted her lashes coyly. "Because you're shy?"

TJ flipped her hands in the air in surrender. "All right! I'll send him the records. You know, you ought to work for the government or something. No one would ever get away with anything."

Paula, hiding her gestures behind TJ's back, gave Mare a thumbs-up sign.

Mare worked hard at keeping a straight face as Erin spoke. "TJ said you were planning to hire an assistant. Any luck with that yet?"

"Yeah, I had an applicant almost right away who looks promising. Young man with a wife and baby. I have another interview set up with him, and if we can get together on a few incidentals, looks like he's the one."

"That'll be great," Paula said. "You need more free time. You keep running around like you have been, and you'll soon be nothing but skin and bones."

Mare was touched that the sometimes-gruff Paula was concerned about her workload.

TJ looked at Erin and Paula. "I've asked Mare to come here to live if she can. Having an assistant would be a big step in that direction."

"Wonderful!" Erin and Paula said together.

"Well, nothing's definite yet," Mare said. "I can't be certain until I see how things work out. But I have high hopes."

"Where will her office be?" Erin said.

"This is a big place, and there are plenty of empty rooms. Mare could have any one she wants."

"Any one?" Mare echoed. She cocked her head at TJ. "Is that a promise?"

"Yeah, that's a promise."

"Then I'll take the one that used to be your father's."

TJ's face blanched, then hardened. "No! That's the only one you can't have."

"You just promised me I could have any I wanted. Are you going to go back on your word?"

"If I had any idea you would choose that one, I would have told you right off you couldn't have it. But no, you had to trick me, and I don't appreciate that." TJ crossed her arms, held her elbows, and seemed to shrink in on herself.

"I wasn't trying to trick you. You should know me better than that. If you had told me I couldn't have that room, I would have argued for it anyway. It's at the end of the house with an outside entrance. People could come in and out to see me without disturbing the rest of the house. It has a screened porch attached to it that would be ideal for me to work in when the weather's right. It's the perfect room for an office."

"Mare's right," Erin said. "It sounds like the ideal spot."

TJ threw Erin a nasty glance. The clamped jaw and lips pressed firmly together left no doubt as to her mood.

Mare was becoming agitated at TJ's hardheaded attitude. And when Mare got agitated, her mouth shifted into another gear. "I didn't think I was coming here as a rental prospect. I expected to have some say in where my office would be. It's also the closest room to your office. And pardon me for thinking this, but I supposed that you and I would like to see each other occasionally during the day."

Mare hadn't shifted her attention from TJ. She saw her eyes narrow when she made the rental remark, but TJ didn't respond. "Have you been in the room since you came back here?"

When TJ kept silent, Paula answered. "No one's been in the room. It's never been unlocked."

"Who has the key?" Mare glanced at Paula, who tilted her head toward TJ.

"May I have the key, TJ?" Mare knew she was treading on dangerous ground. She felt the anxiety coming from Paula and Erin, and TJ's tension almost crackled around her. TJ hadn't said anything, and that obviously put Paula and Erin on edge. Mare knew they had seen some monumental temper outbursts in the past, most of them preceded by a period of speechless anger similar to what was occurring right now.

TJ huddled in her chair, not moving, not saying anything. The stillness in the room pressed against them all, seeming almost to have a life of its own.

Mare's hushed voice nudged the silence, gently edging it away. "TJ, if we can't even talk about a difference of opinion, maybe I need to rethink my coming here to live. It could be a big mistake."

TJ's head jerked up, and Erin and Paula flinched. Paula, uneasy, got up and moved to lean against the counter behind TJ and Mare.

TJ stared wretchedly at Mare as a cheek twitched then the beautiful features contorted. TJ opened her mouth but wasn't able to force the words out. She didn't want the woman she loved to be using the room of a man she hated. Why couldn't Mare understand that? TJ tore her eyes away, lowered her head, and covered her face with both of her hands. Her breath rasped in her throat.

Mare raised a hand to soothe TJ, but Paula stepped forward, grabbed the hand, and shook her head. Mare's heart went out to TJ, but she sat still as had been signaled, feeling that Paula probably was right. No one could predict TJ's reaction.

After a few minutes, TJ's breathing evened out, and she dropped her hands and raised her head, eyes still lowered. She rocked back and forth and interlaced her fingers, but her hands moved anyway, thumbs rolling over each other, over and over. When she finally seemed composed, she lifted her eyes to Mare's.

Mare felt like her heart had backed up and restarted. TJ knew her eyes were a formidable weapon, and even when Mare knew TJ was going to use them on her, she was helpless to defend herself. She just wanted to throw herself at TJ's feet.

"I don't like to be manipulated, and I don't like emotional blackmail. That was my father's most powerful tool." Mare flinched at the hurt in TJ's voice and was dismayed to be compared to the monster TJ's father obviously was. TJ cleared her throat. Her low voice sounded subdued and hesitant. She looked Mare straight in the eye. "But for you I'll compromise."

Paula squealed and threw her hands over her heart. "My God, I'm going to have a heart attack! TJ said the 'C' word!"

Erin blinked and waited for a reaction, and she wasn't disappointed. TJ turned her head slowly and pinned Paula with a cold stare. "You think this is funny?"

"I'm sorry."

Mare watched in fascination as TJ's look drained the blood from Paula's face. She'd heard TJ use that tone before but not to either of her friends. She needed to take the focus off of Paula before TJ said or did anything that she'd regret later. "What do you propose?" she said.

TJ stared a moment longer before turning back to Mare.

"You know I hate that room."

"I know you've turned it into a shrine that embodies your hate for your father, and I don't think that's a healthy situation. I could go in there and redo it, and you'd never recognize it. Whenever you came in, it would seem like a different room. There'd be nothing left to remind you of the bad times." Mare suddenly understood she was bulldozing her way over TJ's objections before she had heard them. "I'm sorry, what are you proposing?"

"You can have the room with four conditions. One, everything in the room must go. Throw it out, give it to some charity, I don't care. Just get rid of it so I'll never see it again. Two, the door to the hall has to be kept closed at all times, and I mean at all times, unless someone is going in or out. Three, no one will use it as a place to hide from me. Four, I'll never step foot in the room, and I'll not be pestered to" — TJ looked directly at each of them — "by anybody. Is that clear?"

All three nodded.

"I want to hear each of you say you promise to abide by these conditions."

"I promise," Mare said and the other two added their promises.

"Paula, the key's in my bedroom in the bottom drawer of the jewelry chest. Would you get it, please?" Paula was halfway to the bedroom by the time TJ finished. She came back quickly with the key and handed it to her.

TJ reached for Mare's hand, turned it over, and placed the key in Mare's palm. Mare closed her fingers around it and slipped the key into a pocket in her jeans.

A nervous twitch tugged at TJ's cheek, and Mare cupped her hand against it. "I know this has been hard for you, sweetheart. But someday I think you'll feel better for it. Thank you for not letting this turn into a wedge between us."

The anger and pain in TJ's eyes slowly dissolved as love's passion replaced them. "I'd give you everything I have if that was the only way to get you here." TJ lifted the chair arm, and Mare moved onto her lap. Erin and Paula quietly left the room.

TJ put her arms around her, and Mare put both hands up to hold the face she loved. She kissed TJ lightly. "I didn't mean that to sound like a threat. I just know we're both pretty hardheaded. If we can't learn to compromise when we disagree, then we have a tough road ahead of us. If I lived someplace else, I could always walk out in a huff."

"If you get in a huff when you live here, I'll just have to hunt you down and 'unhuff' you."

"Umm, that sounds pretty intriguing. I'll try to remember that." Mare put her arms around TJ's neck and snuggled closer against her. "Just think, when I move out here we'll have lots more time together."

"I'm counting on it." TJ sat there, peacefully enjoying the feel of Mare's arms around her neck and the warmth of the body pressed against her own. Long-fingered hands, rarely still, gently moved up and down against Mare's back, sending quiet messages of love.

Mare moaned softly, her heart brimming with the beauty of their companionship.

TJ kissed Mare's hair and laid her head against it. Mare felt the soft, velvety voice coming through TJ's chest. "I can't believe how much I love you. You're so much a part of me, it's like we really are just one person."

"I feel the same way," Mare whispered.

They held each other for a while, until Mare stirred. "I wish I really could stay here forever. But I have to go back to work." She sat up, treated her senses to one more close-up of TJ's face, and leaned into a kiss.

TJ ended the kiss by pulling away with a spurt of laughter. "Don't give me one of those 'light-TJ-up' kind of kisses, then walk out the door. Save it for when you're going to stay and cool me off."

"Sorry. You're just so much fun to kiss."

"I thought the line was, 'You're just so much fun to torment.' "

"Well, sometimes one's the same as the other."

"Humph. You got that right."

When Mare stood up, TJ asked her to push the wall button.

Paula came in to answer the button's summons. "Mare, give Paula the key to the room. She can get started on clearing it out."

Mare handed over the key, and Paula stuck it in her own pocket. "I'll come and help as soon as I can, Paula. Maybe even tonight."

TJ smacked the chair arms. "Don't go tormenting me with words, now."

Mare patted her cheek. "You know I can't promise, but I'll try."

"Hey, TJ, why not ask Mare to come with us to the plant next week? She might be interested in seeing how it works."

"Good idea. You might get back in my good graces, yet." Paula splayed her hand against her chest and widened her eyes in a supposedly innocent look that TJ pointedly ignored. "How about it, Mare? Think you can make it?"

"You'll have to let me know exactly what day and time, and I'll have to see what's on my agenda. Maybe I can rearrange a few things and get someone to cover for me. But, yeah, I can probably make it. With a new assistant on the horizon, I can move some things to a later date. Now, I better be going."

"Okay," TJ said, "we'll let you know the details as soon as we decide." She raised her arms, and they kissed once more before Mare left.

"Wait here, Paula." TJ wheeled over to the window and watched Mare walk to her truck and climb in. As though Mare felt TJ's eyes on her, she glanced at the house and waved before backing up and rolling away.

TJ's cheerful look slowly died as she focused on Paula.

"Am I in trouble, boss?"

"You and Erin both. Ganging up on me like that."

"What? We hardly said anything."

"You didn't have to. Mare and I both knew you were on her side."

"Well, she's a lot smaller than you. We think she should be protected."

"Oh, that's what you think, huh?"

Paula looked at her a bit sheepishly. "Actually when Mare gets her mouth going, I kind of think you're the one who needs protected."

TJ laughed out loud. "Yeah, I think you're right about that." Then her expression sobered. "Listen, I want you to get started on that office, but I don't want to have anything at all to do with it, you understand?"

"I understand. TJ?"

"Yeah?"

"Thanks. About the office, and for bringing Mare out here. She brightens up the whole place. Erin and I both think she's the greatest."

"Thanks, Paula. I think you two guys are the greatest, too. Where is Erin?"

"She went out to see about the horses being brought into the barn and hosed down. It's getting pretty hot out there."

"Yeah, those early morning rides you thought of were a great idea, for the horses and for us. The afternoons have been pretty nasty. Speaking of nasty, we better get back to work."

TJ and Paula started across the kitchen. Paula glanced down at TJ. "I guess when Mare gets here the early morning rides will be out, huh? On the horses, I mean."

TJ slapped Paula in the side. "Erin's right, you're outrageous. We'll worry about that when Mare gets here."

Chapter
Twenty

MARE MADE IT back that afternoon to give Paula a hand clearing the office, and Erin joined them shortly afterward. Paula, while working alone, had managed to sift through part of one of the two filing cabinets and had rescued the deeds and plats of the Meridian ranch holdings. She'd had her fill of paperwork and expressed an opinion that the rest of the files could wait until later, with which the others agreed.

They settled on a system that seemed to be working well. Erin attacked the bookcases, stacking the multicolored, leather-bound tomes in cartons. Paula collected the knickknacks, trophies, mementos, pictures, wall hangings, and other assorted furnishings into other cartons, while Mare investigated the contents of the desk.

"Aaah-choo!" Mare's sneeze rocked the house.

"Gesundheit," Erin said. She paused for a second in her task of pulling books from one of the bookcases. "Where the heck did a sneeze that size come from?"

Mare made a face at her. "From all the darn dust you two are stirring up, that's where." She rubbed her nose and yanked another drawer from the huge black desk, quickly examining its contents.

Paula pointed to a set of pictures standing on a shelf. "Hey, look at this." Others hung against the wall behind them. She waited until Mare and Erin had come over to join her. "That must be TJ's father when he was a young man. He's not as heavyset there as he was later. Who does he remind you of?"

"He looks something like Peter," Mare said.

"Yeah," Erin agreed. "He's taller and slimmer and darker, but give him a beard to go with that moustache, and he and Peter could be brothers. That's amazing."

"Might be part of the reason Peter had so much trouble getting TJ to talk about her father." Mare shook her head at the irony of it. "I'll tell him about this. It might help."

"Sounds good," Paula said, "but let's get moving with this stuff or we'll never get finished." They returned to their efforts and worked without talking for the next few minutes, each lost in her own thoughts.

Mare, never one to sit quietly, broke the silence. "You know, some of the stuff in this desk is valuable. You sure we should throw it all out?" The three drawers she had already emptied were sitting atop the desk. She laid the fourth on the floor and squatted down, poking through its contents. A carton next to her held what she had emptied from the other drawers.

Erin came over and looked in the carton. She saw several gold pen-and-pencil sets, sterling silver cups and flasks, old-fashioned cut-glass inkwells and paperweights, and assorted other expensive items. "Why don't you put them in a separate carton, and we'll donate them to one of the churches? TJ said we could give it away. She didn't insist we throw everything out."

"Yeah," Mare said. "She sure was determined about not keeping anything from this room. But it's understandable." Mare grew sad. She stopped and sank cross-legged to the floor next to the drawer, depressed by the very idea of the beatings TJ endured. "It's hard to imagine anyone treating her like that."

"Paula and I don't have to imagine it," Erin said, her voice hard. "We saw him in action. He was beating TJ like a maniac. She was a grown woman, but he was half again her size. We took her to the hospital, and all the way there she shook so hard I couldn't even keep hold of her. At first I thought she was shaking from fear, but then she spoke in a low, grating voice filled with rage. I've never heard that tone or those words since. She was shaking from hatred. He'd been beating her like that since she was —" Erin's voice turned hoarse. "It hurts like hell to think of her being abused like that even as a young kid."

Paula came over, put an arm around Erin's shoulders, and gave her a quick squeeze. "Nobody will ever hurt her again, not if we have anything to say about it."

"That's for sure."

Mare's eyes were wet with unshed tears. "Maybe clearing out everything in here that reminds her of him will help. But she's got a long way to go to get rid of the hatred he caused."

"Well, this is a start." Erin patted the top of Mare's head. "And it's thanks to you. TJ wouldn't have done this for anyone else. Paula and I tried but never could persuade her."

"Let's hope it helps her," Mare said, then they continued with the cleaning and packing.

Erin's gaze fell for a second time on the drawer Mare was unloading. Something snicked at the back of her mind, and she hesitated before returning to her task, but nothing surfaced. She went again to the bookcase and grabbed a handful of books to put in a carton. When a book wouldn't fit into an opening between two others, she discovered it was too long, so she searched for and found one that was shorter and fit perfectly. As the book slid into place, she shouted, "It's too short!"

Mare and Paula both turned toward her. Paula said, "Are you crazy, Miss Airy? Looks to me like it fits perfectly."

Erin pointed her forefinger at Paula. "Airy? You better not call me that. I don't like it."

Paula raised her arms, made her hands shake, and formed her mouth into a circle. "Oooh, I'm scared." She chuckled at the expression on Erin's face. "Well, it's better than Air-head. Or Mare's initials." She turned to Mare. "Anybody ever call you MT?"

"No one who ever lived to tell about it," Mare said with such sincerity that all three of them laughed. "What were you talking about, anyway, Erin? What's too short?"

Erin walked next to the drawer Mare had just finished clearing out. She reached down and picked it up. "This drawer is too short. Look." She set it on top of one of the three that rested on the desk. Sure enough, it was about six inches shorter. "Look in the opening, Mare. See if there's anything back in there."

From her kneeling position, Mare bent over to look in the opening. "Yeah. There is." She reached in, found an inlaid ring, and pulled. Out slid another, smaller drawer containing papers and pictures. She got to her feet and dumped them on an open spot on the desk.

After Erin picked up the empty drawers and stacked them on the floor, she and Paula joined Mare in inspecting the contents. Mare spread the pictures out. Most of them seemed to be all of the same person at different ages: a baby, an infant, a boy, a preteen. The earlier pictures also had a young woman in them, holding the child. The boy had the same black hair and blue eyes that TJ, her father, and Lance had.

Mare looked from Erin to Paula. "Do you think this is TJ's father when he was a child? Or maybe Lance?"

Erin picked up one of the pieces of paper and read it. She shook her head. "No, I don't think the answer's that easy. This is a birth certificate. The boy's name is Thomas Joseph Meridian Raphaele. His mother's name is Gloria Raphaele, and...his father's name is Thomas Joseph Meridian."

The three stood, speechless, staring at each other.

"How old is he now?" Mare managed to ask.

Erin looked at the certificate. "He's sixteen."

Paula put her hands on her hips. "TJ has a half brother. Wow. Wonder how this is going to hit her? Maybe we shouldn't even tell her. She has this strong, powerful side, but we all know she's still pretty fragile about anything concerning her father."

"I don't see how we can keep it from her," Mare said. "Obviously, the Raphaeles must know something about her. They could pop up at any time. It would be better for her to be prepared. Besides, she has a right to know she has a brother."

"Yeah, I agree." Erin's face vacillated between anguish and frustration. "Every time something good happens to TJ, something else happens to kick her in the gut." She stood a minute, pondering, while the other two waited. "But I don't think we should tell her just yet. I'd like time to investigate this first. That way we can give her the whole story instead of just part of it."

"Sounds good to me," Mare said.

"Me, too," Paula said in a gruff voice. "TJ has enough to contend with without someone causing her more problems."

Erin put the certificate down and pawed through the remaining papers. "Some of these are copies of letters from Tom Meridian to the boy and his mother." She handed some to Mare and Paula.

They read through the letters. Mare looked up. "Pretty sentimental. Seems like Tom Meridian really loved this boy and his mother."

"Yeah." Erin sounded disgruntled. "Shame he couldn't spare some of that for his daughter." She gathered together the papers, letters, and pictures, found a rubber band, and bound them with it. "I'll put these in our bedroom. TJ never goes in there." She addressed Mare. "I'll keep you posted on the investigation. You know who's going to be the one to tell TJ about this, don't you?"

"That's not going to be an easy task. I might need backup. We'll talk about this when you've gotten the information, okay?"

"Okay." Erin stuck the package under her arm. "Time to call a break anyway. It's almost supper time. We can work on this again another day. I'll run this stuff upstairs and be right down. If you two want to wash up and start putting the food out, I'll join you in a few minutes."

"Okay," Paula answered. "Don't forget, we're having our music night tonight. And no excuses from TJ. She *is* going to sing." That thought lightened the mood, and they all went off to their chosen tasks.

TJ, LYING FACE down on the bed, sighed with pleasure. She could feel Mare's knees bent on either side of her waist, and although she had no sensation of Mare, unclothed, sitting across her thighs, she could picture her there in her mind. She always did have a pretty good imagination. Fingers slathered with perfumed oil massaged the juncture of her neck and shoulders, then worked outward and downward, covering every inch of skin.

Each time Mare came to one of the scars on the otherwise unblemished skin, she leaned forward and switched massaging with her fingers to ministrations with tongue and lips before resuming her downward journey. After a prolonged trip, Mare reached the point where TJ's feeling stopped.

Mare leaned her upper body against TJ's back and made a request into her ear. "Do you mind if I continue this fascinating expedition? I know you can't feel my hands, but I can feel you."

"Hmm. You can do anything your little heart desires." TJ lay there dreamily, luxuriating in every rub and stroke. A soft warmth danced through her when Mare leaned down against her back. When Mare changed position and faced the other way, TJ's body suddenly came to full alert. Now Mare was sitting on TJ's back, her knees bent alongside. Moving back and forth in a rocking motion, she stroked her way down the long-legged half of the prone body.

TJ believed that when she lost feeling in the lower half of her body, the upper half had become more sensitive. Although she had no real basis for this belief, the reaction she was experiencing from Mare's rocking against her back seemed to reinforce it. She twisted her neck to look behind her, and the slight glimpse she managed made her groan and flop her face down again. With the exertion of enormous will power, she waited at least three minutes before she licked her dry lips and said hoarsely, "I'll promise you anything if you'll turn me over and do that rocking on my front." Erotic fantasies of sight, touch, and taste blazed through TJ's imagination, deepening her breathing and covering her with a fine sheen of perspiration.

Mare's passionate voice, accompanied by a low chuckle, pumped her adrenaline up even higher. "Your every wish is my command."

The next hour outdid her wildest dreams.

Satiated, the two clung together, damp skin slowly cooling. Mare lay in her favorite spot, turned toward TJ, her head in the hollow of TJ's shoulder, one arm spread across her waist. One of TJ's arms wrapped around her while the other moved a softly caressing hand up and down her side and back.

Mare spoke softly. "I'm so glad I had only that one appointment this afternoon. I miss you so much when we don't have a chance to get together."

The wandering hand stopped and came to Mare's chin. Long fingers tipped Mare's face up. TJ, sending a message of love from affectionate eyes, bent down for a sweet kiss. "Me, too."

"Paula and Erin and I got a lot done toward cleaning out the office, too." TJ tensed and Mare hesitated, then quickly added, "And I loved the music room get together."

She put an elbow down against the bed and pushed up to look into TJ's face. "You know, when Paula said you had a beautiful voice, she wasn't kidding."

TJ relaxed and closed her eyes. A tiny smile tugged at her lips. "Right."

"You do." Mare's hand slapped down against the firm belly bringing TJ's eyes open. "How about singing me to sleep? Nobody's done that since I was a little girl."

"You still are a little girl."

Mare made a face. "Next to you, maybe. How tall are you, anyway?"

"Just about six foot."

"Wow, no wonder it took me so long to oil your whole body." Mare's smile grew impish. "Why don't you sing me 'Rock-a-bye Baby'?"

Newly experienced erotic images suffused TJ's mind this time, and she pulled Mare over on top of her, one hand already searching for sweet spots. "Woman, you just don't know when to quit, do you?"

Chapter
Twenty-One

MARE CLIMBED THE ladder out of the pool and accepted the towel Michael handed her. She dried her face and arms and gave her head a brisk rub, just enough to keep the excess water from running off her hair and down her body. "This is really great, so refreshing. I wonder why the Meridian ranch doesn't have a pool? It would be terrific for TJ." She wrapped the towel around her hips. "And I don't believe Paula or Erin would object, either. I think I'll ask her about that." She walked with Michael to an umbrella table and sat across from him.

"Mare, I've finally finished my examination of TJ's records."

Hope brightened Mare's face. "And?"

Michael reached over and patted her hand. "I wish I could be more optimistic, but I'm no miracle worker. That bullet fragment in TJ's back is wedged against her spinal cord at a level we call T-11. If it could be removed, there are some treatments that might return some feeling and limited use to her legs. But the bullet's in such a precarious position, it's inoperable. There's just no way to get to it without damaging her spinal cord further. I'm sorry."

Mare's face fell. She had harbored some unrealistic hope that her father could help TJ.

"I know you're terribly disappointed, and so am I. I'd love to be able to help her—for your sake, too."

"No, Dad, I'm not disappointed for me. I love TJ no matter what. I'm disappointed for her. For all the obvious reasons, of course. But also for one that might sound a little crazy. TJ loves horses. Everything I read about horseback riding mentions the wonderful sensation of wrapping your legs around such a powerful animal. I see her on Faithful Flag, and I could cry that she can't feel that sensation anymore." Mare sighed. "TJ pats her and hugs her and strokes her, but it's not a true substitute. She can't feel her *seat*. It hurts to see these two magnificent animals who belong together and know that TJ can't experience the full pleasure of that."

Michael nodded in sympathy. "I keep abreast of everything having to do with SCI. If anything shows up, I'll jump right on it."

"Thanks, Dad. Just knowing that you're concerned helps a lot." Mare picked up her watch from the table. "Looks like it's about time to get ready to leave."

"Your visit was a little shorter this time. Too bad your latest prospect for an assistant could only be interviewed today."

"Yeah, that is a shame. But he seems like the perfect candidate. I don't want to let him slip through my fingers. If I had my way, he'd start tomorrow." Mare stood up. "Stay out here, Dad. There's no need for you to shepherd me around now. I think I've finally got the house plan down pat."

She leaned down and kissed his cheek, and he kissed hers. "Okay, Mare, if that makes you happy, then I'm happy to do it." Michael waved as she entered the house to prepare to go home. Her mind was already on the logistics of remodeling the office and moving her belongings to the Meridian ranch in time for her soon-to-be-hired assistant to move his wife and baby into her house. And she was happily making plans for some of the extra time she would free up to spend with TJ.

"DR. GILLESPIE, I had my lawyer look over the contract and the rental agreement, and he said everything's in order." Barry Cassel pulled the papers from his briefcase and handed them to Mare. "Here they are, all properly signed." Close to her own age, Barry was tall and muscular with straight, dark brown hair and hazel eyes. He had a friendly, outgoing manner, and he and Mare had liked each other at once.

Although Barry was a native Texan, after graduation from veterinary school he had worked in Idaho with a fellow graduate. He married his childhood sweetheart, and he and his wife, Berta, had a two-year-old son, Bobby. Barry and Berta decided that they wanted their son, and any future children, to grow up in Texas, so they'd made plans to return.

He and Mare were in her office seated on either side of the desk. "That's great, Barry. Welcome to the practice." Mare offered her hand and they shook. "From now on, please call me Mare. I know most of the people in this town, and they're a pretty good sort. I think you'll be happy you came here."

"I think so, too. Berta and I have already met a few people, and we were impressed by their friendliness. When would you like me to start?"

Mare's cheeks dimpled. "Just as soon as you can. Dr. DiNicola from Sharlesburg will be glad to have another person thrown into the mix, too. We've been covering for each other on alternate Sundays, and your being here will give us some welcome breathing room. Darn animals don't know what Sunday is." Mare's Sharlesburg friend had been doing extra duty on Saturdays, too, to give Mare a break in getting to know her father. But paybacks would come, sooner or later. "I assume you'll be giving two weeks' notice to your current associate?" Barry nodded, and Mare continued, "That will give me more than enough time to get moved. As soon as I'm out, you can start moving in, and I'll expect you in the office two weeks from Monday. How's that?"

"That's fine. The rental agreement doesn't start for two weeks after that, though. Should we prorate the rent for that extra time?"

"No, consider that part of your welcome here." Mare rose and Barry followed. They shook hands again, and Mare walked him to the door. "I'm looking forward to meeting Berta. Anyone married to a vet has to be a very understanding person."

"She is. We'll be seeing you soon." Barry left and Mare leaned against the closed door. "Thank whatever gods that be. An assistant." She put the agreements in her safe, picked up her already packed belongings, and went out the door, heading for the Meridian ranch. *Heading for TJ*, her heart sang. Would she always have this feeling of being only half a person when she wasn't with TJ? And feeling so perfectly complete when she was? She hoped it never stopped.

MARE, TRYING TO do too many things in too little time, was exhausted. She crawled into bed and snuggled up to TJ. She lay quietly in TJ's arms and delighted in the gentle caresses against her back.

Gradually, TJ stilled her hand as she heard Mare's breathing slow and deepen. Son of a gun, she fell asleep! Poor kid must have been dead tired. Disappointed, TJ nevertheless knew that Mare was off the next day and they would have other opportunities. Happy in anticipation of a whole day together, TJ drifted off to sleep, too.

Mare awoke in the middle of the night. At first embarrassed that she had fallen asleep after looking forward to lovemaking, she soon figured that she must have been exhausted and the sleep would do her good. She hesitated to move, lest she wake TJ, but she smiled, picturing in her mind the repose that came to

TJ's gorgeous face only in sleep.

As often happened when waking during the night, Mare started to think more than she wanted to, and she fought against it, hoping only to go back to sleep.

She was so glad Paula and Erin had been able to finish clearing the office. Paula said movers would come Monday to haul everything away, and she'd start painting right after that. Looked like Mare might be able to move out here within the week. Everything seemed to be falling beautifully into place — a "new" father, a new assistant, a new home, and TJ.

A pleasant warmth filled her as she recalled the surprise she and Paula had cooked up for TJ for later today. Erin, delighted when they told her, had even offered a few suggestions. Today, Mare would concentrate on pleasing TJ.

Mare kissed the slope of TJ's breast and snuggled closer as TJ's arm reflexively tightened around her. Then Mare's mind finally quieted, and her breathing slowed to match TJ's as she fell asleep once more.

MARE SLIPPED FROM TJ's embrace in the morning, and got out of bed, still pleading fatigue. The night before, she honestly had been too tired, but this morning she was pretending, believing that restraint now would add enjoyment to their planned time together later in the day.

TJ pouted. "You aren't sick or something are you?"

"No." Mare bent over and planted a swift kiss on the pushed out lip, ducking to avoid TJ's encircling arm. "But don't look so sad. We have a surprise for you."

"What is it?"

"You'll find out later." Mare took some pity on TJ's look of frustration. "I will tell you that once you use your catheter tube and bags this morning, you can dispense with them for a while today." That said, she left a curious TJ and dashed into the bathroom. She showered and dressed, fending off any further questions about the surprise. Mare went in search of Paula and found her in the kitchen stacking a few plates in the dishwasher.

"Erin gave me a hand and everything's ready and packed," Paula said.

"Great." Mare gave her a quick squeeze. "By the time TJ does her exercises and we finish breakfast, we can leave. I told her we have a surprise, so she'll probably try to pump it out of you."

"She won't hear any news from me." Paula dried her hands. "I'll get the exercises started right now. There's coffee made if you want some."

Mare took a mug from the cupboard and poured a cup. "How do you think TJ's going to react to this? Do you see any problems?"

"TJ should be fine. This is a super idea. That last episode you two went through really shook her up. She needs a good experience to replace that." Paula made a thumb's up sign and went to take care of TJ.

All through breakfast, TJ forced herself not to ask Mare anything about the surprise. She just kept throwing daggered looks at her and Paula and Erin, recognizing that the three were in cahoots and determined to torment her. And she was just as determined not to let them.

When breakfast was over, Erin went out the door. Mare and Paula, chatting away, cleared the island. After about ten minutes, Mare took charge of TJ's wheelchair and pushed her out to the barn and up the ramp. Erin brought the saddled Flag toward her.

"What's going on?" TJ said. "Where am I supposed to be riding Flag to?" Mare didn't answer, and TJ saw Paula come bounding into the barn, grab a saddle from the tack room, and take it over to Runny's stall. "Wait a minute." TJ's jaw set and she looked at Erin who still held Flag. "Who's supposed to ride Runny?"

"I'm going to." Mare moved to the side of the chair so TJ could see her. "We're going for a ride somewhere to find out the surprise."

"Mare." TJ looked stern. "Are you sure you want to ride that horse?"

Mare's face grew red, and she glanced away. "I don't...look, TJ, I want to go riding with you."

"Is riding Runny part of the surprise? Or do we just need to go wherever it is on horseback?"

"We just need to go on horseback."

"Okay. Erin, strap me toward the back of the saddle, and Mare can ride with me." She saw Mare's face clear and knew the suggestion appealed to her.

Erin said, "That's a great idea. Paula and I were leery of Mare riding for a while without taking some runs close to home."

"More fun for you, too, boss," Paula called out as she returned Runny's saddle to the tack room. Erin and Mare helped TJ use the hoist to mount Flag, then they strapped her toward the back of the saddle.

Mare managed to mount from the ramp by swinging her leg forward past the saddle horn and settling in front of TJ. Clasping one arm around her, TJ clucked to Flag and they started off.

TJ said, "You mind telling me which way I should direct Flag to go?"

"We're going to the lake. Just aim her that way."

"The surprise is at the lake?"

"Yep."

"And you're not telling me until we get there, right?"

"Right."

TJ reached under Mare's shirt and laid her long hand flat against Mare's bare stomach. Just before her lips locked on the side of Mare's neck, she said in a throaty murmur. "We might not get to the lake."

Mare grabbed the wandering hand and brought it back outside her shirt. "Uh-uh. No hanky-panky until we get to the lake." *Good grief, the woman's voice turns me on. It's no wonder her touch drives me crazy.*

"Hanky-panky?" TJ mocked the expression. "Okay, no hanky-panky. What do you think about a little necking?" TJ moved Mare's hair from the back of her neck and planted a kiss there.

Mare closed her eyes and leaned back against the firm body. "I think we better hurry and get to the lake."

AT LAST, THEY reached their destination. Mare turned her head to watch TJ's eyes widen when she saw a blanket spread on the ground with a tablecloth, picnic basket, cooler, and several firm pillows sitting on it. She gave Mare an extra hug. "So, this is the surprise. A picnic!"

The place chosen was a grassy clearing that abutted the lake, just beyond the ring of trees. One solitary old sentinel stood in the clearing, spreading its boughs over the blanket, its branches reaching to the edge of the water.

"This is a perfect spot. I have only one question."

Mare swung her leg over the saddle horn and slid down to the earth. "What's that?"

"How am I supposed to get off of Flag?" Mare looked up for the raised eyebrow and wasn't disappointed.

"Hand me your cell phone, baby." Mare smirked as TJ mouthed "Baby?" But she pulled the phone from her belt holder and passed it to Mare who punched in some numbers and spoke. "We're here."

She handed the phone back. "Now we have a short wait."

About two minutes later, Erin and Paula showed up in the Rover. They pulled next to Flag and piled out. "Here we are, boss," Paula said, "ready to bring you back to earth."

Erin poked Paula with an elbow. "Behave yourself."

"Well, it sure as hell doesn't take an hour and a half to ride out here from the ranch, even on a slow horse, and Flag isn't slow."

Mare tried for the innocent approach. "We were checking out the scenery."

"Sure," Paula said. "Guess that's why your blouse is buttoned crooked, right?"

Mare looked quickly down at her shirt and saw that it was, indeed, buttoned wrong. She felt a blush start up her cheeks. It turned into a full-fledged red face when she heard TJ's dry response. "She didn't say what scenery."

Everyone laughed, including Mare, and Erin and Paula helped TJ down from Flag. Supporting TJ by draping her arms over their shoulders, they settled her on the blanket with her back against the tree. While Erin held TJ steady, Paula moved the cooler against her one side so she would have something to balance against and put a pillow on her other side. Mare tied Flag's reins to a bush, allowing the palomino room to graze the sweet grass, then loosened the saddle girth.

"How's that, TJ? You comfy?" Erin was squatted next to her, not letting go until she made sure TJ could sit without help. When TJ nodded, Erin kissed her on the cheek and stood up. "Okay, you guys, enjoy. Paula has fixed a feast for you, and there's beer, soda, and a bottle of wine in the cooler. Give us a call when you need us, and we'll be back to help get TJ onto Flag."

"Thanks, both of you." Mare gave them each a hug. "We'll probably be a few hours."

"You know what?" TJ said. They turned to TJ and waited. "If someone would loop a sturdy rope around this limb above me and tie a knot every foot or so, I could probably get on and off Flag with only a little help."

The other three looked at each other in chagrin. Then Mare pointed out something that saved face for them. "We needed to have the picnic basket and cooler brought out anyway." Erin and Paula looked happier at this explanation. "But let's get a rope out here for the visits when we aren't picnicking, okay?"

"Sure thing," Erin pulled a notebook and pencil from her pocket and added that suggestion. She and Paula climbed in the Rover, waved, and left.

"Mare." TJ's seductive voice climbed across her heart. "Come here and let me fix those buttons."

"How about if we eat first?" Mare sat down next to the

basket and opened the lid.

"You and that stomach! Are you always hungry?"

Mare stopped a moment, seeming to give the question serious consideration. "Yeah, I think I am always hungry. But it's not always food I'm hungry for." She looked straight into TJ's eyes. "Most of the time it's something—someone—else." She squealed as TJ rolled onto her side, then her stomach, got her arms under her and "walked" to Mare. She reached for her, but Mare was too quick. She jumped to her feet and stepped over the picnic basket, settling on the far side of it. "No, you don't. Food first. I don't know what you run on, but this body needs some fuel."

TJ rolled onto her back. "Okay, I give up. I've waited this long, I guess a little longer won't kill me. Food first. Wouldn't want you wasting away to nothing from burnout." She propped herself on one elbow. "This is a great surprise. Thanks."

"You've been working so hard, trying to keep things moving for the ranch and the packing plant, I figured it was time for you to relax." Mare dished out the food onto the china plates Paula had provided and handed one to TJ who rolled up onto her side. "You're the most important person in this mix, sweetheart. We don't want you burning out, either."

"That 'most important person' part is a matter of opinion." TJ's hooded eyes left no doubt as to whom she considered the most important. In answer, Mare tossed a wrapped chicken leg at her, which TJ easily caught and set on her plate.

"Eat."

"Yeah, and hurry up about it," TJ said, eating quickly as though she were going to wolf the whole meal.

Mare came back to the other side of the picnic basket to sit cross-legged next to TJ. She reached for one of the pillows and handed it to TJ to lean on. "No, slow down and enjoy it. Or you won't get any dessert."

"Okay, okay, I'm eating slowly. Please notice how well behaved I've been all day, in spite of being mercilessly tormented by a green-eyed vixen." Mare glanced down at the crooked buttoning on her shirt and looked back up with a questioning tilt of her head. TJ grinned and shrugged. "Well, I behaved almost all day. Can't blame a girl for trying."

"Right. So don't go pretending you were the only one being tormented."

"You loved every minute of it."

"Yeah, I guess I did."

When they finished eating, Mare picked up TJ's empty plate, stacked it with hers, and put it into the basket. Then she picked up both sides of the tablecloth, folded them over whatever was left on it, and set it in, too.

She reached into the basket with one hand and grasped the stems of two wineglasses. She froze in that position as TJ's arm encircled her waist. Using the hold for leverage, TJ used her other hand to unbutton Mare's shirt. "That was just an appetizer," she said, capturing a mound's peak between her teeth and teasing with her tongue. She dropped her hand onto Mare's jeans and began stroking deeply.

Mare let go of the glass stems and entangled one hand in the dark hair to pull TJ tighter against her. Her other hand loosened her jeans top as she squirmed to straighten her legs to face TJ's body. "Okay, wine later," she murmured.

THEY LAY NAKED together on the blanket, a gentle breeze from the lake serving to cool the vestiges of their lovemaking. Dampness still lingered where their skin touched. Mare lay on her back, fingers lost in TJ's hair, one hand cupping her cheek. TJ's head rested against Mare's stomach, one long arm wrapped underneath her thighs while the other hand stroked up and down Mare's side and hip.

"Does that hand ever stay still?" Mare's lazy question hung in the air.

The hand stopped. "Do you want it to?"

"No, never."

There was a deep chuckle and the hand returned to its gentle stroking.

"TJ, do you know how to swim?"

"Yeah."

"You want to give the lake a try?"

"You planning on carrying me over there?"

"Come on, it's only about twenty feet with a slight incline. We're practically in it already. You can roll down there. Let go of me and I'll show you." TJ loosened her grasp on Mare's legs and raised her head. Mare scooted out from under her and laid out flat on the ground. She started rolling and traveled right up to the water's edge.

"See?" She waved to TJ. "It's easy. Come on."

TJ turned the upper half of her body and lined it up with the shoreline. She rolled slowly down the incline just as Mare had, surprised at how easily her body moved across the grass. She stopped at the edge of the water and looked up at Mare who was now standing. "Not a bad idea. But I'm not too sure I can stay afloat. My legs will probably weigh me down."

"In the water you won't weigh anywhere near what you weigh out of the water, so I can help hold you up. I'll support your legs. Come on, give me your hands." Mare took hold of TJ's hands and dragged her the last couple of feet across the grass and into the water. She kept pulling her until the water was up to her chest, then moved TJ's hands to her shoulders. "You okay so far?"

"Yeah, as long as I hold onto you. This feels pretty good. They kept taking me into the pool at the hospital for therapy, but I was too depressed to give a damn. I don't feel that way now, thanks to you." She pulled herself closer to Mare, wound long arms around her neck, and kissed her soundly.

Hugging TJ's body tightly and holding the kiss, Mare sank below the surface of the water, then rose again to the air. Their lips broke apart and Mare said, "You look like a different person with your hair plastered back like that."

"Different? How?"

Mare shivered with delight as TJ's velvet voice skittered through her. "I'm not sure. Younger? More rakish? Not quite your usual sober self."

"Sober am I?" TJ tickled Mare's ribs.

"Look out, now. Tickling me out in the middle of the water is not a good idea unless you're sure you can swim."

"Mmm. You have a point. Maybe I should try this instead."

"TJ, stop! I'm warning you, you better stop. You better...ohhh, don't stop. Don't ever stop." TJ's mouth closed on Mare's as her knees buckled, and she and TJ went below the surface again. Mare's hands and body joined TJ's, and they locked together in the throes of passion. Mare finally remembered they needed air to live and managed to find enough strength in her legs to straighten up. Their mouths stayed fastened together until their bodies quieted, then they pulled their lips apart, panting.

"You could have killed us, woman," Mare said with a gasp.

TJ put her head on Mare's shoulder and clung to her. "I thought we did die. Wasn't that heaven we just visited?"

"Yes, yes, yes! Sure felt like heaven to me. What is it about water that is so sexy?"

"Moments like this, maybe? You know what? I think we're ready for that wine now. We have a few things to celebrate today."

Mare pulled TJ back to the shore and helped her roll back to the blanket. She went to Flag and pulled several towels from the saddlebag. Back at TJ's side, she used a towel to dry off TJ's face and throat, then moved to her collarbone.

"I can do that, you know."

Mare's hands froze. "You want me to stop?"

"No, never."

Mare continued with enthusiasm, kissing each part as she dried it. When she finished, she helped TJ get dressed, then dried herself and dressed while TJ, her eyes filled with love, observed her.

"I love to watch you, Mare. Every movement you make is so smooth and graceful. Just like you. What did I ever do to deserve you?"

Mare finished buttoning her shirt — correctly, this time — while TJ pushed herself back up against the tree beside the cooler. "I ask myself that same question almost every day. I guess the two of us just got very, very lucky."

She lifted the wineglasses from the picnic basket, and TJ pulled the wine from the cooler. Mare moved next to her and held the glasses while TJ filled them, then set the bottle back. TJ held her glass out. "To us."

Mare clinked her glass against TJ's. "To us."

They sat side by side, shoulders touching, and drank their wine as the mid-afternoon sun reflected from the glassy surface of the lake.

TJ glanced down at Mare. "We'll have more time to spend days together like this when you get your new assistant and can move to the ranch."

"Boy, am I looking forward to that. Barry has a great resumé, a terrific personality, and talks like a dedicated worker. I know he'll be an asset to the practice, and the additional free time that will give me seems almost too good to be true. Running two offices should be a real boost for everybody as well."

"Mare, we have several suites of rooms in the ranch house. I want you to pick out a suite for your own."

Mare sat forward to look into TJ's face. "Why?"

"I want you to stay with me every second, of every minute, of every hour, of every day, forever. But I don't want you ever to stay with me just because you feel obligated to. Or, you might need some room," TJ said, "if you're ever in one of those huffs you talked about and could use someplace to be alone for a while." She looked down and picked up Mare's hand that had been resting on her thigh. "Are you all right with that?"

TJ's eyes swept up and Mare's heart flip-flopped once again. She saw a tiny glint of satisfaction, and she punched a slightly startled TJ in the arm. "Yes, I'm all right with that, but you know what your eyes do to me, and still you pin me with them. Have you no mercy at all?"

TJ's lips parted. "Well, I — "

The voice was interrupted as Mare's mouth sealed the lips, then forced them apart with a tasting tongue.

At last the kiss ended, and Mare kept her body against TJ's where it seemed to belong.

TJ said, "Time to call home, I guess." Mare sighed and nodded, and TJ made the call.

Touching their heads together, they held hands like young lovers and murmured endearments as they waited for Erin and Paula to arrive.

Chapter
Twenty-Two

"WELL, BOSS-LADY, what now?" Paula threw the last files onto the desk in front of TJ, a grin pulling itself onto her face. They had just covered every inch of the packing plant work areas, and Paula had reason to be proud. The first start-up on the new machinery had gone well, and the few workers who were in the plant had no difficulties in using it or rectifying the simulated breakdowns. As soon as the final inspections were completed, the plant would be operational.

TJ was pleased to see Paula so happy. Paula had put an awful lot of work into getting the plant up and running. In fact, without Paula and Erin, the rejuvenation of Meridianville would have been impossible. "Where are Mare and Erin?"

"Hoping I can convince you to call it a day."

"Hmm. That might be possible, on one condition."

"Which is?"

"It's late and I think we all deserve to celebrate. Let's stop at that bar on the road out of town, get a bite to eat, and have a few drinks."

"Sounds like a plan to me. Who's the designated driver?"

"You and Erin can toss for it." TJ opened her briefcase and inserted the files Paula had dropped on the desk.

"Oh great," Paula said with a moan. "I never win when we toss for it."

"You could just ask Erin to drive for a change, you know." TJ looked over her shoulder as she wheeled out of the door. "This is your celebration, after all."

"Good point, well presented, and you can tell her." Erin actually took the fact pretty well that she had been made designated driver. They all piled into the van: Paula and Mare in the rear, Erin and TJ up front. Morale within the quartet was high. Things on the ranch, at the factory, and in town were going well. Life was treating them all kindly for a change. Erin knew she'd be the only one sober by the end of the evening, but she didn't begrudge Paula her night out.

The bar wasn't far from the factory site, ten minutes at the most. Since it was still early in the evening, it wasn't that crowded when they arrived. Like most bars in smaller towns, it was dimly lit, with smoke-clouded air, and the wail of a country singer came from the jukebox.

They immediately found a table that TJ's chair could fit beneath, and a somewhat tired-looking waitress named Sal came for their order. TJ dove in first, ordering a jug of beer, cutting off any remarks by telling them all that they were having a real drink not some fancy cocktail concoction. She also requested chips and nuts and whatever else Sal could lay her hands on. Glad to oblige the obviously happy group, Sal made to leave, but Erin stopped her, asked for a large cola, and told her she was setting a limit on the amount of beer that would cross the bar for the table tonight.

TJ scowled across at her but didn't argue. She knew the rules. She was the one who had established them. They all knew that whoever was driving made the decisions. If Erin told them they were leaving, they left, no arguments, and if she told someone they had had enough then they stopped. Anybody who didn't play by the rules would pay a nasty forfeit when they finally sobered up. If they should get arrested, then they were left for the night in the care of the local law.

Both Erin and Paula had paid the forfeit more than once, and neither of them cared to pay it again. There was the time several years ago when they'd ignored TJ's "it's time to go," and they'd spent a very uncomfortable night sitting outside their hotel because TJ had told the manager not to let them in. She hadn't even relented when it rained, though she did send out raincoats for them.

But they had gotten her back, a year later, just before TJ's accident, when TJ over-imbibed and wouldn't come along when told. She ended up cleaning Erin and Paula's apartment for a week and also doing the laundry and cooking. The cooking part of the agreement got changed to restaurant or take-out after the initial taste of what TJ had put in front of them.

The rules had been carefully explained to Mare, and she agreed to stick to them.

An ice-cold jug of beer and three glasses appeared on the table, and Paula did the honors by pouring the first drink. She waited until Sal got back with Erin's cola and the snacks before she made the first toast of the evening. Paula stood and raised the glass in her hand.

"To the loves of our life and a job well done," she said. She took a deep drink as the others repeated the toast.

In the two hours they sat there, the bar steadily got busier. The noise level rose, and it became increasingly difficult to see through the layer of smoke hanging in the air. Erin checked her watch again, wondering what time to call it quits on the happy group. It was just after eight-thirty. She'd give them another half an hour.

Mare rose unsteadily to her feet and smiled down at TJ who was gazing lovingly up at her. "I'll be back in a few minutes, sweetie." TJ tangled her hand in Mare's and squeezed tightly. Mare would have appreciated a more open display of affection but recognized that those around them probably wouldn't.

"Hurry back," TJ said, and her lower lip drooped in a pout. "I'll miss you." Mare returned the squeeze, then tottered off toward the restrooms, weaving between those who were dancing to the country music, and showing more grace and expertise than should have been granted to her by the amount of alcohol she had consumed. TJ propped her jaw in her hand and watched Mare's shapely body disappear from sight.

Erin felt a heavy weight on her shoulder and looked to her left. Paula now rested her head on Erin's shoulder as she talked to TJ who was still gazing in the direction that Mare had disappeared. Erin decided it was time to get her lady home to bed. "TJ!" She waved a hand to get her attention. "TJ!"

TJ turned her head slowly toward Erin. "Hmm?"

"Last one, then we go. Okay?"

"Sure," TJ said and went back to gazing after Mare.

Mare made it through the maze of people, eventually breaking through the dancers, and spied the facilities she was after. She edged her way around a group of four rather loud men, not recognizing them in the smoky atmosphere. She pushed the women's restroom door open, squinted at the bright light, and groaned. She was really going to regret this tomorrow. A few minutes later she exited the restroom to trek back to her table. She had put one foot on the dance floor when a hand grabbed her shoulder and turned her around.

"Hello there, Doc." Mare blearily looked up and recognized Nick Lanson, a local troublemaker. He hollered over the music, "You gonna let me and my buddies buy you a drink?"

Uh-oh. She smiled at him and then carefully removed his hand. Equally loudly, she said, "Thanks for your offer, but I'm with friends." She turned and made as rapid an exit as possible across the dance floor.

TJ beamed when she saw Mare appear through the crowd. She grabbed hold of her hand and pulled her down into a chair. "You're back!" She inclined her head toward Erin. "The big, bad lady over there says we have to go."

"Yes," Erin said, "and the big, bad lady is sticking to her guns."

"No fair," Mare said. "We were just starting to have fun."

"Ah, ah, ah," Paula said with a pronounced slur to her words. "Remember the rules."

NICK WATCHED MARE walk away from him and turned back to his friends. Juan was nearly in tears, he was laughing so hard. Miguel wasn't much better. Tony, the youngest of the four, strolled up to him and draped an arm around his shoulders.

"Nice try, Nick," he shouted, "but I'd say the doc's brush-off was better." In the years that they'd hung around together, Tony had nearly a hundred percent success when it came to the ladies, and Nick had a rather less auspicious track record. Juan and Miguel normally kept out of the competition that had sprung up between the other two. Tony let his gaze wander over in the direction the doctor had disappeared. His eyes fixed on a parting in the crowd, and he saw her sitting down at a table full of women. "Oh, looky there. I wonder if that's some of her new friends from the Meridian ranch." His face turned dark when he thought about the buckshot fired into the side of his truck by some maniac out there. Chief Jackson had let them off with a warning to stay away from the ranch, but that didn't satisfy Tony.

Nick looked over at the younger man and said, "Twenty says you can't get her to have a drink with you either."

Tony let a rakish smile cross his face. "I'll take that bet, but you double it if she walks out of here with me. Why don't you guys come run interference with her girl friends?" And maybe they could stir up a little trouble for that Meridian crowd.

The others agreed, and the four men made their way through the dancers.

Erin spotted them first as they crossed the dance floor. She wholeheartedly wished that she'd suggested they leave earlier. They'd had this problem before when they'd gone out as a threesome. At other times, in other places, a lot of men had tried to pick them up, TJ especially. They had come up with inventive ways of dealing with the problem, and of course, there was the direct way of just telling them they were gay. But they had no idea how the town would react to that tidbit of information, so they didn't want to give it out just yet. She looked at her inebriated companions, trying to figure out whether she would get any assistance from them, but it didn't look hopeful.

Tony walked up behind Mare while his three friends spread themselves around the table. "Ladies," he said in greeting.

Mare was disturbed that Nick and his friends had followed her. She knew this could be trouble. None of them had a love for the Meridian family for starters, and the guys weren't known for their good manners.

TJ saw Mare's unease and wondered what it was about.

Now that Tony had the attention of everybody at the table, he tried to turn his charm on Mare.

"I just wanted to apologize for my friend's earlier behavior and wondered whether I could buy you and your group a drink."

Mare gave him a polite smile, knowing that antagonizing this man and his friends wasn't a good idea. She was rapidly beginning to sober up. "That's a really nice offer, Tony, but I'm afraid we were just leaving."

With that, Erin stood up and pulled the unsteady Paula with her.

Tony looked shocked at the immediate brush-off, but he didn't give up. "Come on, one more won't make a difference."

Erin intervened in a firm voice. "As my friend said, it was a nice offer, but we really do need to get going. Some other time, maybe."

TJ was a trifle drunker than she usually allowed herself to get, but she could tell that the man questioning Mare was trouble. She caught his fleeting glance toward his friends, one of whom was trying to hide a growing smirk. Even through the alcohol haze, alarm bells went off in TJ's head as the fake pleasantry on the face of the man Mare had called Tony faltered, and anger showed through. "Some other time?" He put a hand on Mare's shoulder, his hold scarily intimate. "No, we want to buy you a drink now. Just one won't hurt."

Mare shuddered as his hand came into contact with her shoulder. "Look, thanks, but we're just not interested."

Nick was grinning openly and elbowing his buddies, and it didn't take a rocket scientist to see that the men were goading one another on while embarrassing Tony for his lack of success in hitting on them.

Mare continued to look at Tony, then down at his hand, which he finally removed. "As I said, guys, thanks for the offer but we're leaving." Mare stood up, walked behind TJ's chair, and pulled it from beneath the table. "Goodnight."

Erin breathed a sigh of relief. It looked as though they were going to get out of the bar without a major scene. She put an arm around Paula's waist and slowly turned her toward the door.

When he saw the wheelchair, Tony's attention switched

immediately to TJ. "Hey, you're that crippled Meridian. I thought these women were from the Meridian ranch, but I didn't think the owner was here, too, you bitch!"

He said it loud enough that the other patrons in the bar noticed something was happening. "Your family turned this town into a cesspool when you abandoned it." A snarl further marred his countenance. "My old man committed suicide because of you. You took away his job, and he couldn't support us no more. You ruined my family's life, and you come back here to lord it over us? We're supposed to bow down and kiss your ass? I don't think so."

TJ turned the chair and saw that the man, so engrossed with raving at her, now had a bruising grip on Mare's arm and was actually shaking her. His voice lowered into a growl. "Next time we hit your ranch, I'm gonna put some buckshot into those damn horses of yours, just like someone did to my truck."

The idiot was threatening three objects of TJ's deepest affection: her lover, her horses, and her ranch.

Tony's friends were nodding their heads in agreement with his tirade. They didn't seem to be taking any notice of TJ, apparently assuming that the wheelchair meant she was no threat.

She glanced behind her and saw Erin holding up Paula. The others in the bar didn't look as though they were going to interfere. She guessed that left her to straighten this guy out.

Because all eyes were on Mare and her noisy antagonist, nobody but Tony noticed when TJ rolled up beside him. Reaching up, she took hold of his thumb at the joint where it attached to his hand and twisted. The movement put pressure on the ligaments and tendons, which she knew caused excruciating pain.

"Yow!" he yelped. He let go of Mare's arm. TJ pulled his thumb downward, and he could do nothing but follow.

"Hi," she said as a pair of drunken slits for eyes came down to her level. Her voice was low and menacing, barely loud enough for him to hear. "The only part of Meridianville that's a cesspool is whatever spot you're standing on, you useless piece of shit." She twisted his thumb again to hammer home her point.

Tony looked at her in amazement. He seemed stunned that a woman in a wheelchair was crushing his thumb.

"You do know I could break this appendage without thinking about it, don't you?" He nodded rapidly, and she smiled sweetly at him. "You come anywhere near anything that belongs to me, and it won't be your thumb that gets broken, stud. Your friends will be calling you 'Joanie.' You got that?"

He gave another rapid jerk of his head. Suddenly, someone kicked the jukebox, and it went silent. The other occupants of the bar muttered quietly, but everyone had stopped to watch the altercation between TJ and the big bruiser.

"Now," TJ said loudly, "my friend said we're leaving, and we'd appreciate it if we could do it without being disturbed." She relaxed her hold a little as though she were moving away. Tony's face took on a look of relief and the pressure eased. "You bitch!" He squealed in pain as her hold tightened again.

"Oh, and when a woman says no, that's exactly what she means." She gave one more twist. "Got it?" Tony nodded frantically. TJ released his hand, turned her chair, and waited for Mare to wheel her to the exit.

The bar patrons remained quiet as the four women reached the door, and then the absurdity of what they had seen took over. Everyone in the bar roared with laughter at the man who'd been brought to his knees by a cripple holding his thumb — and they hadn't heard anything but the last interchange of words.

Mare pushed the chair into the cool night air and took a deep breath. "My God, TJ. Where the hell did you learn to do that?"

"The boardroom, though I think it looks more impressive now that I'm in the wheelchair."

"Woman, you're incorrigible," Mare said.

Erin had already opened the van and helped Paula into the back. "Hey, you two coming?" she asked. "I'd like to get away from here before you cause any more trouble." She said it with humor in her voice, but underneath she was concerned. The look on the man TJ had just made a fool of hadn't been pleasant. Erin wanted to get out of here before he decided to come after them.

"Yeah, we're coming." Mare pushed TJ the last few yards to the van.

IN THE BAR, Tony was fuming. He gave Juan a shove. "Go watch them. Let me know when they leave the parking lot." The jukebox started back up as he turned to the other two men. "That Meridian bitch is not getting away with making a fool outta me in front of the whole bar. We already owe her a lesson for messing with our families. Last time didn't hurt her enough. We'll get her good this time."

Nick and Miguel agreed with him. They remembered how miserable life had turned for them when their parents' jobs had disappeared. Nick's father had deteriorated into a typical drunk who beat his wife and kids and finally drank himself to death.

Miguel's father had done his best, trying to eke out an existence on a rented parcel of land, but his fun-loving wife, tired of never having any money or the nice things it would buy, deserted her husband and son. Juan's family stayed together, but his association with the other three led him into always looking for trouble, same as they did. They all gloried in the bad reputations they'd built.

Tony's voice turned even nastier. "And that other one with the dark hair looks like the one who shot at us and messed up my truck. They're both gonna pay." He did a double shot from the round Nick provided and ordered another round. He saw Juan returning. "They leave?"

Juan hurried over and tossed back both of his double shots before answering. "Yeah. Took off in a van."

ERIN STARTED THE van and looked both ways before driving onto the main road back toward the ranch. Paula usually drove the bulky van. Erin was more accustomed to handling the Land Rover. After a few moments behind the larger steering wheel, she became more comfortable. She glanced at Mare who was sitting quietly next to her. "You okay?" she asked.

"Yeah, I'm fine. Just have one hell of a hangover playing with my head. It's amazing how quickly you can sober up when trouble starts, huh?"

"Oh yeah. But somehow I get the feeling that guy got more than he expected."

"Yep. Don't think he was prepared for the terror on two wheels back there, do you?"

"Uh-uh." Erin glanced into the rearview mirror. "Gods, would you look at those two?"

Mare turned and looked over her shoulder. Paula had slumped sideways in the back seat and was now fast asleep, cuddling TJ who was gently snoring, head rested against the cool glass of the window.

"I think our girls had a good night, don't you?" Mare said.

"I think we all had a good night until the end, and I think the only person who enjoyed that was TJ."

"Yeah, she did seem to get an awful lot of pleasure from bringing that guy down to her level, didn't she?"

"That's our TJ for you." Erin brought her full attention back to the road. The headlights of the van sliced through the thick blackness, letting her know where they were. Another twenty minutes, and they would have to wake the sleeping beauties in the back and get them into their own beds.

THE DANCERS AND drinkers in the bar had returned to their own pursuits and were no longer paying any attention to Tony and his buddies. Tony turned back to Nick and the other two, a dark scowl on his face. "That Meridian bitch isn't getting away with this. Think I'm gonna take the truck for a spin. Anybody coming?"

Nick shook his head. Tony was a hotheaded fool before he'd had a drink, and afterwards he was worse. Going after the women would only cause more trouble in the long run. Things had taken a turn upwards in the town since the Meridian ranch had reopened, and Nick didn't feel he had a bone to pick with them anymore. Besides, in the past Chief Jackson had turned a blind eye to their antics, but now his support couldn't be relied on. "Why don't we just forget about it for tonight, have a few beers, and enjoy ourselves?"

Tony sneered at the suggestion. "You wimping out on us, Nick? Scared of a group of women?" Miguel and Juan stood next to Tony showing their support for their slighted friend.

Nick raised a glass. "No, that's not it. I just don't see why we have to go chasing after them right away and spoil our night out. Sit down, have a drink."

Tony stepped forward and roughly pushed Nick in the shoulder. "That woman's going to pay for showing me up in front of all these people. And she's gonna pay now." He turned and walked over to the door. "You with me or not?"

Nick shrugged, upended his bottle of beer, and drained the dregs before placing it on a nearby table and following Tony out the door. Miguel and Juan shuffled after them.

NEARLY HOME, ERIN relaxed. The road was almost empty at this time of night. Only a couple of vehicles had passed, traveling in the opposite direction. Bright lights blinded her as she looked in the rearview mirror. She lifted her hand and angled the mirror so the glare no longer affected her eyes. A minute later the glare hadn't dissipated, but now she could make out the dark form of a truck close behind them. A sense of unease settled in her stomach, and she sped up slightly. The truck behind sped up, too.

Mare shook herself out of her thoughts as she felt the van accelerate. She turned toward Erin and saw her looking worriedly at the rearview mirror. "Everything okay?"

"I'm not sure. Some jerk is tailgating us."

Mare looked over her shoulder, past TJ and Paula, and out the back window.

"What do you think?" She faced back to the front.

"I think those guys from the bar couldn't take no for an answer, and although TJ's show was pretty good, I bet they didn't appreciate it." A rough jolt threw the van forward. Mare braced her arms on the dash to keep herself in her seat. A startled exclamation erupted from the back. Mare looked and saw Paula picking herself out of the space between the front and back seats. TJ had grabbed the back of the front seat.

"What the hell was that?" she said. Another jolt threw them all forward again.

Erin struggled to control the van as the hits from behind crashed into them. "I think those guys from the bar were a little pissed at us." She looked to the side as the headlights disappeared from behind them and made their way up the left side of the van. She slammed on the brakes, hoping to force the truck in front of them, but a split second later the truck followed suit. "Uh, guys, I think we're in trouble." Erin saw it coming this time. She swerved, taking the van off of the blacktop to avoid another slam.

TONY FILLED THE truck with a whooping yell as he urged the vehicle forward and into the van. Juan had pulled a six-pack of beer from an Igloo cooler that had been in the back of the truck, and all of the men were drinking.

"Hit 'em again, Tony." Juan rolled down the window and threw out an empty bottle, before cracking open another.

Tony complied and put his foot down on the accelerator. Another set of yells echoed through the truck.

"ANYBODY HAVE ANY ideas?" Desperate, Erin narrowly avoided the truck again.

"How far are we from the ranch?" TJ leaned forward and braced her arms against the back of the front seat.

"About five miles," Erin said through gritted teeth.

"The entrance to Abner's ranch isn't far away," said Mare. "See if you can swing in. We should be safe up there. I doubt if they want to carry on this game with witnesses."

Paula was digging through her backpack, which they had left under the rear seat of the van while they were in the bar. With a cry of triumph, she held aloft her cell phone. "I'll get the police." She tried to punch in the emergency number.

With quick glances to her left, Erin saw the men in the truck shaking fists and clutching beers. Tony, the driver, faked a move toward the van. Erin steered sharply to the right to avoid impact. He swerved over again as soon as Erin swung back onto the road. The two vehicles hit broadside, violently rattling the occupants of both.

Erin resisted the urge to ram the bigger truck back. She knew that was a fight the van couldn't win.

Now the two vehicles were side by side, and Tony tried to force them off the road. The dark stretch of blacktop in front of them had a steep embankment to either side.

"Ah hell," Erin shouted as she strained to turn the steering wheel. "Hold on tight! I can't keep us on the road!" For a second the pressure eased as the truck again swerved away. She sighed in relief, but then the truck came careening back at high speed. The shockingly strong impact shook her grip off of the steering wheel. A sharp, agonizing pain washed over her. Her wrist had snapped. She heard screams and recognized they were hers. Vaguely, she saw Mare try to grab the steering wheel.

Mare lunged further across Erin, but she couldn't get a firm hold of the steering wheel. The vehicle tipped and started to go over the steep embankment. She heard Paula shouting into her cell phone.

TJ experienced the same helpless frustration she had felt when Mare fell from the horse. Here she was, yet again, unable to do anything. She heard Erin scream and then felt herself sliding across the back seat as the van tipped. Oh hell, why hadn't she and Paula put the blasted seatbelts on? She grabbed blindly and found a strap. Without time to put it on properly, she wrapped it around herself and grabbed a tight hold on Paula. There was a moment of weightlessness. The van tumbled, throwing everyone about, then slammed to an abrupt halt.

TONY CACKLED LOUDLY as the van went over the embankment. "Payback's a bitch, ain't it?"

His buddies hooted and hollered as they all looked back, trying to see the carnage they'd caused. When Tony turned to face front, a bright light shone into the truck. "Oh shit. Wrong side of the road!" Tony swung hard to the left to avoid the oncoming vehicle. The truck shot off the other side of the road. It charged forward down the embankment and smashed into the trunk of a tree.

Silence descended along the midnight-black stretch of road.

MARE OPENED HER eyes. A full, pounding pain thumped in her head, which she knew had nothing to do with the amount of alcohol she'd consumed. She swallowed to get rid of the thick, brackish taste in her mouth and recognized the taste as blood. Her bleary mind began to make sense of her surroundings. The first thing she noticed was grass beneath her hands.

She struggled to sit up, groaning as the pain worsened. Raising a hand, she pushed hair from her eyes and forehead and felt the wetness of blood trickling from a shallow cut. Her breathing increased as she understood she'd been thrown from the van. Frantically she looked around and saw the vehicle twenty feet away where it had come to a stop. Lying on its side, it was facing down the steep embankment. A small stand of trees had arrested its plunge.

"Oh, sweet Jesus. TJ!" She scrambled to her feet, ignoring the multitude of aches and pains her body shouted out to her. She heard the thud of running footsteps and gave a startled yell as a hand caught hold of her. At once, she realized she had been falling.

"Hey, hey, take it easy. Sit down, you're hurt." Gentle hands lowered her to the ground.

"My friends are in the van. I have to help them."

"Mare? Is that you?"

Mare looked up into the face of Chuck MacMasters. "Oh, Chuck, thank the Lord. Some idiots ran us off the road on purpose."

"Yeah, I know. I saw it happen. They went off the other side of the road after I couldn't get out of their way. Tree stopped 'em. Missy's called the police and an ambulance."

"TJ and her friends are in the van."

"I'll go check it out and make sure they're okay."

"I'm coming with you." Even though her insides were trembling, she tried for a tone of voice that would assure the rancher she wouldn't take no for an answer. He nodded and carefully helped her to her feet.

The police car's siren wailed in the distance. "They got here quickly," Chuck said as Mare hobbled along by his side. He kept a wary eye on her as they approached the van.

"Paula phoned them before we were run off the road. We were hoping to make it to Abner's place." A deep groaning started off to the side of the van, and Mare and Chuck hurried over, trying to find the source in the long grass that hadn't been flattened by the skidding van. Mare caught sight of the familiar form of Paula on the ground. She was coming around, and Mare breathed a sigh of relief. One down, two to go. "Paula, lie still.

Help's on the way."

"Mare?" Paula let out another groan. "Erin? TJ?"

"We haven't gotten to them yet. You just stay here. I'm going to find out how they are." More rustling footsteps were approaching through the grass. She looked up and saw Chuck's wife, Missy.

"Who was it, and how are they?" Chuck said.

"It was Tony Yarrow and his bunch of rowdies. Tony was driving. He didn't make it. The other damn fools seem okay, just look shook up."

"How about if you stay with the lady here, while Mare and I go find the rest of her friends." He helped Mare to her feet again, and they went straight toward the van. The siren shut off as the police car pulled to the edge of the embankment. The flashing lights illuminated the accident scene somewhat. Doors opened and slammed shut, and two figures appeared at the top of the slope.

"Everybody okay down there?" Chief Jackson shouted.

Chuck said, "We got a few injuries down here, Curt. We still have to check the van."

"Did the truck get away?"

"Nope, came straight at me on the road then turned off. Ended up against a tree over on the other side."

"Okay, I'll go take a look. Ambulance is on the way. Shouldn't be too long."

As Chuck slowed to speak to the chief, Mare left his side and hurried to the van. The back door on the driver's side had been ripped off, which no doubt was how Paula ended up outside the vehicle. She clambered up the underside of the van, wincing as more bruises made themselves known. The driver's door was intact, though the window was missing. Mare reached over and felt around, coming into contact with Erin who was still strapped in by the seatbelt.

The darkness made it impossible to see how badly Erin might be injured. "Chuck, we need some light down here," she yelled over her shoulder. She heard Chuck holler to the chief, and she climbed up the rest of the way and sat with her legs dangling in the doorway that the back door should have protected. She peered into the deep, dark interior. "TJ?" She could just make out a dark form huddled at the bottom but was loath to jump in when she didn't know what was beneath her.

Another siren wail throbbed in the distance, and Mare knew that was the ambulance rushing toward them. She quickly glanced up the embankment and saw that some other cars and trucks had stopped to offer assistance. Several men made their way down toward them, and two of the cars turned in the road so that their headlights shed light on the scene.

She heard a scrabbling behind her. Chuck appeared and offered her a long-handled flashlight. Mare took a deep breath and clicked on the light. She checked Erin first. Erin was unconscious with a large bump on her forehead. Her swollen right wrist dangled grotesquely. Another deep breath, and Mare guided the beam of light to illuminate the back seat of the van. TJ lay crumpled and a dark stain covered the side of her white shirt. From this distance, she wasn't even sure that TJ was breathing.

Mare fought hard to keep her emotions under control. TJ needed her. "Chuck, when that ambulance gets here, you bring them straight over to the van, you hear me?"

"You got it," he said.

Mare braced her arms on either side of the opening and slowly lowered herself in, carefully placing her feet where they would do least damage, until she was surrounded on all sides by the van. She stood still for a moment, letting her weight settle before she crouched down and extended her hand to TJ's neck. Her fingers searched for a pulse. She couldn't find one. Panic built within her. She forced herself to take another deep breath and felt again, concentrating hard. There it was! Only a faint flutter against her fingers, but it was there. She quickly made an assessment of TJ's injuries. The bloody shirt indicated there was some damage to her side, probably from the broken window crushed underneath her. She didn't like TJ's position either. Her head was curled toward her chest, cramping her airway, and the arm she was lying on was curled at an unnatural angle.

Another light appeared, and Mare gazed upward toward a woman she didn't recognize, but a uniform that she did. "You need to get Erin, in the front, out first. TJ here has a previous spinal injury and will need an extrication device and collar before we try to move her."

"You a doc?"

"A veterinarian."

"Better than nothing," murmured the woman before she disappeared.

Mare felt the van move as other people climbed onto it. Another medic, this one male, appeared near the opening as she leaned over TJ, protecting her from anything that might fall from above. She kept her right hand in constant contact with her, trying to reassure TJ that she was still there. She waited as pieces of equipment were handed into the front seat of the van. The medic calmly and efficiently directed those helping him to get

Erin out. A stiff neck collar was handed to him, then an extraction device that he slipped behind her and fastened her into to keep her back and neck stable. Within a few minutes, they were ready to lift Erin clear. The van rocked again as they moved her out, and then for several seconds Mare was left alone with TJ.

"Ma'am?" Mare looked up as the male paramedic reappeared. "I need you to come up here so I can get down to your friend." Mare quickly climbed up and on top of the van. "My partner tells me your friend already has a spinal injury." He looked up at Mare as he checked TJ's pulse. "Can you tell me what level?"

"T-11. She was shot just over twenty months ago and still has bullet fragments embedded in her spine." She moved aside as another medic scrambled up beside her.

"Hey there," he said. "I've sent Billy and Janice off with the van driver."

"How was she?" Mare said.

"She'll be fine. Has a nasty bump to the head and a fractured wrist."

The medic below called out, "Marcus, I need oxygen and an IV line with fluid." Marcus reached into his medical bag and handed down the requested items.

Mare refused to get down from the van while they were working on TJ, though several people asked her to. As long as she wasn't in the way of the medics, she wasn't leaving. More and more people arrived at the scene.

It seemed an age before they were ready to get TJ out. Fearful, but feeling numb with shock, Mare jumped down and stood back with Chuck and Missy. The team worked smoothly together, following a well-orchestrated plan. Once they were ready to move TJ, they had her out in minutes.

It broke Mare's heart to see her like this. Her once tan skin was grayish-white, with a sheen of clammy-looking perspiration. A collar encased her neck, and her head was strapped tightly to a short backboard. Drip lines ran, one into each arm, and a square pad of gauze was bandaged to her side to slow the bleeding.

As soon as they lifted TJ to move her to the ambulance, Mare felt her legs buckle. Reaction to the crash finally hit home, now that she no longer had to be strong. A wave of darkness tunneled her vision, and she felt hands clasp hold of her. Then nothing.

Chapter
Twenty-Three

THE OVERPOWERING ODOR of antiseptic roused TJ to consciousness. She had come to hate that smell just after the shooting. Four months of immobility in a spinal rotational bed, unable to move even her head, had given her an almost pathological hatred of hospitals. Her dislike hadn't lessened, either, when she had been moved into her own room and into a normal hospital bed. She had to be having a nightmare, because there was no way on earth she would have willingly returned to this setting.

The next thing to assault her senses was the humming of electricity and the beeping of machinery that kept an annoyingly persistent beat with her heart. She heard the quiet murmur of voices and the gentle squeak of rubber-soled footwear on the highly polished floor.

This nightmare was frighteningly real. Her mind turned that thought over. Was she in bed at the ranch? Now she noticed the pounding of her head, and a groan escaped her mouth. God, they must have had a good time last night for her to have a hangover like this. Her eyes were still closed and felt glued together. She tried to lift her head into a more comfortable position but found she couldn't move it at all. Her eyes flew open, and panic gripped her as she realized this wasn't a nightmare. It was hard, cold reality. She felt a hand clutch hers and squeeze, but her throat was constricted with the panic that was building within her.

MARE SAT CURLED up in a comfortable chair that some kind soul had brought into the room where TJ was placed after she had been stabilized in the ER. And what an experience that had been.

Mare had awakened in the back of Chuck's truck on the way to the hospital, her head resting across Missy's thigh. She tried to sit up immediately, but Missy prevented that, telling her to rest until they got to medical help.

"Where are they taking TJ? I need to be there."

Missy gently stroked Mare's golden locks from her face. "Calm down, Mare, honey. We're right behind them. The chief's giving us an escorted run to the hospital. We'll be there soon."

Missy was right. Within five minutes, they arrived at the Emergency Room entrance. Chuck and Missy took Mare into the chaos that was the ER. It wasn't that late at night, but any time in an ER is busy. Nurses and doctors moved about with controlled speed, dealing with patient inquiries as they sped past.

People surrounded the reception desk. Chuck and Missy guided her in that direction, but Mare pulled off and went to find Paula and Erin and, most important, TJ. She wandered the department looking into rooms and curtained-off areas, unnoticed by the busy staff. She discovered a frantic Paula first and went to the exam table to envelop her in a tight hug. Tears fell in torrents down their faces.

"Do you know how Erin and TJ are?" Paula's voice was hoarse from crying.

"Not yet," Mare said, still holding tight. "I only just got here. Are you okay?"

Paula scrubbed the tears from her face. "Broke my damn leg, but apart from that just a few bruises. You?"

"I got roughed up here and there, banged my head, but don't remember much of the accident. I'm going to see if I can find TJ and Erin. Will you be okay by yourself for a while?"

"Yeah, just let me know as soon as you find out what's going on."

"I'll be back as soon as I can."

After one last squeeze, Mare stepped outside the cubicle. Through the portal window of double doors, she saw what looked like a mini operation theater with several doctors and nurses at work. One of the nurses turned from the table, came through the doors, and moved to rush by. Mare grabbed the nurse's shoulder, swung her around, and looked into cool, professional eyes. "Is that one of the victims who was just brought in from the van crash?"

"Yes it is. Excuse me, but I need to get these to the labs." And she was gone.

After only a moment's hesitation, Mare pushed the swinging door open and walked in.

"I'm fine," Erin was saying. "Now get me off of this damn table." Mare felt the tears begin again as she heard Erin's harsh voice berating the doctors and nurses.

"Miss Scott," one of the medical personnel said, "we need to assess your condition before we let you up. The more you argue, the longer it'll take and the longer you'll be on this table."

Mare thought listening in to this little drama could be fun, but she knew Erin would be anxious for news of Paula, TJ, and herself. "Hey, Erin," she said when she saw the combative look on her face. "Let the doctors do their job."

Several of the doctors and nurses looked up. One walked over, a scowl on her face. "Miss, you can't be in here."

"She stays or I get off this damn table now!" Erin yelled, lifting her hand toward Mare.

Mare ignored the nurse. She walked straight over to Erin and grabbed the raised hand. "Hey there. Paula sent me on a search mission for you." Relief crossed Erin's bruised face.

"She okay?"

"Yep. Broke her leg, but she's going to be fine. She's in the third cubicle down the hall from this area."

"And TJ?"

"Haven't found her in this rabbit warren yet."

"Excuse me, ma'am." Mare didn't pay the speaker any attention.

Erin said, "I'm sure she'll be fine. What about you? You look almost as bad as I feel."

The nurse cleared her throat. "Ma'am!"

Mare held up a hand. "Give me a second! I just banged my head and I'm a little bruised, but I'll be fine as soon as I find that woman of mine. You're going to be good for the doctors while I go find her, right?"

"Sure." She gave a hasty glance at another nurse who had entered the area and was steaming in their direction. Quickly she said, "Thanks for letting me know Paula's okay."

"That's enough," the new nurse said. "Get out of here."

"Yeah, yeah," Erin said. "I'll join Paula as soon as they finish with me here. You'll come back and let me know how TJ is when you find her?"

"I'll do better than that." Mare bent down and placed a tender kiss on Erin's bruised forehead.

Two sets of firm hands took hold of Mare's upper arms and gracefully propelled her backwards toward the door.

Mare called out, "Don't worry. I'll take you to see her."

And she kept that promise. She found TJ in the trauma room down the hall. The nurses were more insistent that she stay out and physically restrained her when she tried to enter. Just over an hour later, a doctor came out looking for TJ's relatives. Mare explained to him that as far as she knew, TJ had no living relatives. Though she was unsure, she thought Paula or Erin would be considered her next of kin, and that led to a meeting in Paula's curtained-off area. Erin, cleared of any major injury, was already there, wrist in a fiberglass splint.

The doctor was a tallish fellow named Barnes, and although he must have spoken to relatives before, he had a somewhat nervous disposition. He cleared his throat several times as Mare sat down in the chair next to Paula's bed. Erin was snuggled up next to her partner, staring intently at the doctor.

"Your friend's condition is quite serious at the moment. As you probably already know, her previous injuries make it difficult to assess the damage done in this accident." The shock must have shown on their faces. He moved closer and ran a hand across his chin. "Please, don't misunderstand me. Her life isn't in danger. But we have some decisions that need to be made, and made rather quickly." He pulled out X-ray films and scans from a holder he had brought with him. Walking over to the viewer, he clipped them up and turned on the backlight.

"We thought at first that she might have sustained a new injury to her spinal cord." He carried on hurriedly as he heard Mare's gasp. "But an MRI scan has shown us that that hasn't happened. It looks as though several fragments from her previous injury have moved, causing new symptoms of spinal cord injury to appear."

"What do you mean—new symptoms of injury?" Mare asked.

"By comparing test results to her old notes, several reaction responses have changed, becoming slower, or in one case, disappearing altogether."

Mare couldn't believe what she was hearing. Her gaze traveled to Erin and Paula. They were just as shocked as she was. Paula turned pasty white, and Mare could see the tears brimming in Erin's eyes. "So, what you're saying is that her injury has gotten worse?"

"Essentially, yes. But the reason these fragments weren't removed in the first place was because of their positioning. Now that they've shifted, there might be a chance they can be extracted. That raises another problem—finding someone to perform the operation."

Mare felt as though she had just been given the switch to turn on a light. For the first time since the doctor had started talking, hope stirred. "That won't be a problem. Call Michael Gillis over in Springerly. He'll do it."

The doctor paused. "Miss, Dr. Gillis is one of the top surgeons in his field, but he won't be able to drop what he's doing and perform the operation. These things cost an incredible amount of money and need a lot of preparation."

Paula spoke up this time, catching onto the fact that the doctor didn't know whom he was treating. "Money isn't a factor."

Mare got up slowly. "And Dr. Gillis *will* drop what he's doing and come running. He's my father, and he already has copies of TJ's medical records. Now I'd like to see TJ, then I'll phone my father, and we'll get this show rolling."

It was obvious that Dr. Barnes didn't have a clue what to do next. Mare took hold of his arm and steered him out into the hall and back to TJ's room.

Of course, it wasn't as easy as just phoning Michael, although he did arrive at the hospital within an hour of receiving Mare's call. TJ had other injuries to consider as well. The bleeding that Mare had seen when TJ was in the van came from a deep laceration to her side. She'd lost a lot of blood from that, and it had required internal as well as external stitches to close it. She was unconscious, and the reason for that baffled them all. Yes, she had hit her head, but the CT scan hadn't shown a fracture or swelling to the brain.

Michael decided to risk moving TJ back to his hospital unit at Springerly. He had better equipment set up for just such a patient.

After completing arrangements, Michael had an ambulance sent from Springerly the next morning. He had followed behind it, and he directed attendants as they loaded TJ carefully inside. He and Mare drove to Springerly while Paula and Erin decided they would need to return to Meridian when they were discharged later that day.

So here Mare was, two days later, still waiting for TJ to wake up. The only benefit to her continued unconsciousness was that Michael had been able to perform several tests to find out the extent of the newer SCI symptoms.

A moan coming from TJ's bed woke Mare from the doze she had fallen into. She sat bolt upright, leaned over, and took a tight hold of TJ's hand. "TJ? Sweetie, you back with us?" Mare felt TJ's hand clamp vise-like over her own. TJ's heart rate increased rapidly, as did the beep of the machine recording it. Mare looked closely at TJ who was, at this moment, face down with her chest rising and falling rapidly. Mare slipped to the floor so she could see TJ's face. TJ's eyes were scrunched closed, her mouth slightly open. A cold sweat dripped from her face.

Mare grimaced. Ah, hell on earth.

Her hand scrabbled around for the call button, and she pressed it twice, hoping that her father was close by. That done, she adjusted the bed slightly, using the electric controls, so it was inclined instead of horizontal. She gently caressed TJ's face. "TJ, open your eyes for me." She got no response. Continuing to gently stroke her face, Mare carried on. "I need you to slow your breathing down, honey." The door behind her opened, and she looked up to her father's concerned face.

"Everything okay?" he asked as he got near.

"Dad, she's awake but something's wrong."

WRONG? SOMETHING WAS more than wrong. To TJ's mind she wasn't in this hospital with Mare but in some small, private ward in a hospital two years previous. She was back there, reliving every agonizing minute of the time when she discovered not only that she had lost the use of her legs, but also that Lance, her beautiful, loving brother was dead. She remembered every second of that time in vivid detail, every word in stereo surround-sound, and she couldn't live through it again...

The other time, she had awakened facing the hospital ceiling, her head, arms, and legs secured to the bed. A hand had grabbed hold of her shoulder, and she recalled how Erin's face came into view, fuzzy at first, wobbling above her, then coming into focus. TJ had known from that moment that something was seriously wrong. She hadn't been bothered at the time that she couldn't feel her legs, hadn't been bothered that the parts of her body she could feel were screaming in agony. Her one thought was for her brother. Erin had burst into tears before she could say anything. Paula had barely been able to speak as emotion crowded her throat.

"God, TJ, it's good to see those baby blues again. We thought we might have lost you." Paula had her arms around the sobbing Erin.

TJ had tried to speak but her throat was dry, and it took her several attempts before she got her croaked question out. "Lance?" Paula didn't have to say anything. Her head dropped to Erin's shoulder, fresh tears pouring down her face.

TJ's life had lost all meaning in that one piercing moment of time. A black hole opened in her soul. All she had worked for, all she had ever hoped for—for herself and for Lance—was gone. The desolate cry that erupted from her soul scarred both Paula and Erin for life.

And now here she was...again. She started screaming.

Chapter
Twenty-Four

ERIN WOKE, STARTLED from her sleep by the echoing of a nightmare she no longer remembered. She adjusted her position and rolled so that her head was nestled once more in the crook of Paula's shoulder. Although Paula was still deeply asleep, her arm wrapped around Erin and pulled her in closer. Erin snuggled a bit more before settling down, but her mind was wide-awake and refused to let her sleep.

Her finger idly painted nonsense patterns on Paula's stomach. They had been released from the hospital the day before yesterday, after a night of suffering the ministrations of the nursing staff. She'd been on the verge of discharging herself when they relented and made sure she was put in a room with Paula. Erin wasn't sure, but she thought that Mare's father had something to do with that.

They also got to see TJ the morning they were discharged, before she was transferred to Springerly. She looked so small, attached to all the machines monitoring her. It brought back bad memories for Erin and Paula. But this time TJ had Mare there for her, and they hoped that would make a difference. Because, if Erin were honest with herself, she wasn't sure that she or Paula could go through such agonizing emotions a second time.

Paula whispered, "Are you going to lay there brooding all night, or are you going to tell me what's wrong?"

Erin tilted her head back. She strained upwards and felt Paula respond, leaning down to place a gentle, loving kiss on her lips. God, what would she have done if she had lost Paula?

Erin dropped her head and hugged Paula tighter, sharply sucking in a breath as she forgot and put pressure on her injured wrist.

"Sweetie, are you okay?" Paula said.

"Yeah, I'm fine. Just thinking about things. I want to go see TJ and Mare today. You think Bill will let one of the men drive us up to Springerly?"

"I'm sure that won't be a problem. We'll give him a call first thing in the morning." Paula rubbed soothing circles on Erin's exposed back. Erin snuggled tighter, and Paula smiled indulgently, knowing that within minutes Erin would be asleep now that her concerns had been addressed. It had been the same the first time TJ had been injured. Erin would lie awake for hours, then ask for the simplest of wishes — like going to see TJ, or going riding — and when Paula agreed, she'd be asleep in minutes.

They had talked about it, and Erin couldn't explain why these insignificant things bothered her. Paula rather thought that it wasn't them so much as the person they concerned. Ever since TJ had saved her from those thugs in college, Erin had taken it upon herself to look after TJ. And when she couldn't, she needed to be doing something for her. Paula thought it likely that Erin was feeling responsible for the crash, though she had done everything she could to prevent it.

Paula hadn't been able to get her to talk about it yet. She would though. Best not to let her avoid it for much longer. Another glance down assured her that Erin was once again asleep. In a few more hours, she silently promised, they'd get up and go see if their warrior had decided to rejoin them.

WHEN PAULA REQUESTED a driver to take them to Springerly, Bill assigned one of the men, Mike, to be at Erin and Paula's beck and call until they got their casts off. During the ride, Erin sat in the front next to Mike, while Paula had the whole back seat to herself, her leg raised onto it. They phoned the hospital before they left but were told that Mare was asleep and Michael was attending to a patient and couldn't be disturbed. Although they dug for more information on TJ, all they learned was that she was in stable condition.

Mike parked at the entrance to the hospital, hopped out quickly, and ran around to open the door for Paula. She slid herself forward and took the crutches that Mike lifted from the floor. "Thanks Mike. Go take yourself to the movies or something. We're going to be a few hours. We'll give you a call when we need to be picked up."

They were a pair to behold as they walked, or in Paula's case hobbled, into the hospital. With their assortment of bruises, they looked as though they had been in the ring with a heavyweight boxer. But they ignored the curious looks they got and made their way straight to the Gillis Clinic, which took up the entire sixth floor.

The clinic had its own physical therapy department, hydrotherapy pool, and specialized nurses, therapists, and counselors who looked after only those on the unit. In addition, the unit had one of the most experienced medical and orthopedic teams to deal with spinal cord injury.

Erin and Paula were impressed when they stepped from the elevator. With a carpeted floor and bright artwork hung from the walls, it didn't look like your average hospital unit. There was an information station directly in front of them. The young woman who sat behind the desk smiled in greeting and asked how she could help.

"We'd like to see TJ Meridian," Erin said.

"Are you relatives?"

"Not exactly." Paula wondered whether they were going to have an argument about getting in.

"In that case, may I just take your names? I'll make sure Miss Meridian can have visitors." The woman's even gaze didn't falter, but Paula could tell that she'd defend this desk and admittance to the unit with zeal if challenged. They gave her their names and got an immediate response. "Miss Scott, Miss Tanner, of course. Dr. Gillis has already put you on the admitting list. Sorry to delay you. Miss Meridian is down the corridor, room 604, fourth door on the right. Go right on in. No doctors are with her at this time."

"Thanks for your help." Erin and Paula moved in the direction the woman had pointed.

Erin pushed the door open slowly, not wanting to disturb Mare if she were still sleeping, but she needn't have bothered. Mare was wide awake and sitting in a comfortable chair. She turned as Erin opened the door and held it for Paula to hobble in on her crutches.

"Hey, there. How's she doing?" Paula said as she made her way over to Mare. Erin rushed to pull up another chair for Paula to sit in. TJ was lying on her back, head still securely strapped to prevent movement.

"She finally woke up last night, thank goodness," Mare said. "But she was a mess. She went totally berserk, screaming for her brother. Dad had to sedate her. She's been kind of restless ever since."

Erin sat on the arm of Mare's chair and wrapped an arm around her shoulder. "She was real bad last time when she woke up and found out about Lance. I guess this brings back too many terrible memories. What about you? Are you okay?"

Mare lifted her hand and patted Erin's arm. "Much better, now that I know she's going to wake up. She had me scared there for a while."

Paula leaned forward and held a hand out to Mare. When Mare took it, Paula squeezed gently and said, "You do know this is going to be very hard, don't you? I know it's different this time because TJ has you and something to look forward to, but — and it's a big but — she's not going to handle being in the hospital again very well. You know all about her condition. She has some very hard decisions to make, and it's going to be tough."

"I know," Mare said in a sad tone. "But don't worry. I'm here for the long term. She's not getting rid of me that easily."

For the next hour, they spoke only occasionally before TJ began to stir. Everyone tensed as they waited to see what would happen.

TJ mumbled a few unintelligible words, and Mare stood up and leaned over so the first thing TJ would see was her face. Tears trickled down her cheeks as TJ's eyes stayed open but seemed unfocused. "Hey there, beautiful, good to have you back."

"Where am I?" TJ murmured.

Mare opened her mouth to answer, but felt her heart plummet when TJ's eyes closed and stayed that way.

"She's just asleep again," Paula said.

"Probably takes the sedation awhile to wear off," Erin said. "I'll let the nurse know." She returned in a flash. "The nurse left word for Michael. She said it's natural for TJ to fall back to sleep. When she wakes again, she should be more alert."

They settled back to wait, talking in low voices. The first indication TJ had reawakened was her faint whisper.

"Mare?"

Mare jumped up and laid a hand on TJ's cheek. She noticed that her eyes were focused this time and she was fighting her restraints. "Yep. Try not to move just yet, sweetie."

"What happened?"

"What's the last thing you remember?"

TJ's gaze left Mare's face and roamed the ceiling. Mare could actually see her trying to remember. "The bar, I remember the bar."

"Okay, that's good. Well, on the way home we had an accident." Mare saw the buildup of panic in TJ's eyes. "Hey, hey." She leaned closer to TJ. "Everybody's all right. We got a little banged up, but we're fine. You're the one who had us worried." With the hand that wasn't caressing TJ's cheek, she waved Erin and Paula forward.

TJ's face broke into a smile as Erin and Paula appeared above her. "Boy, you two look like crap."

"Well, kiddo, you don't look so great yourself. You lose a fight or something?" Paula said.

"Yeah," Erin said. "Thought we told you to leave the big ones to us."

"Next time, I will." TJ looked back to Mare. "So, what's the deal here? And when can I get out of this contraption?"

Her voice was steady, but Mare could hear the fear in it. She didn't hesitate in her answer. "TJ, you got really banged up in the crash. You have a brand new cut on your side, dislocated your shoulder..." Now she did falter slightly.

"And?" TJ said slowly.

"And, hell, maybe I should get Dad in here. He can explain it better." For some reason, Mare didn't want to be the one telling TJ she would be spending quite a while in the hospital.

TJ pinned Mare with her eyes, sensing her reluctance to tell her the whole truth. "No, tell me now."

"TJ?" Erin stepped forward. "It's complicated. Let Mare get Michael. He'll be able to tell you what your options are."

TJ closed her eyes and felt the frustration building. It was starting again. People telling her lies, refusing to admit how bad things were because they were afraid of what her reaction might be. "Tell me what the hell is going on, or I'll get the nurse in here and sign a discharge form."

She'd do it, too, Mare thought, but she was stopped from having to say anything more because Michael opened the door and came in. "Morning, honey. Ladies." He nodded to Erin and Paula. "How's my favorite patient this morning?" He walked to Mare's side, wrapped an arm around her, and gazed down at TJ. "Good morning, young lady. Good to see you awake. How are you feeling?"

"I'd feel a lot better if somebody would tell me what the hell is wrong and why I'm strapped down to this thing."

"Okay, that's not a problem. I have all your charts in here. We just need to tilt your bed so you can see the scans." He pressed the buzzer near the bed, and within a minute, a nurse walked in.

She smiled at Mare who was now known around the unit. "Well, hello there," she said to TJ when she saw she was awake. TJ just glared back. The nurse said, "Dr. Gillis?" in a pleasant tone.

"Morning, Nancy. Could you adjust TJ's bed to forty-five degrees for me?" Michael walked over to the X-ray display and began putting up TJ's scans.

Nancy worked her way around the bed, securing extra straps around TJ's body to keep her immobile when they tilted the bed. After a few minutes, TJ's bed was tilted so her only view wasn't of the ceiling. Now, although she was still unable to move her head, she could see most of her room. Erin and Paula were in her peripheral vision, as was Mare.

Michael stood in front of her with the scans displayed for her viewing. "Your old scans from the original injury are on the left, and the ones taken a few days ago after the accident are on the right." Mare pulled a chair closer to TJ's bed so that she could sit and still keep hold of TJ's hand.

TJ stared hard at the scans. The nervous feeling she always got when she knew something wasn't right gnawed at her stomach.

Michael said, "The trauma doctor who dealt with your case in Sharlesburg managed to get your scans and records through a computer linkup with the hospital that treated you originally. I have the actual scans so I can be more accurate in my diagnosis." Michael looked over to make sure TJ was following what he was saying, then carried on. "The bullet fragments previously left in your spine are now calcified and show up as white on the later scans, but they're the darker shadows on the earlier ones. As you can see, they've moved."

"What does that mean?" TJ asked, though she didn't really want to hear the reply.

"Your spine from T-9 down to just below T-12 is unstable, and we'll need to operate to stabilize it. But the bullet fragments have shifted and are now in a position where we could possibly extract them." He waited to see if TJ would say anything, but she didn't.

Mare winced at the grasp TJ had on her hand. She heard TJ's breathing pick up before the monitor's beep registered the change. "You okay? TJ?" She stood up and cupped TJ's cheek. When TJ opened her eyes, Mare saw a depth of pain within them that she had never seen before. Mare felt a hand on her shoulder and looked up as Michael spoke again.

"TJ, you have to make a decision here. I can go in and stabilize the spine with rods and leave the fragments. The residual effects that the doctor in Sharlesburg noticed are most likely due to bruising, not any further injury. Or I can remove the fragments and stabilize the spine."

TJ swallowed nervously. "What will removing the fragments do?"

"I have to say that no matter what decision you make, it'll mean a significant time here at the hospital."

"Just tell me. If you take the fragments out, what will happen?"

"I'm not sure. Maybe nothing, but with steroid treatments there's an outside possibility that you may regain some feeling."

"Would I be able to walk?" TJ's voice was quiet.

"Honestly, I don't think so. However, we may be able to retrieve bladder control and some of the lower body functions. But none of this is guaranteed, and there are other side effects you should know about before you make your decision."

"Such as?"

"The major side effect you could experience is pain. If you do regain any feeling, it's likely to be a very slow process, and very painful. It's a possibility that you wouldn't regain any feeling at all, and be left with a constant pins-and-needles sensation. Or you might be in permanent pain for the rest of your life."

Not even the incessant noise of the machinery disturbed the room's oppressive atmosphere. Erin had her arm wrapped around Paula, holding her tight. They had known what was coming, as had Mare. What they hadn't known was what TJ's reaction would be. Erin was unsure whether the lack of reaction was good or bad. She knew how to deal with TJ's outbursts but had never quite managed the silences. She was beginning to feel uncomfortable, wondering whether she and Paula should have stayed away while TJ was given the news. She looked at Paula's concerned face and saw the same questions echoing in her eyes. She felt Paula shrug slightly. She didn't know what TJ was thinking any more that Erin did.

Mare watched in frustration as TJ once again closed her eyes, denying her those windows to her deepest feelings and thoughts, closing herself off from the support that Mare could provide. Mare's emotions were bouncing erratically, heading who knows where. One second she was overwhelmed with joy that her father might be able to help TJ. The next she was frightened by what TJ would have to go through. She knew TJ looked strong, knew that the wall she'd built between herself and everybody, including to some extent Erin and Paula, looked unbreachable to most, but she'd seen the fragile shell it actually was. If TJ went through with the operation to remove the fragments, it would be hard and stressful on them all.

TJ couldn't just go out on Flag to forget all her worries — there would be no escape from her situation. Lack of activity would lead to depression no matter how well things were going with her treatment. Mare knew TJ would be thinking of all this, and she needed to let her know she wouldn't be alone through whatever trials lay ahead. Right now, though, TJ was closing her out, dealing with it on her own as she always had before.

"I'd like to be alone, please." TJ's voice, though quiet, echoed through the silence, startling them all from their thoughts.

Paula moved first. She maneuvered herself to her feet, using the crutches and Erin for support. "We'll be back to see you later. Okay, love?" she said, before hopping to the door. She got no reply from TJ, but then she hadn't expected one.

Mare was more than a little dismayed at TJ's request and would have argued with her had it not been for the pressure of her father's hand on her shoulder. She whispered, "I'll be just outside if you need me," and placed a loving, gentle kiss on TJ's forehead.

"Can you turn off the lights?" TJ asked.

Michael Gillis looked back over his shoulder when he heard the request, flipped the switch, and threw the room into semi-darkness. He exited and closed the door softly behind him.

TJ opened her eyes as the click of the door signaled that she was alone. She stared up toward the ceiling, her thoughts tumbling over and over. What should she do? Should she take the risk? Could she go through the pain all over again? Well, she didn't have much choice about that part, did she? Whatever she decided, she was going to be there for some time. Weeks and weeks, probably months in the hospital. Just like the last time.

Suddenly a fierce need for Mare's comforting touch rocked her. Could Mare stand to be around her while she went through this? Or would she drive Mare away? Oh, she hoped not. She felt the call button under her finger and pressed it.

Chapter
Twenty-Five

MARE SAW PAULA and Erin had commandeered one of two couches at the end of the hall from TJ's room. Paula had her leg propped on the low table in front of her. Mare joined them and sat quietly with her thoughts until her father appeared with a tray of coffee. Mare took a sip of the hot beverage and looked over at Paula and Erin. "What do you think she'll decide?"

"I have no idea," Erin said.

Paula shook her head. "I couldn't say, either, but I'll tell you that whatever decision she makes, she'll need you by her side."

"She'll have that," Mare said, "no matter what happens. I'd go to hell and back with TJ."

"It might take that," Michael said.

Mare looked at him sharply. "But that won't change my mind." Her gaze quickly moved to the hallway as the buzzer sounded from TJ's room.

"Go on," Michael said. "It's you she's calling for."

Mare put her coffee on the table and stood up. As she walked toward TJ's room, the corridor got longer and longer, until finally, she reached the door.

MICHAEL SET HIS empty cup on the tray and locked his straightforward gaze on Erin. "How long have you and Paula been with TJ?"

"We've known her since college. After she inherited the corporation from her father, she hired us to work for her." Erin leaned her head back against the couch.

"You've been through this with her before, then, when her brother was killed?"

Head still back, Erin closed her eyes and nodded, strain evident in her drawn face. She reopened her eyes and met Michael's. "And it wasn't pretty. In fact, it was damn ugly — for all of us. She spent months in the hospital, getting more and more depressed. Counseling didn't help her. Paula and I couldn't help her. All she wanted was to join Lance. She tried to commit suicide."

"The marks on her wrists."

A note of surprise sounded in Paula's voice. "You don't miss much, do you, Doc?"

Michael swung his gaze to Paula. "TJ is doubly important to me. She's not only my patient, but also Mare's partner and friend. I'm determined not to miss anything that bears on her recovery. What can you two tell me about her reactions to her first injury that might be helpful now?"

Paula looked toward Erin who began speaking. "Before the accident, TJ sat on top of the world. She'll tell you herself she always loved power and action. Being in charge of Meridian Corporation, she had her hands full of both. She was a take-charge person and had a broad enough vision to be aware of what each company did. Her vision was also specific enough to know to give bonuses and pats on the back to people when they deserved them."

Paula said, "If she had been the only one injured, I think she would have coped a lot better. She's tough in some ways, not so tough in others, especially when it comes to heavy emotions. She doted on her brother Lance, and his death changed her into a different person. She just shut herself down. Whatever anyone at the hospital told her to do, she did, but like a zombie. None of it meant anything to her. For months she was in a deep depression, either screaming and throwing things, or totally ignoring us and everybody else."

Michael's eyes filled with sympathy. "And you two suffered, right?"

Erin and Paula nodded without even consulting each other, and Erin continued. "You got that right. For months we were walking on eggshells, reluctant to let TJ get worse, but leery of stirring up her anger by pushing her to improve. After a while, the situation affected our own relationship, and we had to have a number of heart-to-heart talks between ourselves to even keep trying to help her. I'm not sure we could go through that again." Paula squeezed Erin's forearm, and Erin lifted her head from the couch back. Moving gently, she brushed Paula's cheek with the fingers of her good hand. "Some people are too important to risk losing."

After a moment, Paula spoke softly as though only to Erin. "TJ's too important to risk, too."

Erin stared deeply into Paula's dark eyes and finally nodded. "You're right, love. We'll be here for her, no matter what. TJ is family." She took a deep breath and continued. "When TJ tried suicide, we convinced her doctors that she needed to go somewhere to get back into life, to become involved again. We knew she had been trying to get people to separate their idea of her from their experiences with her father, and Meridianville was one of the places on her list to be revived. We got the idea that we could bring her out to the ranch with Flag. She's always been obsessed with horses, and we thought her interaction with Flag might help wake up her emotions. But it wasn't working very well. She stayed depressed."

"Until Mare showed up?" Michael said.

"That's right," Paula said. "Mare brought TJ back to life, got her involved again. You might say she picked us all up from the depths."

Michael rested his elbows on his thighs and interlaced his fingers. "Maybe this time, with Mare to help her, TJ will have a better reaction."

Paula said, "Your daughter has TJ in the palm of her hand. If anyone can help her, Mare can."

"Let's just hope TJ lets her." Erin sounded wistful.

"Well, we'll be right behind her to back her up, come hell or high water."

"But with TJ," Erin said, "you can never be sure which is which."

MARE PUSHED OPEN the door and stepped into the darkened room. She walked over to TJ and reached out immediately to touch her cheek.

TJ looked up, anguish on her face. "Will you hold me for a while?"

The pained voice almost broke Mare's heart. Tears sprang from her eyes. "Of course I will." She bent and kissed TJ, then adjusted the bed back down to its horizontal position. She climbed onto the bed, laid her arm across TJ, and held her as close as the restraints allowed.

They closed their eyes and lay still, surrounded by the shielding armor of their love. But the oppressive silence pummeled them with unanswered questions, unaddressed options — clamoring for satisfaction — until it forced them from their shelter.

TJ sighed, and they both opened their eyes. Important issues needed to be resolved. "What do you think, Mare?" TJ's brow furrowed. "Should I go ahead with the operation?"

Mare clasped her hand. "You're the only one who can make

that decision. I can only tell you that, no matter what, I'll be here for you. I love you. In my mind and in my soul, you and I are connected forever and nothing will ever change that."

TJ raised their hands and kissed Mare's smaller one. "You've done so much for me. You brought me back to life. Not only by loving me, but by letting me love you."

Deep affection streamed from Mare's expressive eyes. "You don't have to say anything, sweetheart."

"Please, Mare. I've been thinking and thinking about this. I know you've heard most of it before, in bits and pieces, but I need to put it all together and tell it to you. Consider yourself my therapist for a few minutes."

"Okay, I can do that."

TJ dropped her gaze and spoke in a lower voice. "My parents smothered any love I had for them: my father through abuse and my mother through just not caring. Lance was the only person in my family I truly loved, and he was the only one I believed truly loved me. When I lost him, my whole world went dark." TJ raised her eyes for a brief moment, lifted her hand from Mare's, and placed it on Mare's cheek. Mare pressed her own hand against it for support.

TJ continued in a halting voice. "Being paralyzed at the same time was just one more burden I couldn't handle. That's when I tried suicide. I just wanted to go wherever Lance was. I ached for that unconditional love we'd had for each other." TJ gathered strength from an occasional glance at Mare's concerned face.

Mare waited silently as TJ spoke in fits and starts. Reliving this ordeal on top of everything else had to be agonizing. How she wished she could have been with TJ then. Maybe she could have helped her through that unbearable loss.

TJ wanted to turn her head and hide from the terrible truths being told but tight strapping kept her tortured face exposed. "This life seemed too cruel," she said, "too filled with darkness. Erin and Paula made heroic efforts to chase that darkness, but they just weren't able to bring me completely back. I still yearned to leave this hellhole called life. Most people run from death. I embraced it."

Mare turned her head and kissed the palm of TJ's hand, then brought it down and held it in hers. Tears oozed from her eyes, and she swallowed hard, hoping to contain her emotions. "I love you, TJ," she whispered.

A softness spread across the strong face, bringing the beginnings of a gentle smile. "Then you came along — this beautiful, caring, generous, feisty person who didn't try to edge cautiously into my life. You jumped in with both feet." TJ paused and took several deep breaths. "You didn't pussyfoot around TJ Meridian's monumental temper. It never even fazed you. That in itself was a miracle of huge proportions. No one else had ever reacted to me that boldly, and you piqued my interest right away."

"Mostly I didn't know enough to be scared of you," Mare said. "Thanks for not tossing me out on my ear."

"I tried that, but it didn't work." TJ raised her magnificent eyes, and her smile brought an answering one to Mare's face. "After I'd spent months looking inward, you forced me to look outward. As naturally as the sun rises everyday, you brought light into my life and held back the darkness. You captured my heart, my mind, and my soul. I fell in love with you." Mare pulled TJ's hand against her pounding heart.

TJ said, "And, as if that weren't enough of a miracle, you fell in love with me, too." Now TJ's eyes brimmed, and her voice thickened. "You taught me *how* to love — that intimacy doesn't mean taking, it means giving."

The tears slowly spilled over. "I thought my physical disability made me half a person, but I was wrong. My emotional disability was causing that, and you freed me from it."

Mare lifted her hand from TJ's for a moment and reached for some tissues from the bedside table. Sniffling, she wiped TJ's tears, then her own.

"So, no matter what happens, you've made my life as good as it gets." The larger hand, once again clasped with the smaller, tensed. "I'm going to have the operation to remove the bullet fragments and hope for the best." TJ's jaw set with determination. "I'll cope with whatever happens. With you at my side, I can handle anything."

Mare released TJ's hand and pushed herself farther up the bed to lean over. "You know I'll always be at your side." She worked hard to look mischievous, to give a lift to TJ in this heart-wrenching decision. "I'm grafted there in case you hadn't noticed." Mare's voice went hoarse. "At least my soul is."

Putting a hand on each side of TJ's face, she bathed TJ with the look of love pouring from within and kissed her deeply. TJ's injured side and shoulder prevented her from hugging Mare as she wanted to, but she returned Mare's kiss with abandon.

"Ahhh, Mare, I ache to show you how much I love you."

TJ's seductive voice brought further tears from Mare's eyes. She dried their faces again, patting TJ's as she did so. "Shush now. We'll have plenty of time together when we get you back home. You just concentrate on that. Paula's got everything just about ready for me to move in at the ranch." Mare chuckled through her tears. "You should see her supervising the people she hired to help her while she's hobbling around with that cast. I tried telling her she should keep her leg elevated, and she said, 'The damn leg's elevated all night long, and that should be enough.' You know Paula, there's no slowing her down when she's on a mission."

"She's a tough cookie, all right. I'm glad Paula and Erin will be there at the ranch to keep you company until I get back."

"They're both wonderful. We couldn't ask for two better friends."

"That's for sure. They've always stood by me."

"But I won't be spending much time with them at the ranch. Don't you think my free time will be spent basically living here at the hospital with you?"

A knock came on the hospital room door and a nurse poked her head in. "Miss Meridian, there's a delegation of people here who would like to speak to you for just a moment." Ignoring the fact that Mare was on the bed with TJ, she looked down at the clipboard she held. "They're from Meridianville. Will you see them?"

"I'll see them in two minutes," TJ said, and the nurse departed.

"A delegation?" TJ looked at Mare, who shrugged.

"I don't know anything about it."

TJ sighed. "Hope there aren't any problems. How do I look?"

"You look fine. Of course, you would look fine to me if you were covered with slime."

"Slime? Yuck!" TJ made a face at Mare. "You have such a way with words, Dr. Gillespie."

"I try. But let's make ourselves presentable." She slipped off the bed and pulled the chair over to TJ's bedside.

Another knock came at the door, and the nurse reappeared. "Ready for your visitors?" TJ said yes, and four men from Meridianville entered the room. All were dressed in white shirts, ties, and suits. Mayor Steve Armando led the group. He and the others nodded to Mare, then Armando walked over to shake TJ's hand. "Miss Meridian, TJ, I've brought a few people from our town council to visit you. You already know Abner Stirkle." Abner inclined his head in greeting. "Maybe you remember Lew Sturgis, the town solicitor, and Carlos Sandos, who owns the grocery store. You worked with them at the Town Meeting." The two men came forward and shook hands with TJ.

Mare's curiosity was in high gear. What were these men doing here? And in such a formal group? She hoped they weren't bringing TJ any trouble.

Armando said, "First, I'd like to say how sorry we all were to hear about your accident. Seems those troublemakers were the same bunch who vandalized your ranch. Chief Jackson looked the other way when that happened because feelings ran so high against the Meridians. He let them off with only a warning. We shouldn't have let him get away with that, and we've decided to put him on half pay for six months as a reprimand. We're hoping it will show him that we don't want our police to play favorites."

"I think that's a wise choice," TJ said. "The law should protect everyone, including people you might not like." Lying flat on her back, she had a problem seeing everyone. "Could you all move closer, please? I like to see my visitors." At her request, they crowded next to the bed, alongside Mare's chair, where they came into contact with TJ's powerful gaze.

Armando continued. "When we learned of the accident and who was involved, we called a special Town Meeting." Armando rubbed the back of his neck, and his face flushed a bit. "I know when you first came here, we didn't think too highly of you. We were judging you by our dislike of your father and what he had done to the town. But now we know we were wrong. You've been more than generous. You saved all of us from the contamination spill. You've opened up the ranch and the packing plant and are offering our people honest employment." He looked into the faces of his friends, and they nodded their support.

Mare breathed easier now that she realized the group wasn't here to complain.

"You're putting Meridianville back on its feet, and all you asked was a fair chance to hire people. We spoke about all this at the meeting, and we decided we should do something to show our appreciation and gratitude. We don't want you to believe that those young thugs had anything to do with the way the rest of us feel about the Meridian name now."

"No more S.O.B. connected with it?"

A couple of the men turned red for a moment, and Mare choked back a laugh.

"No more S.O.B.," Armando said. "Instead, we have a token for you to show our sincerity. Lew?"

Lew Sturgis pulled out a 7 x 14" package he had been carrying in a plastic bag. He said, "Abner's a bit of a metal craftsman, and he made this up for us to present to you, on behalf of the town." He handed the gift to TJ. "We don't want you to think of this as just an object, Miss Meridian. This symbolizes the love and gratitude of the whole town. We all voted for it."

TJ lifted the package in front of her, and her hands shook, the only sign of her emotions. "Mare, would you please open this for me?" Mare stood up and took the package from TJ. She removed the ribbon and gift-wrapping and handed TJ a plaque. Mounted at the bottom of the mahogany plaque was a large brass key, heavily embellished, with the name "TJ Meridian" engraved on it. Above the key, a brass rectangle was fastened to the wood and was etched with the following message: "This Key to the Town of Meridianville is presented to Taylor Jade Meridian in recognition of her priceless contributions to our well-being. She is truly our number one citizen."

TJ's lips quivered, and her eyes filled with tears. She put a hand against her lips to quiet them and handed the plaque to Mare to read. Soon two people had tears running down their cheeks, and even the men had to blink their eyes and look away. The tissue box got called into duty again.

At last, TJ got some control over her voice. "I don't know how to thank you."

Abner patted TJ's arm. "No need for you to be thanking us. We're here to thank you. Took us a while to see who you really were. We want you to know you've opened our eyes to how unfair we were to think you were painted with the same colors your father was. Yours are a helluva lot truer."

"Thanks, Abner." TJ acknowledged each man in turn. "Thank you all."

Mayor Armando cleared his throat. "Abner's right. No need for thanks. We'll be going now. Just remember, that key gives you access to anyone, at anytime, for anything you need that we can help you with. We all hope and pray that you recover quickly and get home soon."

Each man shook hands with TJ and Mare, and they said their good-byes, and left.

Mare held the plaque so TJ could see it. "You want me to stand here for an hour or so and just hold this so you can admire it?" Her cheeks dimpled.

"Sure! But I won't put you through such torture. Lay it on the table where I can reach it to look at once in a while." TJ's eyes filled. "I can't believe they did this." She began to cry in earnest.

"Hey, I think I might buy some stock in a tissue company." Mare gave a handful to TJ. She barely got her little quip out before her own tears came, and she had to grab a handful for herself. She set the plaque on the table, pulled her chair as close to the bed as she could, and sat down.

Pushing the button to lower TJ's bed as far as it would go, Mare leaned in until her head lay next to, and touched, TJ's. She put her hand against TJ's strong jaw. "I'm so glad they recognized your true worth."

TJ, tears still flowing, closed her hand around Mare's, moved it to her lips, and kissed it, then moved it back alongside her jaw. TJ would have been embarrassed to cry so openly in front of anyone else, but Mare didn't seem like "anyone else." She was an extension of TJ, body and soul. Mare waited until TJ finished crying, then pushed herself up enough to reach her and dry her face with kisses.

"Do you know what this means to me, Mare? I feel like I've been fighting a battle forever to divorce my father's life from mine. This is the first indication that I'm succeeding. My first victory." Although hoarse from crying, TJ's voice radiated hope.

"There will be lots more to come, TJ. I know that as well as I know you."

TJ took hold of Mare's hand once again and raised their joined hands in the air. "To victory. And to us."

Keeping their hands together in the air, Mare joined her lips to TJ's waiting mouth, and they wordlessly declared their love. When they parted, they smiled into each other's eyes as Mare echoed, "To victory. And to us."

FORTHCOMING TITLES

published by
Yellow Rose Books

Snow Moon Rising

by Lori L. Lake

Mischka Gallo, a proud Roma woman, knows horses, dancing, and travel. Every day since her birth, she and her extended family have been on the road in their *vardo* wagons meandering mostly through Poland and eastern Germany. She learned early to ignore the taunts and insults of all those who call her people "Gypsies" and do not understand their close-knit society and way of life.

Pauline "Pippi" Stanek has lived a settled life in a small German town along the eastern border of Poland and Germany. In her mid-teens, she meets Mischka and her family through her brother, Emil Stanek, a World War I soldier who went AWOL and was adopted by Mischka's troupe. Mischka and Pippi become fast friends, and they keep in touch over the years. But then the Second World War heats up, and all of Europe is in turmoil. Men are conscripted into the Axis or the Allied armies, "undesirables" are turned over to slave labor camps, and with every day that passes, the danger for Mischka, Emil, and their families increases. The Nazi forces will not stop until they've rounded up and destroyed every Gypsy, Jew, dissident, and homosexual.

On the run and separated from her family, Mischka can hardly comprehend the obstacles that face her. When she is captured, she must use all her wits just to stay alive. Can Mischka survive through the hell of the war in Europe and find her family?

In a world beset by war, two women on either side of the conflagration breach the divide—and save one another. *Snow Moon Rising* is a stunning novel of two women's enduring love and friendship across family, clan, and cultural barriers. It's a novel of desperation and honor, hope and fear at a time when the world was split into a million pieces.

Coming June 2006

OTHER SURTEES AND DUNNE TITLES

to be published by

Yellow Rose Books

Many Roads to Travel

TJ Meridian is a woman with a pain-filled past. She has no family to speak of. Her mother died when she was little, and her abusive father is now also dead. Her brother was killed in the same robbery that left TJ paralyzed and in a wheelchair. During TJ's recovery, her two friends Paula and Erin were the only "family" in her life — until she moved back to her childhood home and met the town veterinarian, Mare Gillespie.

Mare changed TJ's life, and TJ changed hers as well. Without each other, Mare would never have found her father, and TJ might not have ever learned about a half-brother. But the road they travel toward finding family and creating family is not smooth. In this sequel to *True Colours*, TJ must learn and truly believe that her inability to walk doesn't make her a lesser person. Mare needs to trust that sometimes things can't be fixed, and that all she can do is offer support and be understanding. TJ's dear friends Paula and Erin have to discover that it's okay to let go of people and let them continue on their own journeys.

Together, TJ and Mare — and Paula and Erin as well — must work through the problems of the past. Can they overcome old ghosts and discover new depths to their relationships? Each has a road of her own to travel. Will they ultimately find ways to journey together?

Coming June 2006

OTHER YELLOW ROSE TITLES
You may also enjoy:

INFINITE LOOP
by Meghan O'Brien

When shy software developer, Regan O'Riley is dragged into a straight bar by her workmates, the last person she expects to meet is the woman of her dreams. Off-duty cop, Mel Raines is tall, dark and gorgeous but has no plans to enter a committed relationship any time soon. Despite their differing agendas, Mel and Regan can't deny an instant, overwhelming attraction. Both their lives are about to change drastically, when a tragedy forces Mel to rethink her emotional isolation and face inner demons rooted in her past. She cannot make this journey alone, and Regan's decision to share it with her has consequences neither woman expects. More than an erotic road novel, *Infinite Loop* explores the choices we make, the families we build, and the power of love to transform lives.

ISBN 1-932300-42-2

THE BLUEST EYES IN TEXAS
by Linda Crist

Kennedy Nocona is an out, liberal, driven attorney, living in Austin, the heart of the Texas hill country. Dallasite Carson Garret is a young paralegal overcoming the loss of her parents, and coming to terms with her own sexual orientation.

A chance encounter finds them inexplicably drawn to one another, and they quickly find themselves in a long distance romance that leaves them both wanting more. Circumstances at Carson's job escalate into a series of mysteries and blackmail that leaves her with more excitement than she ever bargained for. Confused, afraid, and alone, she turns to Kennedy, the one person she knows can help her. As they work together to solve a puzzle, they confront growing feelings that neither woman can deny. Can they overcome the outside forces that threaten to crush them both?

ISBN 978-1-932300-48-2

Other YELLOW ROSE Publications

About the Authors:

Karen is a single 30-something who has served around the world with the Royal Navy as a medic for the past fourteen years. In her spare time she enjoys reading science fiction; especially David Webers Honor Harrignton series, watching TV shows, her favourites right now are Battlestar Galatica and Grey's Anatomy, photography and playing golf to a halfway decent standard. She currently resides on the Rock of Gibraltar where she works in the last Royal Naval Hospital.

Nann Dunne lives in Southeastern Pennsylvania and shares her home with family members. She's an author, editor, and online-newsletter publisher, with 30 years of experience in editing. She's been writing fiction since 1998 and has four published books. Her free online newsletter, Just About Write (www.justaboutwrite.com), presents articles on writing, editing, and marketing, while it promotes lesbian authors, poets, book reviews, and publishers. Nann reads excerpts aloud from her books at http://www.nanndunne.com.

Printed in the United States
72751LV00007B/88-93

9 781932 300529